In the Shadow of Boulder Ridge

Left to right: Henry Hasse, Rah Hoffman, Clark Ashton Smith, Paul Freehafer, and Emil Petaja.

IN THE SHADOW OF BOULDER RIDGE

The Complete California Tales of Clark Ashton Smith

Edited by Ronald S. Hilger

Introduction by Marc Laidlaw

Hippocampus Press

New York

Published by Hippocampus Press
P.O. Box 641, New York, NY 10156.
www.hippocampuspress.com

Cover illustration © 2024 by Gregory Nemec
Cover design by Jason Van Hollander incorporating title design
by Daniel V. Sauer
Hippocampus Press logo designed by Anastasia Damianakos

First Paperback Edition
1 3 5 7 9 8 6 4 2

ISBN 978-1-61498-444-3 trade paperback
ISBN 978-1-61498-454-2 ebook

Contents

5

The Golden State of Clark Ashton Smith

Clark

Ashton

Smith

C

A

S

California

Auburn

Sierras

As a young Southern Californian with aspirations of being a writer, nothing seemed more boring to me than California. It was a place whose history was almost completely glossed over in school, owing to the fact that once you sanitize textbooks to eliminate discussions of slavery, indigenous displacements, and massacres, there's not much left to talk about, beyond brief mentions of acorn flour, adobe, and *atl-atls*. I envied horror writers such as H. P. Lovecraft and Stephen King, who grew up in the diagonally opposed corner of the country, steeped in witchcraft and warfare. Was it any wonder that their stories so often took place in the vividly drawn environs of New England, while a California fantasist like Clark Ashton Smith escaped the West Coast into Zothique, Xiccarph, and Hyperborea . . . and took me with him?

And yet, as I grew older, and began to appreciate the effects of environment on my own extrapolations, I became more interested in

Smith as the resident of a place, as a body that had lived and moved through time and through this world, observing, assimilating, transmuting, and recording his altered observations in the form of stories and poetry. Revisiting these stories, I find that what most interests me now is not the delirious, hallucinatory dimensions that Smith dreamt up, but the California that dreamt him up. I went through this collection looking for signs of the man himself, hoping to catch him in the act of observing and recording. What elements of his surroundings did he consider worth casting in print, transmitting to others?

From my teens, I knew Smith was associated with the town of Auburn, California, although I had no knowledge of Auburn itself and was unaware that it lay in the shadow of the Sierra Nevada range, where I had camped and backpacked as a kid. When I first read "The Return of the Sorcerer," its Oakland setting barely registered; I envisioned it taking place in some more atmospheric city typical of weird horror. Boston or London would have served just as well, for all the relevance of the San Francisco Bay Area to the story.

On the other hand, "The Devotee of Evil" takes place specifically in Auburn, and from the memoirs appended to this collection ("The Arcana of Arkham-Auburn") I learned that the "old Larcom house" described by Smith was based on an actual structure in Auburn. And while Auburn itself is not described in any detail, once the narrator reaches the grounds of the Larcom house, we are taken through "a veritable tangle of Cherokee rose-vines, arbutus, lilac, ivy and crepe-myrtle, half-overshadowed by the great cypresses and somber evergreen oaks." I cherish this glimpse of Smith's own observations, which suddenly ground us in his world. I find these more interesting and less arbitrary than the realm of pure evil that soon takes precedence.

Whenever Smith has good reason to evoke the California setting for story purposes, he shares an indulgence in his physical and sensory world. The cornerstone of his regional fiction must surely be "Genius Loci," where descriptions of the woods and water around "the foot-hill environs of the tiny hamlet of Bowman" are the entire point of the story. The characters move through the landscape on foot and even by car. That car is one of the few clues as to the time period of the tale, which might otherwise have been set at a much earlier date. "Genius Loci" is all about landscape, and Smith invests the fringes of Auburn with the imaginative power that he normally expends on more psychedelic milieux (something about a lengthy steepage in Smith's prose makes a word like *milieux* seem *de rigueur*, not to mention *steepage* [is that even a word? I doubt he would have cared, so nor do I, as long as it earns an extra penny from Farnsworth Wright]). I love how these passages give glimpses of Smith himself, zooming about Sierra foothills by automobile or striding along on foot, with occasional treks (by train?) to San Francisco (which is featured occasionally in these stories, although never with as much detail as I would like, just brief mentions of streetcars and ferries). From "Genius Loci" we derive sparing mentions of Bear River, the "smoky autumn twilight," an assortment of little details that make the boggy "locus" itself more believable. Was this a place Smith himself glimpsed, perhaps? Did he extrapolate his evil pool from a cheerful sunny marsh?

Ultimately, I found myself wishing that Smith had not felt quite so driven to appeal to the expectations of the pulp magazine readership. In the pair of "Singing Flame" stories, we are treated to gorgeous descriptions of Crater Ridge, an area of the Sierra Nevada that not only enflames Smith's imagination but his senses: "mountain sun-flowers, wild currant-bushes, and a few sturdy, wind-warped pines and supple tamaracks." From the vegetable realm we proceed to the mineral: "its outcroppings of rough, nodular stone and enormous rubble-heads have all the air of scoriac remains . . . They look like the slag and refuse of Cyclopean furnaces . . . shapes of limitless grotesquery. . . . The hill is an odd interlude among the granite sheets and crags, and the fir-clothed ravines and valleys of this region." Smith is a weird naturalist, a John Muir of the bizarre, and I wish he would throw himself down here and give me more and more of this natural world. But his narrative impulses take him elsewhere, to the hallucinatory realm of Ydmos and the Temple of Flame, where (much to the delight of fans of this sort of thing) he comes completely unmoored from reality and seems to be trying to anticipate the Frank R. Paul cover he hopes his story will merit.

As a teenage superfan of Klarkash-Ton, it was exactly this sort of thing that enchanted me, and I would have chafed had ol' Philip Hastane spent more than a few sentences gazing on "the remote, luminous blue of the Nevada Mountains, and the soft green of willows in the valley at my feet. It was an aloof, silent world, and I heard no sound other than the dry, crackling noise of cicadas among the—" *"Get on to the Singing Flame already!"* teenage me would have complained. And yet now I could happily ramble all afternoon with Clark below the "titan battlements of Castle Peak," and never once felt I had missed out because we did not pass through the remains of some cosmic portal into a world of exotic, invented sensations.

"The Secret of the Cairn" is more rewarding in its balance of Sierran detail and visionary imagery. We begin in the high Sierras, on "the shore of a tiny sapphire tarn, in a valley sheltered by hemlocks and granite crags." *Yes!* And here we stay, through all the visitations and mysteries that follow. "There were a few tiny patches of alpine phlox within the circle of occultly altered space around the cairn." *Perfect!* An alien scent mingles with the smell of burning juniper, an unearthly light strobes against a background of granite peaks and dark pines. We straddle both worlds now. It's not one of Smith's finest stories, but as a capsule containing essences of both "infinite spheres" and "the lonely Sierras," it is easy to swallow.

The most insanely compelling of these Californian stories also has hilariously little of California in it. "The Eternal World" gives us a momentary glimpse through a laboratory window before the story really begins. The protagonist says farewell to Earth, to its mountain solitude and its rugged gulleys, "threaded by the brawling silver of a tiny stream."

"He saw the granite-sheeted slope beyond, and the two nearer peaks of the Sierras, whose slatey azure was tipped by the first autumn snow; and saw the pass between them that lay in a line with his apparent route through the space-time continuum." And that's it: We are about to rocket straight down that line and into what is surely one of Smith's wildest imaginings, a story of Stapeldonian vastness. Does this brief glimpse out the lab window make the rest of the story somehow more believable? *Not by a long shot.* Does this matter? *Not in the least.* But for all the mind-fracturing images to follow, it is the "brawling silver" and the view of the pass that hang in my mind's eye. I feel I have peered through that window. It's the last time in the story that I can believe my senses. *Brawling silver indeed!*

Sometime in the mid-'90s, when I lived in San Francisco, I thought to take a look at this mysterious Auburn, which had occupied a space in my imagination for so long that it might as well have been fully imaginary. I had some notion of tracking down CAS-specific sites in the Sierra foothills, so I turned to local literary/landscape expert Don Herron for advice. Herron said that, by coincidence, that very weekend a casual "WeirdCon" was being held in Lake of the Pines, just outside Auburn— a gathering which might include a tour of Smith's old homestead.

Two days later, among a group of new friends (including the editor of this collection, Ron Hilger), I clambered out of a van at the top of a hot, dry field and surveyed the spot that had at one time been the site of Smith's cabin. I could not clearly associate the landscape with any of Smith's stories (the tales in this collection were not as readily accessible at that time and I hadn't read much CAS at all in the previous fifteen years), but it was easy to imagine Smith himself hiking about here fifty years earlier.

As we tramped through the tall straw-colored grass and foxtail stickers, I experienced mild paranoia about the presence of spotted deer ticks, as one typically does in such terrain. I knew that toward the end of his life Smith had suffered from a mysterious weakness and wasting, never diagnosed. And given my anxiety about tick-borne illnesses, which are often accompanied by just such weakness and wasting, I began to wonder if Smith might have been the victim of such an ailment.

Slowly, inevitably, anxiety and dread turned into an idea for a story.

What if Smith had been the host of a tick from this very field?

What if, in the process of infecting him with the disease that eventually took his life, the tick drank and grew fat on the blood of Clark Ashton Smith?

What if that tick then leapt from Smith's ankle, returned to the weedy field and went dormant?

Slept among the roots, dozed, waited, and decades later . . . woke, warmed by new bodies in the field?

What if it leapt to another ankle (mine?!), and in drinking, some of the Smith-inflected compounds traveled from its (to me) loathsome little body into my (to the tick) equally loathsome larger one?

What if Clark's dreams, compressed like a zip-file into his DNA, were thus unloaded into mine?

A story germ, but hardly its fruition. With further development and less ego, one might imagine an unsuspecting surveyor, out staking the site for tract homes. A pragmatic sort who suddenly finds himself suffering visions of worlds too bizarre to describe, outré dimensions impinging on his blueprints. His visionary fit might prove curable with the right sort of antibiotics . . . but only if some Auburn physician, more familiar with "the old Smith homestead," recognizes the symptoms in time.

But why write such a story? Who would ever appreciate this extremely inbred little idea apart from the sort of rabid Smith fan who might take the time to read the introduction, of all things, to a collection of Smith's California-set works?

In any event, ticks are a cumbersome vehicle for weird blood-borne visions (and for visions straight out of the videogame Bloodborne, take a gander at "The Ninth Skeleton"!), especially when Clark Ashton Smith's own words already do the job so effectively.

Go thou, then, and be infected. It is absolutely not necessary to visit that weedy field, or indeed any part of the Golden State, to catch glimpses of the weird and beautiful region that Clark Ashton Smith spent so much energy escaping.

—MARC LAIDLAW

Los Angeles, California
March 2024

A Note on the Text

Clark Ashton Smith was a native Californian who lived the vast majority of his life in the Sierra Nevada foothills, near the gold-rush town of Auburn. An only child from a poor family, Smith grew up on the outskirts of town in a small cabin lacking both electricity and running water. Shy and precocious, the young Smith was often subjected to teasing and bullying from his more affluent classmates—an observation corroborated by fellow Auburnites including Helen Sully, Robert Elder, and Gene Scott. Later in life Smith would be described as an oddball, a reclusive hermit, and even as a ladies' man about town by some of the gossip-mongers of Auburn. For these and other reasons Smith often complained of being an outsider in his own hometown and spoke of his desire to quit California, and even the entire country altogether. In a letter to R. H. Barlow of 16 May 1937, Smith writes (speaking of the death of H. P. Lovecraft):

> Truly, as you suggest, America has killed her finest artists. And when she hasn't killed them, she has driven them into exile, as in the case of Hearn and Bierce. Personally I am goddamned sick of the killing process (I seem to die hard) and have fully and absolutely made up my mind to quit the hell-bedunged and heaven-bespitted country when my present responsibilities are over. I haven't any definite plans, but will probably gravitate toward the orient. Anyway, I shall remove myself from Auburn, California and the USA., even if I have to stow away aboard a tramp steamer. [. . .] I could never live in any modern city, and am more of an "outsider" than HPL. His "outside-ness" was principally in regard to time-period; mine is one of space, too.

Another example comes from a letter to August Derleth, dated 21 April 1937.

The risk [of wildfire] becomes worse hereabouts every year, because of the tindery dryness over a period of six or sometimes even eight months, and the god-damned carelessness of autoists, hunters, and other tobacco addicts—not to mention the professional incendiaries. This is one reason (not the only one) why I have thought of quitting California. Of course, it is my native state, and I am attached to the scenery. But there is an increasing destruction and pollution of landscape beauties, and a growing influx of undesirable humans bringing with them filth and pestilence. . . . Apart from this, the local attitude toward art and literature is discouraging.

This collection of tales set in California was conceived as a means to bring together many of Smith's weird tales that do not fall into other story cycles such as Averoigne or Zothique, thus allowing the inclusion of many of Smith's most famous tales, such as "The City of the Singing Flame," "Beyond the Singing Flame," "Genius Loci," "The Devotee of Evil," "The Return of the Sorcerer," and many others. The "Singing Flame" text that appeared in *Out of Space and Time* was based on tearsheets from *Tales of Wonder,* whose editor Walter Gillings combined "The City of the Singing Flame" with its sequel, "Beyond the Singing Flame," in order to create a novelette of 15,000 words. In restoring the texts for these tales it was decided best to separate them back into their original forms in order to present "Pure Smith" rather than this patched-together amalgam. "The Return of the Sorcerer" is another popular Smith tale that passed through many revisions and titles before achieving publication, mostly due to the gruesome nature of the story. Featuring twin brothers who were both practitioners of the dark arts, along with some fine quotations and ritualistic exorcisms from Lovecraft's *Necronomicon,* this tale was adapted for television as an episode for *Rod Serling's Night Gallery* starring Vincent Price and Bill Bixby. Although this campy version takes extensive liberties with the original conception and introduces both a sexy female assistant and a black goat as a dinner guest, it still remains quite grotesque and entertaining.

As in the previous Hippocampus collections by Clark Ashton Smith, the texts included in this volume all utilize the newly corrected and restored texts as prepared by Scott Connors and myself. In addition to

Scott, I would also like to express my gratitude to Jason Van Hollander, Derrick Hussey, S. T. Joshi, Marc Laidlaw, Gregory Nemec, and David E. Schultz for their friendly and professional expertise in the preparation of this, and previous volumes.

In the introduction to *The Averoigne Chronicles* I discussed the autobiographical significance of the many poets Smith used as protagonists throughout this series. His California stories contain a similar, if not more pronounced autobiographical tendency, most notably in the recurring character of Philip Hastane. Smith uses Hastane as a protagonist in "The Devotee of Evil," which is set in Smith's hometown of Auburn and describes Hastane as a novelist. Smith refers to this story in his letter to Lovecraft dated 11 March 1930: "There really is an old house, reputed to be haunted, in the locality I have described in 'The Devotee.' It is, however, currently occupied by a quite respectable lady."

"The Hunters from Beyond" also features Hastane as the main character. He describes himself in the story as follows: "Though I had been for years a professional writer of stories that often dealt with occult phenomena, with the weird and the spectral . . ." Philip Hastane also makes an appearance in both "The City of the Singing Flame" and its sequel, "Beyond the Singing Flame," once again presented as a writer of weird fiction.

A lesser example of this autobiographical tendency is found in "Genius Loci," in which the narrator of the tale, known only as "Murray," purchases an uncultivated ranch near the tiny hamlet of Bowman (which is located a few miles east of Auburn) and "retired for the privacy so essential to prolonged literary effort." Primarily known as a poet and author of highly imaginative fantasy and weird fiction, Clark Ashton Smith was not commonly viewed as a regional writer; however, in passages such as the following excerpt from "Genius Loci" he certainly proved himself capable of capturing on paper both the appearance and atmosphere of the natural Californian landscape:

"It is a very strange place," said Amberville, "but I scarcely know how to convey the impression it made upon me. It will all sound so simple and ordinary. There is nothing but a sedgy meadow, surrounded on three sides by slopes of yellow pine. A dreary little stream flows in from the open end, to lose itself in a *cul-de-sac* of cat-tails and boggy ground. The stream, running slowly and more slowly, forms a stagnant pool of some extent, from which several sickly-looking alders seem to fling themselves backwards, as if unwilling to approach it. A dead willow leans above the pool, tangling its wan, skeleton-like reflection with the green scum that mottles the water. There are no blackbirds, no kildees, no dragon-flies even, such as one usually finds in a place of that sort. It is all silent and desolate. The spot is evil—it is unholy in a way that I simply can't describe."

Finally, we find an even more obvious autobiographical example in "The Ninth Skeleton" where the protagonist is meeting his fiancé, Guenevere, "midway between her parents' home at Newcastle and my cabin on the northeastern extremity of the Ridge, near Auburn." This is an obvious reference to both his cabin on Boulder Ridge and to his lady-friend Genevieve Sully. Clark Ashton Smith was by all accounts an intensely private man who was openly critical of both small-town gossip and biographers, whom he often compared to "jackals and hyenas," so it would be best not to delve too deeply into his personal affairs. Suffice it to say that his relationship with Mrs. Sully was easily the most significant he would have with a woman prior to his marriage to Carol Dorman in 1954; and, while the romantic nature of their relationship would not endure, they nevertheless remained lifelong friends. In fact, Genevieve is credited with encouraging Smith to try his hand at writing fiction rather than poetry, as indicated in her letter included in Donald Sidney-Fryer's bio-bibliography *Emperor of Dreams* (1978):

> After a few days of short walks, we proposed a longer walk—to Crater Ridge—where we had gone many times in the past, but now we were going with a companion who came under a spell of strange thought, transforming the scene into a foreboding and grotesque landscape, which Clark later used in his now famous story "The City of the Singing Flame." Clark wandered about among the boulders, studying the rocks and general terrain. We could all see that he was deeply affected by the place.
>
> Later in the afternoon while Clark was still feeling a strange influence, after we had sat down to look at the views which combine to make this place especially beautiful, I suddenly suggested that he use his powers of

writing for fiction, which would be more remunerative than poetry. His financial situation at the time was critical, and some practical advice seemed in order. This prodding led to Clark's writing of weird fiction and, thus, the walk to Crater Ridge started the flow of work which has made Clark the well-known writer that he is.

Smith used the High Sierras as a setting for many of his California tales such as "The Secret of the Cairn," "A Star Change," "The Eternal World," and what may be his best-known story, "The City of the Singing Flame." Smith mentions this practice to H. P. Lovecraft in a letter of c. 27 January 1931, which begins with this playful heading: "At the apex of the Singing Flame, in the Titan city beyond the trans-dimensional columns."

I am enclosing a new trans-dimensional story, "The City of the Singing Flame," in which I have utilized Crater Ridge (the place where I found the innominable Eikon) as a spring-board. Some day I must look for those two boulders "with a vague resemblance to broken-down columns." If you and other correspondents cease to hear from me thereafter, you can surmise what has happened! The description of the Ridge, by the way, has been praised for its realism by people who know the place.

The indicated description follows:

I had gone for a walk on Crater Ridge, which lies a mile or less to the north of my cabin near Summit. Though differing markedly in its character from the usual landscapes roundabout, it is one of my favorite places. It is exceptionally bare and desolate, with little more in the way of vegetation than mountain sun-flowers, wild currant-bushes, and a few sturdy, wind-warped pines and supple tamaracks. Geologists deny it a volcanic origin; yet its outcroppings of rough, nodular stone and enormous rubble-heaps have all the air of scoriac remains—at least, to my non-scientific eye. They look like the slag and refuse of Cyclopean furnaces, poured out in pre-human years, to cool and harden into shapes of limitless grotesquery. Among them are stones that suggest the fragments of primordial bas-reliefs, or small prehistoric idols and figurines; and others that seem to have been graven with lost letters of an indecipherable script. Unexpectedly, there is a little tarn lying on one end of the long, dry Ridge—a tarn that has never been fathomed. The hill is an odd interlude among the granite sheets and crags, and the fir-clothed ravines and valleys of this region.

For more information regarding Crater Ridge and other aspects of Smith's life and legacy, the interested reader would do well to search out the documentary *Clark Ashton Smith: The Emperor of Dreams*. This invaluable source of first-hand information features much footage from Crater Ridge and Smith's hometown of Auburn as well as interviews from well-known writers and others who knew and admired Smith, such as Donald Sidney-Fryer, S. T. Joshi, Harlan Ellison, Cody Goodfellow, Richard Stanley, William Dorman, Scott Connors, and many others. Released in 2018 and directed by Darin Coehlo Spring, this film is currently available from Hippocampus Press.

In the Shadow of Boulder Ridge closes with the poem "Soliloquy in an Ebon Tower," a 100-line poem in blank verse that was probably the final version of the well-known fragment "The Sorcerer Departs," and was included as the centerpiece of the 1951 Arkham House collection *The Dark Chateau*. Many years ago I wrote to Donald Sidney-Fryer asking him about his feelings regarding the significance of this poem. The following is a quotation from his response: "Thank you for calling attention to this remarkable poem. It is readily apparent that this poem was very important to CAS because he worked on it for many years and wrote several drafts. In my opinion this poem represents Smith's *intellectual* poetic testament, philosophically and imaginatively expressed. In much the same way, 'O Golden-Tongued Romance' represents his *romantic* poetic testament, aesthetically and emotionally expressed." The poem opens with the poet musing alone in his cabin on Boulder Ridge and deals with his philosophical justification for a lifetime of literary effort that has left him with little recognition or financial reimbursement. As such, this beautiful and insightful poem seems the perfect selection to culminate this collection of California tales.

Finally, "The Arcana of Arkham-Auburn" is included as an appendix. This facetious memoir details two visits by Rah Hoffman, Emil Petaja, Paul Freehafer, and Henry Hasse with the "Bard of Auburn" at his cabin on Boulder Ridge and exhibits a very rare and personal (if somewhat whimsical) account of Smith entertaining guests at his home.

Clark Ashton Smith would never "quit" California as he often considered, but did leave Auburn after his marriage to Carol Dorman in 1954 and took up residence at her home in Pacific Grove, where he would pass away on 14 August 1961. It is perhaps fitting to imagine that in much the same way he utilized the High Sierras as a springboard into other planets and dimensions, Clark Ashton Smith would transcend this world and take his rightful place treading the stars as the Emperor of Dreams.

Philip Hastane

THE DEVOTEE OF EVIL

The old Larcom house was a mansion of considerable size and dignity, set among cypresses and oaks on the hill behind Auburn's Chinatown, in what had once been the aristocratic section of the village. At the time of which I write, it had been unoccupied for several years and had begun to present the signs of dilapidation and desolation which untenanted houses so soon display. The place had a tragic history and was believed to be haunted. I had never been able to secure any first-hand or precise accounts of the spectral manifestations that were accredited to it. But certainly it possessed all the necessary antecedents of a haunted house. The first owner, Judge Peter Larcom, had been murdered beneath its roof back in the seventies by a maniacal Chinese cook; one of his daughters had gone insane; and two other members of the family had died accidental deaths. None of them had prospered: their legend was one of sorrow and disaster.

Some later occupants, who had purchased the place from the one surviving son of Peter Larcom, had left under circumstances of inexplicable haste after a few months, moving permanently to San Francisco. They did not return even for the briefest visit; and beyond paying their taxes, they gave no attention whatever to the place. Everyone had grown to think of it as a sort of historic ruin, when the announcement came that it had been sold to Jean Averaud, of New Orleans.

My first meeting with Averaud was strangely significant, for it revealed to me, as years of acquaintance would not necessarily have done, the peculiar bias of his mind. Of course, I had already heard some odd rumors about him: his personality was too signal, his advent too mysterious, to escape the usual fabrication and mongering of village tales. I had been told that he was extravagantly rich, that he was a recluse of the most eccentric type, that he had made certain very singular changes in the inner structure of the old house; and last, but not least, that he lived with a beautiful mulatress, who never spoke to anyone and who was thought to be his mistress as well as his housekeeper. The man himself had been described to me by some as an unusual but harmless lunatic, and by others as an all-round Mephistopheles.

I had seen him several times before our initial meeting. He was a sallow, saturnine Creole, with the marks of race in his hollow cheeks and feverish eyes. I was struck by his air of intellect, and by the fiery fixity of his gaze—the gaze of a man who is dominated by one idea to the exclusion of all else. Some medieval alchemist, who believed himself to be on the point of attaining his objective after years of unrelenting research, might have looked as he did.

I was in the Auburn library one day, when Averaud entered. I had taken a newspaper from one of the tables and was reading the details of an atrocious crime—the murder of a woman and her two infant children by the husband and father, who had locked his victims in a clothes-closet, after saturating their garments with oil. He had left the woman's apron-string caught in the shut door, with the end protruding, and had set fire to it like a fuse.

Averaud passed the table where I was reading. I looked up, and saw his glance at the headlines of the paper I held. A moment later he returned and sat down beside me, saying in a low voice:

"What interests me in a crime of that sort, is the implication of unhuman forces behind it. Could any man, on his own initiative, have conceived and executed anything so gratuitously fiendish?"

"I don't know," I replied, somewhat surprised by the question and by my interrogator. "There are terrifying depths in human nature—gulfs of instinct and impulse more abhorrent than those of the jungle."

"I agree. But how could such impulses, unknown to the most brutal progenitors of man, have been implanted in his nature, unless through some ulterior agency?"

"You believe, then, in the existence of an evil force or entity—a Satan or an Ahriman?"

"I believe in evil—how can I do otherwise when I see its manifestations everywhere? I regard it as an all-controlling power; but I do not think that the power is personal, in the sense of what we know as personality. A Satan? No. What I conceive is a sort of dark vibration, the radiation of a black sun, of a center of malignant aeons—a radiation that can penetrate like any other ray—and perhaps more deeply. But probably I don't make my meaning clear at all."

I protested that I understood him; but, after his burst of communicativeness, he seemed oddly disinclined to pursue the conversation. Evidently he had been prompted to address me; and no less evidently, he regretted having spoken with so much freedom. He arose; but before leaving, he said:

"I am Jean Averaud—perhaps you have heard of me. You are Philip Hastane, the novelist. I have read your books and I admire them. Come and see me some time—we may have certain tastes and ideas in common."

Averaud's personality, the conception he had avowed, and the intense interest and value which he so obviously attached to these conceptions, made a singular impression on my mind, and I could not forget him. When, a few days afterward, I met him on the street, and he repeated his invitation with a cordialness that was unfeignedly sincere, I could do no less than accept. I was interested, though not altogether attracted, by his bizarre, well-nigh morbid individuality, and was impelled by a desire to learn more concerning him. I sensed a mystery of no common order—a mystery with elements of the abnormal and the uncanny.

The grounds of the old Larcom place were precisely as I remembered them, though I had not found occasion to pass them for some time. They were a veritable tangle of Cherokee rose-vines, arbutus, lilac, ivy and crepe-myrtle, half-overshadowed by the great cypresses and somber evergreen oaks. There was a wild, half-sinister charm about

them—the charm of rampancy and ruin. Nothing had been done to put
the place in order, and there were no outward repairs on the house itself,
where the white paint of bygone years was being slowly replaced by
mosses and lichens that flourished beneath the eternal umbrage of the
cypresses. There were signs of decay in the roof and pillars of the front
porch; and I wondered why the new owner, who was reputed to be so
rich, had not already made the necessary restorations.

I raised the gargoyle-shapen knocker and let it fall with a dull, lugubrious clang. The house remained silent; and I was about to knock again,
when the door opened slowly and I saw for the first time the mulatress
of whom so many village rumors had reached me.

The woman was more exotic than beautiful, with fine, mournful
eyes and bronze-colored features of a semi-negroid irregularity. Her figure, though, was truly perfect, with the curving lines of a lyre and the
supple grace of some feline animal. When I asked for Jean Averaud, she
merely smiled and made signs for me to enter. I surmised at once that
she was dumb.

Waiting in the gloomy library to which she conducted me, I could
not refrain from glancing at the volumes with which the shelves were
congested. They were an ungodly jumble of tomes that dealt with an-
thropology, ancient religions, demonology, modern science, history,
psychoanalysis and ethics. Interspersed with these, were a few romances
and volumes of poetry. Beausobre's monograph on Manichaeism was
flanked with Byron and Poe; and *Les Fleurs du mal* jostled a late treatise
on chemistry.

Averaud entered, after some minutes, apologizing extravagantly for
his delay. He said that he had been in the midst of certain labors when
I came; but he did not specify the nature of these labors. He looked even
more hectic and fiery-eyed than when I had seen him last. He was pa-
tently glad to see me, and eager to talk.

"You have been looking at my books," he observed immediately.
"Though you might not think so at first glance, on account of their

seeming diversity, I have selected them with a single object: the study of evil in all its aspects, ancient, medieval and modern. I have traced it in the demonologies and religions of all peoples; and, more than this, in human history itself. I have found it in the inspiration of poets and romancers who have dealt with the darker impulses, emotions and acts of man. Your novels have interested me for this reason: you are aware of the baneful influences which surround us, which so often actuate or influence us. I have followed the workings of these agencies even in chemical reactions, in the growth and decay of trees, flowers, minerals. I feel that the processes of physical decomposition, as well as the similar mental and moral processes, are due entirely to them.

"In brief, I have postulated a monistic evil, which is the source of all death, deterioration, imperfection, pain, sorrow, madness and disease. This evil, so feebly counteracted by the powers of good, allures and fascinates me above all things. For a long time past, my life-work has been to ascertain its true nature, and trace it to its fountain-head. I am sure that somewhere in space there is the center from which all evil emanates."

He spoke with a wild air of excitement, with a morbid and semimaniacal intensity. His obsession convinced me that he was more or less unbalanced; but there was a delusive logic in the development of his ideas.

Scarcely waiting for me to reply, he continued his monologue:

"I have learned that certain localities and buildings, certain arrangements of natural or artificial objects, are more favorable to the reception of evil influences than others. The laws that determine the degree of receptivity are obscure to me; but at least I have verified the fact itself. As you know, there are houses or neighborhoods notorious for a succession of crimes or misfortunes; and there are also articles, such as certain jewels, whose possession is accompanied by disaster. Such places and things are receivers of evil. I have a theory, however, that there is always more or less interference with the direct flow of the malignant force; and that pure, absolute evil has never yet been manifested.

"By the use of some device which would create a proper field or form a receiving station, it should be possible to evoke this absolute evil. Under such conditions, I am sure that the dark vibration would become a visible and tangible thing, comparable to light or electricity."

He eyed me with a gaze that was disconcertingly keen and exigent. Then:

"I will confess that I have purchased this old mansion and its grounds mainly on account of their baleful history. The place is unusually liable to the influences of which I have spoken. I am now at work on an apparatus by means of which, when it is perfected, I hope to manifest in their essential purity the radiations of malign force."

At this moment, the mulatress entered and passed through the room on some household errand. I thought that she gave Averaud a look of maternal tenderness, watchfulness and anxiety. He, on his part, seemed hardly to be aware of her presence, so engrossed was he in the strange ideas and the stranger project he had been expounding. However, when she had gone, he remarked:

"That is Fifine, the one human being who is really attached to me. She is mute, but highly intelligent and affectionate. All of my people, an old Louisiana family, are long departed, and my wife is doubly dead to me."

A spasm of obscure pain contracted his features, and vanished. He resumed his monologue; and at no future time did he again refer to the presumably tragic tale at which he had hinted.

For at least an hour he discoursed on the theme of universal evil, the researches and experiments he had made, and those which he planned to make. There was much that he told me—a strange medley of the scientific and the mystic—into which I should not care to enter here. I assented tactfully to all that he said, but ventured to point out the possible dangers of his evocative experiments, if they should prove successful. To this, with the fervor of an alchemist or a religious devotee, he replied that it did not matter—that he was prepared to accept any and all consequences.

I took my leave, after promising to return for another talk. Of course, I considered now that Averaud was a madman; but his madness was of a most uncommon and picturesque variety. It seemed significant, in a way, that he should have chosen me for a confidant. All others who met him found him uncommunicative and taciturn to an extreme degree. I suppose he had felt the ordinary human need of unbosoming himself to someone; and had selected me as the only person in the neighborhood who was potentially sympathetic.

I saw him several times during the month that followed. He was indeed a strange psychological study; and I encouraged him to talk without reserve—though such encouragement was hardly necessary. Each time I called, he poured forth a brilliant though erratic discourse on his favorite subject. He also gave me to understand that his invention was progressing favorably. And one day he said, with abruptness:

"I will show you my mechanism, if you care to see it."

I protested my eagerness to view the invention, and he led me forthwith into a room to which I had not been admitted before. The chamber was large, triangular in form, and tapestried with curtains of some sullen black fabric. It had no windows. Clearly, the internal structure of the house had been changed in making it; and the queer village tales, emanating from carpenters who had been hired to do the work, were now explained. Exactly in the center of this room, there stood on a low tripod of brass the apparatus of which Averaud had so often spoken.

The contrivance was quite fantastic, and presented the appearance of some new, highly complicated musical instrument. I remember that there were many wires of varying thickness, stretched on a series of concave sounding-boards of some dark, unlustrous metal; and above these, there depended from three horizontal bars a number of square, circular and triangular gongs. Each of these appeared to be made of a different material; some were bright as gold, or translucent as jade; others were black and opaque as jet. A small hammer-like instrument hung opposite each gong, at the end of a silver wire.

Averaud proceeded to expound the scientific basis of his mecha-nism. He spoke of the vibrational properties of the gongs, whose sound-pitch was designed to neutralize all other cosmic vibrations than those of evil. His theorem was oddly lucid in its outré and extravagant devel-opment. But I shall not enlarge upon it, since, in the light of later events, it seemed to afford but a partial and insufficient explanation of phenom-ena which, at bottom, were perhaps inexplicable by the human mind. He ended his peroration:

"I need one more gong to complete the instrument; and this I hope to invent very soon. The triangular room, draped in black, and without windows, forms the ideal surroundings for my experiment. Apart from this room, I have not ventured to make any change in the house or its grounds, for fear of deranging some propitious element or collocation."

More than ever, I thought that he was mad. And, though he had professed on many occasions to abhor the evil which he planned to evoke, I felt an inverted fanaticism in his attitude. In a less scientific age, he would have been a devil-worshipper, a partaker in the abominations of the Black Mass; or would have given himself to the study and practice of sorcery. His was a religious soul that had failed to find good in the scheme of things; and lacking it, was impelled to make of evil itself an object of secret reverence.

In a sudden gleam of clairvoyance, he observed:

"I fear you think I am insane. Would you like to watch an experi-ment? Even though my invention is not completed, I may be able to convince you that my design is not altogether the fantasy of a disordered brain."

I consented. He turned on the lights in the dim room. Then he went to an angle of the wall and pressed a hidden spring or switch. The wires on which the tiny hammers were strung began to oscillate, till each of the hammers touched lightly its companion gong. The sound they made was dissonant and disquieting to the last degree—a diabolic percussion unlike anything I have ever heard, and exquisitely painful to the nerves.

I felt as if a flood of finely broken glass were pouring into my ears.

The swinging of the hammers grew swifter and heavier; but, to my surprise, there was no corresponding increase of loudness in the sound. On the contrary, the clangor became slowly muted, till it was no more than an undertone which seemed to be coming from an immense depth or distance—an undertone still full of disquietude and torment, like the sobbing of far-off winds in hell, or the murmur of demonian fires on coasts of eternal ice.

Said Averaud at my elbow:

"To a certain extent, the combined notes of the gongs are beyond human hearing in their pitch. With the addition of the final gong, even less sound will be audible."

While I was trying to digest this difficult idea, I noticed a partial dimming of the light above the tripod and its weird apparatus. A vertical shaft of faint shadow, surrounded by a penumbra of still fainter gloom, was forming in the air. The tripod itself, and the wires, gongs and hammers, were now a trifle indistinct, as if seen through some obscuring veil. The central shaft and its penumbra seemed to widen; and looking down at the floor, where the outer adumbration, conforming to the room's outline, crept toward the walls, I saw that Averaud and myself were now within its ghostly triangle.

At the same time, there surged upon me an intolerable depression, together with a multitude of sensations which I despair of conveying in language. My very sense of space was distorted and deformed, as if some unknown dimension had somehow been mingled with ours. There was a feeling of dreadful and measureless descent, as if the floor were sinking beneath me into some nether pit; and I seemed to pass beyond the room in a torrent of swirling, hallucinative images, visible but invisible, felt but intangible, and more awful, more accurst than that hurricane of lost souls beheld by Dante.

Down, still down, I appeared to go, in the bottomless and phantom hell that was impinging upon reality. Death, decay, malignity, madness,

gathered in the air and pressed me down like Satanic incubi in that ecstatic horror of descent. I felt that there were a thousand forms, a thousand faces about me, summoned from the gulfs of perdition. And yet I
saw nothing but the white face of Averaud, stamped with a frozen and
abominable rapture as he fell beside me.

Somehow, like a dreamer who forces himself to awaken, he began
to move away from me. I seemed to lose sight of him for a moment, in
the cloud of nameless, immaterial horrors that threatened to take on the
further horror of substance. Then I realized that Averaud had turned
off the switch, and that the oscillating hammers had ceased to beat on
those infernal gongs. The double shaft of shadow faded in mid-air, the
burden of despair and terror lifted from my nerves, and I no longer felt
the damnable hallucination of nether space and descent.

"My God!" I cried. "What was it?"

Averaud's look was full of a ghastly, gloating exultation as he turned
to me.

"You saw and felt it, then?" he queried—"that vague, imperfect
manifestation of the perfect evil which exists somewhere in the cosmos?
I shall yet call it forth in its entirety, and know the black, infinite, reverse
raptures which attend its epiphany."

I recoiled from him with an involuntary shudder. All the hideous
things that had swarmed upon me beneath the cacophonous beating of
those accursed gongs, drew near again for a moment; and I looked with
fearful vertigo into hells of perversity and corruption. I saw an inverted
soul, despairing of good, which longed for the baleful ecstasies of perdition. No longer did I think him merely mad: for I knew the thing which
he sought and could attain; and I remembered, with a new significance,
that line of Baudelaire's poem—*"L'enfer dont dont mon coeur se plait."*

Averaud was unaware of my revulsion, in his dark rhapsody. When
I turned to leave, unable to bear any longer the blasphemous atmosphere of that room, and the sense of strange depravity which emanated
from its owner, he pressed me to return as soon as possible.

"I think," he exulted, "that all will be in readiness before long. I want you to be present in the hour of my triumph."

I do not know what I said, or what excuses I made to get away from him. I longed to assure myself that a world of unblasted sunlight and undefiled air could still exist. I went out; but a shadow followed me; and execrable faces leered or mowed from the foliage as I left the cypress-shaded grounds.

For days afterwards, I was in a condition verging upon neurotic disorder. No one could come as close as I had been to the primal effluence of evil, and go thence unaffected. Shadowy noisome cobwebs draped themselves on all my thoughts, and presences of unlineamented fear, of shapeless horror, crouched in the half-litten corners of my mind but would never fully declare themselves. An invisible gulf, bottomless as Malebolge, seemed to yawn before me wherever I went.

Presently, though, my reason re-asserted itself; and I wondered if my sensations in the black triangular room had not been largely a matter of suggestion or auto-hypnosis. I asked myself if it were credible that a cosmic force of the sort postulated by Averaud could really exist; or, granting its existence, could be evoked by any man through the absurd intermediation of a musical device. The nervous terrors of my experience faded a little in memory; and, though a disturbing doubt still lingered, I assured myself that all I had felt was of purely subjective origin. Even then, it was with supreme reluctance, with an inward shrinking only to be overcome by violent resolve, that I returned to visit Averaud once more.

For an even longer period than usual, no one answered my knock. Then there were hurrying footsteps, and the door was opened abruptly by Fifine. I knew immediately that something was amiss, for her face bore a look of unnatural dread and anxiety, and her eyes were wide, with the whites showing blankly, as if she gazed upon horrific things. She tried to speak, and made that ghastly inarticulate sound which the mute are able to make on occasion, as she plucked my sleeve and drew me after her along the somber hall toward the triangular room.

The door was open; and as I approached it, I heard a low, dissonant, snarling murmur, which I recognized as the sound of the gongs. It was like the voice of all the souls in a frozen hell, uttered by lips congealing slowly toward the ultimate torture of silence. It sank and sank till it seemed to be issuing from pits below the nadir.

Fifine shrank back on the threshold, imploring me with a pitiful glance to precede her. The lights were all turned on; and Averaud, clad in a strange medieval costume, in a black gown and cap such as Faustus might have worn, stood near the percussive mechanism. The hammers were all beating with a frenzied rapidity; and the sound became still lower and tenser as I approached. Averaud did not even see me: his eyes, abnormally dilated, and flaming with infernal luster like those of one possessed, were fixed upon something in mid-air.

Again the soul-congealing hideousness, the sense of eternal falling, of myriad harpy-like, incumbent horrors, rushed upon me as I looked and saw. Vaster and stronger than before, a double column of triangular shadow had materialized and was becoming more and more distinct. It swelled, it darkened, it enveloped the gong-apparatus, and towered to the ceiling. The inner column grew solid as ebony or sable marble; and the face of Averaud, who was standing well within the broad penumbral shadow, became dim as if seen through a film of Stygian water.

I must have gone utterly mad for awhile. I remember only a teeming delirium of things too frightful to be endured by a sane mind, that peopled the infinite gulf of hell-born illusion into which I sank with the hopeless precipitancy of the damned. There was a sickness inexpressible, a vertigo of irremeable descent, a pandemonium of ghoulish phantoms that reeled and swayed about the column of malign omnipotent force which presided over all. Averaud was only one more phantom in this delirium, when with arms outstretched in the agonizing rapture of his perverse adoration, he stepped toward the inner column and passed into it till he was lost to view. And Fifine was another phantom when she ran by me to the wall and turned off the switch that operated those demoniacal hammers.

As one who re-emerges from a swoon, I saw the fading of the dual pillar, till the light was no longer sullied by any tinge of that satanic radiation. And where it had been, Averaud still stood beside the baleful instrument he had designed. Erect and rigid he stood, in a strange immobility; and I felt an incredulous horror, a chill awe, as I went forward and touched him with a faltering hand. For that which I saw and touched was no longer a human being but an ebon statue, whose face and brow and fingers were black as the Faust-like raiment or the sullen curtains. Charred as by sable fire, or frozen by black cold, the features bore the commingled ecstasy and pain of Lucifer in his ultimate hell of ice. For an instant, the supreme evil which Averaud had worshipped so madly, which he had summoned from the vaults of incalculable space, had made him one with itself; and passing, it had left him petrified into an image of its own essence. The form that I touched was harder than marble; and I knew that it would endure to all time as a testimony of the infinite Medusean power that is death and corruption and darkness.

Fifine had now thrown herself at the feet of the image and was clasping its insensible knees. With her frightful muted moaning in my ears, I went forth for the last time from that chamber and from that mansion. Vainly, through delirious months and madness-ridden years, I have tried to shake off the infrangible obsession of my memories. But there is a fatal numbness in my brain, as if it too had been charred and blackened a little in that moment of overpowering nearness to the dark ray that came from pits beyond the universe. On my mind, as upon the face of the black statue that was Jean Averaud, the impress of awful and forbidden things has been set like an everlasting seal.

THE HUNTERS FROM BEYOND

I have seldom been able to resist the allurement of a book-store, particularly one that is well supplied with rare and exotic items. Therefore I turned in at Toleman's to browse around for a few minutes. I had come to San Francisco for one of my brief, biannual visits; and had started early that idle forenoon to an appointment with Cyprian Sincaul, the sculptor, a second or third cousin of mine, whom I had not seen for several years. His studio was only a block from Toleman's, and there seemed to be no especial object in reaching it ahead of time. Cyprian had offered to show me his collection of recent sculptures; but, remembering the smooth mediocrity of his former work, amid which were a few banal efforts to achieve horror and grotesquerie, I did not anticipate anything more than an hour or two of vaguely dismal boredom.

The little shop was empty of customers. Knowing my proclivities, the owner and his one assistant became tacitly non-attentive after a word of recognition, and left me to rummage at will among the curiously laden shelves. Wedged in between other but less alluring titles, I found a deluxe edition of Goya's *Proverbes*. I began to turn the heavy pages, and was soon engrossed in the diabolic art of these nightmare-nurtured drawings.

It has always been incomprehensible to me that I did not shriek aloud with mindless, overmastering terror, when I happened to look up from the volume, and saw the thing that was crouching in a corner of the book-shelves before me. I could not have been more hideously startled if some hellish conception of Goya had suddenly come to life and emerged from one of the pictures in the folio.

What I saw was a forward-slouching, vermin-grey figure, wholly devoid of hair or down or bristles, but marked with faint, etiolated rings like those of a serpent that has lived in darkness. It possessed the head and brow of an anthropoid ape, a semi-canine mouth and jaw, and arms ending in twisted hands whose black hyena talons nearly scraped the floor. The thing was infinitely bestial, and, at the same time, macabre; for its parchment skin was shrivelled, corpse-like, mummified, in a manner impossible to convey; and from eye-sockets well-nigh deep as those of a skull, there glimmered evil slits of yellowish phosphorescence, like burning sulfur. Fangs that were stained as if with poison or gangrene, issued from the slavering, half-open mouth; and the whole attitude of the creature was that of some maleficent monster in readiness to spring.

Though I had been for years a professional writer of stories that often dealt with occult phenomena, with the weird and the spectral, I was not at this time possessed of any clear and settled belief regarding such phenomena. I had never before seen anything that I could identify as a phantom, nor even an hallucination; and I should hardly have said off-hand that a book-store on a busy street, in full summer daylight, was the likeliest of places in which to see one. But the thing before me was assuredly nothing that could ever exist among the permissible forms of a sane world. It was too horrific, too atrocious, to be anything but a creation of unreality.

Even as I stared across the Goya, sick with half-incredulous fear, the apparition moved toward me. I say that it moved—but its change of position was so instantaneous, so utterly without effort or visible transition, that the verb is hopelessly inadequate. The foul specter had seemed five or six feet away—but now it was stooping directly above the volume that I still held in my hands, with its loathsomely lambent eyes peering upward at my face, and a grey-green slime drooling from its mouth on the broad pages. At the same time I breathed an insupportable fetor, like a mingling of rancid serpent-stench with the mouldiness of antique charnels and the fearsome reek of newly decaying carrion. In a frozen timelessness that was perhaps no more than a second or two, my heart appeared to suspend its beating, while I beheld the ghastly face with a clearness too obscene for depiction. Gasping, I let the Goya drop with a resonant bang on the floor, and even as it fell, I saw that the vision had vanished.

"What is wrong, Mr. Hastane? Are you ill?" Toleman, a tonsured gnome with shell-rimmed goggles, had rushed forward to retrieve the fallen volume. From the meticulousness with which he examined the binding in search of possible damage, I knew that his chief solicitude was concerning the Goya. It was plain that neither he nor his clerk had seen the phantom; nor could I detect aught in their demeanor to indicate that they had noticed the mephitic odor that still lingered on the air like an exhalation from broken graves. And, as far as I could tell, they did not even perceive the greyish slime that still polluted the open folio.

I do not remember how I managed to make my exit from the shop. My mind had become a seething blur of muddled horror, of crawling, sick revulsion from the supernatural vileness I had beheld, together with the direst apprehension for my own sanity and safety. I recall only that I found myself on the street above Toleman's, walking with feverish rapidity toward my cousin's studio, with a neat parcel containing the Goya volume under my arm. Evidently, in an effort to atone for my clumsiness, I must have bought and paid for the book by a sort of automatic impulse, without any real awareness of what I was doing.

I came to the building in which was my destination but went on around the block several times before entering. All the while I fought desperately to regain my self-control and equipoise. I remember how difficult it was even to moderate the pace at which I was walking, or refrain from breaking into a run; for it seemed to me that I was fleeing all the time from an invisible pursuer. I tried to argue with myself, to convince the rational part of my mind that the apparition had been the product of some evanescent trick of light and shade, or a temporary dimming of eyesight. But such sophistries were useless; for I had seen the gargoylish terror all too distinctly, in an unforgettable fullness of grisly detail.

What could the thing mean? I had never used narcotic drugs nor abused alcohol. My nerves, as far as I knew, were in sound condition. But either I had suffered a visual hallucination that might mark the beginning of some obscure cerebral disorder, or had been visited by a spectral phenomenon, by something from realms and dimensions that are past the normal scope of human perception. It was a problem either for the alienist or the occultist.

Though I was still damnably upset, I contrived to regain a nominal composure of my faculties. Also, it occurred to me that the unimaginative portrait-busts and tamely symbolic figure-groups of Cyprian Sincaul might serve admirably to sooth my shaken nerves. Even his grotesques would seem sane and ordinary by comparison with the blasphemous gargoyle that had drooled before me in the bookshop.

I entered the studio-building, and climbed a worn stairway to the second floor, where Cyprian had established himself in a somewhat capacious suite of rooms. As I went up the stairs, I had the peculiar feeling that somebody was climbing them just ahead of me; but I could neither see nor hear anyone; and the hall above was no less silent and empty than the stairs.

Cyprian was in his atelier when I knocked. After an interval which seemed unduly long, I heard him call out, telling me to enter. I found him wiping his hands on an old cloth, and surmised that he had been modeling. A sheet of light burlap had been thrown over what was plainly an ambitious but unfinished group of figures, which occupied the center of the long room. All around were other sculptures, in clay, bronze, marble, and even the terra-cotta and steatite which he sometimes employed for his less conventional conceptions. At one end of the room there stood a heavy Chinese screen.

At a single glance, I realized that a great change had occurred, both in Cyprian Sincaul and his work. I remembered him as an amiable, somewhat flabby-looking youth, always dapperly dressed, with no trace of the dreamer or visionary. It was hard to recognize him now, for he had become lean, harsh, vehement, with an air of pride and penetration that was almost Luciferian. His unkempt mane of hair was already shot with white; and his eyes were electrically brilliant with a strange knowledge, and yet somehow were vaguely furtive, as if there dwelt behind them a morbid and macabre fear.

The change in his sculpture was no less striking. The respectable tameness and polished mediocrity were gone; and in their place, incredibly, was something little short of genius. More unbelievable still, in view of the laboriously ordinary grotesques of his earlier phase, was the trend that his art had now taken. All around me were frenetic, murderous demons, satyrs mad with nympholepsy, ghouls that seemed to sniff the odors of the charnel, lamias voluptuously coiled about their victims, and less namable things that belonged to the outland realms of evil myth and malign superstition.

Sin, horror, blasphemy, diablerie—the lust and malice of pandemonium—all had been caught with impeccable art. The potent nightmarishness of these creations was not calculated to reassure my trembling nerves; and all at once I felt an imperative desire to escape from the studio, to flee from the baleful throng of frozen cacodemons and chiselled chimeras.

My expression must have betrayed my feeling to some extent.

"Pretty strong work, aren't they?" said Cyprian, in a loud, vibrant voice, with a note of harsh pride and triumph. "I can see that you are surprised—you didn't look for anything of the sort, I dare say."

"No, candidly, I didn't," I admitted. "Good Lord, man, you will become the Michelangelo of diabolism if you go on at this rate. Where on earth do you get such stuff?"

"Yes, I've gone pretty far," said Cyprian, seeming to disregard my question. "Further even than you think, probably. If you could know what I know, could see what I have seen, you might make something really worth while out of your weird fiction, Philip. You are very clever and imaginative, of course. But you've never had any experience."

I was startled and puzzled. "Experience? What do you mean?"

"Precisely that. You try to depict the occult and the supernatural without even the most rudimentary first-hand knowledge of them. I tried to do something of the same sort in sculpture, years ago, without knowledge; and doubtless you recall the mediocre mess that I made of it. But I've learned a thing or two since then."

"Sounds as if you had made the traditional bond with the Devil, or something of the sort," I observed, with a feeble and perfunctory levity.

Cyprian's eyes narrowed slightly, with a strange, secret look.

"I know what I know. Never mind how or why. The world in which we live isn't the only world; and some of the others lie closer at hand than you think. The boundaries of the seen and the unseen are sometimes interchangeable."

Recalling the malevolent phantom, I felt a peculiar disquietude as I listened to his words. An hour before, his statement would have impressed me as mere nebular theorizing; but now it assumed an ominous and terrifying significance.

"What makes you think I have had no experience of the occult?" I asked.

"Your stories hardly show anything of the kind—anything factual or personal. They are all palpably made up. When you've argued with a ghost, or watched the ghouls at meal-time, or fought with an incubus, or suckled a vampire, you may achieve some genuine characterization and color along such lines."

For reasons that should be fairly obvious, I had not intended to tell anyone of the unbelievable thing at Toleman's. Now, with a singular mixture of emotions, of compulsive, eerie terrors and desire to refute the animadversions of Cyprian, I found myself describing the phantom.

He listened with an inexpressive look, as if his thoughts were occupied with other matters than my story. Then, when I had finished:

"You are becoming more psychic than I imagined. Was your apparition anything like one of these?"

With the last words, he lifted the sheet of burlap from the muffled group of figures beside which he had been standing.

I cried out involuntarily with the shock of that appalling revelation, and almost tottered as I stepped back. Before me, in a monstrous semi-circle, were seven creatures who might all have been modeled from the loathly gargoyle that had confronted me across the folio of Goya draw-ings. Even in several that were still amorphous or incomplete, Cyprian had conveyed with a damnable art the peculiar mingling of primal bes-tiality and mortuary putrescence that had signalized the phantom. The seven monsters had closed in on a cowering, naked girl, and were all clutching foully toward her with their hyena claws. The stark, frantic, insane terror on the face of the girl, and the slavering hunger of her assailants, were alike unbearable. The group was a masterpiece, in its consummate power of technique—but a masterpiece that inspired loathing rather than admiration. And, following my recent experience, the sight of it affected me with indescribable alarm. It seemed to me that I had gone astray from the normal, familiar world into a land of detest-able mystery, of prodigious and unnatural menace.

Held by an abhorrent fascination, it was hard for me to wrench my eyes away from the figure-piece. At last I turned from it to Cyprian him-self. He was regarding me with a cryptic air, beneath which I suspected a covert gloating.

"How do you like my little pets?" he inquired. "I am going to call the composition 'The Hunters from Beyond.'"

Before I could answer, a woman suddenly appeared from behind the Chinese screen. I saw that she was the model for the girl in the un-finished group. Evidently she had been dressing, and was now ready to leave, for she wore a tailored suit and a smart toque. She was beautiful, in a dark, semi-Latin fashion; but her mouth was sullen and reluctant, and her wide, liquid eyes were wells of strange terror as she gazed at Cyprian, myself and the uncovered statue-piece.

Cyprian did not introduce me. He and the girl talked together in low tones for a minute or two, and I was unable to overhear more than half of what they said. I gathered, however, that an appointment was being made for the next sitting. There was a pleading, frightened note in the girl's voice, together with an almost maternal concern; and Cyprian seemed to be arguing with her or trying to reassure her about something. At last she went out, with a queer, supplicative glance at me—a glance whose meaning I could only surmise and could not wholly fathom.

"That was Marta," said Cyprian. "She is half Irish, half Italian. A good model; but my new sculptures seem to be making her a little nervous." He laughed abruptly, with a mirthless, jarring note that was like the cachinnation of a sorcerer.

"In God's name, what are you trying to do here?" I burst out. "What does it all mean? Do such abominations really exist, on earth or in any hell?"

He laughed again, with an evil subtlety, and became evasive all at once. "Anything may exist, in a boundless universe with multiple dimensions. Anything may be real—or unreal. Who knows? It is not for me to say. Figure it out for yourself, if you can—there's a vast field for speculation—and perhaps for more than speculation."

With this, he began immediately to talk of other topics. Baffled, mystified, with a sorely troubled mind and nerves that were more unstrung than ever by the black enigma of it all, I ceased to question him. Simultaneously, my desire to leave the studio became almost overwhelming—a mindless, whirlwind panic that prompted me to run pell-mell from the room and down the stairs into the wholesome normality of the common, twentieth century streets. It seemed to me that the rays which fell through the skylight were not those of the sun but of some darker orb; that the room was touched with unclean webs of shadow where shadow should not have been; that the stone Satans, the bronze lamias, the terra-cotta satyrs, and the clay gargoyles had somehow increased in number and might spring to malignant life at any instant.

Hardly knowing what I said, I continued to converse for awhile with Cyprian. Then, excusing myself on the score of a nonexistent luncheon appointment, and promising vaguely to return for another visit before my departure from the city, I took my leave.

I was surprised to find my cousin's model in the lower hall, at the foot of the stairway. From her manner, and her first words, it was plain that she had been waiting for me.

"You are Mr. Philip Hastane, aren't you?" she said, in an eager, agitated voice. "I am Marta Fitzgerald. Cyprian has often mentioned you; and I believe that he admires you a lot.

"Maybe you'll think me crazy," she went on, "but I had to speak to you. I can't stand the way that things are going here; and I'd refuse to come to the place any more, if it wasn't that I . . . like Cyprian so much.

"I don't know what he has done—or what has been done to him—but he is altogether different from what he used to be. His new work is so horrible—you can't imagine how it frightens me. The sculptures he does are more hideous, more hellish all the time. Ugh! those drooling, dead-grey monsters in that new group of his—I can hardly bear to be in the studio with them. It isn't right for anyone to depict such things. Don't you think they are awful, Mr. Hastane? They look as if they had broken loose from hell—and make you think that hell can't be very far away. It is wrong and wicked for anyone to . . . even imagine them; and I wish that Cyprian would stop. I am afraid that something will happen to him—to his mind—if he goes on. And I'll go mad, too, if I have to see those monsters many more times. My God! No one could keep sane in that studio."

She paused, and appeared to hesitate. Then:

"Can't you do something, Mr. Hastane? Can't you talk to him, and tell him how wrong it is, and how dangerous to his mental health? You must have a lot of influence with Cyprian—you are his cousin, aren't you? And he thinks you are very clever too. I wouldn't ask you, if I hadn't been forced to notice so many things that aren't as they should be.

"I wouldn't bother you either, if I knew anyone else to ask. He has shut himself up in that awful studio for the past year; and he hardly ever sees anybody. You are the first person that he has invited to see his new sculptures. He wants them to be a complete surprise for the critics and the public, when he holds his next exhibition.

"But you'll speak to Cyprian, won't you, Mr. Hastane? I can't do anything to stop him—he seems to exult in the mad horrors he creates. And he merely laughs at me when I try to tell him the danger. However, I think that those things are making him a little nervous sometimes— that he is growing afraid . . . of his own morbid imagination. Perhaps he will listen to you."

If I had needed anything more to unnerve me, the desperate pleading of the girl and her dark, obscurely baleful hintings would have been enough. I could see that she loved Cyprian, that she was frantically anxious concerning him, and hysterically afraid; otherwise, she would not have approached an utter stranger in this fashion.

"But I haven't any influence with Cyprian," I protested, feeling a queer embarrassment. "And what am I to say to him, anyway? Whatever he is doing is his own affair, not mine. His new sculptures are magnificent—I have never seen anything more powerful of the kind. And how could I advise him to stop doing them? There would be no legitimate reason—he would simply laugh me out of the studio. An artist has the right to choose his own subject-matter, even if he takes it from the nether pits of Limbo and Erebus."

The girl must have pleaded and argued with me for many minutes in that deserted hall. Listening to her, and trying to convince her of my inability to fulfill her request, was like a dialogue in some futile and tedious nightmare. During the course of it, she told me a few details that I am unwilling to record in this narrative; details that were too morbid and too shocking for belief, regarding the mental alteration of Cyprian, and his new subject-matter and method of work. There were direct and oblique hints of a growing perversion; but somehow it seemed that much more was being held back; that even in her most horrifying disclosures she was not wholly frank with me. At last, with some sort of hazy promise that I would speak to Cyprian, would remonstrate with him, I succeeded in getting away from her, and returned to my hotel.

The afternoon and evening that followed were tinged as by the tyrannous adumbration of an ill dream. I felt that I had stepped from the solid earth into a gulf of seething, menacing, madness-haunted shadow, and was lost henceforward to all rightful sense of location or direction. It was all too hideous—and too doubtful and unreal. The change in Cyprian himself was no less bewildering, and hardly less horrifying, than the vile phantom of the bookshop, and the demon sculptures that displayed a magisterial art. It was as if the man had become possessed by some Satanical energy or entity.

Everywhere that I went, I was powerless to shake off the feeling of an intangible pursuit, of a frightful, unseen vigilance. It seemed to me that the worm-grey face and sulphurous eyes would reappear at any moment; that the semi-canine mouth with its gangrene-dripping fangs might come to slaver above the restaurant table at which I ate, or upon the pillow of my bed. I did not dare to reopen the purchased Goya volume, for fear of finding that certain pages were still defiled with a spectral slime.

I went out, and spent the evening in cafés, in theaters, wherever people thronged and lights were bright. It was after midnight when I finally ventured to brave the solitude of my hotel bedroom. Then there were endless hours of nerve-wrung insomnia, of shivering, sweating apprehension beneath the electric bulb that I had left burning. Finally, a little before dawn, by no conscious transition and with no premonitory drowsiness, I fell asleep.

I remember no dreams—only the vast incubus-like oppression that persisted even in the depth of slumber, as if to drag me down with its formless, ever-clinging weight in gulfs beyond the reach of created light or the fathoming of organized entity.

It was almost noon when I awoke, and found myself staring into the verminous, apish, mummy-dead face and hell-illumined eyes of the gargoyle that had crouched before me in the corner at Toleman's. The thing was standing at the foot of my bed; and behind it as I stared, the wall of the room, which was covered with a floral paper, dissolved in an infinite vista of greyness, teeming with ghoulish forms that emerged like monstrous, misshapen bubbles from plains of undulant ooze and skies of serpentining vapor. It was another world—and my very sense of equilibrium was disturbed by an evil vertigo as I gazed. It seemed to me that my bed was heaving dizzily, was turning slowly, deliriously toward the gulf—that the feculent vista and the vile apparition were swimming beneath me—that I would fall toward them in another moment and be precipitated forever into that world of abysmal monstrosity and obscenity.

In a start of profoundest alarm, I fought my vertigo, fought the sense that another will than mine was drawing me, that the unclean gargoyle was luring me by some unspeakable mesmeric spell, as a serpent is said to lure its prey. I seemed to read a nameless purpose in its yellow-slitted eyes, in the soundless moving of its oozy, chancrous lips; and my very soul recoiled with nausea and revulsion as I breathed its pestilential fetor.

Apparently, the mere effort of mental resistance was enough. The vista and the face receded; they went out in a swirl of daylight. I saw the design of tea-roses on the wallpaper beyond; and the bed beneath me was sanely horizontal once more. I lay sweating with my terror, all adrift on a sea of nightmare surmise, of unearthly threat and whirlpool madness; till the ringing of the telephone bell recalled me automatically to the known world.

I sprang to answer the call. It was Cyprian, though I should hardly have recognized the dead, hopeless tones of his voice, from which the mad pride and self-assurance of the previous day had wholly vanished.

"I must see you at once," he said. "Can you come to the studio?"

I was about to refuse, to tell him that I had been called home suddenly, that there was no time, that I must catch the noon train—anything to avert the ordeal of another visit to that place of mephitic evil—

when I heard his voice again.

"You simply must come, Philip. I can't tell you about it over the phone, but a dreadful thing has happened: Marta has disappeared."

I consented, telling him that I would start for the studio as soon as I had dressed. The whole environing nightmare had closed in, had deepened immeasurably with his last words; but remembering the haunted face of the girl, her hysteric fears, her frantic pleas and my vague promise, I could not very well decline to go.

I dressed and went out with my mind in a turmoil of abominable conjecture, of ghastly doubt, and apprehension all the more hideous because I was unsure of its object. I tried to imagine what had happened, tried to piece together the frightful, evasive, half-admitted hints of unknown terror into a tangible coherent fabric; but found myself involved in a chaos of shadowy menace.

I could not have eaten any breakfast, even if I had taken the necessary time. I went at once to the studio, and found Cyprian standing aimlessly amid his baleful statuary. His look was that of a man who has been stunned by the blow of some crushing weapon, or has gazed on the very face of Medusa. He greeted me in a vacant manner, with dull, toneless words. Then, like a charged machine, as if his body rather than his mind were speaking, he began at once to pour forth the atrocious narrative.

"They took her," he said, simply. "Maybe you didn't know it, or weren't sure of it; but I've been doing all my new sculptures from life—even that last group. Marta was posing for me this forenoon—only an hour ago—or less. I had hoped to finish her part of the modelling today; and she wouldn't have had to come again for this particular piece. I hadn't called the Things this time, since I knew she was beginning to fear them more and more. I think she feared them on my account more than her own . . . and they were making me a little uneasy too, by the boldness with which they sometimes lingered when I had ordered them to leave—and the way they would sometimes appear when I didn't want them.

"I was busy with some of the final touches on the girl-figure, and wasn't even looking at Marta, when suddenly I knew that the Things were there. The smell told me, if nothing else—I guess you know what the smell is like. I looked up, and found that the studio was full of them—they had never before appeared in such numbers. They were surrounding Marta, were crowding and jostling each other, were all reaching toward her with their filthy talons; but even then, I didn't think that they could harm her. They aren't material beings, in the sense that we are; and they really have no physical power outside of their own plane. All that they do have is a sort of snaky mesmerism, and they'll always try to drag you down to their own dimension by means of it. God help anyone who yields to them; but you don't have to go, unless you are weak, or willing. I've never had any doubt of my power to resist them; and I didn't really dream they could do anything to Marta.

"It startled me, though, when I saw the whole crowding hell-pack, and I ordered them to go pretty sharply. I was angry—and somewhat alarmed, too. But they merely grimaced and slavered, with that slow, twisting movement of their lips that is like a voiceless gibbering; and then they closed in on Marta, just as I represented them doing in that accursed group of sculpture. Only there were scores of them now, instead of merely seven.

"I can't describe how it happened, but all at once their foul talons had reached the girl; they were pawing her, were pulling at her hands, her arms, her body. She screamed—and I hope I'll never hear another scream so full of black agony and soul-unhinging fright. Then I knew that she had yielded to them—either from choice, or from excess of terror—and knew that they were taking her away.

"For a moment, the studio wasn't there at all—only a long, grey, oozing plain, beneath skies where the fumes of hell were writhing like a million ghostly and distorted dragons. Marta was sinking into that ooze—and the Things were all about her, were gathering in fresh hundreds from every side, were fighting each other for place, were sinking with her like bloated, misshapen fen-creatures into their native slime.

Then everything vanished—and I was standing here in the studio—all alone with these damned sculptures."

He paused for a little, and stared with dreary, desolate eyes at the floor. Then:

"It was awful, Philip, and I'll never forgive myself for having anything to do with those monsters. I must have been a little mad; but I've always had a strong ambition to create some real stuff in the field of the grotesque and visionary and macabre. I don't suppose you ever suspected, back in my stodgy phase, that I had a veritable appetence for such things. I wanted to do in sculpture what Poe and Lovecraft and Baudelaire have done in literature, what Rops and Goya did in pictorial art.

"That was what led me into the occult, when I realized my limitations. I knew that I had to *see* the dwellers of the invisible worlds before I could depict them. I wanted to do it. I longed for this power of vision and representation more than anything else. And then, all at once, I found that I had the power of summoning the unseen. . . .

"There was no magic involved, in the usual sense of the word—no spells and circles, no pentacles and burning gums from old sorcery books. At bottom, it was just will-power, I guess—a will to divine the Satanic, to summon the innumerable malignities and grotesqueries that people other planes than ours, or mingle unperceived with humanity.

"You've no idea what I have beheld, Philip. These statues of mine—these devils, vampires, lamias, satyrs—were all done from life, or, at least from recent memory. The originals are what the occultists would call elementals, I suppose. There are endless worlds, contiguous to our own, or co-existing with it, that such beings inhabit. All the creations of myth and fantasy, all the familiar spirits that sorcerers have evoked, are resident in these worlds.

"I made myself their master, I levied upon them at will. Then, from a dimension that must be a little lower than all others, a little nearer the ultimate nadir of hell, I called the innominate beings who posed for this new figure-piece.

"I don't know what they are—but I have surmised a good deal. They are hateful as the worms of the Pit, they are malevolent as harpies, they drool with a poisonous hunger not to be named or imagined. But I believed that they were powerless to do anything outside of their own sphere; and I've always laughed at them when they tried to entice me—even though that snakish mental pull of theirs was rather creepy at times. It was as if soft, invisible, gelatinous arms were trying to drag you down from the firm shore into a bottomless bog.

"They are hunters—I am sure of that—the hunters from Beyond. God knows what they will do to Marta now that they have her at their mercy. That vast, viscid, miasma-haunted place to which they took her is awful beyond the imagining of a Satan. Perhaps—even there—they couldn't harm her body. But bodies aren't what they want—it isn't for human flesh that they grope with those ghoulish claws, and gape and slaver with those gangrenous mouths. The brain itself—and the soul, too—is their food: they are the creatures who prey on the minds of madmen and madwomen, who devour the disembodied spirits that have fallen from the cycles of incarnation, have gone down beyond the possibility of rebirth.

"To think of Marta in their power—it is worse than hell or madness. Marta loved me—and I loved her, too, though I didn't have the sense to realize it, wrapped as I was in my dark, baleful ambition and impious egotism. She was afraid for me—and I believe she surrendered voluntarily to the Things. She must have thought that they would leave me alone—if they secured another victim in my place."

He ceased, and began to pace idly and feverishly about. I saw that his hollow eyes were alight with torment, as if the mechanical telling of his horrible story had in some manner served to re-quicken his crushed mind. Utterly and starkly appalled by his hideous revelations, I could say nothing, but could only stand and watch his torture-twisted face.

Incredibly, his expression changed, with a wild, startled look that was instantly transfigured into joy. Turning to follow his gaze, I saw that

Marta was standing in the center of the room. She was nude, except for a Spanish shawl that she must have worn while posing. Her face was bloodless as the marble of a tomb, and her eyes were wide and blank, as if she had been drained of all life, of all thought or emotion or memory—as if even the knowledge of horror had been taken away from her. It was the face of the living dead, the soulless mask of ultimate idiocy; and the joy faded from Cyprian's eyes as he stepped toward her.

He took her in his arms, he spoke to her with a desperate, loving tenderness, with cajoling and caressing words. She made no answer, no movement of recognition or awareness, but stared beyond him with her blank eyes, to which the daylight and the darkness, the void air and her lover's face, would henceforward be the same. He and I both knew, in that instant, that she would never again respond to any human voice, or to human love or terror; that she was like an empty cerement, retaining the outward form of that which the worms have eaten in their mausolean darkness. Of the noisome pits wherein she had been, of that bournless realm and its pullulating phantoms, she could tell us nothing: her agony had ended with the terrible mercy of complete forgetfulness.

Like one who confronts the Gorgon, I was frozen by her wide and sightless gaze. Then, behind her, where stood an array of carven Satans and lamias, the room seemed to recede, the walls and floors dissolved in a seething, unfathomable gulf, amid whose pestilential vapors the statues were mingled in momentary and loathsome ambiguity with the ravening faces, the hunger-contorted forms that swirled toward us from their ultra-dimensional limbo like a devil-laden hurricane from Malebolge. Outlined against that boiling measureless cauldron of malignant storm, Marta stood like an image of glacial death and silence in the arms of Cyprian. Then, once more, after a little, the abhorrent vision faded, leaving only the diabolic statuary.

I think that I alone had beheld it; that Cyprian had seen nothing but the dead, mindless face of Marta. He drew her close, he repeated his hopeless words of tenderness and cajolery. Then, suddenly, he released her with a vehement sob of despair. Turning away, while she stood and still looked on with unseeing eyes, he snatched a heavy sculptor's mallet from the table on which it was lying, and proceeded to smash with furious blows the newly-modelled group of gargoyles, till nothing was left but the figure of the terror-maddened girl, crouching above a mass of cloddish fragments and formless, half-dried clay.

THE FROZEN WATERFALL

I returned on a winter day to the mountain stream, upon whose banks we roamed so long ago, when the rich azaleas leaned above it with their load of bloom, and butterflies more white than their blossoms were on the wing. And I sought the many-stranded waterfall that plunged from a mossy boulder beneath the flowering branches, where once we loitered and loved each other well, and listened to the splashing of the stream. And now the azaleas were bare, and their leaves had long flown adown the torrent, and the foamy tresses of the fall had turned to gleaming ice, and all hung in silence like downward-pointing blades that never dropped.

And seeing it, I thought of deterred desires and aspirations, of violent longings checked and frozen in their course. And I found in the waterfall the symbol I had sought; and finding it, I was doubly sad. . . . For was it not the symbol of my soul?

THE CITY OF THE SINGING FLAME

Foreword

We had been friends for a decade or more, and I knew Giles Angarth as well as anyone could purport to know him. Yet the thing was no less a mystery to me than to others at the time, and it is still a mystery. Sometimes I think that he and Ebbonly had designed it all between them as a huge, insoluble hoax; that they are still alive, somewhere, and are laughing at the world that has been so sorely baffled by their disappearance. And sometimes I make tentative plans to re-visit Crater Ridge and find, if I can, the two boulders mentioned in Angarth's narrative as having a vague resemblance to broken-down columns. In the meanwhile no one has uncovered any trace of the missing men or has heard even the faintest rumor concerning them; and the whole affair, it would seem, is likely to remain a most singular and exasperating riddle.

Angarth, whose fame as a writer of fantastic fiction will probably outlive that of most other modern magazine contributors, had been spending that summer among the Sierras, and had been living alone till the artist Felix Ebbonly went to visit him. Ebbonly, whom I had never met, was well known for his imaginative paintings and drawings; and he had illustrated more than one of Angarth's novels. When neighboring campers became alarmed over the prolonged absence of the two men and the cabin was searched for some possible clue, a package addressed to me was found lying on the table; and I received it in due course of time, after reading many newspaper speculations regarding the double vanishment. The package contained a small, leather-bound notebook. Angarth had written on the fly-leaf:

Dear Hastane,

    You can publish this journal sometime, if you like. People will think it the last and wildest of all my fictions—unless they take it for one of your own. In either case, it will be just as well. Good-bye.

Faithfully,

Giles Angarth.

    I am now publishing the journal, which will doubtless meet the reception he predicted. But I am not so certain myself, as to whether the tale is truth or fabrication. The only way to make sure will be to locate the two boulders; and anyone who has ever seen Crater Ridge, and has wandered over its miles of rock-strewn desolation, will realize the difficulties of such a task.

The Journal

July 31st, 1930. I have never acquired the diary-keeping habit—mainly, no doubt, because of my uneventful mode of existence, in which there has seldom been anything to chronicle. But the thing which happened this morning is so extravagantly strange, so remote from mundane laws and parallels, that I feel impelled to write it down to the best of my understanding and ability. Also, I shall keep account of the possible repetition and continuation of my experience. It will be perfectly safe to do this, for no one who ever reads the record will be likely to believe it.

    I had gone for a walk on Crater Ridge, which lies a mile or less to the north of my cabin near Summit. Though differing markedly in its character from the usual landscapes roundabout, it is one of my favorite places. It is exceptionally bare and desolate, with little more in the way of vegetation than mountain sun-flowers, wild currant-bushes, and a few sturdy, wind-warped pines and supple tamaracks. Geologists deny it a volcanic origin; yet its outcroppings of rough, nodular stone and enormous rubble-heaps have all the air of scoriac remains—at least, to my non-scientific eye. They look like the slag and refuse of Cyclopean furnaces, poured out in pre-human years, to cool and harden into shapes

of limitless grotesquery. Among them are stones that suggest the fragments of primordial bas-reliefs, or small prehistoric idols and figurines;
and others that seem to have been graven with lost letters of an indecipherable script. Unexpectedly, there is a little tarn lying on one end of
the long, dry Ridge—a tarn that has never been fathomed. The hill is an
odd interlude among the granite sheets and crags, and the fir-clothed
ravines and valleys of this region.

It was a clear, windless morning, and I paused often to view the
magnificent perspectives of varied scenery that were visible on every
hand—the titan battlements of Castle Peak; the rude masses of Donner
Peak, with its dividing pass of hemlocks; the remote, luminous blue of
the Nevada Mountains, and the soft green of willows in the valley at my
feet. It was an aloof, silent world, and I heard no sound other than the
dry, crackling noise of cicadas among the currant-bushes.

I strolled on in a zig-zag manner for some distance, and coming to
one of the rubble-fields with which the Ridge is interstrewn, I began to
search the ground closely, hoping to find a stone that was sufficiently
quaint and grotesque in its form to be worth keeping as a curiosity. I
had found several such in my previous wanderings. Suddenly I came to
a clear space amid the rubble, in which nothing grew—a space that was
round as an artificial ring. In the center were two isolated boulders,
queerly alike in shape, and lying about five feet apart. I paused to examine them. Their substance, a dull, greenish-grey stone, seemed to be different from anything else in the neighborhood; and I conceived at once
the weird, unwarrantable fancy that they might be the pedestals of vanished columns, worn away by incalculable years till there remained only
these sunken ends. Certainly the perfect roundness and uniformity of
the boulders was peculiar; and though I possess a smattering of geology,
I could not identify their smooth, soapy material.

My imagination was excited, and I began to indulge in some rather
overheated fantasies. But the wildest of these was a homely commonplace in comparison with the thing that happened when I took a single

step forward in the vacant space immediately between the two boulders. I shall try to describe it to the utmost of my ability; though human language is naturally wanting in words that are adequate for the delineation of events and sensations beyond the normal scope of human experience.

Nothing is more disconcerting than to miscalculate the degree of descent in taking a step. Imagine then what it was like to step forward on level, open ground, and find utter nothingness underfoot! I seemed to be going down into an empty gulf, and at the same time the landscape before me vanished in a swirl of broken images and everything went blind. There was a feeling of intense, hyperborean cold, and an indescribable sickness and vertigo possessed me, due, no doubt, to the profound disturbance of equilibrium. Also—either from the speed of my descent or for some other reason—I was totally unable to draw breath. My thoughts and feelings were unutterably confused, and half the time it seemed to me that I was falling *upward* rather than downward, or was sliding horizontally or at some oblique angle. At last I had the sensation of turning a complete somersault; and then I found myself standing erect on solid ground once more, without the least shock or jar of impact. The darkness cleared away from my vision, but I was still dizzy, and the optical images I received were altogether meaningless for some moments.

When finally I recovered the power of cognizance, and was able to view my surroundings with a measure of perception, I experienced a mental confusion equivalent to that of a man who might find himself cast without warning on the shore of some foreign planet. There was the same sense of utter loss and alienation which would assuredly be felt in such a case—the same vertiginous, overwhelming bewilderment, the same ghastly sense of separation from all the familiar environmental details that give color and form and definition to our lives and even determine our very personalities.

I was standing in the midst of a landscape which bore no degree or manner of resemblance to Crater Ridge. A long, gradual slope, covered with violet grass and studded at intervals with stones of monolithic size and shape, ran undulantly away beneath me to a broad plain with sinuous, open meadows and high, stately forests of an unknown vegetation whose predominant hues were purple and yellow. The plain seemed to end in a wall of impenetrable, golden-brownish mist, that rose with phantom pinnacles to dissolve on a sky of luminescent amber in which there was no sun.

In the foreground of this amazing scene, not more than two or three miles away, there loomed a city whose massive towers and mountainous ramparts of red stone were such as the Anakim of undiscovered worlds might build. Wall on beetling wall, and spire on giant spire, it soared to confront the heavens, maintaining everywhere the severe and solemn lines of a wholly rectilinear architecture. It seemed to whelm and crush down the beholder with its stern and crag-like imminence.

As I viewed this city, I forgot my initial sense of bewildering loss and alienage, in an awe with which something of actual terror was mingled; and, at the same time, I felt an obscure but profound allurement, the cryptic emanation of some enslaving spell. But after I had gazed awhile, the cosmic strangeness and bafflement of my unthinkable position returned upon me; and I felt only a wild desire to escape from the maddeningly oppressive bizarrerie of this region and regain my own world. In an effort to fight down my agitation, I tried to figure out if possible what had really happened.

I had read a number of trans-dimensional stories—in fact, I had written one or two myself; and I had often pondered the possibility of other worlds or material planes which may co-exist in the same space with ours, invisible and impalpable to human senses. Of course, I realized at once that I had fallen into some such dimension. Doubtless, when I took that step forward between the boulders, I had been precipitated into some sort of flaw or fissure in space, to emerge at the bottom in this alien sphere—in a totally different kind of space. It sounded simple enough in a way—but not simple enough to make the *modus operandi* anything but a brain-racking mystery.

In a further effort to collect myself, I studied my immediate surroundings with a close attention. This time, I was impressed by the arrangement of the monolithic stones I have spoken of, many of which were disposed at fairly regular intervals in two parallel lines running down the hill, as if to mark the course of some ancient road obliterated by the purple grass. Turning to follow its ascent, I saw right behind me two columns, standing at precisely the same distance apart as the two odd boulders on Crater Ridge, and formed of the same soapy, greenish-grey stone! The pillars were perhaps nine feet high, and had been taller at one time, since the tops were splintered and broken away. Not far above them, the mounting slope vanished from view in a great bank of the same golden-brown mist that enveloped the remoter plain. But there were no more monoliths—and it seemed as if the road had ended with those pillars.

Inevitably I began to speculate as to the relationship between the columns in this new dimension and the boulders in my own world. Surely the resemblance could not be a matter of mere chance. If I stepped between the columns, could I return to the human sphere by a reversal of my precipitation therefrom? And if so, by what inconceivable beings from foreign time and space had the columns and boulders been established as the portals of a gateway between the two worlds? Who could have used the gateway, and for what purpose? My brain reeled before the infinite vistas of surmise that were opened by such questions.

However, what concerned me most was the problem of getting back to Crater Ridge. The weirdness of it all, the monstrous walls of the nearby town, the unnatural hues and forms of the outlandish scenery, were too much for human nerves; and I felt that I should go mad if forced to remain long in such a milieu. Also, there was no telling what hostile powers or entities I might encounter if I stayed. The slope and plain were devoid of animate life, as far as I could see; but the great city was presumptive proof of its existence. Unlike the heroes in my own tales, who were wont to visit the fifth dimension or the worlds of Algol with perfect *sang froid,* I did not feel in the least adventurous; and I shrank back with man's instinctive recoil before the unknown. With one fearful glance at the looming city and the wide plain with its lofty, gorgeous vegetation, I turned and stepped back between the columns.

There was the same instantaneous plunge into blind and freezing gulfs, the same indeterminate falling and twisting, that had marked my descent into this new dimension. At the end I found myself standing, very dizzy and shaken, on the same spot from which I had taken my forward step between the greenish-grey boulders. Crater Ridge was swirling and reeling about me as if in the throes of earthquake; and I had to sit down for a minute or two before I could recover my equilibrium.

I came back to the cabin like a man in a dream. The experience seemed, and still seems, incredible and unreal; and yet it has overshadowed everything else, and has colored and dominated all my thoughts. Perhaps by writing it down I can shake it off a little. It has unsettled me more than any previous experience in my whole life, and the world about me seems hardly less improbable and nightmarish than the one that I have penetrated in a fashion so fortuitous.

August 2nd. I have done a lot of thinking in the past few days—and the more I ponder and puzzle, the more mysterious it all becomes. Granting the flaw in space, which must be an absolute vacuum, impervious to air, ether, light and matter, how was it possible for me to fall into it? And having fallen in, how could I fall out—particularly into a sphere that has no certifiable relationship with ours? . . . But, after all, one process would be as easy as the other, in theory. The main objection is: how could one move in a vacuum, either up or down or backward or forward? The whole thing would baffle the comprehension of an Einstein; and I do not feel that I have even approached the true solution.

Also, I have been fighting the temptation to go back, if only to convince myself that the thing really occurred. But, after all, why shouldn't I go back? An opportunity has been vouchsafed to me such as no man may ever have been given before; and the wonders I shall see and the secrets I shall learn are beyond imagining. My nervous trepidation is in-excusably childish under the circumstances.

August 3rd. I went back this morning, armed with a revolver. Some-how, without thinking that it might make a difference, I did not step in the very middle of the space between the boulders. Undoubtedly as a result of this, my descent was more prolonged and impetuous than be-fore, and seemed to consist mainly of a series of spiral somersaults. It must have taken me minutes to recover from the ensuing vertigo; and when I came to, I was lying on the violet grass.

This time, I went boldly down the slope and keeping as much as I could in the shelter of the bizarre purple and yellow vegetation, I stole toward the looming city. All was very still; and there was no breath of wind in those exotic trees, which appeared to imitate in their lofty up-right boles and horizontal foliage the severe architectural lines of the Cyclopean buildings.

I had not gone far when I came to a road in the forest—a road paved with stupendous blocks of stone at least twenty feet square. It ran to-ward the city. I thought for awhile that it was wholly deserted—perhaps disused; and I even dared to walk upon it, till I heard a noise behind me and turning saw the approach of several singular entities. Terrified, I sprang back and hid myself in a thicket, from which I watched the passing of those creatures, wondering fearfully if they had seen me. Apparently my fears were groundless, for they did not even glance at my hiding-place.

It is hard for me to describe or even visualize them now, for they were totally unlike anything that we are accustomed to think of as hu-man or animal. They must have been ten feet tall and they were moving along with colossal strides that took them from sight in a few instants beyond a turn of the road. Their bodies were bright and shining, as if encased in some sort of armor; and their heads were equipped with high, curving appendages of opalescent hues which nodded above them like fantastic plumes, but may have been antennae or other sense-organs of a novel type.

Trembling with excitement and wonder, I continued my progress through the richly-colored undergrowth. As I went on, I perceived for the first time that there were no shadows anywhere. The light came from all portions of the sunless amber heaven, pervading everything with a soft, uniform luminosity. All was motionless and silent, as I have said before; and there was no evidence of bird, insect or animal life in all this preternatural landscape. But when I had advanced to within a mile of the city (as well as I could judge the distance in a realm where the very proportions of objects were unfamiliar) I became aware of something which at first was recognizable as a vibration rather than a sound. There was a queer thrilling in my nerves, the disquieting sense of some unknown force or emanation flowing through my body. This was perceptible for some time before I heard the music; but having heard it, my auditory nerves identified it at once with the vibration.

It was faint and far-off, and seemed to emanate from the very heart of the Titan city. The melody was piercingly sweet and resembled at times the singing of some voluptuous feminine voice. However, no human voice could have possessed the unearthly pitch, the shrill, perpetually sustained notes that somehow suggested the light of remote worlds and stars translated into sound.

Ordinarily I am not very sensitive to music; I have even been reproached for not reacting more strongly to it. But I had not gone much farther when I realized the peculiar mental and emotional spell which the far-off sound was beginning to exert upon me. There was a siren-like allurement which drew me on, forgetful of the strangeness and potential perils of my situation; and I felt a slow, drug-like intoxication of brain and senses. In some insidious manner, I know not how nor why, the music conveyed the ideas of vast but attainable space and altitude, of superhuman freedom and exultation; and it seemed to promise all the impossible splendors of which my imagination has vaguely dreamt.

The forest continued almost to the city walls. Peering from behind the final boscage, I saw their overwhelming battlements in the sky above me, and noted the flawless jointure of their prodigious blocks. I was near the great road, which entered an open gate large enough to admit the passage of behemoths. There were no guards in sight; and several more of the tall, gleaming entities came striding along and went in as I watched. From where I stood, I was unable to see inside the gate, for the wall was stupendously thick. The music poured from that mysterious entrance in an ever-strengthening flood, and sought to draw me on with its weird seduction, eager for unimaginable things.

It was hard to resist, hard to rally my will-power and turn back. I tried to concentrate on the thought of danger—but the thought was tenuously unreal. At last I tore myself away and retraced my footsteps, very slowly and lingeringly, till I was beyond reach of the music. Even then, the spell persisted, like the effects of a drug; and all the way home I was tempted to return and follow those shining giants into the city.

August 5th. I have visited the new dimension once more. I thought I could resist that summoning music; and I even took some cotton-wadding along with which to stuff my ears if it should affect me too strongly. I began to hear the supernal melody at the same distance as before, and was drawn onward in the same manner. But this time I entered the open gate!

I wonder if I can describe that city. I felt like a crawling ant upon its mammoth pavements, amid the measureless Babel of its buildings, of its streets and arcades. Everywhere there were columns, obelisks and the perpendicular pylons of fane-like structures that would have dwarfed those of Thebes and Heliopolis.

And the people of the city! How is one to depict them, or give them a name? I think that the gleaming entities I first saw are not the true inhabitants, but are only visitors—perhaps from some other world or dimension, like myself. The real people are giants too; but they move slowly, with solemn, hieratic paces. Their bodies are nude and swart, and their limbs are those of caryatides—massive enough, it would seem, to uphold the roofs and lintels of their own buildings. I fear to describe them minutely: for human words would give the idea of something monstrous and uncouth; and these beings are not monstrous but they have merely developed in obedience to the laws of another evolution than ours, the environmental forces and conditions of a different world.

Somehow, I was not afraid when I saw them—perhaps the music had drugged me till I was beyond fear. There was a group of them just inside the gate, and they seemed to pay me no attention whatever as I passed them. The opaque, jet-like orbs of their huge eyes were impassive as the carven eyes of andro-sphinxes, and they uttered no sound from their heavy, straight, expressionless lips. Perhaps they lack the sense of hearing; for their strange, semi-rectangular heads were devoid of anything in the nature of external ears.

I followed the music, which was still remote and seemed to increase little in loudness. I was soon overtaken by several of those beings whom I had previously seen on the road outside the walls; and they passed me quickly and disappeared in the labyrinth of buildings. After them there came other beings, of a less gigantic kind, and without the bright shards or armor worn by the first-comers. Then, overhead, two creatures with long, translucent, blood-colored wings, intricately veined and ribbed, came flying side by side and vanished behind the others. Their faces, featured with organs of unsurmisable use, were not those of animals; and I felt sure that they were beings of a high order of development.

I saw hundreds of those slow-moving, somber entities whom I have identified as the true inhabitants. But none of them appeared to notice me. Doubtless they were accustomed to seeing far weirder and more unusual kinds of life than humanity. As I went on, I was overtaken by dozens of improbable-looking creatures, all going in the same direction as myself, as if drawn by the same siren melody.

Deeper and deeper I went into the wilderness of colossal architecture, led by that remote, ethereal, opiate music. I soon noticed a sort of gradual ebb and flow in the sound, occupying an interval of ten minutes or more; but by imperceptible degrees it grew sweeter and nearer. I wondered how it could penetrate that manifold maze of builded stone and be heard outside the walls.

I must have walked for miles, in the ceaseless gloom of those rectangular structures that hung above me, tier on tier, at an awful height in the amber zenith. Then, at length, I came to the core and secret of it all. Preceded and followed by a number of those chimerical entities, I emerged on a great square in whose center was a temple-like building more immense than the others. The music poured, imperiously shrill and loud, from its many-columned entrance.

I felt the thrill of one who approaches the sanctum of some hierarchal mystery, when I entered the halls of that building. People who must have come from many different worlds or dimensions, went with me and before me along the titanic colonnades whose pillars were graven with indecipherable runes and enigmatic bas-reliefs. Also, the dark, colossal inhabitants of the town were standing or roaming about, intent, like all the others, on their own affairs. None of these beings spoke, either to me or to one another; and though several eyed me casually, my presence was evidently taken for granted.

There are no words to convey the incomprehensible wonder of it all. And the music? I have utterly failed to describe that, also. It was as if some marvellous elixir had been turned into sound-waves—an elixir conferring the gift of superhuman life, and the high, magnificent dreams which are dreamt by the Immortals. It mounted in my brain like a supernal drunkenness as I approached the hidden source.

I do not know what obscure warning prompted me now to stuff my ears with cotton ere I went any farther. Though I could still hear it, still feel its peculiar, penetrant vibration, the sound became muted when I had done this; and its influence was less powerful henceforward. There is little doubt that I owe my life to this simple and homely precaution.

The endless rows of columns grew dim for awhile as the interior of some long, basaltic cavern; and then, at some distance ahead, I perceived the glimmering of a soft light on the floor and pillars. The light soon became an overflooding radiance, as if gigantic lamps were being lit in the temple's heart; and the vibrations of the hidden music pulsed more strongly in my nerves.

The hall ended in a chamber of immense, indefinite scope, whose walls and roof were doubtful with unremoving shadows. In the center, amid the pavement of mammoth blocks, there was a circular pit above which seemed to float a fountain of flame that soared in one perpetual, slowly lengthening jet. This flame was the sole illumination; and also it was the source of the wild, unearthly music. Even with my purposely deafened ears, I was wooed by the shrill and starry sweetness of its singing; and I felt the voluptuous lure and the high, vertiginous exaltation.

I knew immediately that the place was a shrine, and that the transdimensional beings who accompanied me were visiting pilgrims. There were scores of them—perhaps hundreds; but all were dwarfed in the cosmic immensity of that chamber. They were gathered before the flame in various attitudes of worship; they bowed their exotic heads, or made mysterious gestures or adoration with unhuman hands and members. And the voices of several, deep as booming drums, or sharp as the stridulation of giant insects, were audible amid the singing of the fountain.

Spell-bound, I went forward and joined them. Enthralled by the music and by the vision of the soaring flame, I paid as little heed to my outlandish companions as they to me.

The fountain rose and rose, till its light flickered on the limbs and features of throned, colossal statues behind it—heroes or gods or demons from the earlier cycles of alien time, staring in stone from a dusk of illimitable mystery. The fire was white and dazzling, it was pure as the central flame of a star; it blinded me, and when I turned my eyes away, the air was filled with webs of intricate color, with swiftly changing arabesques whose numberless, unwonted hues and patterns were such as no mundane eye had ever beheld. I felt a stimulating warmth that filled my very marrow with intenser life.

The music mounted with the flame; and I understood now its re-current ebb and flow. As I looked and listened, a mad thought was born in my mind—the thought of how marvellous and ecstatical it would be to run forward and leap headlong into the singing fire. The music seemed to tell me that I should find in that moment of flaring dissolu-tion all the delight and triumph, all the splendor and exaltation it had promised from afar. It besought me, it pleaded with tones of supernal melody; and despite the wadding in my ears, the seduction was well-nigh irresistible.

However, it had not robbed me of all sanity. With a sudden start of terror, like one who has been tempted to fling himself from a high prec-ipice, I drew back. Then I saw that the same dreadful impulse was shared by some of my companions. The two entities with scarlet wings, whom I have previously mentioned, were standing a little apart from the rest of us. Now, with a great fluttering, they rose and flew toward the flame like moths toward a candle. For a brief moment the light shone redly through their half-transparent vans, ere they disappeared in the leaping incandescence, which flared briefly and then burned as before.

Then, in rapid succession, a number of other beings who repre-sented the most divergent trends of biology, sprang forward and immo-lated themselves in the flame. There were creatures with translucent bodies, and some that shone with all the hues of the opal; there were winged colossi, and titans who strode as with seven-league boots; and there was one being with useless abortive wings, who crawled rather than ran, to seek the same glorious doom as the rest. But among them there were none of the city's people: these merely stood and looked on, impassive and statue-like as ever.

I saw that the fountain had now reached its greatest height and was beginning to decline. It sank steadily but slowly to half its former eleva-tion. During this interval there were no more acts of self-sacrifice; and several of the beings beside me turned abruptly and went away, as if they had overcome the lethal spell. One of the tall, armored entities, as he left, addressed me in words that were like clarion-notes, with unmistakable accents of warning. By a mighty effort of will, in a turmoil of conflicting emotions, I followed him. At every step, the madness and delirium of the music strove with my instincts of self-preservation. More than once I started to go back. My homeward journey was blurred and doubtful as the wanderings of a man in an opium-trance; and the music sang behind me and told me of the rapture I had missed, of the flaming doom whose brief instant was better than aeons of mortal life.

August 9th. I have tried to go on with a new story, but have made no progress. Anything that I can imagine, or frame in language, seems flat and puerile beside the world of unsearchable mystery to which I have found admission. The temptation to return is more cogent than ever, the call of that remembered music is sweeter than the voice of a loved woman. And always I am tormented by the problem of it all, and tantalized by the little which I have perceived and understood. What forces are these whose existence and working I have merely apprehended? Who are the inhabitants of the city? And who are the beings that visit the enshrined flame? What rumor or legend has drawn them from outland realms and ulterior planets to that place of inenarrable danger and destruction? And what is the fountain itself, and what the secret of its lure and its deadly singing? These problems admit of infinite surmise, but no conceivable solution.

I am planning to go back once more—but not alone. Someone must go with me this time, as a witness to the wonder and the peril. It is all too strange for credence—I must have human corroboration of what I have seen and felt and conjectured. Also, another might understand where I have failed to do more than apprehend.

Who shall I take? It will be necessary to invite someone here from the outer world—someone of high intellectual and aesthetic capacity. Shall I ask Philip Hastane, my fellow fiction-writer? Hastane would be too busy, I fear. But there is the Californian artist, Felix Ebbonly, who has illustrated some of my fantastic novels. Ebbonly would be the man to see and appreciate the new dimension, if he can come. With his bent for the bizarre and unearthly, the spectacle of that plain and city, the Babelian buildings and arcades, and the temple of the flame, will simply enthrall him. I shall write immediately to his San Francisco address.

August 12th. Ebbonly is here—the mysterious hints in my letter, regarding some novel pictorial subjects along his own line, were too provocative for him to resist. Now I have explained fully and given him a detailed account of my adventures. I can see that he is a little incredulous, for which I hardly blame him. But he will not remain incredulous for long, for tomorrow we shall visit together the city of the singing flame.

August 13th. I must concentrate my disordered faculties, I must choose my words and write with exceeding care. This will be the last entry in my journal, and the last writing I shall ever do. When I have finished, I shall wrap the journal up and address it to Philip Hastane, who can make such disposition of it as he sees fit.

I took Ebbonly into the other dimension today. He was impressed, even as I had been, by the two isolated boulders on Crater Ridge.

"They look like the guttered ends of columns established by pre-human gods," he remarked. "I begin to believe you now."

I told him to go first, and indicated the place where he should step. He obeyed without hesitation, and I had the singular experience of seeing a man melt into utter, instantaneous nothingness. One moment he was there—and the next, there was only bare ground, and the far-off tamaracks whose view his body had obstructed. I followed, and found him standing in speechless awe on the violet grass.

"This," he said at last, "is the sort of thing whose existence I have hitherto merely suspected, and have never even been able to hint in my most imaginative drawings."

We spoke little as we followed the lines of monolithic boulders toward the plain. Far in the distance, beyond those high and stately trees with their sumptuous foliage, the golden-brown vapors had parted, showing the pale vistas of an immense horizon; and past the horizon were range on range of gleaming orbs and fiery, flying motes in the depth of that amber heaven. It was as if the veil of another universe than ours had been drawn back.

We crossed the plain, and came at length within ear-shot of the siren music. I warned Ebbonly to stuff his ears with cotton-wadding, but he refused.

"I don't want to deaden any new sensations which I may experience," he observed.

We entered the city. My companion was in a veritable rhapsody of artistic delight when he beheld the enormous buildings and the people. I could see, too, that the music had taken hold upon him: his look soon became fixed and dreamy as that of an opium-eater. At first he made many comments on the architecture and the various beings who passed us, and called my attention to details which I had not perceived before. However, as we drew nearer to the temple of the flame, his observational interest seemed to flag, and was replaced by more and more of an ecstatic inward absorption. His remarks became fewer and briefer; and he did not even seem to hear my questions. It was evident that the sound had wholly bemused and bewitched him.

Even as on my former visit, there were many pilgrims going toward the shrine—and few that were coming away from it. Most of them belonged to evolutionary types that I had seen before. Among those that were new to me, I recall one gorgeous creature with golden and cerulean wings like those of a giant lepidopter, and scintillating, jewel-like eyes that must have been designed to mirror the glories of some Edenic world.

I too felt, as before, the captious thraldom and bewitchment, the insidious, gradual perversion of thought and instinct, as if the music were working in my brain like a subtle alkaloid. Since I had taken my usual precaution, my subjection to the influence was less complete than that of Ebbonly; but nevertheless it was enough to make me forget a number of things—among them, the initial concern which I had felt when my companion refused to employ the same mode of protection as myself. I no longer thought of his danger or my own, except as something very distant and immaterial.

The streets were like the prolonged and wildering labyrinth of a nightmare. But the music led us forthrightly; and always there were other pilgrims. Like men in the grip of some powerful current, we were drawn to our destination.

As we passed along the hall of gigantic columns and neared the abode of the fiery fountain, a sense of our peril quickened momentarily in my brain, and I sought to warn Ebbonly once more. But all my protests and remonstrances were futile: he was deaf as a machine, and wholly impervious to anything but the lethal music. His expression and his movements were those of a somnambulist. Even when I seized and shook him with such violence as I could muster, he remained oblivious.

The throng of worshippers was larger than upon my first visit. The jet of pure, incandescent flame was mounting steadily as we entered, and it sang with the white ardor and ecstasy of a star alone in space. Again, with ineffable tones, it told me the rapture of a moth-like death in its lofty soaring, the exultation and triumph of a momentary union with its elemental essence.

The flame rose to its apex; and even for me, the mesmeric lure was well-nigh irresistible. Many of our companions succumbed; and the first to immolate himself was the giant lepidopterous being. Four others, of diverse evolutional types, followed in appallingly swift succession.

In my own partial subjection to the music, my own effort to resist that deadly enslavement, I had almost forgotten the very presence of Ebbonly. It was too late for me to even think of stopping him, when he ran forward in a series of leaps that were both solemn and frenzied, like the beginning of some sacerdotal dance, and hurled himself headlong into the flame. The fire enveloped him, it flared up for an instant with a more dazzling whiteness; and that was all.

Slowly, as if from benumbed brain-centers, a horror crept upon my conscious mind, and helped to annul the perilous mesmerism. I turned, while many others were following Ebbonly's example, and fled from the shrine and from the city. But somehow the horror diminished as I went; and more and more, I found myself envying my companion's fate, and wondering as to the sensations he had felt in that moment of fiery dissolution . . .

Now, as I write this, I am wondering why I came back again to the human world. Words are futile to express what I have beheld and experienced; and the change that has come upon me, beneath the play of incalculable forces in a world of which no other mortal is even cognizant. Literature is nothing more than the shadow of a shadow; and life, with its drawn-out length of monotonous, reiterative days, is unreal and without meaning now in comparison with the splendid death which I might have had—the glorious doom which is still in store. I have no longer any will to fight the ever-insistent music which I hear in memory. And—there seems to be no reason at all why I should fight it. Tomorrow, I shall return to the city.

Beyond the Singing Flame

When I, Philip Hastane, gave to the world the journal of my friend Giles Angarth, I was still doubtful as to whether the incidents related therein were fiction or verity. The trans-dimensional adventures of Angarth and Ebbonly, the city of the Flame with its strange residents and pilgrims, the immolation of Ebbonly, and the hinted return of the narrator himself for a like purpose, after making the last entry in his diary, were very much the sort of thing that Angarth might have imagined in one of the fantastic novels for which he had become so justly famous.

Add to this the seemingly impossible and incredible nature of the whole tale, and my hesitancy in accepting it as veridical will easily be understood.

However, on the other hand, there was the unsolved and eternally recalcitrant enigma offered by the disappearance of the two men. Both were well-known, the one as a writer, the other as an artist; both were in flourishing circumstances, with no serious cares or troubles; and their vanishment, all things considered, was difficult to explain on the ground of any motive less unusual or extraordinary than the one assigned in the journal.

At first, as I have hinted in my foreword to the published diary, I thought that the whole affair might well have been devised as a somewhat elaborate practical joke; but this theory became less and less tenable as weeks and months went by and linked themselves slowly into a year, without the reappearance of the presumptive jokers.

Now, at last, I can testify to the truth of all that Angarth wrote—and more. For I, too, have been in Ydmos, the City of Singing Flame, and have known also the supernal glories and raptures of the Inner Dimension. And of these I must tell, however falteringly and stumblingly, with mere human words, ere the vision fades. For these are things which neither I nor any other shall behold or experience again: since Ydmos itself is now a riven ruin, and the Temple of the Flame has been blasted to its foundations in the basic rock, and the fountain of singing fire has been stricken at its source, and the Inner Dimension has perished like a broken bubble, in the great war that was made upon Ydmos by the rulers of the Outer Lands. . . .

After editing and publishing Angarth's journal, I was unable to forget the peculiar and tantalizing problems it had raised. The vague but infinitely suggestive vistas opened by the tale were such as to haunt my imagination recurrently with a hint of half-revealed or hidden mysteries; and I was troubled by the possibility of some great mystic meaning behind it all—some cosmic actuality of which the narrator had perceived merely the external veils and fringes.

As time went on, I found myself pondering it perpetually, and more and more I was possessed by an overwhelming wonder, and a sense of something which no mere fiction-weaver would have been likely to invent through the unassisted workings of his own fantasy.

In the early summer of 1931, after finishing a new novel of interplanetary adventure, I felt able for the first time to take the necessary leisure for the execution of a project that had often occurred to me. Putting all my affairs in order, and knitting all the loose ends of my literary labors and correspondence, in case I should not return, I left Auburn ostensibly for a week's vacation, and actually went to Summit with the idea of investigating closely the milieu in which Angarth and Ebbonly had disappeared from human ken.

With strange emotions, I visited the forsaken cabin south of Crater Ridge that had been occupied by Angarth, and saw the rough, home-made table of pine boards upon which my friend had written his journal and had left the sealed package containing it to be forwarded to me after his departure.

There was a weird and brooding loneliness about the place, as if the non-human infinitudes had already claimed it for their own. The unlocked door had sagged inward from the pressure of high-piled winter snows, and fir-needles had sifted across the sill to strew the unswept floor. Somehow, I know not why, the bizarre narrative became more real and more credible to me, while I stood there, as if an occult intimation of all that had happened to its author still lingered around the cabin.

This mysterious intimation grew stronger when I came to visit Crater Ridge itself, and to search amid its miles of pseudo-volcanic rubble for the two boulders so explicitly described by Angarth as having a likeness to the pedestals of ruined columns.

Many of my readers, no doubt, will remember his description of the Ridge; and there is no need to enlarge upon it with reiterative detail, other than that which bears upon my own adventures.

Following the northward path which Angarth must have taken from his cabin, and trying to retrace his wanderings on the long, barren hill, I combed it thoroughly from end to end and from side to side, since he had not specified the location of the boulders. After two mornings spent in this manner without result, I was almost ready to abandon the quest and dismiss the queer, soapy, greenish-grey column-ends as one of Angarth's most provocative and deceptive fictions.

It must have been the formless, haunting intuition of which I have spoken, that made me renew the search on the third morning. This time, after crossing and re-crossing the hill-top for an hour or more, and weaving tortuously to and fro among the cicada-haunted wild currant bushes and sun-flowers on the dusty slopes, I came at last to an open, circular, rock-surrounded space that was totally unfamiliar, and which I had somehow missed it in all my previous roamings. It was the place of which Angarth had told; and I saw with an inexpressible thrill the two rounded, worn-looking boulders that were situated in the center of the ring.

I believe that I trembled a little with excitement as I went forward to inspect the curious stones. Bending over, but not daring to enter the bare, pebbly space between them, I touched one of them with my hand, and received a sensation of preternatural smoothness, together with a coolness that was inexplicable, considering that the boulders and the soil about them must have lain unshaded from the sultry August sun for many hours.

From that moment, I became fully persuaded that Angarth's account was no mere fable. Just why I should have felt so certain of this, I am powerless to say. But it seemed to me that I stood on the threshold of an ultramundane mystery, on the brink of uncharted gulfs; and I looked about at the familiar Sierran valleys and mountains, wondering that they still preserved their wonted outlines, and were still unchanged by the contiguity of alien worlds, were still untouched by the luminous glories of arcanic dimensions.

Being convinced that I had indeed found the gateway between the worlds, I was prompted to strange reflections. What, and where, was this other sphere to which my friend had attained entrance? Was it near at hand, like a secret room in the structure of space? Or was it, in reality, millions or trillions of light-years away by the reckoning of astronomic distance, in a planet of some ulterior galaxy? After all, we know little or nothing of the actual nature of space; and perhaps, in some way that we cannot imagine, the infinite is doubled upon itself in places, with dimensional folds and tucks, and short-cuts whereby the distance to Algenib or Aldebaran is but a step. Perhaps, also, there is more than one infinity. The spatial "flaw" into which Angarth had fallen might well be a sort of super-dimension, abridging the cosmic intervals and connecting universe with universe.

However, because of this very certitude that I had found the interspheric portals, and could follow Angarth and Ebbonly if I so desired, I hesitated before trying the experiment, mindful of the mystic danger and irrefragable lure that had overcome the others. I was consumed by imaginative curiosity, by an avid, well-nigh feverish longing to behold the wonders of this exotic realm; but I did not purpose to become a victim to the opiate power and fascination of the Singing Flame.

I stood for a long time, eyeing the odd boulders and the barren, pebble-littered spot that gave admission to the unknown. At length, I went away, deciding to defer my venture till the following morn. Visualizing the weird doom to which the others had gone so voluntarily, and even gladly, I must confess that I was afraid. On the other hand, I was drawn by the fateful allurement that leads an explorer into far places. . . and perhaps by something more than this.

I slept badly that night, with nerves and brain excited by formless, glowing premonitions, by intimations of half-conceived perils and splendors and vastnesses. Early the next morning, while the sun was still hanging above the Nevada Mountains, I returned to Crater Ridge.

I carried a strong hunting-knife and a Colt revolver, and wore a filled cartridge-belt, and also a knapsack containing sandwiches and a thermos bottle of coffee. Before starting, I had stuffed my ears tightly with cotton soaked in a new anaesthetic fluid, mild but efficacious, which would serve to deafen me completely for many hours. In this way, I felt that I should be immune to the demoralizing music of the fiery fountain.

I peered about on the rugged landscape with its varied and far-flung vistas, wondering if I should ever see it again. Then, resolutely, but with the eerie thrilling and shrinking of one who throws himself from a high cliff into some bottomless chasm, I stepped forward into the space between the greyish-green boulders.

My sensations, generally speaking, were similar to those described by Angarth in his diary. Blackness and illimitable emptiness seemed to wrap me round in a dizzy swirl as of rushing wind or milling water, and I went down and down in a spiral descent whose duration I have never been able to estimate. Intolerably stifled, and without even the power to gasp for breath, in the chill, airless vacuum that froze my very muscles and marrow, I felt that I should lose consciousness in another moment, and descend into the greater gulf of death or oblivion.

Something seemed to arrest my fall, and I became aware that I was standing still, though I was troubled for some time by a queer doubt as to whether my position was vertical, horizontal or upside-down in relation to the solid substance that my feet had encountered.

Then the blackness lifted slowly like a dissolving cloud, and I saw the slope of violet grass, the rows of irregular monoliths running downward from where I stood, and the grey-green columns near at hand, and the titan, perpendicular city of red stone that was dominant above the high and multi-colored vegetation of the plain.

It was all very much as Angarth had depicted it; but somehow, even then, I became aware of differences that were not immediately or clearly definable, of scenic details and atmospheric elements for which his account had not prepared me. And, at the moment I was too thoroughly disequilibrated and overpowered by the vision of it all to even speculate concerning the character of these differences.

As I gazed at the city with its crowding tiers of battlements and its multitude of overlooming spires, I felt the invisible threads of a secret attraction, was seized by an imperative longing to know the mysteries hidden behind the massive walls and the myriad buildings. Then, a moment later, my gaze was drawn to the remote, opposite horizon of the plain, as if by some conflicting impulse whose nature and origin were undiscoverable.

It must have been because I had formed so clear and definite a picture of the scene from my friend's narrative, that I was surprised and even a little disturbed as if by something wrong or irrelevant, when I saw in the far distance the shining towers of what seemed to be another city—a city of which Angarth had not written. The towers rose in serried lines, reaching for many miles in a curious arc-like formation, and were sharply defined against a blackish mass of cloud that had reared behind them and was spreading out on the luminous amber sky in sullen webs and sinister, crawling filaments.

Subtle disquietude and repulsion seemed to emanate from the far-off, glittering spires, even as attraction emanated from those of the nearer city. I saw them quiver and pulse with an evil light, like living and moving things, through what I assumed to be some refractive trick of the atmosphere. Then, for an instant, the black cloud behind them glowed with dull, angry crimson throughout its whole mass, and even its questing webs and tendrils were turned into lurid threads of fire.

The crimson faded, leaving the cloud inert and lumpish as before. But from many of the vanward towers, lines of red and violet flame had leaped, like out-thrust lances at the bosom of the plain beneath them, and they were held thus for at least a minute, moving slowly across a wide area, before they vanished. In the spaces between the towers, I now perceived a multitude of gleaming, restless particles, like armies of militant atoms, and wondered if perchance they were living things. If the idea had not appeared so fantastical, I could have sworn even then that the far city had already changed its position and was advancing toward the other on the plain.

Apart from the fulguration of the cloud and the flames that had sprung from the towers, and the quiverings which I deemed a refractive phenomenon, the whole landscape before and about me was unnaturally still. On the strange amber air, on the Tyrian-tinted grasses, on the proud, opulent foliage of the unknown trees, there lay the dead calm that precedes the stupendous turmoil of typhonic storm or seismic cataclysm. The brooding sky was permeated with intuitions of cosmic menace, was weighed down by a dim, elemental despair.

Alarmed by this ominous atmosphere, I looked behind me at the two pillars which, according to Angarth, were the gateway of return to the human world. For an instant, I was tempted to go back. Then, I turned once more to the nearby city; and the feelings I have mentioned were lost in an oversurging awesomeness and wonder. I felt the thrill of a deep, supernal exaltation before the magnitude of the mighty buildings; a compelling sorcery was laid upon me by the very lines of their construction, by the harmonies of a solemn architectural music. I forgot my impulse to return to Crater Ridge, and started down the slope toward the city.

Soon the boughs of the purple and yellow forest arched above me like the altitudes of Titan-builded aisles, with leaves that fretted the rich heaven in gorgeous arabesques. Beyond them, ever and anon, I caught glimpses of the piled ramparts of my destination; but looking back, in the direction of that other city on the horizon, I found that its fulgurating towers were now lost to view.

I saw, however, that the masses of the great, somber cloud were rising steadily on the sky; and once again they flared to a swart, malignant red, as if with some unearthly form of sheet-lightning; and though I could hear nothing with my deadened ears, the ground beneath me trembled with long vibrations as of thunder. There was a queer quality in the vibrations, that seemed to tear my nerves and set my teeth on edge with its throbbing, lancinating discord, painful as broken glass or the torment of a tightened rack.

Like Angarth before me, I came to the paved, Cyclopean highway. Following it, in the stillness after the unheard peals of thunder, I felt another and subtler vibration, which I knew to be that of the Singing Flame in the temple at the city's core. It seemed to soothe and exalt and bear me on, to erase with soft caresses the ache that still lingered in my nerves from the torturing pulsations of the thunder.

I met no one on the road, and was not passed by any of the transdimensional pilgrims such as had overtaken Angarth. And when the accumulated ramparts loomed above the highest trees, and I came forth from the wood in their very shadow, I saw that the great gate of the city was closed, leaving no crevice through which a pygmy like myself might obtain entrance.

Feeling a profound and peculiar discomfiture, such as one would experience in a dream that had gone wrong, I stared at the grim, unrelenting blankness of the gate, which seemed to be wrought from one enormous sheet of somber and lusterless metal. Then I peered upward at the sheerness of the wall, which rose above me like an alpine cliff, and saw that the battlements were seemingly deserted.

Was the city forsaken by its people, by the guardians of the Flame? Was it no longer open to the pilgrims who came from outlying lands to worship the Flame, and to immolate themselves? With a curious reluctance, after lingering there for many minutes in a sort of stupor, I turned away to retrace my steps.

In the interim of my journey, the black cloud had drawn immeasurably nearer, and was now blotting half the heaven with two portentous wing-like formations. It was a sinister and terrible sight; and it lightened again with that ominous, wrathful flaming, with a detonation that beat upon my deaf ears like waves of disintegrative force, and seemed to lacerate the inmost fibers of my body.

I hesitated, fearing that the storm would burst upon me before I could reach the inter-dimensional portals. I saw that I should be exposed to an elemental disturbance of unfamiliar character and supreme violence.

Then, in mid-air, before the imminent, ever-rising cloud, I perceived two flying creatures, whom I can compare only to gigantic moths. With bright, luminous wings, upon the ebon forefront of the storm, they approached me in level but precipitate flight, and would have crashed headlong against the shut gate if they had not checked themselves with sudden and easy poise.

With hardly a flutter, they descended and paused on the ground beside me, supporting themselves on queer, delicate legs that branched at the knee-joints in floating antennae and waving tentacles. Their wings were sumptuously mottled webs of pearl and madder and opal and orange, and their heads were circled by a series of convex and concave eyes, and were fringed with coiling, horn-like organs from whose hollow ends there hung aerial filaments.

I was more than startled, more than amazed by their aspect; but somehow, by an obscure telepathy, I felt assured that their intentions toward me were friendly. I knew that they wished to enter the city, and knew also that they understood my predicament.

Nevertheless, I was not prepared for what happened. With movements of utmost celerity and grace, one of the giant moth-like beings stationed himself at my right hand, and the other at my left. Then, before I could even suspect their intention, they enfolded my limbs and body with their long tentacles, wrapping me round and round as if with powerful ropes; and carrying me between them as if my weight were a mere trifle, they rose in air and soared at the mighty ramparts!

In that swift and effortless ascent, the wall seemed to flow downward beside and beneath us like a wave of molten stone. Dizzily I watched the falling away of the mammoth blocks in endless recession. Then we were level with the broad ramparts, were flying across the unguarded parapets and over a canyon-like space toward the immense rectangular buildings and numberless square towers.

We had hardly crossed the walls, when a weird and flickering glow was cast on the edifices before us by another lightening of the great cloud. The moth-like beings paid no apparent heed, and flew steadily on into the city with their strange faces toward an unseen goal; but, turning my head to peer backward at the storm, I beheld an astounding and appalling spectacle.

Beyond the city ramparts, as if wrought by black magic or the toil of genii, another city had reared, and its high towers were moving swiftly forward beneath the rubescent dome of the burning cloud! A second glance, and I perceived that the towers were identical with those I had beheld afar on the plain. In the interim of my passage through the woods, they had travelled over an expanse of many miles by means of some unknown motive-power, and had closed in on the city of the Flame.

Looking more closely, to determine the manner of their locomotion, I saw that they were not mounted on wheels, but on short, massy legs like jointed columns of metal, that gave them the stride of ungainly colossi. There were six or more of these legs to each tower, and near the tops of the towers were rows of huge eye-like openings, from which issued the bolts of red and violet flame I have mentioned before. The many-colored forest had been burned away by these flames in a league-wide swath of devastation, even to the walls, and there was nothing but a stretch of black, vaporing desert between the mobile towers and the city. Then, even as I gazed, the long, leaping beams began to assail the craggy ramparts, and the topmost parapets were melting like lava beneath them.

It was a scene of utmost terror and grandeur; but, a moment later, it was blotted from my vision by the buildings among which we had now plunged.

The great lepidopterous creatures who bore me went on with the speed of eyrie-questing eagles. In the course of that amazing flight, I was hardly capable of conscious thought or volition; I lived only in the breathless and giddy freedom of aerial movement, of dream-like levitation above the labyrinthine maze of stone immensitudes and marvels.

Also, I was without conscious cognizance of much that I beheld in that stupendous Babel of architectural imageries; and only afterwards, in the more tranquil light of recollection, could I give coherent form and meaning to many of my impressions. My senses were stunned by the vastness and strangeness of it all; and I realized but dimly the cataclysmic ruin that was being loosed upon the city behind us, and the doom from which we were fleeing. I knew that war was being made with unearthly weapons and engineries, by inimical powers that I could not imagine, for a purpose beyond my conception; but to me, it all had the elemental confusion and vague, impersonal horror of some cosmic catastrophe.

We flew deeper and deeper into the city. Broad, platform roofs and terrace-like tiers of balconies flowed away beneath us, and the pavements raced like darkling streams at some enormous depth. Severe cubicular spires and square monoliths were all about and above us; and we saw on some of the roofs the dark, Atlantean people of the city, moving slowly and statuesquely, or standing in attitudes of cryptic resignation and despair, with their faces toward the flaming cloud. All were weaponless, and I saw no engineries anywhere, such as might be used for purposes of military defense.

Swiftly as we flew, the climbing cloud was swifter, and the darkness of its intermittently glowing dome had overarched the town, its spidery filaments had meshed the further heavens and would soon attach themselves to the opposite horizon. The buildings darkened and lightened with the recurrent fulguration; and I felt in all my tissues the painful pulsing of the thunderous vibrations.

Dully and vaguely, I realized that the winged beings who carried me between them were pilgrims to the temple of the Flame. More and more I became aware of an influence that must have been that of the starry music emanating from the temple's heart. There were soft, soothing vibrations in the air, that seemed to absorb and nullify the tearing discords of the unheard thunder. I felt that we were entering a zone of mystic refuge, of sidereal and celestial security; and my troubled senses were both lulled and exalted.

The gorgeous wings of the giant lepidopters began to slant downward. Before and beneath us, at some distance, I perceived a mammoth pile which I knew at once for the temple of the Flame. Down, still down we went, in the awesome space of the surrounding square; and then I was borne in through the lofty, ever-open entrance, and along the high hall with its thousand columns.

It was like some corridor in a Karnak of titan worlds. Pregnant with strange balsams, the dim, mysterious dusk enfolded us; and we seemed to be entering realms of premundane antiquity and transstellar immensity, to be following a pillared cavern that led to the core of some ultimate star.

It seemed that we were the last and only pilgrims; and also that the temple was deserted by its guardians; for we met no one in the whole extent of that column-crowded gloom. After awhile, the dusk began to lighten, and we plunged into a widening beam of radiance, and then into the vast central chamber in which soared the fountain of green fire.

I remember only the impression of shadowy, flickering space, of a vault that was lost in the azure of infinity, of colossal and Memnonian statues that looked down from Himalaya-like altitudes; and, above all, the dazzling jet of flame that aspired from a pit in the pavement and rose in air like the visible rapture of gods.

But all this I saw and knew for an instant only. Then I realized that the beings who bore me were flying straight toward the flame on level wings, without the slightest pause or flutter of hesitation!

There was no room for fear, no time for alarm, in the dazed and chaotic turmoil of my sensations. I was stupefied by all that I had experienced; and, moreover, the drug-like spell of the Flame was upon me, even though I could not hear its fatal singing. I believe that I struggled a little, by some sort of mechanical muscular revulsion, against the tentacular arms that were wound about me. But the lepidopters gave no heed; and it was plain that they were conscious of nothing but the mounting fire and its seductive music.

I remember, however, that there was no sensation of actual heat, such as might have been expected, when we neared the soaring column. Instead, I felt the most ineffable thrilling in all my fibers, as if I were being permeated by waves of celestial energy and demiurgic ecstasy. Then we entered the Flame.

Like Angarth before me, I had taken it for granted that the fate of all those who flung themselves into the Flame was an instant though blissful destruction. I expected to undergo a briefly flaring dissolution, followed by the nothingness of utter annihilation. The thing which really happened was beyond the boldest reach of speculative thought, and to give even the meagerest idea of my sensations would beggar the resources of language.

The Flame enfolded us like a green curtain, blotting from view the great chamber. Then it seemed to me that I was caught and carried to supercelestial heights, in an upward-rushing cataract of quintessential force and deific rapture and all-illuminating light. It seemed that I, and also my companions, had achieved a god-like union with the Flame; that every atom of our bodies had undergone a transcendental expansion, was winged with ethereal lightness; that we no longer existed, except as one divine, indivisible entity, soaring beyond the trammels of matter, beyond the limits of time and space, to attain undreamable shores.

Unspeakable was the joy, and infinite was the freedom of that ascent, in which we seemed to overpass the zenith of the highest star. Then, as if we had risen with the Flame to its culmination, had reached its very apex, we emerged and came to a pause.

My senses were faint with exaltation, my eyes were blind with the glory of the fire; and the world on which I now gazed was a vast arabesque of unfamiliar forms, and bewildering hues from another spectrum than the one to which our eyes are habituated. It swirled before my dizzy eyes like a labyrinth of gigantic jewels, with interweaving rays and tangled lusters; and only by slow degrees was I able to establish order and distinguish detail in the surging riot of my perceptions.

All about me were endless avenues of super-prismatic opal and jacinth, arches and pillars of ultra-violet gems, of transcendent sapphire, of unearthly ruby and amethyst, all suffused with a multi-tinted splendor. I appeared to be treading on jewels; and above me was a jewelled sky.

Presently, with recovered equilibrium, with eyes adjusted to a new range of cognition, I began to perceive the actual features of the landscape. I, with the two moth-like beings still beside me, was standing on a million-flowered grass, among trees of a paradisal vegetation, with fruit, foliage, blossoms and trunks whose very forms were beyond the conception of tri-dimensional life. The grace of their drooping boughs, of their fretted fronds, was inexpressible in terms of earthly line and contour; and they seemed to be wrought of pure, ethereal substance, half-translucent to the empyrean light, which accounted for the gem-like impression I had first received.

I breathed a nectar-laden air; and the ground beneath me was ineffably soft and resilient, as if it were composed of some higher form of matter than ours. My physical sensations were those of the utmost buoyancy and well-being, with no trace of fatigue or nervousness, such as might have been looked for after the unparalleled and marvellous events in which I had played a part. I felt no sense of mental dislocation or confusion; and apart from my ability to recognize unknown colors and non-Euclidean forms, I began to experience a queer alteration and extension of tactility, through which it seemed that I was able to touch remote objects.

The radiant sky was filled with many-colored suns, like those that might shine on a world of some multiple solar system. But strangely, as I gazed, their glory became softer and dimmer, and the brilliant luster of the trees and grass was gradually subdued, as if by encroaching twilight.

I was beyond surprise, in the boundless marvel and mystery of it all, and nothing, perhaps, would have seemed incredible. But if anything could have amazed me or defied belief, it was the human face—the face of my vanished friend, Giles Angarth, which now emerged from among the waning jewels of the forest, followed by that of another man whom I recognized from photographs I had seen as Felix Ebbonly.

They came out from beneath the gorgeous boughs and paused before me. Both were clad in lustrous fabrics, finer than Oriental silk and of no earthly cut or pattern. Their look was both joyous and meditative; and their faces had taken on a hint of the same translucency that characterized the ethereal fruits and blossoms.

"We have been looking for you," said Angarth. "It occurred to me that after reading my journal, you might be tempted to try the same experiments, if only to make sure whether the account was truth or fiction. This is Felix Ebbonly, whom I believe you have never met."

It surprised me when I found that I could hear his voice with perfect ease and clearness; and I wondered why the effect of the drug-soaked cotton should have died out so soon in my auditory nerves. Yet such details were trivial, in face of the astounding fact that I had found Angarth and Ebbonly; that they, as well as I, had survived the unearthly rapture of the Flame.

"Where are we?" I asked, after acknowledging his introduction. "I confess that I am totally at a loss to comprehend what has happened."

"We are now in what is called the Inner Dimension," explained Angarth. "It is a higher sphere of space and energy and matter than the one into which we were precipitated from Crater Ridge; and the only entrance is through the Singing Flame in the city of Ydmos. The Inner Dimension is born of the fiery fountain, and sustained by it; and those who fling themselves into the Flame are lifted thereby to this superior plane of vibration. For them, the outer worlds no longer exist. The nature of the Flame itself is not known, except that it is a fountain of pure energy, springing from the central rock beneath Ydmos, and passing beyond mortal ken by virtue of its own ardency."

He paused, and seemed to be peering attentively at the winged entities, who still lingered at my side. Then, he continued:

"I haven't been here long enough to learn very much, myself; but I have found out a few things; and Ebbonly and I have established a sort of telepathic communication with the other beings who have passed through the Flame. Many of them have no spoken language, nor organs of speech; and their very methods of thought are basically different from ours, because of their divergent lines of sense-development, and the varying conditions of the worlds from which they come. But we are able to communicate a few images.

"The persons who came with you are trying to tell me something," he went on. "You and they, it seems, are the last pilgrims who will enter Ydmos and attain the Inner Dimension. War is being made on the Flame and its guardians by the rulers of the Outer Lands, because so many of their people have obeyed the lure of the singing fountain and have vanished into the higher sphere; and even now their armies have closed in upon Ydmos, and are blasting the city's ramparts with the force-bolts of their moving towers."

I told him what I had seen, comprehending now much that had been obscure heretofore. He listened gravely; and then said:

"It has long been feared that such war would be made sooner or later. There are many legends in the Outer Lands, concerning the Flame and the fate of those who succumb to its attraction; but the truth is not known, or is guessed only by a few. Many believe, as I did, that the end is destruction; and even by some who suspect its existence, the Inner Dimension is hated, as a thing that lures idle dreamers away from worldly reality. It is regarded as a lethal and pernicious chimera, or a mere poetic dream, or a sort of opium paradise.

"There are a thousand things to tell you, regarding the inner sphere, and the laws and conditions of being to which we are now subject, after the revibration of all our component atoms and electrons in the Flame. But at present there is no time to speak further, since it is highly probable that we are all in grave danger—that the very existence of the Inner Dimension, as well as our own, is threatened by the inimical forces that are destroying Ydmos. There are some who say that the Flame is impregnable, that its pure essence will defy the blasting of all inferior beams, and its source remain impenetrable to the dire lightnings of the Outer Lords. But most are fearful of disaster, and expect the failure of the fountain itself when Ydmos is riven to the central rock.

"Because of this imminent peril, we must not tarry longer. There is a way which affords egress from the inner sphere to another and remoter cosmos in a second infinity—a cosmos unconceived by mundane astronomers, or by the astronomers of the worlds about Ydmos. The majority of the pilgrims, after a term of sojourn here, have gone on to the worlds of this other universe; and Ebbonly and I have waited only for your coming before following them. We must make haste, and delay no more, or doom will overtake us."

Even as he spoke, the two moth-like entities, seeming to resign me to the care of my human friends, arose on the jewel-tinted air and sailed in long, level flight above the paradisal perspectives whose remoter avenues were lost in glory. Angarth and Ebbonly had now stationed themselves beside me; and one took me by the left arm, and the other by the right.

"Try to imagine that you are flying," said Angarth. "In this sphere, levitation and flight are possible through will-power; and you will soon acquire the ability. We shall support and guide you, however, till you have grown accustomed to the new conditions, and are independent of such help."

I obeyed his injunction, and formed a mental image of myself in the act of flying. I was amazed by the clearness and verisimilitude of the thought-picture, and still more by the fact that the picture was becoming an actuality! With little sense of effort, but with exactly the same feeling that characterizes a levitational dream, the three of us were soaring from the jeweled ground, were slanting easily and swiftly upward through the glowing air.

Any attempt to describe the experience would be foredoomed to futility: since it seemed that a whole range of new senses had been opened up in me, together with corresponding thought-symbols for which there are no words in human speech. I was no longer Philip Hastane, but a larger and stronger and freer entity, differing as much from my former self as the personality developed beneath the influence of hashish or kava would differ.

The dominant feeling was one of immense joy and liberation, coupled with a sense of imperative haste, of the need to escape into other realms where the joy would endure eternal and unthreatened. My visual perceptions, as we flew above the burning, lucent woods, were marked by intense aesthetic pleasure, as far above the normal delight afforded by agreeable imagery as the forms and colors of this world were beyond the cognition of normal eyes. Every changing image was a source of veritable ecstasy; and the ecstasy mounted as the whole landscape began to brighten again, and returned to the flashing, scintillating glory it had worn when I first beheld it.

We soared at a lofty elevation, looking down on numberless miles of labyrinthine forest, on long luxurious meadows, on voluptuously folded hills, on palatial buildings, and waters that were clear as the pristine lakes and rivers of Eden. It all seemed to quiver and pulsate like one living, effulgent, ethereal entity: and waves of radiant rapture passed from sun to sun in the splendor-crowded heaven.

As we went on, I noticed again, after an interval, that partial dimming of the light, that somnolent, dreamy saddening of the colors, to be
followed by another period of ecstatic brightening. The slow, tidal
rhythm of this process appeared to correspond to the rising and falling
of the Flame, as Angarth had described it in his journal; and I suspected
immediately that there was some connection.

No sooner had I formulated this thought, when I became aware that
Angarth was speaking. And yet I am not sure whether he spoke, or
whether his worded thought was perceptible to me through another
sense than that of physical audition. At any rate, I was cognizant of his
comment:

"You are right. The waning and waxing of the fountain and its music
is perceived in the Inner Dimension as a clouding and lightening of all
visual images."

Our flight began to swiften, and I realized that my companions were
employing all their psychic energies in an effort to redouble our speed.
The lands below us blurred to a cataract of streaming color, a sea of
flowing luminosity; and we seemed to be hurtling onward like stars
through the fiery air.

The ecstasy of that endless soaring, the anxiety of that precipitate
flight from an unknown doom, are incommunicable. But I shall never
forget them, and never forget the state of ineffable communion and understanding that existed between the three of us. The memory of it all is
housed in the deepest and most abiding cells of my brain.

Others were flying beside and above and beneath us now, in the
fluctuant glory: pilgrims of hidden worlds and occult dimensions, proceeding as we ourselves toward that other cosmos of which the inner
sphere was the ante-chamber. These beings were strange and outré beyond belief in their corporeal forms and attributes; and yet I took no
thought of their strangeness, but felt toward them the same conviction
of fraternity that I felt toward Angarth and Ebbonly.

Now, as we still went on, it appeared to me that my two companions were telling me many things; were communicating, by what means I am not sure, much that they had learned in their new existence. With a grave urgency, as if perhaps the time for imparting this information might well be brief, ideas were expressed and conveyed which I could never have understood amid terrestrial circumstances; and things that were inconceivable in terms of the five senses, or in abstract symbols of philosophic or mathematic thought, were made plain to me as the letters of the alphabet.

Certain of these data, however, are roughly conveyable or suggestible in language. I was told of the gradual process of initiation into the life of the new dimension, of the powers gained by the neophyte during his term of adaptation, of the various recondite aesthetic joys experienced through a mingling and multiplying of all the perceptions: of the control acquired over natural forces and over matter itself, so that raiment could be woven and buildings reared solely through an act of volition.

I learned also of the laws that would control our passage to the further cosmos, and the fact that such passage was difficult and dangerous for anyone who had not lived a certain length of time in the Inner Dimension. Likewise, I was told that no one could return to our present plane from the higher cosmos, even as no one could go backward through the Flame into Ydmos.

Angarth and Ebbonly had dwelt long enough in the Inner Dimension (they said) to be eligible for entrance to the worlds beyond; and they thought that I too could escape through their assistance, even though I had not yet developed the faculty of spatial equilibrium necessary to sustain those who dared the interspheric path and its dreadful sub-jacent gulfs alone.

There were boundless, unforeseeable realms, planet on planet, universe on universe, to which we might attain, and among whose prodigies and marvels we could dwell or wander indefinitely. In these worlds, our brains would be attuned to the comprehension or apprehension of vaster and higher scientific laws, and states of entity beyond those of our present dimensional milieu.

I have no idea of the duration of our flight; since, like everything else, my sense of time was completely altered and transfigured. Relatively speaking, we may have gone on for hours; but it seemed to me that we had crossed an area of that supernal terrain for whose transit many years or centuries might well have been required.

Even before we came within sight of it, a clear pictorial image of our destination had arisen in my mind, doubtless through some sort of thought-transference. I seemed to envision a stupendous mountain-range, with alp on celestial alp, higher than the summer cumuli of earth; and above them all the horn of an ultra-violet peak whose head was enfolded in a hueless and spiral cloud, touched with the sense of invisible chromatic overtones, that seemed to come down upon it from skies beyond the zenith. I knew that the way to the outer cosmos was hidden in the high cloud.

On, on, we soared; and at length the mountain-range appeared on the far horizon, and I saw the paramount peak of ultra-violet with its dazzling crown of cumulus. Nearer still we came, till the strange volutes of cloud were almost above us, towering to the heavens and vanishing among the vari-colored suns. We saw the gleaming forms of pilgrims who preceded us, as they entered the swirling folds.

At this moment, the sky and the landscape had flamed again to their culminating brilliance, they burned with a thousand hues and lusters; so that the sudden, unlooked-for eclipse which now occurred was all the more complete and terrible.

Before I was conscious of anything amiss, I seemed to hear a despairing cry from my friends, who must have felt the oncoming calamity through a subtler sense than any of which I was yet capable.

Then, beyond the high and luminescent alp of our destination, I saw the mounting of a wall of darkness, dreadful and instant and positive and palpable, that rose everywhere and toppled like some Atlantean wave upon the irised suns and the fiery-colored vistas of the Inner Dimension.

We hung irresolute in the shadowed air, powerless and hopeless before the impending catastrophe, and saw that the darkness had surrounded the entire world and was rushing upon us from all sides. It ate the heavens, it blotted the outer suns; and the vast perspectives over which we had flown appeared to shrink and shrivel like a blackened paper. We seemed to wait alone for one terrible instant, in a center of dwindling light on which the cyclonic forces of night and destruction were impinging with torrential rapidity.

The center shrank to a mere point—and then the darkness was upon us like an overwhelming maelstrom—like the falling and crashing of cyclopean walls. I seemed to go down with the wreck of shattered worlds in a roaring sea of vortical space and force, to descend into some infrastellar pit, some ultimate limbo to which the shards of forgotten suns and systems are flung. Then, after a measureless interval, there came the sensation of violent impact, as if I had fallen among these shards, at the bottom of the universal night.

I struggled back to consciousness with slow, prodigious effort, as if I were crushed beneath some irremovable weight, beneath the lightless and inert débris of galaxies. It seemed to require the labors of a Titan to lift my lids; and my body and limbs were heavy as if they had been turned to some denser element than human flesh; or had been subjected to the gravitation of a grosser planet than the earth.

My mental processes were benumbed and painful and confused to the last degree; but at length I realized that I was lying on a riven and tilted pavement, among gigantic blocks of fallen stone. Above me, the light of a livid heaven came down among overturned and jagged walls that no longer supported their colossal dome. Close beside me, I saw a fuming pit, from which a ragged rift extended through the floor, like the chasm wrought by an earthquake.

I could not recognize my surroundings for a time; but at last, with a toilsome groping of thought, I understood that I was lying in the ruined temple of Ydmos. The pit whose grey and acrid vapors rose beside me was that from which the fountain of singing flame had issued.

It was a scene of stupendous havoc and devastation. The wrath that had been visited upon Ydmos had left no wall nor pylon of the temple standing. I stared at the blighted heavens from an architectural ruin in which the remains of On and Angkor would have been mere rubble-heaps.

With herculean effort, I turned my head away from the smoking pit, whose thin, sluggish fumes curled upward in phantasmal coils where the green ardor of the Flame had soared and sung. Not until then did I perceive my companions. Angarth, still insensible, was lying near at hand; and just beyond him I saw the pale, contorted face of Ebbonly, whose lower limbs and body were pinned down by the rough and broken pediment of a fallen pillar.

Striving as in some eternal nightmare to throw off the leaden-clinging weight of my inertia, and able to bestir myself only with the most painful slowness and laboriousness, I got somehow to my feet and went over to Ebbonly. Angarth, I saw at a glance, was uninjured, and would presently regain consciousness; but Ebbonly, crushed by the monolithic mass of stone, was dying swiftly; and even with the help of a dozen men, I could not have released him from his imprisonment; nor could I have done anything to palliate his agony. He tried to smile, with gallant and piteous courage, as I stooped above him.

"It's no use—I'm going in a moment," he whispered. "Good-bye, Hastane—and tell Angarth good-bye for me, too." His tortured lips relaxed, his eyelids dropped, and his head fell back on the temple pavement. With an unreal, dream-like horror, almost without emotion, I saw that he was dead. The exhaustion that still beset me was too profound to permit of thought or feeling; it was like the first reaction that follows the awakening from a drug-debauch. My nerves were like burnt-out wires, my muscles dead and unresponsive as clay, my brain was ashen and gutted as if a great fire had burned within it and gone out.

Somehow, after an interval of whose length my memory is uncertain, I managed to revive Angarth, and he sat up dully and dazedly. When I told him that Ebbonly was dead, my words appeared to make no impression upon him; and I wondered for awhile if he had understood. Finally, rousing himself a little with evident labor and difficulty, he peered at the body of our friend, and seemed to realize in some measure the horror of the situation. But I think he would have remained there for hours, or perhaps for all time, in his utter despair and lassitude, if I had not taken the initiative.

"Come," I said, with an attempt at firmness. "We must get out of this."

"Where to?" he queried, dully. "The Flame has failed at its source; and the Inner Dimension is no more. I wish I were dead, like Ebbonly— I might as well be, judging from the way I feel."

"We must find our way back to Crater Ridge," I said. "Surely we can do it, if the inter-dimensional portals have not been destroyed."

Angarth did not seem to hear me, but he followed obediently when I took him by the arm and began to seek an exit from the temple's heart among the roofless halls and overturned columns.

My recollections of our return are dim and confused, and are full of the tediousness of some interminable delirium. I remember looking back at Ebbonly, lying white and still beneath the massive pillar that would serve as an eternal monument for him; and I recall the mountainous ruins of the city, in which it seemed that we were the only living beings—a wilderness of chaotic stone, of fused, obsidian-like blocks, where streams of molten lava still ran in the mighty chasms, or poured like torrents adown unfathomable pits that had opened in the ground. And I remember seeing amid the wreckage the charred bodies of those dark colossi who were the people of Ydmos and the warders of the Flame.

Like pygmies lost in some shattered fortalice of the giants, we stumbled onward, strangling in mephitic and metallic vapors, reeling with weariness, dizzy with the heat that emanated everywhere to surge upon us in buffeting waves. The way was blocked by overthrown buildings, by toppled towers and battlements, over which we climbed precariously and toilsomely; and often we were compelled to divagate from our direct course by enormous rifts that seemed to cleave the foundations of the world.

The moving towers of the wrathful Outer Lords had withdrawn, their armies had disappeared on the plain beyond Ydmos, when we staggered over the riven and shapeless and scoriac crags that had formed the city's ramparts. Before us there was nothing but desolation—a fire-blackened and vapor-vaulted expanse in which no tree or blade of grass remained.

Across this waste we found our way to the slope of violet grass above the plain, which had lain beyond the path of the invader's bolts. There the guiding monoliths, reared by a people of whom we were never to learn even the name, still looked down upon the fuming desert and the mounded wrack of Ydmos. And there, at length, we came once more to the greyish-green columns that were the gateway between the worlds.

Auburn Area

THE ROOT OF AMPOI

A circus had arrived in Auburn. The siding at the station was crowded with long lines of cars from which issued a medley of exotic howls, growls, snarls and trumpetings. Elephants and zebras and dromedaries were led along the main streets; and many of the freaks and performers wandered about the town.

Two bearded ladies passed with the graceful air and walk of women of fashion. Then came a whole troupe of midgets, trudging along with the look of mournful, sophisticated children. And then I saw the giant, who was slightly more than eight feet tall and magnificently built, with no sign of the disproportion which often attends giantism. He was merely a fine physical specimen of the ordinary man, somewhat more than life-size. And even at first glance, there was something about his features and his gait which suggested a seaman.

I am a doctor; and the man provoked my medical curiosity. His abnormal bulk and height, without trace of acromegaly, was something I had never happened to meet before.

He must have felt my interest, for he returned my gaze with a speculative eye; and then, lurching in sailor-like fashion, he came over to me.

"I say, sir, could a chap buy a drink in this 'ere town?" He queried cautiously.

I made a quick decision.

"Come with me," I replied. "I'm an allopath; and I can tell without asking that you're a sick man."

We were only a block from my office. I steered the giant up the stairs and into my private sanctum. He almost filled the place, even when he sat down at my urging. I brought out a bottle of rye and poured a liberal glassful for him. He downed it with manifest appreciation. He had worn an air of mild depression when I first met him; now he began to brighten.

"You wouldn't think, to look at me, that I wasn't always a bloomin' giant," he soliloquized.

"Have another drink," I suggested.

After the second glass, he resumed a little mournfully: "No, sir, Jim Knox wasn't always a damn circus freak."

Then, with little urging on my part, he told me his story.

*　　*　　*

Knox, an adventurous Cockney, had followed half the seas of the world as a common sailor and boatswain in his younger years. He had visited many strange places, had known many bizarre experiences. Before he had reached the age of thirty, his restless and daring disposition led him to undertake an incredibly fantastic quest.

The events preceding this quest were somewhat unusual in themselves. Shipwrecked by a wild typhoon in the Banda Sea, and apparently the one survivor, Knox had drifted for two days on a hatch torn from the battered and sinking vessel. Then, rescued by a native fishing-proa, he had been carried to Salawatti.

The Rajah of Salawatti, an old and monkey-like Malay, was very nice to Knox. The Rajah was a teller of voluminous tales; and the boatswain was a patient listener. On this basis of congeniality, Knox became an honored guest for a month or more in the Rajah's palace. Here, among other wonders detailed by his host, he heard for the first time the rumor of a most remarkable Papuan tribe.

This unique tribe dwelt on a well-nigh inaccessible plateau of the Arfak Mountains. The women were nine feet tall and white as milk; but the men, strangely, were of normal stature and darker hue. They were friendly to the rare travelers who reached their domains; and they would trade for glass beads and mirrors the pigeons' blood rubies in which their mountain slopes abounded. As proof of the latter statement, the

Rajah showed Knox a large, flawless, uncut ruby, which he claimed had come from this region.

Knox was hardly inclined to credit the item about the giant women; but the rubies sounded far less improbable. It was characteristic of him that, with little thought of danger, difficulty, or the sheer absurdity of such a venture, he made up his mind at once to visit the Arfak Mountains.

Bidding farewell to his host, who mourned the loss of a good listener, he continued his odyssey. By means that he failed to specify in his history, Knox procured two sackfuls of mirrors and glass beads, and managed to reach the coast of northwestern New Guinea. At Andai, in Arfak, he hired a guide who purported to know the whereabouts of the giant Amazons, and struck boldly inland toward the mountains.

The guide, who was half Malay and half Papuan, bore one of the sacks of baubles on his shoulders; and Knox carried the other. He fondly hoped to return with the two sacks full of smouldering dark-red rubies.

It was a little known land. Some of the peoples were reputed to be headhunters and cannibals; but Knox found them friendly enough. But somehow, as they went on, the guide began to exhibit a growing haziness in his geography. When they reached the middle slopes of the Arfak range, Knox realized that the guide knew little more than he himself regarding the location of the fabulous ruby-strewn plateau.

They went on through the steepening forest. Before them, above trees that were still tall and semi-tropical, arose the granite scarps and crags of a high mountain-wall, behind which the afternoon sun had disappeared. In the early twilight, they camped at the foot of a seemingly insuperable cliff.

Knox awoke in a blazing yellow dawn, to discover that his guide had departed, taking one of the sacks of trinkets—which, from a savage viewpoint, would constitute enough capital to set the fellow up in business for life. Knox shrugged his shoulders and swore a little. The guide wasn't much of a loss; but he didn't like having his jewel-purchasing power diminished by half.

He looked at the cliffs above. Tier on tier they towered in the glow of dawn, with tops scarce distinguishable from the clouds about them. Somehow, the more he looked, the surer he became that they were the cliffs which guarded the hidden plateau. With their silence and inaccessible solitude, their air of eternal reserve and remoteness, they couldn't be anything else but the ramparts of a realm of titan women and pigeons' blood rubies.

He shouldered his pack and followed the granite wall in search of a likely starting-place for the climb he had determined to attempt. The upright rock was smooth as a metal sheet, and didn't offer a toehold for a spider monkey. But at last he came to a deep chasm which formed the bed of a summer-dried cataract. He began to ascend the chasm, which was no mean feat in itself, for the stream-bed was a series of high shelves, like a giant stairway.

Half the time he dangled by his fingers without a toehold, or stretched on tiptoe and felt precariously for a finger-grip. The climb was a ticklish business, with death on the pointed rocks below as the penalty of the least miscalculation.

He dared not look back on the way he had climbed in that giddy chasm. Toward noon, he saw above him the menacing overhang of a huge crag, where the straitening gully ceased in a black-mouthed cavern.

He scrambled up the final shelf into the cave, hoping that it led, as was likely, to an upper entrance made by the mountain torrent. By the light of struck matches, he scaled a slippery incline. The cave soon narrowed; and Knox could often brace himself between the walls, as if in a chimney's interior.

After long upward groping, he discerned a tiny glimmering ahead, like a pin-prick in the solid gloom. Knox, nearly worn out with his efforts, was immensely heartened. But again the cave narrowed, till he could squeeze no farther with the pack on his back. He slid back a little distance and removed the sack, which he then proceeded to push before him up a declivity of forty-five degrees. In those days, Knox was of average height and somewhat slender; but even so, he could barely wriggle through the last ten feet of the cavern.

He gave the sack a final heave and landed it on the surface without. Then he squirmed through the opening and fell exhausted in the sunlight. He lay almost at the fountain-head of the dried stream, in a saucer-like hollow at the foot of a gentle slope of granite beyond whose bare ridge the clouds were white and near.

Knox congratulated himself on his gifts as an alpine climber. He felt no doubt whatever that he had reached the threshold of the hidden realm of rubies and giant women. Suddenly, as he lay there, several men appeared against the clouds, on the ridge above. Striding like mountaineers, they came toward him with excited jabberings and gestures of amazement; and he rose and stood awaiting them.

Knox must have been a singular spectacle. His clothing and face were bestreaked with dirt and with the stains of parti-colored ores acquired in his passage through the cavern. The approaching men seemed to regard him with a sort of awe.

They were dressed in short reddish-purple tunics, and wore leather sandals. They did not belong to any of the lowland types: their skin was a light sienna, and their features were good even according to European standards. All were armed with long javelins but seemed friendly. Wide-eyed, and apparently, somewhat timorous, they addressed Knox in a language which bore no likeness to any Melanesian tongue he had ever heard.

He replied in all the languages of which he had the least smattering; but plainly they could not understand him. Then he untied his sack, took out a double handful of beads, and tried to convey by pantomime the information that he was a trader from remote lands.

The men nodded their heads. Beckoning him to follow them, they returned toward the cloud-rimmed ridge. Knox trudged along behind them, feeling quite sure that he had found the people of the Rajah's tale.

Topping the ridge, he saw the perspectives of a long plateau, full of woods, streams and cultivated fields. In the mild and slanting sunlight, he and his guides descended a path among flowering willow-herbs and rhododendrons to the plateau. There it soon became a well-trodden road, running through forests of dammar and fields of wheat. Houses of rough-hewn stone with thatched roofs, evincing a higher civilization than the huts of the Papuan sea-board, began to appear at intervals.

Men, garbed in the same style as Knox's guides, were working in the fields. Then Knox perceived several women, standing together in an idle group. Now he was compelled to believe the whole story about the hidden people, for these women were eight feet or more in height and had the proportions of shapely goddesses! Their complexion was not of a milky fairness, as in the Rajah's tale, but was tawny and cream-like and many shades lighter than that of the men. Knox felt a jubilant excitement as they turned their calm gaze upon him and watched him with the air of majestic statues. He had found the legendary realm; and he peered among the pebbles and grasses of the wayside, half expecting to see them intersown with rubies. None was in evidence, however.

A town appeared, circling a sapphire lake with one-storied but well-built houses laid out in regular streets. Many people were strolling or standing about; and all the women were tawny giantesses, and all the men were of average stature, with umber or sienna complexions.

A crowd gathered about Knox; and his guides were questioned in a quite peremptory manner by some of the titan females, who eyed the boatswain with embarrassing intentness. He divined at once the respect and obeisance paid to these women by the men, and inferred the superior position which they held. They all wore the tranquil and assured look of empresses.

Knox was led to a building near the lake. It was larger and more pretentious than the others. The roomy interior was arrayed with roughly pictured fabrics and furnished with chairs and couches of ebony. The general effect was rudely sybaritic and palatial, and much enhanced by the unusual height of the ceilings.

In a sort of audience-room, a woman sat enthroned on a broad dais. Several others stood about her like a bodyguard. She wore no crown, no jewels, and her dress differed in no wise from the short kilts of the other women. But Knox knew that he had entered the presence of a queen. The woman was fairer than the rest, with long rippling chestnut hair and fine oval features. The gaze that she turned upon Knox was filled with a feminine mingling of mildness and severity.

The boatswain assumed his most gallant manner, which must have been a little nullified by his dirt-smeared face and apparel. He bowed before the giantess; and she addressed him with a few soft words in which he sensed a courteous welcome. Then he opened his pack and selected a mirror and a string of blue beads, which he offered to the queen. She accepted the gifts gravely, showing neither pleasure nor surprise.

After dismissing the men who had brought Knox to her presence, the queen turned and spoke to her female attendants. They came forward and gave Knox to understand that he must accompany them. They led him to an open court, containing a huge bath fed by the waters of the blue lake. Here, in spite of his protests and strugglings, they undressed him as if he had been a little boy. Then they plunged him into the water and scrubbed him thoroughly with scrapers of stiff vegetable fiber. One of them brought him a brown tunic and a pair of sandals in lieu of his former raiment.

Though somewhat discomfited and abashed by his summary treatment, Knox couldn't help feeling like a different man after his renovation. And when the women brought in a meal of taro and millet-cake and roast pigeon, piled on enormous platters, he began to forgive them for his embarrassment.

Two of his fair attendants remained with him during the meal; and afterwards they gave him a lesson in their language by pointing at various objects and naming them. Knox soon acquired a knowledge of much domestic nomenclature.

The queen herself appeared later and proceeded to take a hand in his instruction. Her name, he learned, was Mabousa. Knox made an apt pupil; and the day's lesson was plainly satisfactory to all concerned. Knox realized more clearly than before that the queen was a beautiful woman; but he wished that she was not quite so large and imposing. He felt so juvenile beside her. The queen, on her part, seemed to regard Knox with a far from unfavorable gravity. He saw that she was giving him a good deal of thought and consideration.

Knox almost forgot the rubies of which he had come in search; and when he remembered them, he decided to wait till he had learned more of the language before broaching the subject.

A room in the palace was assigned to him; and he inferred that he could remain indefinitely as Mabousa's guest. He ate at the same table with the queen and her half-dozen attendants. It seemed that he was the only man in the establishment. The chairs were all designed for giant-esses, with one exception, which resembled the high chair in which a child sits at table amongst its elders. Knox occupied this chair.

Many days went by; and he learned enough of the language for all practical purposes. It was a tranquil but far from unpleasant life. He soon grew familiar with the general conditions of life in the country ruled by Mabousa, which was called Ondoar. It was quite isolated from the world without, for the mountain walls around it could be scaled only at the point which Knox had so fortuitously discovered. Few strangers had ever obtained entrance. The people were prosperous and contented, leading a pastoral existence under the benign but absolute matriarchy of Mabousa. The women governed their husbands by sheer virtue of phys-ical superiority; but there seemed to be fully as much domestic amity as in the households of countries where a reverse dominion prevails.

Knox wondered greatly about the superior stature of the women, which struck him as being a strange provision of nature. Somehow he did not venture to ask any questions; and no one volunteered to tell him the secret.

He kept an eye open for rubies, and was puzzled by the paucity of these gems. A few inferior rubies, as well as small sapphires and emeralds, were worn by some of the men as ear-ring pendants, though none of the women were addicted to such ornaments. Knox wondered if they didn't have a lot of rubies stored away somewhere. He had come there to trade for red corundum and had carried a whole sack-load of the requisite medium of barter up an impossible mountainside; so he was loath to relinquish the idea.

One day he resolved to open the subject with Mabousa. For some reason, he never quite knew why, it was hard to speak of such matters to the dignified and lovely giantess. But business was business.

He was groping for suitable words, when he suddenly noticed that Mabousa too had something on her mind. She had grown uncommonly silent and the way she kept looking at him was disconcerting and even embarrassing. He wondered what was the matter; also, he began to wonder if these people were cannibalistic. Her gaze was so eager and avid.

Before he could speak of the rubies and his willingness to buy them with glass beads, Mabousa startled him by coming out with a flatly phrased proposal of marriage. To say the least, Knox was unprepared. But it seemed uncivil, as well as unpolitic, to refuse. He had never been proposed to before by a queen or a giantess, and he thought it would be hardly the proper etiquette to decline a heart and hand of such capacity. Also, as Mabousa's husband, he would be in a most advantageous position to negotiate for rubies. And Mabousa was undeniably attractive, even though she was built on a grand scale. After a little hemming and hawing, he accepted her proposal, and was literally swept off his feet as the lady gathered him to the gargantuan charms of her bosom.

The wedding proved to be a very simple affair: a mere matter of verbal agreement in the presence of several female witnesses. Knox was amazed by the ease and rapidity with which he assumed the bonds of holy matrimony.

He learned a lot of things from his marriage with Mabousa. He found at the wedding-supper that the high chair he had been occupying at the royal table was usually reserved for the queen's consort. Later, he learned the secret of the women's size and stature. All the children, boys and girls, were of ordinary size at birth; but the girls were fed by their mothers on a certain root which caused them to increase in height and bulk beyond the natural limits.

The root was gathered on the highest mountain slopes. Its peculiar virtue was mainly due to a mode of preparation whose secret had been carefully guarded by the women and handed down from mother to daughter. Its use had been known for several generations. At one time the men had been the ruling sex; but an accidental discovery of the root by a down-trodden wife named Ampoi had soon led to a reversal of this domination. In consequence the memory of Ampoi was highly venerated by the females, as that of a savioress.

Knox also acquired much other information, on matters both social and domestic. But nothing was ever said about rubies. He was forced to decide that the plenitude of these jewels in Ondoar must have been sheer fable; a purely decorative addition to the story of the giant Amazons.

His marriage led to other disillusionments. As the queen's consort, he had expected to have a share in the government of Ondoar, and had looked forward to a few kingly prerogatives. But he soon found that he was merely a male adjunct of Mabousa, with no legal rights, no privileges other than those which she, out of wifely affection, might choose to accord him. She was kind and loving, but also strong-minded, not to say bossy; and he learned that he couldn't do anything or go anywhere without first consulting her and obtaining permission.

She would sometimes reprimand him, would often set him right on some point of Ondoarian etiquette, or the general conduct of life, in a sweet but strict manner; and it never occurred to her that he might even wish to dispute any of her mandates. He, however, was irked more and more by this feminine tyranny. His male pride, his manly British spirit, revolted. If the lady had been of suitable size he would, in his own phrase, "have knocked her about a little." But, under the circumstances, any attempt to chasten her by main strength hardly seemed advisable.

Along with all this, he grew quite fond of her in his fashion. There were many things that endeared her to him; and he felt that she would be an exemplary wife, if there were only some way of curbing her deplorable tendency to domineer.

Time went on, as it has a habit of doing. Mabousa seemed to be well enough satisfied with her spouse. But Knox brooded a good deal over the false position in which he felt that she had placed him, and the daily injury to his manhood. He wished that there were some way of correcting matters, of asserting his natural rights and putting Mabousa in her place.

One day he remembered the root on which the women of Ondoar were fed. Why couldn't he get hold of some of it and grow big himself like Mabousa, or bigger? Then he would be able to handle her in the proper style. The more he thought about it, the more this appealed to him as the ideal solution of his marital difficulties.

The main problem, however, was to obtain the root. He questioned some of the other men in a discreet way, but none of them could tell him anything about it. The women never permitted the men to accompany them when they gathered the stuff; and the process of preparing it for consumption was carried on in deep caverns. Several men had dared to steal the food in past years; two of them, indeed, had grown to giant stature on what they had stolen. But all had been punished by the women with life-long exile from Ondoar.

All this was rather discouraging. Also, it served to increase Knox's contempt for the men of Ondoar, whom he looked upon as a spineless, effeminate lot. However, he didn't give up his plan. But, after much deliberation and scheming, he found himself no nearer to a solution of the problem than before.

Perhaps he would have resigned himself, as better men have done, to an inevitable life-long henpecking. But at last, in the birth of a female baby to Mabousa and himself, he found the opportunity he had been seeking.

The child was like any other girl infant, and Knox was no less proud of it, no less imbued with the customary parental sentiments, than other fathers have been. It did not occur to him till the baby was old enough to be weaned and fed on the special food, that he would now have in his own home a first-rate chance to appropriate some of this food for his personal use.

The simple and artless Mabousa was wholly without suspicion of such unlawful designs. Male obedience to the feministic law of the land was so thoroughly taken for granted that she even showed him the strange foodstuff and often fed the child in his presence. Nor did she conceal from him the large earthen jar in which she kept her reserve supply.

The jar stood in the palace kitchen, among others filled with more ordinary staples of diet. One day, when Mabousa had gone to the country on some political errand, and the waiting-women were all preoccupied with other than culinary matters, Knox stole into the kitchen and carried away a small bagful of the stuff, which he then hid in his own room. In his fear of detection, he felt more of an actual thrill than at any time since the boyhood days when he had pilfered apples from London street-barrows behind the backs of the vendors.

The stuff looked like a fine variety of sage, and had an aromatic smell and spicy taste. Knox ate a little of it at once but dared not indulge himself to the extent of a full meal for fear that the consequences would be visible. He had watched the incredible growth of the child, which had gained the proportions of a normal six-year old girl in a fortnight under the influence of the miraculous nutrient; and he did not wish to have his theft discovered, and the further use of the food prevented, in the first stage of his own development toward gianthood.

He felt that some sort of seclusion would be advisable till he could attain the bulk and stature which would ensure a position as master in his own household. He must somehow remove himself from all female supervision during the period of growth.

This, for one so thoroughly subject to petticoat government, with all his goings and comings minutely regulated, was no mean problem. But again fortune favored Knox: for the hunting season in Ondoar had now arrived; a season in which many of the men were permitted by their wives to visit the higher mountains and spend days or weeks in tracking down a certain agile species of alpine deer, known as the *okloh*.

Perhaps Mabousa wondered a little at the sudden interest shown by Knox in *okloh*-hunting, and his equally sudden devotion to practice with the javelins used by the hunters. But she saw no reason for denying him permission to make the desired trip; merely stipulating that he should go in company with certain other dutiful husbands, and should be very careful of dangerous cliffs and crevasses.

The company of other husbands was not exactly in accord with Knox's plan; but he knew better than to argue the point. He had contrived to make several more visits to the palace pantry, and had stolen enough of the forbidden food to turn him into a robust and wife-taming titan. Somehow, on that trip among the mountains, in spite of the meek and law-abiding males with whom he was condemned to go, he would find chances to consume all he had stolen. He would return a conquering Anakim, a roaring and swaggering Goliath; and everyone, especially Mabousa, would stand from under.

Knox hid the food, disguised as a bag of millet meal, in his private supply of provisions. He also carried some of it in his pockets, and would eat a mouthful or two whenever the other men weren't looking. And at night, when they were all sleeping quietly, he would steal to the bag and devour the aromatic stuff by the handful.

The result was truly phenomenal, for Knox could watch himself swell after the first square meal. He broadened and shot up inch by inch, to the manifest bewilderment of his companions, none of whom, at first, was imaginative enough to suspect the true reason. He saw them eyeing him with a sort of speculative awe and curiosity, such as a civilized people would display before a wild man from Borneo. Obviously they regarded his growth as a kind of biological anomaly, or perhaps as part of the queer behavior that might well be expected from a foreigner of doubtful antecedents.

The hunters were now in the highest mountains, at the northernmost end of Ondoar. Here, among stupendous riven crags and piled pinnacles, they pursued the elusive *okloh*; and Knox began to attain a length of limb that enabled him to leap across chasms over which the others could not follow.

At last one or two of them must have gotten suspicious. They took to watching Knox, and one night they surprised him in the act of devouring the sacred food. They tried to warn him, with a sort of holy horror in their demeanor, that he was doing a dreadful and forbidden thing, and would bring upon himself the direst consequences.

Knox, who was beginning to feel as well as look like an actual giant, told them to mind their own business. Moreover, he went on to express his frank and uncensored opinion of the sapless, decadent and effeminate males of Ondoar. After that the men left him alone, but murmured fearfully among themselves and watched his every movement with apprehensive glances. Knox despised them so thoroughly, that he failed to attach any special significance to the furtive disappearance of two members of the party. Indeed, at the time, he hardly noticed that they had gone.

After a fortnight of alpine climbing, the hunters had slain their due quota of long-horned and goat-footed *okloh*; and Knox had consumed his entire store of the stolen food and had grown to proportions which, he felt sure, would enable him to subdue his domineering helpmeet and show her the proper inferiority of the female sex. It was time to return: Knox's companions would not have dreamt of exceeding the limit set by the women, who had enjoined them to come back at the end of a fortnight; and Knox was eager to demonstrate his new-won superiority of bulk and brawn.

As they came down from the mountains and crossed the cultivated plain, Knox saw that the other men were lagging behind more and more, with a sort of fearfulness and shrinking timidity. He strode on before them, carrying three full-sized *okloh* slung over his shoulders, as a lesser man would have carried so many rabbits.

The fields and roads were deserted, and none of the titan women were in sight anywhere. Knox wondered a little about this; but feeling himself so much the master of the general situation, he did not over-exert his mind in curious conjectures.

However, as they approached the town, the desolation and silence became a trifle ominous. Knox's fellow-hunters were obviously stricken with dire and growing terror. But Knox did not feel that he should lower his dignity by even asking the reason.

They entered the streets, which were also strangely quiet. There was no evidence of life, other than the pale and frightened faces of a few men that peered from windows and furtively opened doors.

At last they came in sight of the palace. Now the mystery was explained, for apparently all the women of Ondoar had gathered in the square before the building! They were drawn up in a massive and appallingly solid formation, like an army of giant Amazons; and their utter stillness was more dreadful than the shouting and tumult of battlefields. Knox felt an unwilling but irresistible dismay before the swelling thews of their mighty arms, the solemn heaving of their gargantuan bosoms, and the awful and austere gaze with which they regarded him in unison.

Suddenly he perceived that he was quite alone—the other men had faded away like shadows, as if they did not even dare to remain and watch his fate. He felt an almost undeniable impulse to flee; but his British valor prevented him from yielding to it. Pace by pace he forced himself to go on toward the embattled women.

They waited for him in stony silence, immovable as caryatides. He saw Mabousa in the front rank, her serving-women about her. She watched him with eyes in which he could read nothing but unutterable reproach. She did not speak; and somehow the jaunty words with which he had intended to greet her were congealed on his lips.

All at once, with a massed and terrible striding movement, the women surrounded Knox. He lost sight of Mabousa in the solid wall of titanesses. Great, brawny hands were grasping him, tearing the spear from his fingers and the *okloh* from his shoulders. He struggled as became a doughty Briton. But one man, even though he had eaten the food of giantesses, could do nothing against the whole tribe of eight-foot females.

Maintaining a silence more formidable than any outcry, they bore him through the town and along the road by which he had entered On-doar, and up the mountain path to the outmost ramparts of the land. There, from the beetling crag above the gully he had climbed, they lowered him with a tackle of heavy ropes to the dry torrent-bed two hundred feet below, and left him to find his way down the perilous mountain-side and back to the outer world that would accept him henceforward only as a circus freak.

THE NINTH SKELETON

I t was beneath the immaculate blue of a morning in April that I set out to keep my appointment with Guenevere. We had agreed to meet on Boulder Ridge, at a spot well known to both of us, a small and circular field surrounded with pines and full of large stones, midway between her parents' home at Newcastle and my cabin on the northeastern extremity of the Ridge, near Auburn.

Guenevere is my fiancé. It must be explained that at the time of which I write, there was a certain amount of opposition on the part of her parents to the engagement—an opposition since happily withdrawn. In fact, they had gone so far as to forbid me to call, and Guenevere and I could see each other only by stealth, and infrequently.

The Ridge is a long and rambling moraine, heavily strewn in places with boulders, as its name implies, and with many out-croppings of black volcanic stone. Fruit-ranches cling to some of its slopes, but scarcely any of the top is under cultivation, and much of the soil, indeed, is too thin and stony to be arable. With its twisted pines, often as fantastic in form as the cypresses of the California coast, and its gnarled and stunted oaks, the landscape has a wild and quaint beauty, with more than a hint of the Japanesque in places.

It is perhaps two miles from my cabin to the place where I was to meet Guenevere. Since I was born in the very shadow of Boulder Ridge, and have lived upon or near it for most of my thirty-odd years, I am familiar with every rod of its lovely and rugged extent, and, previous to that April morning, would scarcely have refrained from laughing if anyone had told me I could possibly lose my way . . . Since then—well, I assure you, I should not feel inclined to laugh . . .

Truly, it was a morning made for the trysts of lovers. Wild bees were humming busily in the patches of clover and in the ceanothus bushes with their great masses of white flowers, whose strange and heavy perfume intoxicated the air. Most of the spring blossoms were abroad: cyclamen, yellow violet, poppy, wild hyacinth, and woodland star; and the green of the fields was opalescent with their colors. Between the emerald of the buckeyes, the grey-green of the pines, the golden and dark and bluish greens of the oaks, I caught glimpses of the snow-white Sierras to the east, and the faint blue of the Coast Range to the west, beyond the pale and lilac levels of the Sacramento valley. Following a vague trail, I went onward across open fields where I had to thread my way among clustering boulders.

My thoughts were all of Guenevere, and I looked only with a casual and desultory eye at the picturesqueness and vernal beauty that environed my path. I was half-way between my cabin and the meeting-place, when I became suddenly aware that the sunlight had darkened, and glanced up, thinking, of course, that an April cloud, appearing unobserved from beyond the horizon, had passed across the sun. Imagine, then, my surprise when I saw that the azure of the entire sky had turned to a dun and sinister brown, in the midst of which the sun was clearly visible, burning like an enormous round red ember. Then, something strange and unfamiliar in the nature of my surroundings, which I was momentarily at a loss to define, forced itself upon my attention, and my surprise became a growing consternation. I stopped and looked about me, and realized, incredible as it seemed, that I had lost my way; for the pines on either hand were not those that I had expected to see. They were more gigantic, more gnarled, than the ones I remembered; and their roots writhed in wilder and more serpentine contortions from a soil that was strangely flowerless, and where even the grass grew only in scanty tufts. There were boulders large as druidic monoliths, and the forms of some of them were such as one might see in a nightmare. Thinking, of course, that it must all be a dream, but with a sense of utter bewilderment which seldom if ever attends the absurdities and monstrosities of nightmare, I sought in vain to orient myself and to find some familiar landmark in the bizarre scene that lay before me.

A path, broader than the one I had been following, but running in what I judged to be the same direction, wound on among the trees. It was covered with a grey dust, which, as I went forward, became deeper and displayed footprints of a singular form—footprints that were surely too attenuate, too fantastically slender, to be human, despite their five toe-marks. Something about them, I know not what, something in the nature of their very thinness and elongation, made me shiver. Afterwards, I wondered why I had not recognized them for what they were; but at the time, no suspicion entered my mind—only a vague sense of disquietude, an indefinable trepidation.

As I proceeded, the pines amid which I passed became momentarily more fantastic and more sinister in the contortions of their boughs and boles and roots. Some were like leering hags; others were obscenely crouching gargoyles; some appeared to writhe in an eternity of hellish torture; others were convulsed as with a satanic merriment. All the while, the sky continued to darken slowly, the dun and dismal brown that I had first perceived turning through almost imperceptible changes of tone to a dead funereal purple, wherein the sun smouldered like a moon that had risen from a bath of blood. The trees and the whole landscape were saturated with this macabre purple, were immersed and steeped in its unnatural gloom. Only the rocks, as I went on, grew strangely paler; and their forms were somehow suggestive of headstones, of tombs and monuments. Beside the trail, there was no longer the green of vernal grass—only an earth mottled by drying algae and tiny lichens the color of verdigris. Also there were patches of evil-looking fungi with stems of a leprous pallor and blackish heads that drooped and nodded loathsomely.

The sky had now grown so dark that the whole scene took on a semi-nocturnal aspect, and made me think of a doomed world in the twilight of a dying sun. All was airless and silent; there were no birds, no insects, no sighing of the pines, no lisping of leaves: a baleful and pre-ternatural silence, like the silence of the infinite void.

The trees became denser, then dwindled, and I came to a circular field. Here, there was no mistaking the nature of the monolithal boul-ders—they were headstones and funeral monuments, but so enor-mously ancient that the letterings or figures upon them were well-nigh effaced; and the few characters that I could distinguish were not of any known language. About them there was the hoariness and mystery and terror of incomputable Eld. It was hard to believe that life and death could be as old as they. The trees around them were inconceivably gnarled and bowed as with an almost equal burden of years. The sense of awful antiquity that these stones and pines all served to convey in-creased the oppression of my bewilderment, confirmed my disquietude. Nor was I reassured when I noticed on the soft earth about the head-stones a number of those attenuate footprints of which I have already spoken. They were disposed in a fashion that was truly singular, seeming to depart from and return to the vicinity of each stone.

Now, for the first time, I heard a sound other than the sound of my own footfalls in the silence of this macabre scene. Behind me, among the trees, there was a faint and evil rattling. I turned and listened; there was something in these sounds that served to complete the demoraliza-tion of my unstrung nerves; and monstrous fears, abominable fancies, trooped like the horde of a witches' sabbat through my brain.

The reality that I was now to confront was no less monstrous! There was a whitish glimmering in the shadow of the trees, and a human skel-eton, bearing in its arms the skeleton of an infant, emerged and came toward me! Intent as on some ulterior cryptic purpose, some charnel errand not to be surmised by the living, it went by with a tranquil pace, an effortless and gliding tread, in which, despite my terror and stupefac-tion, I perceived a certain horrible and feminine grace. I followed the apparition with my eyes as it passed among the monuments without pausing and vanished in the darkness of the pines on the opposite side of the field. No sooner had it gone, than a second, also bearing in its arms an infant skeleton, appeared and passed before me in the same direction and with the same abominable and loathsome grace of movement.

A horror that was more than horror, a fear that was beyond fear, petrified all my faculties, and I felt as if I were weighted down by some ineluctable and insupportable burden of nightmare. Before me, skeleton after skeleton, each precisely like the last, with the same macabre lightness and ease of motion, each carrying its pitiful infant, emerged from the shadow of the ancient pines and followed where the first had disappeared, intent as on the same cryptic errand. One by one they came, till I had counted eight! Now I knew the origin of the bizarre footprints whose attenuation had disturbed and troubled me.

When the eighth skeleton had passed from sight, my eyes were drawn as by some irresistible impulsion to one of the nearer headstones, beside which I was amazed to perceive what I had not noticed before: a freshly opened grave, gaping darkly in the soft soil. Then, at my elbow, I heard a low rattling, and the fingers of a fleshless hand plucked lightly at my sleeve. A skeleton was beside me, differing only from the others through the fact that it bore no infant in its arms. With a lipless and ingratiating leer, it plucked again at my sleeve, as if to draw me toward the open grave, and its teeth clicked as if it were trying to speak. My senses and my brain, aswirl with vertiginous terror, could endure no more: I seemed to fall and fall through deeps of infinite eddying blackness with the clutching terror of those fingers upon my arm, till consciousness was left behind in my descent.

When I came to, Guenevere was holding me by the arm, concern and puzzlement upon her sweet oval face, and I was standing among the boulders of the field appointed for our rendezvous.

"What on earth is the matter with you, Herbert?" she queried anxiously. "Are you ill? You were standing here in a daze when I came, and didn't seem to hear or see me when I spoke to you. And I really thought you were going to faint when I touched your arm."

THE OLD WATERWHEEL

Often, on homeward ways, I come
   To a deserted orchard, old and lone,
Unplowed, untrod, with wilding grasses grown
Through rows of pear and plum.

There, in a never-ceasing round,
In the slow stream, by noon, by night, by dawn,
An ancient, hidden water-wheel turns on
With a sad, reiterant sound.

Most eerily it comes and dies,
And comes again, when on the horizon's breast
The ruby of Antares seems to rest,
Fallen from star-fraught skies:

A dolent, drear, complaining note
Whose all-monotonous cadence haunts the air
Like the recurrent moan of a despair
Some heart has learned by rote;

Heavy, and ill to hear, for one
Within whose breast, today, tonight, tomorrow,
Like the slow wheel, an ancient, darkling sorrow
Turns and is never done.

Genius Loci

"It is a very strange place," said Amberville, "but I scarcely know how to convey the impression it made upon me. It will all sound so simple and ordinary. There is nothing but a sedgy meadow, surrounded on three sides by slopes of yellow pine. A dreary little stream flows in from the open end, to lose itself in a *cul-de-sac* of cat-tails and boggy ground. The stream, running slowly and more slowly, forms a stagnant pool of some extent, from which several sickly-looking alders seem to fling themselves backwards, as if unwilling to approach it. A dead willow leans above the pool, tangling its wan, skeleton-like reflection with the green scum that mottles the water. There are no blackbirds, no kildees, no dragon-flies even, such as one usually finds in a place of that sort. It is all silent and desolate. The spot is evil—it is unholy in a way that I simply can't describe. I was compelled to make a drawing of it, almost against my will, since anything so outré is hardly in my line. In fact, I made two drawings. I'll show them to you, if you like."

Since I had a high opinion of Amberville's artistic abilities, and had long considered him one of the foremost landscape painters of his generation, I was naturally quite eager to see the drawings. He, however, did not even pause to await my avowal of interest, but began at once to open his portfolio. His facial expression, the very movements of his hands, were somehow eloquent of a strange mixture of compulsion and repugnance as he brought out and displayed the two water-color sketches he had mentioned.

I could not recognize the scene depicted from either of them. Plainly it was one that I had missed in my desultory rambling about the foothill environs of the tiny hamlet of Bowman, where, two years before, I had purchased an uncultivated ranch and had retired for the privacy so essential to prolonged literary effort. Francis Amberville, in the one fortnight of his visit, through his flair for the pictorial potentialities of landscape, had doubtless grown more familiar with the neighborhood than I. It had been his habit to roam about in the forenoon, armed with sketching-materials; and in this way he had already found the theme of more than one lovely painting. The arrangement was mutually convenient, since I, in his absence, was wont to apply myself assiduously to an antique Remington.

I examined the drawings attentively. Both, though of hurried execution, were highly meritorious, and showed the characteristic grace and vigor of Amberville's style. And yet, even at first glance, I found a quality that was more than alien to the spirit of his work. The elements of the scene were those he had described. In one picture, the pool was half hidden by a fringe of mace-reeds, and the dead willow was leaning across it at a prone, despondent angle, as if mysteriously arrested in its fall toward the stagnant waters. Beyond, the alders seemed to strain away from the pool, exposing their knotted roots as if in eternal effort. In the other drawing, the pool formed the main portion of the foreground, with the skeleton tree looming drearily at one side. At the water's further end, the cat-tails seemed to wave and whisper among themselves in a dying wind; and the steeply barring slope of pine at the meadow's terminus was indicated as a wall of gloomy green that closed in the picture, leaving only a pale margin of autumnal sky at the top.

All this, as the painter had said, was ordinary enough. But I was impressed immediately by a profound horror that lurked in these simple elements and was expressed by them as if by the balefully contorted features of some demoniac face. In both drawings, this sinister character was equally evident, as if the same face had been shown in profile and front view. I could not trace the separate details that composed the impression; but ever, as I looked, the abomination of a strange evil, a spirit of despair, malignity, desolation, leered from the drawings more openly and hatefully. The spot seemed to wear a macabre and Satanic grimace. One felt that it might speak aloud, might utter the imprecations of some gigantic devil, or the raucous derision of a thousand birds of ill omen. The evil conveyed was something wholly outside of humanity—more ancient than man. Somehow—fantastic as this will seem—the meadow had the air of a vampire, grown old and hideous with unutterable infamies. Subtly, indefinably, it thirsted for other things than the sluggish trickle of water by which it was fed.

"Where is the place?" I asked, after a minute or two of silent inspection. It was incredible that anything of the sort could really exist—and equally incredible that a nature so robust as Amberville should have been sensitive to its quality.

"It's in the bottom of that abandoned ranch, a mile or less down the little road toward Bear River," he replied. "You must know it. There's a small orchard about the house, on the upper hillside; but the lower portion, ending in that meadow, is all wild land."

I began to visualize the vicinity in question. "Guess it must be the old Chapman place," I decided. "No other ranch along that road would answer your specifications."

"Well, whoever it belongs to, that meadow is the most horrible spot I have ever encountered. I've known other landscapes that had something wrong with them—but never anything like this."

"Maybe it's haunted," I said, half in jest. "From your description, it must be the very meadow where old Chapman was found dead one morning by his youngest daughter. It happened a few months after I moved here. He was supposed to have died of heart failure. His body was quite cold, and he had probably been lying there all night, since the family had missed him at supper-time. I don't remember him very clearly, but I remember that he had a reputation for eccentricity. For some time before his death, people thought that he was going mad. I forget the details. Anyway, his wife and children left, not long after he died, and no one has occupied the house or cultivated the orchard since.

It was a commonplace rural tragedy."

"I'm not much of a believer in spooks," observed Amberville, who seemed to have taken my suggestion of haunting in a literal sense. "Whatever the influence is, it's hardly of human origin. Come to think of it, though, I received a very silly impression once or twice—the idea that someone was watching me while I did those drawings. Queer—I had almost forgotten that, till you brought up the possibility of haunting. I seemed to see him out of the tail of my eye, just beyond the radius that I was putting into the picture: a dilapidated old scoundrel with dirty grey whiskers and an evil scowl. It's odd, too, that I should have gotten such a definite conception of him, without ever seeing him squarely. I thought it was a tramp who had strayed into the meadow-bottom. But when I turned to give him a level glance, he simply wasn't there. It was as if he melted into the miry ground, the cat-tails, the sedges."

"That isn't a bad description of Chapman," I said. "I remember his whiskers—they were almost white, except for the tobacco juice. A battered antique, if there ever was one—and very unamiable, too. He had a poisonous glare toward the end, which no doubt helped along the legend of his insanity. Some of the tales about him come back to me now. People said that he neglected the care of his orchard more and more. Visitors used to find him in that lower meadow, standing idly about and staring vacantly at the trees and water. Probably that was one reason they thought he was losing his mind. But I'm sure I never heard that there was anything unusual or queer about the meadow—either at the time of Chapman's death, or since. It's a lonely spot, and I don't imagine that anyone ever goes there now."

"I stumbled on it quite by accident," said Amberville. "The place isn't visible from the road, on account of the thick pines. . . . But there's another odd thing: I went out this morning with a strong and clear intuition that I might find something of uncommon interest. I made a bee-line for the meadow, so to speak—and I'll have to admit that the intuition justified itself. The place repels me—but it fascinates me, too. I've simply got to solve the mystery, if it has a solution," he added, with a slightly defensive air. "I'm going back early tomorrow, with my oils, to start a real painting of it."

I was surprised, knowing that predilection of Amberville for scenic brilliance and gaiety which had caused him to be likened to Sorolla. "The painting will be a novelty for you," I commented. "I'll have to come and take a look at the place myself, before long. It should really be more in my line than yours. There ought to be a weird story in it somewhere, if it lives up to your drawings and description."

Several days passed. I was deeply preoccupied, at the time, with the toilsome and intricate problems offered by the concluding chapters of a new novel; and I put off my proposed visit to the meadow discovered by Amberville. My friend, on his part, was evidently engrossed by his new theme. He sallied forth each morning with his easel and oil-colors, and returned later each day, forgetful of the luncheon-hour that had formerly brought him back from such expeditions. On the third day, he did not reappear till sunset. Contrary to his custom, he did not show me what he had done, and his answers to my queries regarding the progress of the picture were somewhat vague and evasive. For some reason, he was unwilling to talk about it. Also, he was apparently loath to discuss the meadow itself, and in answer to direct questions, merely reiterated in an absent and perfunctory manner the account he had given me following his discovery of the place. In some mysterious way that I could not define, his attitude seemed to have changed.

There were other changes, too. He seemed to have lost his usual blitheness. Often I caught him frowning intently, and surprised the lurking of some equivocal shadow in his frank eyes. There was a moodiness, a morbidity, which, as far as our five years' friendship enabled me to observe, was a new aspect of his temperament. Perhaps, if I had not been so preoccupied with my own difficulties, I might have wondered more as to the causation of his gloom, which I attributed readily enough at first to some technical dilemma that was baffling him. He was less and less the Amberville that I knew; and on the fourth day, when he came back at twilight, I perceived an actual surliness that was quite foreign to his nature.

"What's wrong?" I ventured to inquire. "Have you struck a snag? Or is old Chapman's meadow getting on your nerves with its ghostly influences?"

He seemed, for once, to make an effort to throw off his gloom, his taciturnity and ill humor.

"It's the infernal mystery of the thing," he declared, "I've simply got to solve it, in one way or another. The place has an entity of its own— an indwelling personality. It's there, like the soul in a human body, but I can't pin it down or touch it. You know that I'm not superstitious— but, on the other hand, I'm not a bigoted materialist, either; and I've run across some odd phenomena in my time. That meadow, perhaps, is inhabited by what the ancients called a *Genius Loci*. More than once, before this, I have suspected that such things might exist—might reside, inherent, in some particular spot. But this is the first time that I've had reason to suspect anything of an actively malignant or inimical nature. The other influences, whose presence I have felt, were benign in some large, vague, impersonal way—or were else wholly indifferent to human welfare—perhaps oblivious of human existence. This thing, however, is hatefully aware and watchful: I feel that the meadow itself—or the force embodied in the meadow—is scrutinizing me all the time. The place has the air of a thirsty vampire, waiting to drink me in, somehow, if it can. It is a *cul-de-sac* of everything evil, in which an unwary soul might well be caught and absorbed. But I tell you, Murray, I can't keep away from it."

"It looks as if the place *were* getting you," I said, thoroughly astonished by his extraordinary declaration, and by the air of fearful and morbid conviction with which he uttered it.

Apparently he had not heard me, for he made no reply to my observation. "There's another angle," he went on, with a feverish intensity in his voice. "You remember my impression of an old man lurking in the background and watching me, on my first visit. Well, I have seen him again, many times, out of the corner of my eye; and during the last two days, he has appeared more directly, though in a queer, partial way. Sometimes, when I am studying the dead willow very intently, I see his scowling, filthy-bearded face as a part of the bole. Then, again, it will float among the leafless twigs, as if it had been caught there. Sometimes a knotty hand, a tattered coat-sleeve, will emerge through the mantling algae in the pool, as if a drowned body were rising to the surface. Then, a moment later—or simultaneously—there will be something of him among the alders or the cat-tails. These apparitions are always brief, and when I try to scrutinize them closely, they melt like films of vapor into the surrounding scene. But the old scoundrel, whoever or whatever he may be, is a sort of fixture. He is no less vile than everything else about the place—though I feel that he isn't the main element of the vileness."

"Good Lord!" I exclaimed. "You certainly have been seeing things. If you don't mind, I'll come down and join you for a while, tomorrow afternoon. The mystery begins to inveigle me."

"Of course I don't mind. Come ahead." His manner, all at once, for no tangible reason, had resumed the unnatural taciturnity of the past four days. He gave me a furtive look that was sullen and almost unfriendly. It was as if an obscure barrier, temporarily laid aside, had again risen between us. The shadows of his strange mood returned upon him visibly; and my efforts to continue the conversation were rewarded only by half-surly, half-absent monosyllables. Feeling an aroused concern, rather than any offence, I began to note, for the first time, the unwonted pallor of his face, and the bright, febrile luster of his eyes. He looked vaguely unwell, I thought—as if something of his exuberant vitality had gone out of him, and had left in its place an alien energy of doubtful and less healthy nature. Tacitly, I gave up any attempt to bring him back from the secretive twilight into which he had withdrawn. For the rest of the evening, I pretended to read a novel, while Amberville maintained his singular abstraction. Somewhat inconclusively, I puzzled over the matter till bed-time. I made up my mind, however, that I would visit Chapman's meadow. I did not believe in the supernatural; but it seemed apparent that the place was exerting a deleterious influence upon Amberville.

The next morning, when I arose, my Chinese servant informed me that the painter had already breakfasted and had gone out with his easel and colors. This further proof of his obsession troubled me; but I applied myself rigorously to a forenoon of writing.

Immediately after luncheon, I drove down the highway, followed the narrow dirt road that branched off toward Bear River, and left my car on the pine-thick hill above the old Chapman place. Though I had never visited the meadow, I had a pretty clear idea of its location. Disregarding the grassy, half-obliterated road into the upper portion of the property, I struck down through the woods into the little blind valley, seeing more than once, on the opposite slope, the dying orchard of pear and apple trees, and the tumbledown shanty that had belonged to the Chapmans.

It was a warm October day; and the serene solitude of the forest, the autumnal softness of light and air, made the idea of anything malign or sinister seem impossible. When I came to the meadow-bottom, I was ready to laugh at Amberville's notions; and the place itself, at first sight, merely impressed me as being rather dreary and dismal. The features of the scene were those that he had described so clearly, but I could not find the open evil that had leered from the pool, the willow, the alders and the cat-tails in his drawings.

Amberville, with his back toward me, was seated on a folding stool before his easel, which he had placed among the plots of dark green wire-grass in the open ground above the pool. He did not seem to be working, however, but was staring intently at the scene beyond him, while a loaded brush drooped idly in his fingers. The sedges deadened my footfalls; and he did not hear me as I drew near.

With much curiosity, I peered over his shoulder at the large canvas on which he had been engaged. As far as I could tell, the picture had already been carried to a consummate degree of technical perfection. It was an almost photographic rendering of the scummy water, the whitish skeleton of the leaning willow, the unhealthy, half-disrooted alders, and the cluster of nodding mace-reeds. But in it I found the macabre and demoniac spirit of the sketches: the meadow seemed to wait and watch like an evilly distorted face. It was a deadfall of malignity and despair, lying apart from the autumn world around it; a plague-spot of nature, forever accurst and alone.

Again I looked at the landscape itself—and saw that the spot was indeed as Amberville had depicted it. It wore the grimace of a mad vampire, hateful and alert! At the same time, I became disagreeably conscious of the unnatural silence. There were no birds, no insects, as the painter had said; and it seemed that only spent and dying winds could ever enter that depressed valley-bottom. The thin stream that lost itself in the boggy ground was like a soul that went down to perdition. It was part of the mystery, too; for I could not remember any stream on the lower side of the barring hill that would indicate a subterranean outlet.

Amberville's intentness, and the very posture of his head and shoulders, were like those of a man who has been mesmerized. I was about to make my presence known to him; but at that instant there came to me the apperception that we were not alone in the meadow. Just beyond the focus of my vision, a figure seemed to stand in a furtive attitude, as if watching us both. I whirled about—and there was no one. Then I heard a startled cry from Amberville, and turned to find him staring at me. His features wore a wild look of terror and surprise, which had not wholly erased a hypnotic absorption.

"My God!" he said, "I thought you were the old man!"

I cannot be sure whether anything more was said by either of us. I have, however, the impression of a blank silence. After his single exclamation of surprise, Amberville seemed to retreat into an impenetrable abstraction, as if he were no longer conscious of my presence; as if, having identified me, he had forgotten me at once. On my part, I felt a weird and overpowering constraint. That infamous, eerie scene depressed me beyond measure. It seemed that the boggy bottom was trying to drag me down in some intangible way. The boughs of the sick alders beckoned. The pool, over which the bony willow presided like an arboreal Death, was wooing me foully with its stagnant waters.

Moreover, apart from the ominous atmosphere of the scene itself, I was painfully aware of a further change in Amberville—a change that was an actual alienation. His recent mood, whatever it was, had strengthened upon him enormously: he had gone deeper into its morbid twilight, and was lost to the blithe and sanguine personality I had known. It was as if an incipient madness had seized him; and the possibility of this terrified me.

In a slow, somnambulistic manner, without giving me a second glance, he began to work at his painting, and I watched him for a while, hardly knowing what to do or say. For long intervals, he would stop and peer with dreamy intentness at some feature of the landscape. I conceived the bizarre idea of a growing kinship, a mysterious *rapport* between Amberville and the meadow. In some intangible way, it seemed as if the place had taken something from his very soul—and had given something of itself in exchange. He wore the air of one who participates in some unholy secret, who has become the acolyte of an unhuman knowledge. In a flash of horrible definitude, I saw the place as an actual vampire, and Amberville as its willing victim.

How long I remained there, I can not say. Finally I stepped over to him and shook him roughly by the shoulder.

"You're working too hard," I said. "Take my advice, and lay off for a day or two."

He turned to me with the dazed look of one who is lost in some narcotic dream. This, very slowly, gave place to a sullen, evil anger.

"Oh, go to hell!" he snarled. "Can't you see that I'm busy?"

I left him then, for there seemed nothing else to do under the circumstances. The mad and spectral nature of the whole affair was enough to make me doubt my own reason. My impressions of the meadow—and of Amberville—were tainted with an insidious horror such as I had never before felt in any moment of waking life and normal consciousness.

At the bottom of the slope of yellow pine, I turned back with repugnant curiosity for a parting glance. The painter had not moved, he was still confronting the malign scene like a charmed bird that faces a lethal serpent. Whether or not the impression was a double optic image, I have never been sure: but at that instant, I seemed to discern a faint, unholy aura, neither light nor mist, that flowed and wavered above the meadow, preserving the outlines of the willow, the alders, the reeds, the pool. Stealthily it appeared to lengthen, reaching toward Amberville like ghostly arms. The whole image was extremely tenuous, and may well have been an illusion; but it sent me shuddering into the shelter of the tall, benignant pines.

The remainder of that day, and the evening that followed, were tinged with the shadowy horror I had found in Chapman's meadow. I believe that I spent most of the time in arguing vainly with myself, in trying to convince the rational part of my mind that all I had seen and felt was utterly preposterous. I could arrive at no conclusion, other than a conviction that Amberville's mental health was endangered by the damnable thing, whatever it was, that inhered in the meadow. The malign personality of the place, the impalpable terror, mystery and lure, were like webs that had been woven upon my brain, and which I could not dissipate by any amount of conscious effort.

I made two resolves, however: one was, that I should write immediately to Amberville's fiancé, Miss Avis Olcott, and invite her to visit me as a fellow-guest of the artist during the remainder of his stay at Bowman. Her influence, I thought, might help to counteract whatever was affecting him so perniciously. Since I knew her fairly well, the invitation would not seem out of the way. I decided to say nothing about it to Amberville: the element of surprise, I hoped, would be especially beneficial.

My second resolve was, that I should not again visit the meadow myself, if I could avoid it. Indirectly—for I knew the folly of trying to combat a mental obsession openly—I should also try to discourage the painter's interest in the place, and divert his attention to other themes. Trips and entertainments, too, could be devised, at the minor cost of delaying my own work.

The smoky autumn twilight overtook me in such meditations as these; but Amberville did not return. Horrible premonitions, without coherent shape or name, began to torment me as I waited for him. The night darkened; and dinner grew cold on the table. At last, about nine o'clock, when I was nerving myself to go out and hunt for him, he came in hurriedly. He was pale, dishevelled, out of breath; and his eyes held a painful glare, as if something had frightened him beyond endurance.

He did not apologize for his lateness; nor did he refer to my own visit to the meadow-bottom. Apparently he had forgotten the whole ep-isode—had forgotten his rudeness to me.

"I'm through!" he cried. "I'll never go back again—never take an-other chance. That place is more hellish at night than in the daytime. I can't tell you what I've seen and felt—I must forget it, if I can. There's an emanation—something that comes out openly in the absence of the sun, but is latent by day. It lured me, it tempted me to remain this even-ing—and it nearly got me . . . God! I didn't believe that such things were possible—that abhorrent compound of—" He broke off, and did not finish the sentence. His eyes dilated, as if with the memory of something too awful to be described. At that moment, I recalled the poisonously haunted eyes of old Chapman whom I had sometimes met about the hamlet. He had not interested me particularly, since I had deemed him a common type of rural character, with a tendency to some obscure and unpleasant aberration. Now, when I saw the same look in the eyes of a sensitive artist, I began to wonder, with a shivering speculation, whether Chapman too had been aware of the weird evil that dwelt in his meadow. Perhaps, in some way that was beyond human comprehension, he had been its victim. . . . He had died there; and his death had not seemed at all mysterious. But perhaps, in the light of all that Amberville and I had perceived, there was more in the matter than any one had suspected.

"Tell me what you saw," I ventured to suggest.

At the question, a veil seemed to fall between us, impalpable but tenebrific. He shook his head morosely and made no reply. The human terror, which perhaps had driven him back toward his normal self, and had made him almost communicative for the nonce, fell away from Amberville. A shadow that was darker than fear, an impenetrable alien umbrage, again submerged him. I felt a sudden chill, of the spirit rather than the flesh; and once more there came to me the outré thought of his growing kinship with the ghoulish meadow. Beside me, in the lamp-lit room, behind the mask of his humanity, a thing that was not wholly human seemed to sit and wait.

Of the days that followed, I shall offer only a summary. It would be impossible to convey the eventless, phantasmal horror in which we dwelt and moved.

I wrote immediately to Miss Olcott, pressing her to pay me a visit during Amberville's stay, and, in order to insure acceptance, I hinted obscurely at my concern for his health and my need of her coadjutation. In the meanwhile, waiting her answer, I tried to divert the artist by suggesting trips to sundry points of scenic interest in the neighborhood. These suggestions he declined, with an aloof curtness, an air that was stony and cryptic rather than deliberately rude. Virtually, he ignored my existence, and made it more than plain that he wished me to leave him to his own devices. This, in despair, I finally decided to do, pending the arrival of Miss Olcott. He went out early each morning, as usual, with his paints and easel, and returned about sunset or a little later. He did not tell me where he had been; and I refrained from asking.

Miss Olcott came on the third day following my letter, in the afternoon. She was young, lissome, ultra-feminine, and was altogether devoted to Amberville. In fact, I think she was in awe of him. I told her as much as I dared, and warned her of the morbid change in her fiancé, which I attributed to nervousness and overwork. I simply could not bring myself to mention Chapman's meadow and its baleful influence:

the whole thing was too unbelievable, too phantasmagoric, to be offered as an explanation to a modern girl. When I saw the somewhat helpless alarm and bewilderment with which she listened to my story, I began to wish that she were of a more resolute and determined type, and were less submissive toward Amberville than I surmised her to be. A stronger woman might have saved him, but even then I began to doubt whether Avis could do anything to combat the imponderable evil that was engulfing him.

A heavy crescent moon was hanging like a blood-dipt horn in the twilight, when he returned. To my immense relief, the presence of Avis appeared to have a highly salutary effect. The very moment that he saw her, Amberville came out of the singular eclipse that had claimed him, as I feared, beyond redemption, and was almost his former affable self. Perhaps it was all make-believe, for an ulterior purpose; but this, at the time, I could not suspect. I began to congratulate myself on having applied a sovereign remedy. The girl, on her part, was plainly relieved; though I saw her eyeing him in a slightly hurt and puzzled way, when he sometimes fell for a short interval into moody abstraction, as if he had temporarily forgotten her. On the whole, however, there was a transformation that appeared no less than magical, in view of his recent gloom and remoteness. After a decent interim, I left the pair together, and retired.

I rose very late the next morning, having overslept. Avis and Amberville, I learned, had gone out together, carrying a lunch which my Chinese cook had provided. Plainly he was taking her along on one of his artistic expeditions; and I augured well for his recovery from this. Somehow, it never occurred to me that he had taken her to Chapman's meadow. The tenuous, malignant shadow of the whole affair had begun to lift from my mind; I rejoiced in a lightened sense of responsibility; and, for the first time in a week, was able to concentrate clearly on the ending of my novel.

The two returned at dusk, and I saw immediately that I had been mistaken on more points than one. Amberville had again retired into a sinister, saturnine reserve. The girl, beside his darkly looming height and massive shoulders, looked very small, forlorn, and pitifully bewildered and frightened. It was as if she had encountered something altogether beyond her comprehension—something with which she was humanly powerless to cope.

Very little was said by either of them. They did not tell me where they had been—but, for that matter, it was unnecessary to inquire. Amberville's taciturnity, as usual, seemed due to an absorption in some dark mood or sullen reverie. But Avis gave me the impression of a dual constraint—as if, apart from some enthralling terror, she had been forbidden to speak of the day's events and experiences. I knew that they had gone to that accursed meadow; but I was far from sure whether Avis had been personally conscious of the weird and baneful entity of the place, or had merely been frightened by the unwholesome change in her lover beneath its influence. In either case, it seemed obvious that she was wholly subservient to him, I began to damn myself for a fool in having invited her to Bowman—though the true bitterness of my regret was still to come.

A week went by, with the same daily excursions of the painter and his fiancé—the same baffling, sinister estrangement and secrecy in Amberville—the same terror, helplessness, constraint and submissiveness in the girl. How it would all end, I could not imagine; but I feared, from the ominous alteration of his character, that Amberville was heading for some form of mental alienation, if nothing worse. My offers of entertainment and scenic journeys were rejected by the pair; and several blunt efforts to question Avis were met by a wall of almost hostile evasion which convinced me that Amberville had enjoined her to secrecy—and had perhaps, in some sleightful manner, misrepresented my own attitude toward him.

"You don't understand him," she said, repeatedly. "He is very temperamental."

The whole affair was a maddening mystery, but it seemed more and more that the girl herself was being drawn, either directly or indirectly, into the same phantasmal web that had enmeshed the artist.

I surmised that Amberville had done several new pictures of the meadow; but he did not show them to me, nor even mention them. My own recollection of the place, as time went on, assumed an unaccountable vividness that was almost hallucinatory. The incredible idea of some inherent force or personality, malevolent and even vampirish, became an unavowed conviction against my will. The place haunted me like a phantasm, horrible but seductive. I felt an impelling morbid curiosity, an unwholesome desire to visit it again, and fathom, if possible, its enigma. Often I thought of Amberville's notion about a *Genius Loci* that dwelt in the meadow, and the hints of a human apparition that was somehow associated with the spot. Also, I wondered what it was that the artist had seen on the one occasion when he had lingered in the meadow after nightfall, and had returned to my house in driven terror. It seemed that he had not ventured to repeat the experiment, in spite of his obvious subjection to the unknown lure.

The end came, abruptly and without premonition. Business had taken me to the county seat, one afternoon, and I did not return till late in the evening. A full moon was high above the pine-dark hills. I expected to find Avis and the painter in my drawing-room; but they were not there. Li Sing, my factotum, told me that they had returned at dinner-time. An hour later, Amberville had gone out quietly while the girl was in her room. Coming down a few minutes later, Avis had shown excessive perturbation when she found him absent, and had also left the house, as if to follow him, without telling Li Sing where she was going or when she might return. All this had occurred three hours previously; and neither of the pair had yet reappeared.

A black and subtly chilling intuition of evil seized me as I listened to Li Sing's account. All too well I surmised that Amberville had yielded to the temptation of a second nocturnal visit to that unholy meadow.

An occult attraction, somehow, had overcome the fright of his first experience, whatever it had been. Avis, knowing where he was, and perhaps fearful of his sanity—or safety—had gone out to find him. More and more, I felt an imperative conviction of some peril that threatened them both—some hideous and innominable thing to whose power, perhaps, they had already yielded.

Whatever my previous folly and remissness in the matter, I did not delay now. A few minutes of driving at precipitate speed through the mellow moonlight brought me to the piny edge of the Chapman property. There, as on my former visit, I left the car, and plunged headlong through the shadowy forest. Far down, in the hollow, as I went, I heard a single scream, shrill with terror, and abruptly terminated. I felt sure that the voice was that of Avis; but I did not hear it again.

Running desperately, I emerged in the meadow-bottom. Neither Avis nor Amberville was in sight; and it seemed to me, in my hasty scrutiny, that the place was full of mysteriously coiling and moving vapors that permitted only a partial view of the dead willow and the other vegetation. I ran on toward the scummy pool, and nearing it, was arrested by a sudden and twofold horror.

Avis and Amberville were floating together in the shallow pool, with their bodies half hidden by the mantling masses of algae. The girl was clasped tightly in the painter's arms, as if he had carried her with him, against her will, to that noisome death. Her face was covered by the evil, greenish scum; and I could not see the face of Amberville, which was averted against her shoulder. It seemed that there had been a struggle; but both were quiet now, and had yielded supinely to their doom.

It was not this spectacle alone, however, that drove me in mad and shuddering flight from the meadow, without making even the most tentative attempt to retrieve the drowned bodies. The true horror lay in the thing, which, from a little distance, I had taken for the coils of a slowly moving and rising mist. It was *not* vapor, nor anything else that could

conceivably exist—that malign, luminous, pallid emanation that enfolded the entire scene before me like a restless and hungrily wavering
extension of its outlines—a phantom projection of the pale and death-
like willow, the dying alders, the reeds, the stagnant pool and its suicidal
victims. The landscape was visible through it, as through a film; but it
seemed to curdle and thicken gradually in places, with some unholy, terrifying activity. Out of these curdlings, as if disgorged by the ambient
exhalation, I saw the emergence of three human faces that partook of
the same nebulous matter, being neither mist nor plasm. One of these
faces seemed to detach itself from the bole of the ghostly willow; the
second and third swirled upward from the seething of the phantom
pool, with their bodies trailing formlessly among the tenuous boughs.
The faces were those of old Chapman, of Francis Amberville, and Avis
Olcott.

Behind this eerie, wraith-like projection of itself, the actual landscape leered with the same infernal and vampirish air which it had worn
by day. But it seemed now that the place was no longer still—that it
seethed with a malignant secret life—that it reached out toward me with
its scummy waters, with the bony fingers of its trees, with the spectral
faces it had spewed forth from its lethal deadfall.

Even terror was frozen within me for a moment. I stood watching,
while the pale, unhallowed exhalation rose higher above the meadow.
The three human faces, through a further agitation of the curdling mass,
began to approach each other. Slowly, inexpressibly, they merged in one,
becoming an androgynous face, neither young nor old, that melted finally into the lengthening phantom boughs of the willow—the hands of
the arboreal Death, that were reaching out to enfold me. Then, unable
to bear the spectacle any longer, I started to run. . . .

There is little more that need be told, for nothing that I could add
to this narrative would lessen the abominable mystery of it all in any
degree. The meadow—or the thing that dwells in the meadow—has already claimed three victims . . . and I sometimes wonder if it will have a

fourth. I alone, it would seem, among the living, have guessed the secret of Chapman's death, and the death of Avis and Amberville; and no one else, apparently, has felt the malign genius of the meadow. I have not returned there, since the morning when the bodies of the artist and his fiancé were removed from the pool . . . nor have I summoned up the resolution to destroy or otherwise dispose of the four oil paintings and two water-color drawings of the spot that were made by Amberville. Perhaps . . . in spite of all that deters me . . . I shall visit it again.

THE BLACK LAKE

In a land where weirdness and mystery had strongly leagued themselves with eternal desolation, the lake was out-poured at an undiscoverable date of elder aeons, to fill some fathomless gulf far down amid the shadows of snowless, volcanic mountains. No eye, not even the sun's, when he stared vertically upon it for a few hours at midday, seemed able to divine its depths of sullen blackness and unrippled silence. It was for this reason that I found a so singular pleasure in frequently contemplating the strange lake. Sitting for I knew not how long on its bleak basaltic shores, where grew but a few fleshly red orchids, bent above the waters like open and thirsty mouths, I would peer with countless fantastic conjectures and shadowy imaginings, into the alluring mystery of its unknown and inexplorable gulf.

It was at an hour of morning before the sun had surmounted the rough and broken rim of the summits, when I first came, and clomb down through the shadows which filled like some subtler fluid the volcanic basin. Seen at the bottom of the stirless tincture of air and twilight, the lake seemed as dregs of darkness.

Peering for the first time, after the deep and difficult descent, into the so dull and leaden waters, I was at length aware of certain small and scattered gleams of silver, apparently far beneath the surface. And fancying them the metal in some mysterious ledge, or the glints of long-sunken treasure, I bent closer in my eagerness, and finally perceived that what I saw was but the reflection of the stars, which, though the day was full upon the mountains and the lands without, were yet visible in the depth and darkness of that enshadowed place.

144

The Face by the River

It was after the commission of the deed, and during his nation-wide flight from its legal consequences, that Edgar Sylen began to develop an aversion for rivers, and a dread of women's faces. It had never occurred to him before that so many rivers resembled the Sacramento; nor had he imagined that anything sinister could attach itself to the leaning willows and alders along their banks. Now, wherever he went, by some macabre coincidence he was always coming at afterglow of a sullen sunset to the edge of tree-fringed running waters, from which he would recoil with guilty fright and repulsion. Also, he saw resemblances to the dead woman everywhere, in the girls that he passed on the streets of unfamiliar towns and cities. He had never thought, even before he began to see her with the altered vision of enamorment, that Elise belonged to a frequently encountered type. But now, with observational powers that were morbidly sharpened in this one regard, he found that her short oval face with its pallor untouched by rouge, her high, faintly pencilled brows above eyes of deep violet-grey, her full, petulant mouth, or her slender but well-curved figure, were seemingly to be met on every pavement and in every train, street-car, shop, restaurant and hotel.

Sylen was not aware of any consuming remorse for his act, in the usual sense of the word. But certainly he had reason to regret it as a piece of overwhelming and irremediable folly, into which he had been driven by the goading of some devilish fatality. Elise had been his stenographer: the propinquity of business association had drawn them into a more intimate relationship; and he had loved her for awhile, till she became too exacting, too exorbitant in her demands. He was not brutal or cold-blooded, he had never dreamed of killing her at any time; and even when he had tired of her, and even in that last walk at twilight by the river, when she had threatened with bitter, hysterical reproaches to tell his wife of their affair, he had not really wanted to harm the girl. His feeling had been a mixture of alarm at the menace to his domestic security, and a sudden, mad desire to still the intolerable, shrewish clamor of her tedious voice. He hardly knew that he had gripped her by the throat, that he was choking her with ferocious fingers. Such an action was totally foreign to his own conception of himself; and when he realized what he was doing, he had loosed her and pushed her away from him. All he could see at that moment was her frightened face, her throat with the visible marks of his fingers—white as an apparition in the dusk, and appallingly distinct in every detail. He had forgotten that they were so close to the river's edge, had forgotten that the water was very deep below the bank at that particular place. These things he had remembered when he heard the splash of her fall; and he had also remembered, with a numb sense of terror, that neither he nor Elise could swim. Perhaps she had lost consciousness when she fell: for she had sunk immediately, and had not risen to the surface again. The whole scene was dim and confused in Sylen's mind, apart from that final glimpse of her face on the shore. His flight from California was vague to him also; and his first clear memory was that of a newspaper he had seen the next morning in a neighboring state, with pictures of Elise and himself above a lurid conjectural description of the crime. The horror of those headlines, in which he seemed to meet the accusing eyes of a vast multitude of people, was branded ineffaceably upon his brain. Henceforth it was a perpetual miracle to him that he could manage to evade arrest. Like most criminals, he felt that the world was pre-occupied with himself and his crime; and did not realize its manifold oblivion, its absorption in multiform pursuits and interests.

He was stunned by the consequences of the deed, by the break that it entailed with his whole past life, with everything and everyone he had known. His flourishing business, the respectable place he had won in his community, his wife and two children—all were lost beyond recovery through something which, as he had soon persuaded himself, was no more than a fatal accident. The idea of himself as a fugitive from justice, as a vulgar murderer in the eyes of the world, was alien and confusing to the last degree. He retained enough wit, however, to disguise himself with a touch of subtlety, and to double upon his trail in a manner that baffled the police. He bought some second-hand clothing, of the type that would be worn by a laboring-man, and disposed of his neat tailor-made suit by leaving it at night beneath a pile of old lumber. He allowed his beard to grow, and purchased a pair of heavy-rimmed spectacles. These simple measures transformed him from a well-to-do realtor to a socialistic carpenter out of work. In trying to conceal his furtiveness, his perennial fear of observation, he acquired a rough and fierce air that was quite compatible with the role of a discontented workman.

Sylen was well supplied with money. Even when prolonged security had diminished his fear of arrest, he did not dare to linger in any place. A queer, morbid restlessness impelled him to go on. And always, it seemed to him, there was a willow-bordered river to remind him of the scene of his act; and always there were women who resembled Elise. The mere sight of a stream, or a girl with the fancied likeness, even in one feature or detail of costume, would send him toward the nearest railroad station. He tried not to think of Elise, and sometimes succeeded; but any chance resemblance was too much for his nerves. The damnable frequency of such resemblances became one of his chief worries. He could not account for them as part of the natural order of things.

Often, with apparitional suddenness and irrelevance, he would remember Elise as he had seen her in that last moment, when her face had emerged from the twilight with such preternatural pallor and vividness. Even when he managed to forget her, there was a sense of some troublous haunting in the background of his mind. He developed also a physical feeling that he was not alone—that an unseen presence accompanied him wherever he went. But at first he did not connect this feeling with Elise, nor did he associate with her the earliest beginnings of the actual visual hallucination from which he eventually came to suffer.

Sylen was well aware of his growing nervousness, and made desultory efforts to overcome it. He knew, or had been told, that such a condition might lead to insanity. He tried by means of auto-suggestion to dismiss the irrational fears and impressions that dogged him in his wanderings. He felt that he was succeeding to some extent, that his haunting obsessions were growing fainter. Then, simultaneously with this, he began to think that there was something wrong with his eye-sight. He was troubled by a small, blurred image, somewhat to one side in his field of vision—an image that he could not seize or define, and which followed him everywhere, maintaining always the same position. He could even see it when he lay awake in the darkness—as if it were possessed of a pale luminosity. It occurred to him that the glasses he wore were injuring his eyes; and forthwith he discarded them; but the unaccountable blurring still persisted. For some reason, other than his natural fear of optical disease, it made him horribly uneasy. But, for the time being, he did not think so often of Elise. Also, he was not quite so afraid of rivers and women as he had formerly been.

One evening, in a strange city far from the state he had left, Sylen deliberately went for a walk by the shore of a tree-fringed river. He wanted to re-assure himself, wanted to feel that he was mastering his old terrors.

It was still twilight when he neared the water—that deceptive half light which alters the position and proportion of objects in a manner so illusory. All at once, Sylen became aware than the strange blur in his field of vision was now directly before him instead of at one side. Also, the blur had defined itself to a human face, seen as in some diminished perspective, at an interval of vague distance. But the face was unnaturally clear in every feature, and was outlined in luminous pallor against the dark flowing of the stream. It was the face of Elise, even as Edgar Sylen had last seen her. . . .

Sylen was unable afterwards to recollect the circumstances of his flight from the apparition. Any real consciousness of his actions was drowned for awhile by a primordial tide of unreasoning terror. When he came to himself, trembling like an ague patient, he was sitting in the lighted smoker of a moving train. He could not even remember where he was going, till he looked at the ticket which he held in his hand. He no longer saw the face of Elise; but, even as before, there was a blurred image in his field of vision—perhaps not so far to one side as it had been at first.

For several days, it was only at twilight that the image became definite. But all the time it was moving nearer to the center of his vision. Then he saw the face at various hours during the day, and also at night. It was always pale and luminous, it was detached and disembodied, like a face that has been superimposed on a photographic plate. But the clearness of detail was abnormal; even at the remote perspective which it maintained for many days, he could see the horror-widened eyes, the parted lips, and the livid marks of his fingers on the white throat. It appeared to him on the streets, in trains, in restaurants and hotel-lobbies; it came between him and the visages of people when he passed; he saw it in the foliage of trees, and among the faces of actors in the plays or films to which he had gone in the hope of temporary distraction. But at first the haunting was not continual; the face came and went at varying intervals, and left him always with the same paralysing horror, which would wear off in some slight degree before the next appearance.

Sylen had never been a believer in the supernatural. But he knew a little about brain diseases and morbid hallucinations. His fear of the dead woman was more than doubled by a fear of madness. He felt that he was unquestionably headed for some sort of lunacy. At first he tried to reason with himself in the interludes of his panic. Among other things, he went to a public library with the idea of consulting various medical volumes on brain-pathology. He did not repeat his visit: for while he was reading one of the pages in a work of this type, the letters suddenly began to blur and fade; and it seemed to him that he was looking through and beyond them into a shadowy gulf, in which swam the face of Elise.

From that time onward, the appearances of the face were more frequent day by day; till the hour came when he saw it continually. For awhile, he drank soddenly; he sought the anodyne of drugs; but without losing the specter even in the ultimate delirium of his intoxication. Then his mind succumbed to a fear that was utterly beyond reason; and he dwelt henceward in a hell of fantasmal and superstitious terrors. The thing was no longer a mere hallucination, it had come back from the cryptic realms of the dead, from a gulf beyond mortal perception, to freeze his blood and his brain with ghastly intimations of all that is hidden in the depths of death. Perhaps his mind had already given way; for he soon lost the fear of madness in a greater and more abysmal fear of the woman herself, and the unknown world into which he had precipitated her by his crime. In his heedlessness of anything but the apparition, he would stumble against people on the street; and he was often in danger from passing vehicles. But in some miraculous manner, like a somnambulist, he would avoid them without ever knowing his peril or his escape.

The face was nearer now. It sat opposite him at every table, it moved before him along the pavements, it stood at the foot of his bed through the night-time. It was always the same, with widely staring eyes, and lips that were parted in an eternal gasp. Sylen was no longer conscious of what he did or where he went. It was some automatic portion of his brain which enabled him to continue the daily movements and actions of life. He was wholly obsessed by the image of Elise, he lived in a kind of mental catalepsy. Held by a dreadful hypnosis, he watched all day in open sun or rain or shadowy rooms, the thing that was stamped upon his vision; and he watched it during the night, by lamplight or in utter darkness. He slept very little, and when he did sleep, Elise hovered before him in the vistas of his dreams. It was mostly at night, lying awake, that he became aware of the abyss that lay behind and beneath her face—an abyss in which he could see the slow sinking of dim, macabre forms, of corpse-like or skeleton-like things that appeared always to fall and decompose in unfathomable gloom. But the face itself never sank into the abyss.

Sylen knew nothing of time. The moment in which he had last seen Elise was re-lived by him in a virtual eternity through the perpetuation of her visual image. And he knew nothing of the cities through which he passed, nor the route by which he returned on a latter evening, still oblivious of his whereabouts, to the city and the river-side of his crime. He knew only that the face was leading him somewhere, to an end which his palsied faculties could not even imagine.

He stared about him with sightless eyes. Here, in the dusk, beneath the unheeded willows, beside the unrecognized flowing of the Sacramento, the face drew nearer still. The phantom throat was within arms' length for the first time—even as when he had loosed his fingers from the living throat of Elise and had pushed her back toward the water in a sullen twilight many months before.

Sylen did not perceive that he was standing close to the river-brink. He saw only the features of Elise, knew only that her throat was within seeming reach of his fingers once more. It was a mad impulse of frantic fear, of ultimate desperation, which made him clutch at the white phantom, with its changeless eyes and mouth, and the livid, never-fading marks below its chin. . . .

He still saw the face for a little while, when he sank beneath the water. It seemed to swim on a fathomless abyss, where human bones and cadavers were slowly drowning in a darkness that was like the deliquescence of the world and of all past years and eras. The face was very close to him as he went down . . . and then it began to recede in a lessening perspective . . . and then, suddenly, he saw it no longer.

A Dream of Lethe

In the quest of her whom I had lost, I came at length to the shores of Lethe, under the vault of an immense, empty, ebon sky, from which all the stars had vanished one by one. Proceeding I knew not whence, a pale, elusive light as of the wandering moon, or the phantasmal phosphorescence of a dead sun, lay dimly and without luster on the sable stream, and on the black, flowerless meadows. By this light, I saw many wandering souls of men and women, who came, hesitantly or in haste, to drink of the slow, unmurmuring waters. But among all these, there was none who departed in haste, and many who stayed to watch, with unseeing eyes, the calm and waveless movement of the stream. At length in the lily-tall and gracile form, and the still, uplifted face of a women who stood apart from the rest, I saw the one whom I had sought; and, hastening to her side, with a heart wherein old memories sang like a nest of nightingales, was fain to take her by the hand. But in the pale, immutable eyes, and wan, unmoving lips that were raised to mine, I saw no light of memory, nor any tremor of recognition. And knowing now that she had forgotten, I turned away despairingly, and finding the river at my side, was suddenly aware of my ancient thirst for its waters, a thirst I had once thought to satisfy at many diverse springs, but in vain. Stooping hastily, I drank, and rising again, perceived that the light had died or disappeared, and that all the land was like the land of a dreamless slumber, wherein I could no longer distinguish the faces of my companions. Nor was I able to remember any longer why I wished to drink of the waters of oblivion.

THE PHANTOMS OF THE FIRE

It was late summer, and the Georgetown road was deep with dust, which had settled like a dun pall on the bordering chaparral and pines. Since he had walked all the way from Auburn without securing a single lift, the man who was trudging along the road with the broiling afternoon sun on his back was hardly less dusty than the trees. He paused now and then to mop his face with a discolored handkerchief, or to peer rather wistfully at the occasional cars which passed him without offering to stop. His clothing, though not actually ragged, was old and worn, and had the indescribable shapelessness of clothing that has been slept in. He was very thin, stoop-shouldered, and discouraged-looking; his general aspect was almost that of a professional tramp, and the people of the country-side were suspicious of tramps.

"Well, I guess I'll have t' walk all the way," he said to himself, whining a little even in his thoughts. "But it ain't much further now . . . Gosh, but things is hot an' dry." He looked about him at the familiar landscape of parched grass, brushwood and yellow pines with an appraising eye. "Wonder there ain't been more fires—there alluz is at this time o' year."

The man was Jonas McGillicuddy, and he was on his way home after a somewhat prolonged absence. His return was unannounced, and would prove as unexpected to his wife and three children as his departure had been. Tired of trying to extort a living from a small vineyard and pear-orchard of rocky El Dorado land, and tired also of the perennial nagging of his frail, sensitive-nerved and sorely disappointed wife, Jonas had left abruptly, three years before, after a quarrel of more than customary bitterness and acerbity with his helpmeet. Since then, he had heard nothing from his family, for the good and sufficient reason that he had not sought to communicate with them. His various attempts to earn a livelihood had proven scarcely more successful than the fruit-ranching venture, and he had drifted aimlessly and ineffectually from place to place, from situation to situation—a forlorn and increasingly desperate figure. For a man of such shifting, unstable temperament, when all else had failed him, and he had wearied of the hopeless struggle, it was not unnatural to think of returning. Time had softened his memory of his wife's undependable temper, of her shrewish outbursts; but he had not forgotten her motherly ways when she was in a more tractable humor, nor her excellent cooking.

Now, with empty pockets, since his last money had sufficed merely to pay his train-fare to Sacramento, Jonas was nearing the hills in which lay his forest-surrounded ranch beyond Georgetown. The country through which he tramped was sparsely-peopled, and there were great stretches of softly-rolling hills and low valleys that had not known the touch of cultivation. The ranches were often quite isolated. Beyond all, in the hazy blue of the distance, were the vague and spectral snows of the Sierras.

"Gosh, but one of Matilda's pear pies'll taste good," thought the wanderer. His mouth began to water. He was not reflective enough, however, to wonder just what his reception would be, beyond an uneasy surmise that Matilda might give him a terrific scolding for his absence. "But mebbe she'll be mighty glad t'see me, after all," he consoled himself. Then he tried to picture his children, the five-year-old boy and the girl-babies of three and two respectively whom he had last seen.

"Guess they'll have forgotten they had a papa," he mused.

The afternoon had been utterly still and airless, with a sultry brooding in its silence. Now, from the north-east, along the road he was traveling, there came a gust of wind, and with it the unmistakable acrid odor of burnt grass and trees.

"Hell, there has been a fire after all," muttered Jonas, with an uneasy start. He peered anxiously ahead, but could see no smoke above the dun and grey-green hills. "Guess it's all out now, anyway."

He came to the top of the low slope he was climbing, and saw before him the burnt area, which lay on both sides of the road and was of indeterminable extent. The brown foliage of heat-seared oaks and the black skeletons of bushes and pines were everywhere. A few fallen logs and old stumps were still smoking a little, as is their wont for days after the extinguishment of a forest fire. It was a scene of complete and irremediable desolation.

Jonas hurried on, with a sense of growing panic, for he was now little more than a mile from his own property. He thought of the yellow pines that stood so close and tall about his cabin—the pines which he had wished to fell, but had spared at the earnest solicitation of the nature-loving Matilda.

"They're so pretty, Jonas," she had said, pleadingly. "I just can't see them go."

"Hope the fire didn't get into them pines," thought Jonas now. "Gosh, but I wish I'd cut 'em down when I wuz plannin' to. It would have been a lot safer; and I'd have had the money for the wood, too."

The road was strewn in places with ashen leaves, with the charcoal of fallen brands, and several trees had crashed across it, but had now been removed to permit the passage of traffic. It was hotter than ever, in this charred and blackened waste, for the brief gust of wind had fallen. The dust on Jonas' cheeks was runneled with sweat which he no longer paused to wipe away. Irresponsible as he was, a strange gravity had come over the wastrel, and he felt an ever-deepening premonition of calamity.

He came at last to the little by-road which turned off to his ranch from the Georgetown highway. Here, he found with a sinking heart, the fire had also been, and had left nothing but devastation. In spite of his fatigue, he almost ran, with long, shambling steps, and rounding a turn in the by-road, saw that the fire had stopped at the very verge of his own property. The hill-side orchard of stunted pear trees, the straggling vines of Mission and Muscat grapes, were quite as he remembered them; and beyond, in the grove of yellow pines, he could see the wreathing smoke that arose from the chimney of his cabin. Panting heavily, he paused, with a sense of relief and thanksgiving as poignant as anything of which his dulled heart was capable.

The sun had almost touched the horizon, as he climbed the winding road through the orchard and entered the grove above. Aisles of light perceptibly tinged with gold lay between the elongated shadows. Even to the sodden, insensitive Jonas, the beauty of the woodland scene, the magic of the sunset, the high, solemn, dark-green pines and the rich glow sifting among them on manzanita-bushes and beds of brown needles, were not without their charm. He drew a long breath, inhaling the clean balsams that the hot sun had drawn from the forest, and feeling as he did so a vague pleasure.

Now he could see his cabin, a long, four-roomed shack of plain, unpainted boards and weather-darkened shingles. A woman in calico was standing in front of the steps. Two little girls were beside her, and he wondered as to the whereabouts of the boy, who had been a fragile youngster, always ailing and fretful. "Mebbe Bill is sick agin," mused Jonas. He was very glad to be home, but he felt a little doubtful, a trifle tremulous, as to the greeting he would receive from Matilda.

The woman looked up as he approached, shading her eyes with her hand from the last rays of the sun, which fell horizontally through the wood. He could see her apron, which was quite clean, as always, though worn and faded from many washings, like her dress. She did not seem to perceive him, but was apparently staring with great intentness at something among the trees. The children also stared, and huddled closer to her, clinging to the hem of her gown.

Jonas tried to call out: "Hello, Matilda," but his throat was so dry and dusty that the words were no more than a hoarse whisper. He started to clear his throat, but the simple act was never finished, for at that moment, the whole scene before him, the trees, the cabin, the woman and the children, were lost in a roaring sheet of ruddy flame that seemed to come from all sides at once and blot out the entire world and the very sky as it towered full-grown in what could have been no more than the fraction of a second. A blast of intolerable heat, fierce as the breath of a thousand furnaces, blew in Jonas' face and swept him backward like a hurricane. The mighty roaring pounded in his ears like a sea, and was mingled with human screams, as he went down into pitch-black gulfs of unconsciousness.

It was day when Jonas awoke, but he was too confused for a few instants to realize that the light was slanting through the tree-tops from a different direction, or that there was more of it than seemed normal in an ever-green forest. When his wits returned sufficiently to permit the comprehension of the fact that it was morning, he began to notice other things that were equally singular. He found that he was lying on his back among burnt needles, and above him towered the dark boles of fire-swept trees with the pitiful stumps of their cauterized branches. Darkly, indistinctly, in a sort of dull astonishment, he began to remember the events of the previous day, his return at sunset to the cabin, his glimpse of Matilda and the two children, and the all-engulfing sheet of flame. He looked instinctively at his clothes, with the feeling that he must have been badly burnt; but there was no trace of fire on his raiment, and the black ashes about him were cold. Nor, when he reared himself on his elbow and peered around, was there the faintest thread of smoke to indicate a recent conflagration.

He arose and stepped toward the place where the cabin had stood. It was a heap of ashes, from which protruded the ends of charred beams.

"My God!" muttered Jonas. He felt utterly dazed, and his thoughts refused to align themselves, failing to form any sort of intelligible order.

As Jonas spoke, a man arose from where he had been stooping behind the wreckage of the cabin, furtively dropping some object that he held in his hands. Seeing Jonas, the man came forward hastily. He was a gaunt individual in dirty overalls, with the profile and the general air of a somewhat elderly and dilapidated buzzard. Jonas recognized him as Samuel Slocum, one of his neighbors.

"Wal, Jonas McGillicuddy, so you've come back," exclaimed this individual in raucous tones of unfeigned surprise. "Ye're a little too late, though," he went on, without pausing to let Jonas speak. "Everythin' burnt up clean, day before yestiddy."

"But the cabin wuz here las' night," stammered Jonas. "I came through the woods 'bout sunset, an' I saw Matilda an' the children in front o' the steps, jus' as plain as I see you. Then everythin' seemed to go up in a burst o' flame, an' I didn't know nothin' till I woke up jus' now."

"Ye're crazy, Jonas," assured the neighbor. "There weren't no cabin here las' night, an' no Matildy an' no childern, neither. They wuz all burnt up, along with the rest o' the country hereabouts. We heerd yer wife an' babies a-screamin', but the fire wuz all aroun' before ye could say Jack Robinson, an' the trees fell across yer road, an' no one could git in, an' no one could git out . . . I alluz told ye, Jonas, t' cut them yeller pines down."

"My folks wuz all burnt up?" faltered Jonas.

"Wal, yer little boy died a year ago, so they wuz jus' Matildy an' the two gals."

A Good Embalmer

Jonas Turple and Caleb Udley, joint owners of the sole undertaking establishment in Ramsville, were continuing an immemorial dispute.

"You couldn't embalm a salted herring," said Turple, with the air of jocose and rubicund contempt which he usually adopted in referring to his partner's technical abilities and methods. "Look at the job you did on old Aaron Webley, five years ago, when I was away at the embalmers' convention. Of course no one would have been the wiser if the family hadn't decided to transfer him to their home lot in Georgetown, ten months after. The condition of the corpse wasn't much of an advertisement for us. I believe in doing a thorough job, one that will endure and stand up under all vicissitudes. And I tell you, there's nothing like corrosive sublimate, and plenty of it. You can have your Peruvian bark, your camphor and cinnamon and other aromatics, and your sulphate of zinc; but all this stuff is mere trimming if you ask me."

Turple, a large, florid, middle-aged bachelor, who looked more like a restaurant owner than a mortician, terminated his remarks with a resonant sniff and eyed his confrère with semi-jovial belligerence.

"Sulphate of zinc is good enough for me," maintained Caleb Udley, with much acerbity. He was a thin, meager, deacon-like person, alternately bullied by his wife and his business partner. He was, however, more recalcitrant toward the latter than toward the former, and rarely made an attempt to uphold his own views.

"Well, you'll never shoot any of it into me," said Turple. "You'd make a mess of it anyway. I'd certainly hate to be at your mercy and have you try to embalm me, if I were dead."

"Even at that, there are times when I wouldn't mind having the chance," returned Udley, with a tart malice.

"The hell you say. Look here, Caleb, if I should die before you do, and you start your blundering operations on me, I'll simply rise up from the dead."

"But the dead don't rise," said Udley, who was not only something of a Sadducean, but was also rather literal-minded.

II

It is not the function of this story to record in detail, or even in rough outline, the lives of two country undertakers.

For many years after the discussion related above, Turple and Udley pursued the somewhat funereal tenor of their ways. In the face of their perennial disputation, half-humorous, half-contemptuous on one side and wholly acrimonious on the other, it would have been difficult to determine the exact degree of brotherly love which existed between them. Turple continued to deride his confrère's professional capacities and opinions; and Udley never failed to resent the derision. With slight variations, their quotidian quarrel was repeated a thousand times.

The situation was modified only by the admission of a third and younger partner, one Thomas Agdale, into the firm. Agdale, who was comparatively inexperienced, and was also mild-tempered, became the butt of both his seniors; and, in especial, of Udley, who thus succeeded in transferring to another victim some of the scorn and contumely which he himself endured at the hands of Turple.

Even undertakers, however, are not exempt from the common laws of mortality. Turple, who had long shown an apoplectic tendency, but nevertheless had not expected a so sudden and early demise, was found dead one morning in the local hotel-room which he had occupied for more than twenty years. His partners, as was natural, were deeply shocked and surprised by the news; but, since he had omitted to leave any instructions to the contrary, they proceeded to take charge of his body with all due expedition.

The feelings of Udley, when Turple's corpse was laid out before him on the embalming-table, were somewhat peculiar and difficult to analyze. How much of real regret or sorrow they included, I am not prepared to say: but, undeniably, there was a more or less furtive undercurrent of actual triumphancy, of self-vindication if not of vindictiveness. After all of Turple's manifold and life-long aspersions on his capabilities as an embalmer, Udley was now in a position to render the last services to his vilifier. It would not be proper to say that he rejoiced in this situation; but certainly his emotions were those of a wronged man who beholds the final balancing of the scales of justice.

Agdale was present, but Udley had resolved that he himself would perform everything necessary and would utilize the services of Agdale only in the mere lifting of the corpse into the grimly sumptuous casket that had been prepared for it.

The March afternoon was murky and foggy; and the lights had been turned on in the rear room of the undertaking parlor, where Udley and Agdale were about to begin their gruesome task. They gave a semi-nocturnal touch to the macabre scene.

"So I couldn't embalm a salted codfish, hey?" thought Udley to himself, remembering his partner's habitual jest with the sour resentment of one who is wholly without humor. "Well, we'll see about that."

He approached the pursy and somewhat abdominous corpse, and was about to begin the preliminary incisions. These, however, were not made—at least not by Caleb Udley. For, even as he stooped above it, the cadaver stirred, its eyelids fluttered and opened, and that which had been the earthly shell of Jonas Turple sat up suddenly and heavily on the cold slab.

Udley leapt back. His lean frame exuded from head to foot an icy, instantaneous perspiration, and terror had deprived him of the power of thought and reason. Something seemed to have gone wrong with his heart, also; and he felt an awful choking sensation between the intolerably suspended beat. Agdale, who had a superstitious vein, had given one look at the animated corpse and was fleeing from the shop by the back door.

"What did I tell you, Caleb?" Udley was aware that the cadaver had spoken. Its voice seemed to issue from a deep vault, and was hideously muffled, as if it had made its way through some intervening medium of a viscous or semi-liquescent nature. It was not the familiar voice of the living Turple: but one could readily have imagined it as issuing from the lips of Lazarus after his resurrection.

If any further remarks or observations were made by the corpse, they were not heard by Udley. His heart, at the sound of that unnatural voice, had refused to continue its disordered throbbing, and he had fallen dead on the floor.

III

It was two hours later when Agdale mastered his terrors sufficiently to admit of returning. In the meanwhile, he had confided to several of the townspeople, including the doctor who had signed Turple's death-certificate, the unbelievable circumstances which had occasioned his hasty departure. It was a resolute and valiant committee of investigation which finally entered the undertakers' parlors.

The situation which revealed itself here was more mysterious and more remarkable than even the superstitious Agdale had expected. The corpse of Turple was lying decorously in the very same place and position in which it had been laid out by Udley and Agdale; and there was not the faintest hint of life or supernatural re-animation. Dr. Martin needed no more than a glance to re-confirm his original opinion, that the deceased was properly and lawfully dead.

For a few moments, no one noticed Udley. He had been alive when

Agdale fled; and the latter not unnaturally surmised that Udley had followed suit. Somehow, no one had given him much thought.

It was Agdale who made the singular discovery that the new casket
which had been provided for Turple's reception was now occupied—
and that the occupant was Caleb Udley! But it remained for Dr. Martin,
in his official capacity as coroner, to make a discovery that was even
more singular, if possible. *The corpse of Udley had been fully and efficiently
embalmed; and the chief agent employed was corrosive sublimate.* The body of
Turple, however, was still in need of this service.

A Murder
in the Fourth Dimension

The following pages are from a note-book that was discovered lying at the foot of an oak tree beside the Lincoln highway, between Bowman and Auburn. They would have been dismissed immediately as the work of a disordered mind, if it had not been for the unaccountable disappearance, eight days before, of James Buckingham and Edgar Halpin. Experts testified that the handwriting was undoubtedly that of Buckingham. A silver dollar, and a handkerchief marked with Buckingham's initials, were also found not far from the note-book.

Not everyone, perhaps, will believe that my ten years' hatred for Edgar Halpin was the impelling force that drove me to the perfecting of a most unique invention. Only those who have detested and loathed another man with the black fervor of the feeling I had conceived, will understand the patience with which I sought to devise a revenge that should be safe and adequate at the same time. The wrong he had done me was one that must be expiated sooner or later; and nothing short of his death would be sufficient. However, I did not care to hang, not even for a crime that I could regard as nothing more than the mere execution of justice; and, as a lawyer, I knew how difficult, how practically impossible, was the commission of a murder that would leave no betraying evidence. Therefore, I puzzled long and fruitlessly as to the manner in which Halpin should die, before my inspiration came to me.

I had reason enough to hate Edgar Halpin. We had been bosom friends all through our school days and through the first years of our professional life as law-partners. But when Halpin married the one woman I had ever loved with complete devotion, all friendship ceased on my side and was replaced by an ice-like barrier of inexorable enmity. Even the death of Alice, five years after the marriage, made no difference, for I could not forgive the happiness of which I had been deprived—the happiness they had shared during those years, like the thieves they were. I felt that she would have cared for me if it had not been for Halpin—indeed, she and I had been almost engaged before the beginning of his rivalry.

It must not be supposed, however, that I was indiscreet enough to betray my feelings at any time. Halpin was my daily associate in the Auburn law-firm to which we belonged; and I continued to be a most welcome and frequent guest at his home. I doubt if he ever knew that I had cared greatly for Alice: I am secretive and undemonstrative by temperament; and also, I am proud. No one, except Alice herself, ever surmised my suffering; and even she knew nothing of my resentment. Halpin himself trusted me; and nurturing as I did the idea of retaliation at some future time, I took good care that he should continue to trust me. I made myself necessary to him in all ways, I helped him when my heart was a cauldron of seething poisons, I spoke words of brotherly affection and clapped him on the back when I would rather have driven a dagger through him. I knew all the tortures and all the nausea of a hypocrite. And day after day, year after year, I made my varying plans for an ultimate revenge.

Apart from my legal studies and duties, during those ten years, I apprised myself of everything available that dealt with the methods of murder. Crimes of passion allured me with a fateful interest, and I read untiringly the records of particular cases. I made a study of weapons and poisons; and as I studied them, I pictured to myself the death of Halpin in every conceivable way. I imagined the deed as being done at all hours of the day and night, in a multitude of places. The only flaw in these dreams was my inability to think of any spot that would assure perfect safety from subsequent detection.

It was my bent toward scientific speculation and experiment that finally gave me the clue I sought. I had long been familiar with the theory that other worlds or dimensions may co-exist in the same space with ours by reason of a different molecular structure and vibrational rate, rendering them intangible for us. One day, when I was indulging in a murderous fantasy, in which for the thousandth time I imagined myself throttling Halpin with my bare hands, it occurred to me that some unseen dimension, if one could only penetrate it, would be the ideal place for the commission of a homicide. All circumstantial evidence, as well as the corpse itself, would be lacking—in other words, one would have a perfect absence of what is known as the *corpus delicti*. The problem of how to obtain entrance to this dimension was of course an unsolved one; but I did not feel that it would necessarily prove insoluble. I set myself immediately to a consideration of the difficulties to be overcome, and the possible ways and means.

There are reasons why I do not care to set forth in this narrative the details of the various experiments to which I was drawn during the next three years. The theory that underlay my tests and researches was a very simple one; but the processes involved were highly intricate. In brief, the premise from which I worked was, that the vibratory rate of objects in the fourth dimension could be artificially established by means of some mechanism, and that things or persons exposed to the influence of the vibration could be transported thereby to this alien realm.

For a long time, all my experiments were condemned to failure, because I was groping among mysterious powers and recondite laws whose motive-principle I had not wholly grasped. I will not even hint at the basic nature of the device which brought about my ultimate success, for I do not want others to follow where I have gone and find themselves in the same dismal predicament. I will say, however, that the desired vibration was attained by condensing ultra-violet rays in a refractive apparatus made of certain very sensitive materials which I will not name. The resultant power was stored in a kind of battery, and could be emitted from a vibratory disk suspended above an ordinary office chair, exposing everything beneath the disk to the influence of the new vibration.

The range of the influence could be closely regulated by means of an insulative attachment. By the use of the apparatus, I finally succeeded in precipitating various articles into the fourth dimension: a dinner-plate, a bust of Dante, a Bible, a French novel and a house-cat, all disappeared from sight and touch in a few instants when the ultra-violet power was turned upon them. I knew that henceforth they were functioning as atomic entities in a world where all things had the same vibratory rate that had been artificially induced by means of my mechanism.

Before venturing into the invisible domain myself, it was of course necessary to have some way of returning. I invented a second battery and a second vibratory disk, through which, by the use of certain infra-red rays, the vibrations of our own world could be established. By turning the force from the disk on the very same spot where the dinner-plate and the other articles had disappeared, I succeeded in recovering all of them. All were absolutely unchanged; and though several months had gone by, the cat had not suffered in any way from its fourth-dimensional incarceration. The infra-red device was portable; and I meant to take it with me on my visit to the new realm in company with Edgar Halpin. I—but not Halpin—would return anon to resume the threads of mundane existence.

My experiments had all been carried on with utter secrecy. To mask their real nature, as well as to provide myself with the needful privacy, I had built a small laboratory in the woods of an uncultivated ranch that I owned, lying midway between Auburn and Bowman. Here I retired at varying intervals when I had the requisite leisure, ostensibly to conduct some chemical experiments of an educative but far from unusual type. I never admitted anyone to the laboratory; and no great amount of curiosity was evinced by friends and acquaintances regarding its contents or the tests I was carrying on. Never did I breathe a syllable to anyone that could indicate the true goal of my researches.

I shall never forget the jubilation I felt when the infra-red device had proven its practicality by retrieving the plate, the bust, the two volumes and the cat. I was so eager for the consummation of my long-delayed revenge, that I did not even consider a preliminary personal trip into the fourth dimension. I had determined that Edgar Halpin must precede me when I went. I did not feel, however, that it would be wise to tell him anything concerning the real nature of my device, or the proposed excursion.

Halpin, at this time, was suffering from recurrent attacks of terrific neuralgia. One day, when he had complained more than usual, I told him under the seal of confidence that I had been working on a vibratory invention for the relief of such maladies and had finally perfected it.

"I'll take you out to the laboratory tonight, and you can try it," I said. "It will fix you up in a jiffy: all you'll have to do will be to sit in a chair and let me turn on the current. But don't say anything to anybody."

"Thanks, old man," he rejoined. "I'll certainly be grateful if you can do anything to stop this damnable pain. It feels like electric drills boring through my head all the time."

I had chosen my time well, for all things were favorable to the maintenance of the secrecy I desired. Halpin lived on the outskirts of the town; and he was alone for the nonce, his housekeeper having gone away on a brief visit to some sick relative. The night was murky and foggy; and I drove to Halpin's house and stopped for him shortly after the dinner hour, when few people were abroad. I do not think that anyone saw us when we left the town. I followed a rough and little-used byroad for most of the way to my laboratory, saying that I did not care to meet other cars in the thick fog, if I could avoid it. We passed no one, and I felt that this was a good omen and that everything had combined to further my plan.

Halpin uttered an exclamation of surprise when I turned on the lights in my laboratory.

"I didn't dream you had so much stuff here," he remarked, peering about with respectful curiosity at the long array of unsuccessful appliances which I had thrown aside in the course of my labors.

I pointed to the chair above which the ultra-violet vibrator was suspended.

"Take a seat, Ed," I enjoined him. "We'll soon cure everything that ails you."

"Sure you aren't going to electrocute me?" he joked, as he obeyed my direction.

A thrill of fierce triumph ran through me like the stimulation of some rare elixir, when he had seated himself. Everything was in my power now, and the moment of recompense for my ten years' humiliation and suffering was at hand. Halpin was so unsuspecting: the thought of any danger to himself, of any treachery on my part, would have been fantastically incredible to him. Putting my hand beneath my coat, I caressed the hilt of the hunting-knife that I carried.

"All set?" I asked him.

"Sure, Mike. Go ahead and shoot."

I had found the exact range that would involve all of Halpin's body without affecting the chair itself. Fixing my gaze upon him, I pressed the little knob that turned on the current of vibratory rays. The result was practically instantaneous, for he seemed to melt like a puff of thinning smoke. I could still see his outlines for a moment, and the look of a phantasmal astonishment on his face. And then he was gone—utterly gone.

Perhaps it will be a source of wonderment that, having annihilated Halpin as far as all earthly existence was concerned, I was not content merely to leave him in the unseen, intangible plane to which he had been transposed. Would that I had been content to do so. But the wrong I had suffered was hot and cankerous within me, and I could not bear to think that he still lived, in any form or upon any plane. Nothing but absolute death would suffice to assuage my resentment; and the death must be inflicted by my own hand. It now remained to follow Halpin into that realm which no man had ever visited before, and of whose geographical conditions and characteristics I had formed no idea whatever. I felt sure, however, that I could enter it and return safely, after disposing of my victim. The return of the cat left no apparent room for doubt on that score.

I turned out the lights; and seating myself in the chair with the portable infra-red vibrator in my arms, I switched on the ultra-violet power. The sensation I felt was that of one who falls with nightmare velocity into a great gulf. My ears were deaf with the intolerable thunder of my descent, a frightful sickness overcame me, and I was near to losing all consciousness for a moment, in the black vortex of roaring space and force that seemed to draw me nadir-ward through the ultimate pits. Then the speed of my fall was gradually retarded, and I came gently down to something that was solid beneath my feet. There was a dim glimmering of light that grew stronger as my eyes accustomed themselves to it, and by this light I saw Halpin standing a few feet away. Behind him were dark, amorphous rocks and the vague outlines of a desolate landscape of low mounds and primordial treeless flats. Even though I had hardly known what to expect, I was somewhat surprised by the character of the environment in which I found myself. At a guess, I would have said that the fourth dimension would be something more colorous and complex and varied—a land of multifold hues and many-angled forms. However, in its drear and primitive desolation, the place was truly ideal for the commission of the act I had intended.

Halpin came toward me in the doubtful light. There was a dazed and almost idiotic look on his face, and he stuttered a little as he tried to speak.

"W-what h-happened?" he articulated at last.

"Never mind what happened. It isn't a circumstance to what's going to happen now."

I laid the portable vibrator aside on the ground as I spoke.

The dazed look was still on Halpin's face when I drew the hunting-knife and stabbed him through the body with one clean thrust. In that thrust, all the stifled hatred, all the cankering resentment of ten insufferable years was finally vindicated. He fell in a twisted heap, twitched a little, and lay still. The blood oozed very slowly from his side and formed a puddle. I remember wondering at its slowness, even then, for the oozing seemed to go on through hours and days.

Somehow, as I stood there, I was obsessed by a feeling of utter unreality. No doubt the long strain I had been under, the daily stress of indurate emotions and decade-deferred hopes, had left me unable to realize the final consummation of my desire when it came. The whole thing seemed no more than one of the homicidal day-dreams in which I had imagined myself stabbing Halpin to the heart and seeing his hateful body lie before me.

At length, I decided that it was time to effect my return; for surely nothing could be gained by lingering any longer beside Halpin's corpse amid the unutterable dreariness of the fourth-dimensional landscape. I erected the vibrator in a position where its rays could be turned upon myself, and pressed the switch.

I was aware of a sudden vertigo, and felt that I was about to begin another descent into fathomless vortical gulfs. But, though the vertigo persisted, nothing happened, and I found that I was still standing beside the corpse, in the same dismal milieu.

Dumbfoundment and growing consternation crept over me. Apparently, for some unknown reason, the vibrator would not work in the way I had so confidently expected. Perhaps, in these new surroundings, there was some barrier to the full development of the infra-red power. I do not know; but, at any rate, there I was, in a truly singular and far from agreeable predicament.

I do not know how long I fooled in a mounting frenzy with the mechanism of the vibrator, in the hope that something had temporarily gone wrong and could be remedied, if the difficulty were only found. However, all my tinkerings were of no avail: the machine was in perfect working-order, but the required force was wanting. I tried the experiment of exposing small articles to the influence of the rays. A silver coin and a handkerchief dissolved and disappeared very slowly, and I felt that they must have regained the levels of mundane existence. But evidently the vibrational force was not strong enough to transport a human being.

Finally I gave it up and threw the vibrator to the ground. In the surge of a violent despair that came upon me, I felt the need of muscular action, of prolonged movement; and I started off at once to explore the weird realm in which I had involuntarily imprisoned myself.

It was an unearthly land—a land such as might have existed before the creation of life. There were undulating blanks of desolation beneath the uniform grey of a heaven without moon or sun or stars or clouds, from which an uncertain and diffused glimmering was cast upon the world beneath. There were no shadows, for the light seemed to emanate from all directions. The soil was a grey dust in places and a grey viscidity of slime in others; and the low mounds I have already mentioned were like the backs of prehistoric monsters heaving from the primal ooze. There were no signs of insect or animal life, there were no trees, no herbs, and not even a blade of grass, a patch of moss or lichen, or a trace of algae. Many rocks were strewn chaotically through the desolation; and their forms were such as an idiotic demon might have devised in aping the handiwork of God. The light was so dim that all things were lost at a little distance; and I could not tell whether the horizon was near or far.

It seems to me that I must have wandered on for several hours, maintaining as direct a course of progression as I could. I had a compass—a thing that I always carry with me; but it refused to function, and I was driven to conclude that there were no magnetic poles in this new world.

Suddenly, as I rounded a pile of the vast amorphous boulders, I came to a human body that lay huddled on the ground, and saw incredulously that it was Halpin. The blood still oozed from the fabric of his coat, and the pool it had formed was no larger than when I had begun my journey.

I felt sure that I had not wandered in a circle, as people are said to do amid unfamiliar surroundings. How, then, could I have returned to the scene of my crime? The problem nearly drove me mad as I pondered it; and I set off with frantic vigor in an opposite direction from the one I had first taken.

For all intents and purposes, the scene through which I now passed was identical with the one that lay on the other side of Halpin's corpse.

It was hard to believe that the low mounds, the drear levels of dust and ooze and the monstrous boulders, were not the same as those among which I had made my former way. As I went, I took out my watch with the idea of timing my progress; but the hands had stopped at the very moment when I had taken my plunge into unknown space from the laboratory; and though I wound it carefully, it refused to run again.

After walking an enormous distance, during which, to my surprise, I felt no fatigue whatever, I came once more to the body I had sought to leave. I think that I went really mad then, for a little while. . . .

Now, after a duration of time—or eternity—which I have no means of computing, I am writing this pencilled account on the leaves of my note-book. I am writing it beside the corpse of Edgar Halpin, from which I have been unable to flee; for a score of excursions into the dim realms on all sides have ended by bringing me back to it after a certain interval. The corpse is still fresh and the blood has not dried. Apparently, the thing we know as time is well-nigh non-existent in this world, or at any rate is seriously disordered in its action; and most of the normal concomitants of time are likewise absent; and space itself has the property of returning always to the same point. The voluntary movements I have performed might be considered as a sort of time-sequence; but in regard to involuntary things there is little or no time-movement. I experience neither physical weariness or hunger; but the horror of my situation is not to be conveyed in human language; and hell itself can hardly have devised a name for it.

When I have finished writing this narration, I shall precipitate the note-book into the levels of mundane life by means of the infra-red vibrator. Some obscure need of confessing my crime and telling my predicament to others has led me to an act of which I should never have believed myself capable, for I am the most uncommunicative of men by nature. Apart from the satisfying of this need, the composition of my narrative is something to do, it is a temporary reprieve from the desperate madness that will surge upon me soon, and the grey eternal horror of the limbo to which I have doomed myself beside the undecaying body of my victim.

THE RESURRECTION OF THE RATTLESNAKE

N o, as I've told you fellows before, I haven't a red cent's worth of faith in the supernatural."

The speaker was Arthur Avilton, whose tales of the ghostly and macabre had often been compared to Poe, Bierce and Machen. He was a master of imaginative horrors, with a command of diabolically convincing details, of monstrous cobweb suggestions, that had often laid a singular spell on the minds of readers who were not ordinarily attracted or impressed by literature of that type. It was his own boast, often made, that all his effects were secured in a purely ratiocinative, even scientific manner, by playing on the element of subconscious dread, the ancestral superstition latent in most human beings; but he claimed that he himself was utterly incredulous of anything occult or phantasmal, and that he had never in his life known the slightest tremor of fear concerning such things.

Avilton's listeners looked at him a little questioningly. They were John Godfrey, a young landscape painter, and Emil Schuler, a rich dilettante, who played in alternation with literature and music, but was not serious in his attentions to either. Both were old friends and admirers of Avilton, at whose house on Sutter Street, in San Francisco, they had met by chance that afternoon. Avilton had suspended work on a new story to chat with them and smoke a sociable pipe. He still sat at his writing-table, with a pile of neatly written foolscap before him. His appearance was as normal and non-eccentric as his handwriting, and he might have been a lawyer or doctor or chemist, rather than a concocter of bizarre fiction. The room, his library, was quite luxurious, in a sober, gentlemanly sort of fashion, and there was little of the outré in its furnishings.

The only unusual notes were struck by two heavy brass candlesticks on his table, wrought in the form of rearing serpents, and a stuffed rattle-snake that was coiled on top of one of the low bookcases.

"Well," observed Godfrey, "if anything could convince me of the reality of the supernatural, it would be some of your stories, Avilton. I always read them by broad daylight—I wouldn't do it after dark on a bet . . . By the way, what's the yarn you are working on now?"

"It's about a stuffed serpent that suddenly comes to life," replied Avilton. "I'm calling it 'The Resurrection of the Rattlesnake'. I got the idea while I was looking at my rattler this morning."

"And I suppose you'll sit here by candlelight tonight," put in Schuler, "and go on with your cheerful little horror without turning a hair." It was well known that Avilton did much of his writing at night.

Avilton smiled. "Darkness always helps me to concentrate. And, considering that so much of the action in my tales is nocturnal, the time is not inappropriate."

"You're welcome," said Schuler, in a jocular tone. He arose to go, and Godfrey also found that it was time to depart.

"Oh, by the way," said their host, "I'm planning a little week-end party. Would you fellows care to come over next Saturday evening? There'll be two or three others of our friends. I'll have this story off my chest by then, and we'll raise the roof."

Godfrey and Schuler accepted the invitation, and went out together. Since they both lived across the bay, in Oakland, and both were on their way home, they caught the same car to the ferry.

"Old Avilton is certainly a case of the living contradiction, if there ever was one," remarked Schuler. "Of course, no one quite believes in the occult or the necromantic nowadays; but anyone who can cook up such infernally realistic horrors, such thoroughgoing hair-frizzlers as he does, simply hasn't the right to be so cold-blooded about it. I claim that it's really indecent."

"I agree," rejoined his companion. "He's so damnably matter-of-fact that he arouses in me a sort of Hallowe'en impulse: I want to dress up in an old sheet and play ghost or something, just to jar him out of that skeptical complacency of his."

"Ye gods and little ghosties!" cried Schuler. "I've got an inspiration. Remember what Avilton told us about the new story he's writing— about the serpent that comes to life?" He unfolded the prankish idea he had conceived, and the two laughed like mischievous schoolboys plotting some novel deviltry.

"Why not? It should give the old lad a real thrill," chuckled Godfrey. "And he'll think that his fictions are more scientific than he ever dreamed before."

"I know where I can get one," said Schuler. "I'll put it in a fishing-creel, and hide the creel in my valise next Saturday when we go to Avilton's. Then we can watch our chance to make the substitution."

On Saturday evening the two friends arrived together at Avilton's house, and were admitted by a Japanese who combined in himself the roles of cook, butler, housekeeper and valet. The other guests, two young musicians, had already come, and Avilton, who was evidently in a mood for relaxation, was telling them a story, which, to judge from the continual interruptions of laughter, was not at all in the vein for which he had grown so famous. It seemed almost impossible to believe that he could be the author of the gruesome and brain-freezing horrors that bore his name.

The evening went successfully, with a good dinner, cards, and some pre-war Bourbon, and it was after midnight when Avilton saw his guests to their chambers, and sought his own.

Godfrey and Schuler did not retire, but sat up talking in the room they occupied together, till the house had grown silent and it was probable that everyone had fallen asleep. Avilton, they knew, was a sound sleeper, who boasted that even a rivet-factory or a brass orchestra could not keep him awake for five minutes after his head had touched the pillow.

"Now's our chance," whispered Schuler, at last. He had taken from his valise a fishing-creel, in which was a large and somewhat restless gopher-snake, and softly opening the door, which they had left ajar, the conspirators tip-toed down the hall toward Avilton's library, which lay at the farther end. It was their plan to leave the live gopher-snake in the library in lieu of the stuffed rattler, which they would remove. A gopher-snake is somewhat similar to a rattler in its markings; and, in order to complete the verisimilitude, Schuler had even provided himself with a set of rattles, which he meant to attach with thread to the serpent's tail before freeing it. The substitution, they felt, would undoubtedly prove a trifle startling, even to a person of such boiler-plate nerves and unrelenting skepticism as Avilton.

As if to facilitate their scheme, the door of the library stood half-open. Godfrey produced a flashlight, and they entered. Somehow, in spite of their merry mood, in spite of the schoolboy hoax they had planned and the Bourbon they had drunk, the shadow of something dim and sinister and disquieting fell on the two men as they crossed the threshold. It was like a premonition of some unknown and unexpected menace, lurking in the darkness of the book-peopled room where Avilton had woven so many of his weird and spectral webs. They both began to remember incidents of nocturnal horror from his stories—happenings that were ghoulishly hideous or necromantically strange and terrible. Now, such things seemed even more plausible than the author's diabolic art had made them heretofore. But neither of the men could have quite defined the feeling that came over them or could have assigned a reason for it.

"I feel a little creepy," confided Schuler, as they stood in the dark library. "Turn on that flashlight, won't you?"

The light fell directly on the low bookcase where the stuffed rattler had been coiled, but to their surprise, they found the serpent missing from its customary place.

"Where is the damned thing, anyway?" muttered Godfrey. He

turned his light on the neighboring bookcases, and then on the floor and chairs in front of them, but without revealing the object of his search. At last, in its circlings, the ray struck Avilton's writing-table, and they saw the snake, which, in some mood of grotesque humor, Avilton had evidently placed on his pile of manuscript to serve in lieu of a paperweight. Behind it gleamed the two serpentine candlesticks.

"Ah! there you are," said Schuler. He was about to open his creel when a singular and quite unforeseen thing occurred. He and Godfrey both saw a movement on the writing-table, and before their incredulous eyes the rattlesnake coiled on the pile of paper slowly raised its arrow-shaped head and darted forth its forky tongue! Its cold, unwinking eyes, with a fixation of baleful intensity well-nigh hypnotic, were upon the intruders, and as they stared in unbelieving horror, they heard the faint rattling of its tail, like withered seeds in a wind-swung pod.

"My God!" exclaimed Schuler. "The thing is alive!"

As he spoke, the flashlight fell from Godfrey's hand and went out, leaving them in soot-black darkness. As they stood for a moment, half-petrified with astonishment and terror, they heard the rattling again, and then the sound of some object that seemed to strike the floor in falling. Once more, in a few instants, there came the faint rattle, this time almost at their very feet.

Godfrey screamed aloud, and Schuler began to curse incoherently, as they both turned and ran toward the open door. Schuler was ahead, and as he crossed the threshold into the dim-lit hall, where one electric bulb still burned, he heard the crash of his companion's fall, mingled with a cry of such infinite terror, such atrocious agony, that his brain and his very marrow were turned to ice. In the paralyzing panic that overtook him, Schuler retained no faculty except that of locomotion, and it did not even occur to him that it would be possible to stop and ascertain what had befallen Godfrey. He had no thought, no desire, except to put the length of the hall between himself and that accursed library and its happenings.

Avilton, dressed in pajamas, stood at the door of his room. He had been aroused by Godfrey's scream of terror.

"What's the matter?" the story-writer queried, with a look of amiable surprise, which turned to a real gravity when he saw Schuler's face. Schuler was as white as a marble headstone and his eyes were preternaturally dilated.

"The snake!" Schuler gasped. "The snake! The snake! Something awful has happened to Godfrey—he fell with the thing just behind him."

"What snake? You don't mean my stuffed rattler by any chance, do you?"

"Stuffed rattler?" yelled Schuler. "The damned thing is alive! It came crawling after us, rattling under our very feet a moment ago. Then Godfrey stumbled and fell—and he didn't get up."

"I don't understand," purred Avilton. "The thing is a manifest impossibility—really quite contrary to all natural laws, I assure you. I killed that snake four years ago, in El Dorado County, and had it stuffed by an expert taxidermist."

"Go and see for yourself," challenged Schuler.

Avilton strode immediately to the library and turned on the lights. Schuler, mastering a little his panic and his dreadful forebodings, followed at a cautious distance. He found Avilton stooping over the body of Godfrey, who lay quite still in a huddled and horribly contorted position near the door. Not far away was the abandoned fishing-creel. The stuffed rattlesnake was coiled in its customary place on top of the bookshelves.

Avilton, with a grave and brooding mien, removed his hand from Godfrey's heart, and observed:

"He's quite dead—shock and heart-failure, I should think."

Neither he nor Schuler could bear to look very long at Godfrey's upturned face, on which was stamped as with some awful brand or acid an expression of fear and suffering beyond all human capacity to endure.

In their mutual desire to avoid the lidless horror of his dead staring, their eyes fell at the same instant on his right hand, which was clenched in a hideous rigidity and drawn close to his side.

Neither could utter a word when they saw the thing that protruded from between Godfrey's fingers. It was a bunch of rattles, and on the endmost one, where it had evidently been torn from the viper's tail, there clung several shreds of raw and bloody flesh.

A Sierran Sunrise

A SIERRAN SUNRISE

L ook yonder, where the whitened orient skies
     Grow splendid with the radiance of the dawn,
O'er regal mountains that majestic rise
     With misty purple robes about them drawn.

The painting of the masterpiece behold
     That every morn, before our careless eye,
Nature portrays, in crimson and in gold,
     Upon the canvas of the earth and sky.

Mark what unequaled and supernal hues—
     Ever the artist's dream and his despair—
She doth, with art supreme, unrivaled use,
     To limn her vision wonderful and fair.

Long-sought, elusive Beauty here descends,
     And for a moment unto Nature's hand
Her star-caught skill and inspiration lends,
     Whence springs this dawn miraculous and grand.

The Secret of the Cairn

It will be said, by nearly all who peruse this narrative, that I must have been mad from the beginning; that even the first of the phenomena related herein were sensory hallucinations betokening some grave disorder. It is possible that I am mad now, at those times when the gulfward-sliding tide of memory sweeps me away; those times when I am lost anew in the tracts of dreadful light and unknown entity that were opened before me by the last phase of my experience. But I was sane at the outset, and I am still sane enough to write down a sober and lucid account of all that occurred.

My solitary habit of life, as well as my reputation for eccentricity and extravagance, will no doubt be urged against me by many, to support the theory of mental unsoundness. Those who are unconventional enough to credit me with rationality will smile at my story and deem that I have forsaken the province of bizarre pictorial art (in which I have achieved a certain eminence) to invade that of super-scientific fiction.

However, if I wished, I could bring forward much corroborative evidence of the strange visitations. Some of the phenomena were remarked by other people in the locality; though I did not know this at the time, owing to my thorough isolation. One or two brief and obscure notices, giving a somewhat commonplace meteoric explanation, appeared shortly afterwards in metropolitan journals, and were reprinted even more briefly and obscurely in scientific gazettes. I shall not quote them here, since to do so would involve a repetition of details which, in themselves, are more or less doubtful and inconclusive.

I am Dorian Wiermoth. My series of illustrative paintings, based on the poems of Poe, will perhaps be familiar to some of my readers.

For a number of reasons, some of which it is needless to mention, I had decided to spend a whole year in the high Sierras. On the shore of a tiny sapphire tarn, in a valley sheltered by hemlocks and granite crags, I had built a rough cabin and had stocked it plentifully with provisions, books, and the materials of my art. For the time being, I was independent of a world whose charms and enchantments were, to say the least, no longer irresistible.

The region possessed, however, other allurements than those of seclusion. Everywhere, in the stark mountain masses and pinnacles, the juniper-studded cliffs, the glacier-moulded sheets of rock, there was a mingling of grandeur and grotesquery that appealed most intimately to my imagination. Though my drawings and paintings were never, in any sense, literal transcriptions of nature, and were often avowedly fantastic, I had made at all times a careful study of natural forms, realizing that the wildest evocations of the unknown are merely, at bottom, recombinations of known shapes and colors, even as the furthest worlds are compositions of elements familiar to terrene chemistry.

Therefore, I found much that was suggestive in this scenery; much that I could interweave with the arabesques of weirdly imaginative designs; or could render more directly, as pure landscape, in a semi-Japanese style with which I was then experimenting.

The place in which I had settled was remote from the state highway, the railroad, and the path of aeroplanes. My only near neighbors were the mountain crows and jays and chipmunks. Occasionally, in my rambles, I met a fisherman or hunter; but the region was miraculously free of tourists. I began a serene regimen of work and study, which was interrupted by no human agency. The thing that ended my stay so prematurely, came, I am sure, from a sphere that is not mapped by geographers, nor listed by astronomers.

The mystery began, without forewarning or prescience, on a quiet evening in July, after the scimitar-shaped moon had sheathed itself in the firs and hemlocks. I was sitting in my cabin, reading for relaxation a detective story whose title I have since forgotten. The day had been quite warm; there was no wind in that sequestered valley; and the oil lamp was burning steadily between the half-open door and the wide windows.

Then, on the still air, there came a sudden aromatic perfume that filled the cabin like a flooding wave. It was not the resinous odor of the conifers, but a rich and ever-deepening spice that was wholly exotic to the region—perhaps alien to the *Earth*. It made me think of myrrh and sandal and incense; and yet it was none of these, but a stranger thing, whose very richness was pure and supernal as the odors that were said to attend the apparition of the Holy Grail.

Even as I inhaled it, startled, and wondering if I were the victim of some hallucination, I heard a faint music that was somehow allied to the perfume and inseparable from it. The sound, like a breathing of fairy flutes, ethereally sweet, thrilling, eldritch, was all about me in the room; and I seemed to hear it in my inmost brain, as one hears the sea-whisper in a shell.

I ran to the door, I flung it wide open, and stepped out into the azure-green evening. The perfume was everywhere, it arose before me, like the frankincense of veiled altars, from the tarn and the hemlocks, and it seemed to fall from the stilly burning stars above the Gothic trees and granite walls, to the north. Then, turning eastward, I saw the mysterious light that palpitated and revolved in a fan of broad beams upon the hill.

The light was soft, rather than brilliant, and I knew that it could be neither aurora nor aeroplane beacon. It was hueless—and yet somehow it seemed to include the intimation of a hundred colors lying beyond the familiar spectrum. The rays were like the spokes of a half-hidden wheel that turned slowly and more slowly, but did not change its position. Their center, or hub, was behind the hill. Presently they became stationary, except for a slight trembling. Against them, I saw the bowed masses of several mighty junipers.

I must have stood there for a long while, gaping and staring like any yokel who beholds a marvel beyond his comprehension. I still breathed the unearthly odor, but the music had grown fainter with the slackening of the wheel of light, and had fallen to a sub-auditory sighing—the suspicion of a murmur far away in some undiscovered world. Implicitly, though perhaps illogically, I connected the sound and the scent with that unexplained luminance. Whether the wheel was just beyond the junipers, on the craggy hill-top, or a billion miles away in astronomic space, I could not decide; and it did not even occur to me that I could climb the hill and ascertain this particular for myself.

My main emotion was a sort of half-mystic wonder, a dreamy curiosity that did not prompt me to action. Idly I waited, with no clear awareness of the passing of time, till the wheel of rays began once more to revolve slowly. It swiftened, and presently I could no longer distinguish the separate beams. All I could see was a whirling disk, like a moon that spun dizzily but maintained the same position relative to the rocks and junipers. Then, without apparent recession, it grew dim and faded on the sapphire darkness. I heard no longer the remote and flute-like murmur; and the perfume ebbed from the valley like an out-going tide, leaving but elusive wraiths of its unknown spicery.

My sense of wonder sharpened with the passing of these phenomena; but I could form no conclusion as to their origin. My knowledge of natural science, which was far from extensive, seemed to afford no plausible clue. I felt, with a wild thrilling, half-fearful, half-exultant, that the thing I had witnessed was not to be found in the catalogues compiled by human observers.

The visitation, whatever it was, had left me in a state of profound nervous excitement. Sleep, when it came, was intermittent; and the problematic light, perfume, and melody recurred again and again with my dreams with a singular vividness, as if they had stamped themselves upon my brain with more than the force of normal sensory impressions.

I awoke at earliest dawn, filled with a well-nigh feverish conviction that I must visit the eastern hill immediately and learn if any tangible sign had been left by the agency of the turning beams. After a hasty and half-eaten breakfast, I made the ascent, armed with my drawing-pad and pencils. It was a short climb among overbeetling boulders, sturdy tamaracks, and dwarf oaks that took the form of low-growing bushes.

The hill-top itself comprised an area of several hundred yards, roughly elliptic. It fell gently away toward the east, and ended on two sides in sheerly riven cliffs and jagged scarps. There were patches of soil amid the enormous granite folds and out-croppings; but these patches were bare, except for a few alpine flowers and grasses; and the place was given mainly to a number of gnarled and massive junipers, which had rooted themselves by preference in the solid rock. From the beginning, it had been one of my favorite haunts. I had made many sketches of the mightily mortised junipers, some of which, I verily believe, were more ancient than the famed sequoias, or the cedars of Lebanon.

Surveying the scene with eager eyes in the cloudless morning light, I saw nothing untoward at first. As usual, there were deer-tracks in the basins of friable soil; but apart from these, and my own former footprints, there was no token of any visitor. Somewhat disappointed, I began to think that the luminous, turning wheel had been far-off in space, beyond the hill.

Then, wandering on toward the lower levels of the crest, I found, in a sheltered spot, the thing that had previously been hidden from my view by the trees and out-croppings.

It was a cairn of granite fragments—but a cairn such as I had never beheld in all my mountain explorations. Built in the unmistakable form of a star with five blunt angles, it rose waist-high from the middle of a plot of intersifting loam and sand. About it grew a few plants of mountain phlox. On one side were the charred remnants of a tree that had been destroyed by lightning in recent years. On two other sides, forming a right angle, were high walls to which several junipers clung like coiling dragons with tenacious claws, embedded in the riven rock.

On the summit of the strange pile, in the center, I perceived a pale and coldly shining stone with star-like points that duplicated and followed the five angles. This stone, I thought, had been shaped by artificial means. I did not recognize its material; and I felt sure that it was nothing native to the region.

I felt the elation of a discoverer, deeming that I had stumbled on the proof of some alien mystery. The cairn, whatever its purpose, whoever its builders, had been reared during the night; for I had visited this very spot on the previous afternoon, a little before sunset, and would have seen the structure if it had been there at that time.

Somehow, I dismissed immediately and forever all idea of human agency. There occurred to me the bizarre thought that voyagers from some foreign world had paused on the hill and had left that enigmatic pile as a sign of their visit. In this manner, the queer nocturnal manifestations were accounted for, even if not fully explained.

Arrested by the weird enigma of it all, I had paused on the verge of the loamy basin, at a distance of perhaps twelve feet from the cairn itself. Now, my brain on fire with fantastical surmise, I stepped forward to examine the cairn more closely. To my utter dumbfoundment, it appeared to recede before me, preserving the same interval, as I went toward it. Pace after pace I took, but the ground flowed forward beneath me like a treadmill; my moving feet descended in their former tracks; and I was unable to make the least progress toward the goal that was apparently so near at hand! My movements were in no sense impeded, but I felt a growing giddiness, that soon verged upon nausea.

My disconcertment can more readily be imagined than expressed. It seemed obvious that either I or nature had gone suddenly mad. The thing was absurd, impossible—it belied the most elementary laws of dimension. By some incalculable means, a new and arcanic property had been introduced into the space about the cairn.

To test further the presence of this hypothetical property, I abandoned my efforts at direct approach, and began to circle the basin, resuming the attempt from other angles. The pile, I found, was equally unapproachable from all sides: at a distance of twelve feet, the soil began its uncanny treadmill movement when I tried to encroach upon it. The cairn, to all intents and purposes, might have been a million miles away, in the gulf between the worlds!

After a while, I gave up my weird and futile experiments, and sat down beneath one of the overhanging junipers. The mystery maddened me, it induced a sort of mental vertigo as I pondered it. But also, it brought into the familiar order of things the exhilaration of a novel and perhaps supernatural element. It spoke of the veiled infinitudes I had vainly longed to explore; it goaded my feverish fantasy to ungovernable flights.

Recalling myself from such conjectures, I studied with sedulous care the stelliform pile and the soil around it. Surely the beings who had built it would have left their footprints. However, there were no discernible marks of any kind; and I could learn nothing from the arrangement of the stones, which had been piled with impeccable neatness and symmetry. I was still baffled by the five-pointed object on the summit, for I could recall no terrene mineral that resembled its substance very closely. It was too opaque for moonstone or crystal, too lucid and brilliant for alabaster.

At whiles, as I continued to sit there, I was visited by an evanescent whiff of the spicy perfume that had flooded my cabin on the previous night. It came and went like a dying phantom, and I was never quite sure of its presence.

At length I roused myself and made a thorough search of the hilltop, to learn if any other trace had been left by the problematic visitors. In one of the sandy patches of soil, near the northern verge, I saw a curious indentation, like the slender, three-toed footmark of some impossibly gigantic bird. Close at hand was the small hollow from which a loose fragment of stone, doubtless employed in the building of the cairn, had been removed. The three-pointed mark was very faint, as if the maker had trodden there with an airy lightness. But apart from the finding of this doubtful vestige, my search was wholly without result.

During the weeks that ensued, the unearthly riddle upon which I had fallen preoccupied me almost to the point of mania. Perhaps, if there had been anyone with whom I could have discussed it, anyone who could have thrown upon it the calm and sober light of technical knowledge, I might have rid myself of the obsession to some extent. But I was entirely alone; and, to the best of my belief, the neighborhood of the cairn was visited by no other human being at that time.

On several occasions, I renewed my efforts to approach the cairn; but the unheard-of, incredible property of a concealed *extension*, a treadmill *flowing*, still inhered in the space about it, as if established there to guard it from all intrusion. Faced with this abrogation of known geometry, I felt at whiles the delirious horror of one for whom the infinite has declared its yawning gulf amid the supposed solidity of finite things.

I made a pencil drawing of the long, light footmark before it was erased by the Sierran winds; and from that one vestige, like a paleontologist who builds up some extinct monster from a single bone, I tried to reconstruct in my imagination the being that had left it there. The cairn itself was the theme of numerous sketches; and I believe that I formed and debated in turn almost every conceivable theory as to its purpose and the identity of its builders.

Was it a monument that marked the grave of some intercosmic voyager from Algol or Aldebaran? Had it been reared as a token of discovery and possession by a Columbus of Achernar, landing on our planet? Did it indicate the site of a mysterious cache, to which the makers would return at some future time? Was it a landmark between dimensions? a hieroglyphic milepost? a signal for the guidance of other travelers who might pass among the worlds, going from deep to deep?

All conjectures were equally valid—and worthless. Before the wildering mystery of it all, my human ignorance drove me to veritable frenzy.

A fortnight had gone by, and the midsummer month was drawing to its close, when I began to notice certain new phenomena. I have mentioned, I think, that there were a few tiny patches of alpine phlox within the circle of occultly altered space around the cairn. One day, with a startlement that amounted to actual shock, I saw that an extraordinary change had occurred in their pale blossoms. The petals had doubled in number, they were now of abnormal size and heaviness, and were tinged with ardent purple and lambent ruby. Perhaps the change had been going on for some time without my perception; perhaps it had developed overnight. At any rate, the modest little flowers had taken on the splendor of asphodels from some mythologic land!

Beyond all mortal trespass, they flamed in that enchanted area, moated with unseen immensities. Day after day I returned, smitten with the awe of one who witnesses a miracle, and saw them there, ever larger and brighter, as if they were fed by other elements than the known air and earth.

Then, presently, in the berries of a great juniper bough that overhung the ring, I perceived a corresponding change. The tiny, dull-blue globes had enlarged enormously, and were colored with a lucent crimson, like the fiery apples of some exotic paradise. At the same time, the foliage of the bough brightened to a tropic verdancy. But on the main portion of the tree, outside the cryptic circle, the leaves and berries were unaltered.

It was as if something of another world had been intercalated with ours. . . . More and more, I began to feel that the star of lucent, nameless stone that topped the cairn was in some manner the source or key of these unique phenomena. But I could prove nothing, could learn nothing. I could feel sure of only one thing: I was witnessing the action of forces that had never intruded heretofore upon human observation. These forces were obedient to their own laws—which, it appeared, were not altogether synonymous with the laws that man in his presumption has laid down for the workings of nature. The meaning of it all was a secret told in some alien, clueless cipher.

I have forgotten the exact date of those final occurrences, in whose aftermath I was carried beyond the imaginable confines of time and space. Indeed, it seems to me that it would be impossible to date them in terms of terrene chronology. Sometimes I feel that they belong only to the cycles of another world; sometimes, that they never happened; sometimes, that they are still happening—or yet to happen.

I remember, though, that there was a half-moon above the crags and firs on that fatal evening. The air had turned sharp with a prescience of the coming autumn, and I had closed the door and windows and had kindled a fire of dead juniper-wood that was perfuming the cabin with its subtle incense. I heard the soughing of a wind in the higher hemlocks, as I sat before my table, looking over the recent sketches I had made of the cairn and its surroundings, and wondering for perhaps the millionth time if I, or anyone, would ever solve the unearthly riddle.

This time, I began to hear the faint, aerial music, as if in the inmost convolutions of my brain, before I caught the mystic odor. At first, it was little more than the memory of a sound; but it seemed to rise and flow and pour *outward*, slowly, tortuously, as if through the windings of some immeasurable conch, till it was all about me with its labyrinthine murmuring. The cabin—the world outside—the very heavens—were filled with tenuous horns and susurrous flutes that told the incommunicable dreams of a lost elfland.

Then, above the redolence of the clearly burning, smokeless wood, I smelt that other perfume, rich and ethereal, and no less pervasive than on the former occasion. It seemed that the closed doors and windows were no barrier to its advent: it came as if through another medium than the air, another avenue than the space in which we move and have our being.

In a fever of exalted wonder and curiosity, I threw the door open and went out into the sea of unearthly fragrance and melody that over-flowed the world. On the eastern hill, as I had expected, the turning wheel of light was slowing in a stationary position beyond the tower-like junipers. The rays were soft and hueless, as before, but their luster was not diminished by the moon.

This time, I felt an imperative desire to solve the enigma of that visitation: a desire that drew me, stumbling and racing upward among the craggy boulders and low-grown bushes. The music ebbed to a far, faint whisper, the wheel revolved more gradually, as I neared the summit.

A rudiment of that caution which humanity has always felt in the presence of unknown things, impelled me to slacken my reckless pace. Several immense trees and granite out-croppings, however, still intervened betwixt myself and the source of those trembling beams. I stole forward, seeing with an inexpressible thrill, as of some mystic confirmation, that the beams emanated from the site of the stelliform cairn.

It was an easy matter to climb the massive folds of rock and reach a vantage from which I could look directly down on that mysterious area. Crawling flat on my stomach, in a line with the mightiest of the overjutting junipers, I attained my objective, and could peer from behind a heavy bough that grew horizontally along the rock, at the wall's edge.

The loamy basin in which the cairn had been reared was beneath me. Poised in mid-air, level and motionless, and a little to one side of the cairn, there hung a singular vessel that I can liken only to a great open barge with upward curving prow and stern. In its center, above the bulwarks, arose a short mast or slender pillar, topped with a fiery, dazzling disk from which the wheel of beams, as if from a hub, poured vertically and transversely. The whole vessel was made of some highly translucent material, for I could see the dim outlines of the landscape beyond it; and the beams poured earthward through its bottom with little diminution of their radiance. The disk, as well as I could tell from the sharply foreshortened position in which I viewed the barge, was the only semblance of mechanism.

It was as if a crescent moon of milky crystal had come down to flood that shadowy nook with its alien light. And the prow of this moon was no more than six or seven feet from the granite wall that formed my place of vantage!

Four beings, whom I can compare to no earthly creatures, were hovering in air about the cairn, without wings or other palpable support, as if they, like the barge, were independent of terrene gravity. Though little less in stature than men, their whole aspect was slight and imponderable to a degree that is found only in birds or insects. Their bodily plasm was almost diaphanous, with its intricate nerves and veinings dimly visible, like iridescent threads through a gauzy fabric of pearl and faint rose.

One of them, hanging aloft before the wheel of beams, with his head averted from my view, was holding in his long, frail hands the cold and lucent star that had topped the cairn. The others, stooping airily, were lifting and throwing aside the fragments that had been piled with such impeccable symmetry.

The faces of two were wholly hidden; but the third presented a strange profile, slightly resembling the beak and eye of an owl beneath an earless cranium that rose to a lofty ridge aigretted with nodding tassels like the topknots of quail.

The tearing-down of the pile was accomplished with remarkable deftness and speed; and it seemed that the pipy arms of these creatures were far stronger than one would have imagined. During the process of demolition, they stooped lower and lower, till they floated almost horizontally, just above the ground. Soon all the fragments were removed; and the entities began to scoop away with their fingers the soil beneath, whose looseness appeared to evince a previous digging at some recent date.

Breathless and awed before the cryptic vision, I bent forward from my eyrie, wondering what inconceivable treasure, what cache of unguessed glory and mystery, was about to be exhumed by these other-world explorers.

Finally, from the deep hollow they had made in the loamy soil, one of the beings withdrew his hand, holding aloft a small and colorless object. Apparently it was the thing for which they had been searching, for the creatures abandoned their delving, and all four of them swam upward toward the barge as if wafted by invisible wings. Two of them took their stations in the rear part of the vessel, standing behind the mast-like pillar and its wheel of rays. The one who bore the shining, star-shaped stone, and the carrier of the dull, unknown object, posted themselves in the prow, at a distance of no more than nine or ten feet from the crag on which I crouched.

For the first time, I beheld their faces in front view, peering straight toward me with glowing, pale-gold eyes of inscrutable strangeness. Whether or not they saw me, I have never been sure: they seemed to gaze through me and beyond—illimitably beyond—into occulted gulfs, and upon worlds forever sealed to the sight of man.

I discerned more clearly now, in the fingers of the foremost being, the nameless object they had dug from beneath the dismantled cairn. It was smooth, drab, oval, and about the size of a falcon's egg. I might have deemed it no more than a common pebble, aside from one peculiar circumstance: a crack in the larger end, from which issued several short, luminous filaments. Somehow, the thing reminded me of a riven seed with sprouting roots.

Heedless of any possible peril, I had risen to my feet and was staring raptly at the barge and its occupants. After a few moments, I became aware that the wheel of beams had begun to turn gradually, as if in response to an unperceived mechanism. At the same time, I heard the eerie whispering of a million flutes, I breathed a rushing gale of Edenic spices. Faster and faster the rays revolved, sweeping the ground and the air with their phantom spokes, till I saw only a spinning moon that divided the crescent vessel and seemed to cleave asunder the very earth and rocks.

My senses reeled with the dizzy radiance, the everpouring music and perfume. An indescribable sickness mounted through all my being, the solid granite seemed to turn and pitch under my feet like a drunken world, and the heavily buttressed junipers tossed about me against the overturning heavens.

Very swiftly, the wheel, the vessel and its occupants took on a filmy dimness, fading in a manner that is hard to convey, as if, without apparent diminishment of perspective, they were receding into some ultra-geometric space. Their outlines were still before me—and yet they were immeasurably distant. Coincidentally, I felt a terrific suction, an unseen current more powerful than cataracting waters, that seized me as I stood leaning forward from the rock, and swept me past the violently threshing boughs.

I did not fall toward the ground beneath—for there was no longer any ground. With the sensation of being wrenched asunder in the ruin of worlds that had returned to chaos, I plunged into grey and frigid space, that included neither air, earth, stars nor heaven; void, uncreated space, through which the phantom crescent of the strange vessel fell away beneath me, bearing a ghostly moon.

As well as I can recollect, there was no total loss of consciousness at any time during my fall; but, toward the end, there was an increasing numbness, a great dubiety, and a dim perception of enormous arabesques of color that had risen before me, as if created from the grey nothing.

All was misty and two-dimensional, as if this new-made world had not yet acquired the attribute of depth. I seemed to pass obliquely over painted labyrinths. At length, amid soft opals and azures, I came to a winding area of rosy light, and settled into it till the rosiness was all about me.

My numbness gave way to a sharp and painful tingling as of frostbite, accompanied by a revival of all my senses. I felt a firm grasp about my shoulders, and knew that my head and upper body had emerged from the rosiness.

For an instant, I thought that I was leaning horizontally from a slowly plunging cataract of some occult element, neither water, air nor flame, but somehow analogous to all three. It was more tangible than air, but there was no feeling of wetness; it flowed with the soft fluttering of fire, but it did not burn.

Two of the strange, ethereal entities were drawing me out on a luminous golden cliff, from which an airy vegetation, hued as with the rainbows of towering fountains, projected its lightly arching masses into a gold-green abyss. The crescent barge and its wheel of beams, now stationary, were hovering close at hand in a semi-capsized position. Farther away, beyond the delicate trees, I saw the jutting of horizontal towers. Five suns, drowning in their own glory, were suspended at wide intervals in the gulf.

I wondered at the weird inversion of gravity that my position evinced; and then, as if through a normalizing of equilibrium, I saw that the great cliff was really a level plain, and the cataract a gentle stream.

Now I was standing on the shore, with the people of the barge beside me. They were no longer supporting me with their frail, firm hands. I could not guess their attitude, and my brain awoke with a keen electric shock to the eerie terror and wildering strangeness of it all. Surely the world about me was no part of the known cosmos! The very soil beneath me thrilled and throbbed with unnameable energies. All things, it seemed, were composed of a range of elements nearer to pure force than to common matter. The trees were like fountains of supernal pyrotechnics, arrested and made permanent in mid-air. The structures that soared at far intervals, like celestial minarets, were built as of moulded morning cloud and luminescence. I breathed an air that was more intoxicating than the air of alpine heights.

Out of this world of marvel, I saw the gathering of many people similar to the entities beside me. Amid the trees and towers, from the shimmering vistas, they came as if summoned by magic. Their movements were swift and silent as the gliding of phantoms, and they seemed to tread the air rather than the ground. I could not hear even the least whispering among them, but I had the feeling of inaudible converse all about me—the vibrant thrilling of overtones too high for the human ear.

Their eyes of pale gold regarded me with unsearchable intentness. I noted their softly curving mouths, which appeared to express an alien sadness, but perhaps were not sad at all. Beneath their gaze, I felt a queer embarrassment, followed quickly by something that I can describe only as an inward illumination. This illumination did not seem to be telepathic: it was merely as if my mind had acquired, as a concomitant of the new existence into which I had fallen, a higher faculty of comprehension impossible in its normal state. This faculty was something that I drew in from the strange soil and air, the presence of the strange multitude. Even then, my understanding was only partial, and I knew there was much that still eluded me through certain insuperable limitations of my brain.

The beings, I thought, were benignantly disposed, but were somewhat puzzled as to what should be done with me. Inadvertently, in a way without parallel, I had trespassed upon another cosmos than my own. Caught in the pull of some transdimensional vortex wrought by the crescent vessel as it departed from earth, I had followed the vessel to its own world, which adjoined ours in transcendental space.

This much I understood, but the mechanics of my entrance into the supernal realm were somewhat obscure to me. Apparently my fall into the rosy river had been providential, for the stream had revived me with its superaqueous element, and had perhaps served to prevent a sort of frostbite that would otherwise have been incurred by my plunge through an interspatial vacuum.

The purpose of the granite cairn, and the visits made by its builders to earth, were things that I could apprehend but dimly. Something had been planted beneath the cairn, and had been left there for a stated interval, as if to absorb from the grosser mundane soil certain elements or virtues lacking in the soil of this ethereal world. The whole process was based on the findings of an arcanic but severely ordered science; and the experiment was one that had been made before. The lucent stone on the cairn, in some way that I could not grasp, had established around it the guarding zone of fluent treadmill space, on which no earthly denizen could intrude. The unearthly changes of the vegetation within this zone were due to certain mystic emanations from the planted seed.

The nature of the seed eluded me; but I knew that it possessed an

enormous and vital importance. And the time for its transplanting to the
otherworld soil was now at hand. My eyes were drawn to the fingers of
the entity who carried it, and I saw that the seed had swollen visibly, that
the shining rootlets had lengthened from its riven end.

More and more of the people had gathered, lining the shore of that
rosy river, and the intervals of the airy boskage, in a silent multitude.
Some, I perceived, were thin and languid as wasting specters; and their
bodily plasm, as if clouded by illness, was dull and opaque, or displayed
unhealthy mottlings of shadow amid the semi-translucence that was
plainly a normal attribute.

In a clear area, beside the hovering vessel, a hole had been dug in
that Edenic soil. Amid the bewildering flux of my impressions, I had not
noticed it heretofore. Now it assumed a momentous import, as the
bearer of the seed went forward to deposit his charge in that shallow pit,
and bury it with a curious oval spade of crystalline metal beneath the
golden element that was like a mixture of loam and sunset glory.

The crowd had drawn back, leaving a vacant field about the planted
seed. There was a sense of awful and solemn and ceremonial expectation
in the stillness of that waiting people. Dim, sublime, ungraspable images
hovered upon the horizon of my thought like unborn suns; and I trembled with the nearness of some tremendous thaumaturgy. But the purpose of it all was still beyond my comprehension.

Darkly I felt the anticipation of the alien throng . . . and somewhere—in myself or in those about me—a great need and a crying hunger that I could not name.

It seemed that whole months and seasons went by; that the five suns
revolved about us in altered ecliptics, ere the end of the interim of waiting. . . . But time and its passing were perhaps obedient to unknown
laws, like all else in that other sphere, and were not as the hours and
seasons of earthly time.

There came at last the awaited miracle: the pushing of a pale shoot
from the golden sod. Visibly, dynamically it grew, as if fed with the sap

of accelerating years that had turned to mere minutes. From it, there burst a multitude of scions, budding in their turn with irised leafage. The thing was a fountain of unsealed glories, an upward-rushing geyser of emerald and opal that took the form of a tree.

The rate of growth was beyond belief, it was like a legerdemain of gods. From moment to moment the boughs multiplied and lengthened with the leaping of wind-wrought flames. The foliage spread like a blown spray of jewels. The plant became colossal, it towered with a pillar-thick stem, and its leafage meshed the five suns, and drooped down toward the river and above the barge, the crowd, and the lesser vegetation.

Still the tree grew, and its boughs came down in glorious arches and festoons, laden with starlike blossoms. I beheld the faces of those about me in a soft umbrage, along arboreal arcades, as if beneath some paradisal banyan. Then, as the festoons hung nearer, I saw the fruiting of the tree: the small globules, formed as of blood and light, that were left by the sudden withering of the starry blossoms. Swiftly they swelled, attaining the size of pears, and descending till they grew well within my reach—and within the reach of that embowered throng.

It seemed that the marvellous growth had attained its culmination, and was now quiescent. We were domed as if by some fabulous Tree of Life that had sprung from the mated energies of Earth and the celestial Otherworld.

Suddenly I knew the purpose of it all, when I saw that some of the people about me were plucking and devouring the fruit. Many others abstained, however, and I perceived that the sanguine-colored pears were eaten only by the languid, sickly beings I have mentioned before. It seemed that the fruit was a sovereign curative for their illness: even as they devoured it, their bodies brightened, the mottlings of shadow disappeared, and they began to assume the normal aspect of their fellows.

I watched them—and upon me there came a kindred hunger, a profound and mystic craving, together with the reckless vertigo of one who is lost in a world too far and high for human tread. There were doubts that woke within me, but I forgot them even as they woke. There were hands that reached out as if to warn and restrain me, but I disregarded them. One of the luscious, glowing pears hung close before me—and I picked it.

The thing filled my fingers with a sharp, electric tingling, followed by a coolness that I can compare only to snow beneath a summer sun. It was not formed of anything that we know as matter—and yet it was firm and solid to the touch, and it yielded a winy juice, an ambrosial pulp, between my teeth. I devoured it avidly, and a high, divine elation coursed like a golden lightning through all my nerves and fibers.

I have forgotten much of the delirium (if delirium it was) that ensued. . . . There were things too vast for memory to retain. And much that I remember could be told only in the language of Olympus.

I recall, however, the colossal expansion of all my senses, the flowering of thought into stars and worlds, as if my consciousness had towered above its mortal tenement with more than the thaumaturgic spreading of the Tree. It seemed that the life of the strange people had become a province of my being, that I knew from all time the arcana of their wisdom, the preterhuman scale of their raptures and sorrows, of their triumphs and disasters.

Holding all this as an appanage, I rose into spheres ulterior and superior. Infinities were laid before me, I conned them as one cons an unrolled map. I peered down upon the utmost heavens, and the hells that lie contiguous to the heavens; and I saw the perennial process of their fiery transmutation and interchange.

I possessed a million eyes and ears; my nerves were lengthened into nether gulfs, were spun out beyond the suns. I was the master of strange senses, that were posted to oversee the activities of unlit stars and blind planets.

All this I beheld and comprehended with the exultation of a drunken demiurge; and all was familiar to me, as if I had seen it in other cycles.

Then, quickly and terribly, there came the sense of division, the feeling that part of myself no longer shared this empire of cosmic immensitude and glory. My delirium shrank like a broken bubble, and I seemed to lose and leave behind me the colossal, shadowy god that still towered above the stars. I was standing again beneath the Tree, with the transdimensional people about me, and the ruddy fruit still burning in the far-flung arches of leafage.

Here, also, the inexorable doom of division pursued me, and I was no longer one, but *two*. Distinctly I saw myself, my body and features touched with the ethereal radiance of the beings who were native to that world; but *I*, who beheld that *alter ego*, was aware of a dark and iron weight, as if some grosser gravity had claimed me. It seemed that the golden soil was yielding under me like a floor of sunset cloud, and I was plunging and falling through nether emptiness, while that other self remained beneath the Tree.

I awoke with the sultry beams of the midday sun upon my face. The loamy ground on which I lay, the scattered fragments of the cairn beside me, and the rocks and junipers, were irrecognizable as if they had belonged to some other planet than ours. I could not remember them for a long while; and the things I have detailed in this narrative came back to me very tardily, in a broken and disordered sequence.

The manner of my return to Earth is still a mystery. Sometimes I think that the supernal people brought me back in that shining vessel whose mechanism I have never understood. Sometimes, when the madness is upon me, I think that I—or part of myself—was precipitated hither as an aftermath of the eating of the fruit. The energies to whose operation I exposed myself by that act were wholly incalculable. Perhaps, in accord with the laws of a transdimensional chemistry, there was a partial revibration, and an actual separation of the elements of my body, by which I became two persons, in different worlds. No doubt the physicists will laugh at such ideas. . . .

There were no corporeal ill effects from my experience, apart from a minor degree of what appeared to be frostbite, and a curious burning of the skin, mild rather than severe, that might have resulted from a temporary exposure to radioactive matters. But in all other senses, I was, and still am, a mere remnant of my former self. . . . Among other things, I soon found that my artistic abilities had deserted me; and they have not returned after an interim of months. Some higher essence, it would seem, has departed wholly and forever.

I have become as it were, a clod. But often, to that clod, the infinite spheres descend in their terror and marvel. I have left the lonely Sierras and have sought the refuge of human nearness. But the streets yawn with uncharted abysms, and Powers unsuspected by others move for me amid the crowd. Sometimes I am no longer here among my fellows, but am standing with the eaters of the fruit, beneath the Tree, in that mystic otherworld.

A STAR-CHANGE

I

It was on Spanish Mountain, where he had climbed from Donner to escape the society of his fellow-campers, that Lemuel Sarkis first met the people of the planet Mlok.

Since he was far from being an expert mountaineer, he had not cared to assail the crowning castellation of the long, somber ridge, but had contented himself with the lower, more accessible eastern terminus. From this, he could look down on the waters of Frog Lake, lying dark and still at the bottom of a bare declivity.

Among volcanic-looking boulders, well out of the wind that swept the upper ridge, he seated himself in morose contemplation while the mountain shadows lengthened, shaken out like lazy wings, and a pale light crept eastward on the waters of black opal below. The vastness of the solitude, its grim and craggy grandeur, began to have a soothing effect upon Sarkis; and the human trivialities and banalities that had driven him to flight assumed their proper insignificance in the mighty perspectives on which he peered.

He had seen no one, not even a sheepherder or fisherman, in his climb through the forested ravines and up the sunflower-covered slopes. He was startled as well as annoyed when a pebble loosened as if by some unheard foot fall clattered past him and went over the precipice. Someone else had climbed the mountain; and his misanthropic aversion rose in a gall-like bitterness as he turned to survey the intruder.

Instead of the tourist or mountaineer he had expected, he saw two beings who bore not even the remotest appearance to humanity, and, moreover, were obviously unrelated to any species of earth-life. Not only for that first startled moment, but during the entire episode that followed, Sarkis wondered if he had fallen asleep and had been visited by some preposterous dream.

Each of the beings was about four feet high, with a somewhat doubtful division into head and body. Their formation was incredibly flat and two-dimensional; and they seemed to float rather than stand, as if swimming through the air. The upper division, which one accustomed to earthly physical structures would have taken for the head, was much larger than the lower, and more rotund. It resembled the featureless disk of a moonfish, and was fringed with numberless interbranching tendrils or feelers like a floral arabesque. The lower division suggested a Chinese kite. It was marked with unknown goblin features, some of which may have been eyes, of a peculiarly elongated and oblique sort. It ended in three broad, streamer-like members, subdividing into webby tassels, that trailed on the ground but seemed wholly inadequate for the purpose of legs.

The coloration of these beings baffled Sarkis. He received alternate impressions of opal-shot blackness, elusive greyness and blood-bright violet.

Impossible, beyond belief, they hung before him among the rocks, swaying forward with a dreamy slowness, as if attached to the ground by their tasseled streamers. Their fringes of woven tendrils seemed to float toward him, quivering with restless life, and certain of their eyelike features gradually brightened and drew his gaze with the hypnotic gleaming of crystals.

The feeling of divorce from diurnal reality increased upon him; for now he seemed to hear a low, insistent humming, to which he could assign no definite source. It corresponded vaguely with the slow vibration of the fringes in its beat and cadence. He heard it all around him in the air, like a mesh of sound; and yet somehow it was inside his own brain, as if the unused cells were thrilling with a telepathic murmur from worlds unknown to man.

The humming grew louder, it took on a partial coherence and artic-
ulation, as if certain semi-phonetic sounds were repeated over and over
in a long-drawn sequence. Still more articulate it grew, seeming to form
a prolonged vocable. Startlingly it dawned upon him that the vocable
was intended for the English phrase, "Come with us," and he realized
that the beings were trying earnestly to convey an invitation by means
of unearthly vocal organs.

Like one who has been mesmerized, without fear or wonder, he
gave himself up to the impressions that besieged his senses. On the flat,
vacant, moonfish disks, very gradually, dim, intricate lines and masses
limned themselves, growing brighter and more distinct till they began to
suggest an actual picture.

Sarkis could comprehend little enough of what he saw; but he received an idea of immense distance and alien, distorted perspective. In
a blare of exotic light, a sea-like flood of intense color, strange-angled
machineries towered, and structures that might have been either buildings or vegetable growths, receded on a ground of baffling dimension
and doubtful inclination. Through this baroque scenery, there floated
forms that bore a slight and incoherent resemblance to the beings who
confronted him: a resemblance like the broken hint of natural shapes
maintained in the utmost perversions of cubism. Together with these
forms, as if convoyed by them, there moved another figure having an
equally remote and dubious likeness to a human being.

Somehow, Sarkis divined that this latter figure was intended for
himself. The scene was a picture of some foreign world or dimension
which these fantastic creatures invited him to visit! Alike in all its details,
the tableau was duplicated on the disks.

With curious lucidity and coolness, he pondered the invitation.
Should he accept it? And if he did accept, what would happen? Of
course, it was all a dream—and dreams were tricky things, with a habit
of vanishing if one tried consciously to fathom their elusive vistas. But—
supposing it were not a dream? From what world, then, had these beings

emerged, and by what mode of transit were they enabled to visit the earth? Surely they could not have come from any planet of the solar system: their utter strangeness seemed to argue that they were children of another galaxy, or at least of another sun than ours.

The beings appeared to perceive his hesitation. The pictures on their bodies faded, and were slowly replaced by others, as if they sought to woo him with the varied sceneries of their native world. At the same time, the humming noise resumed; and after awhile, the equivocal monotone began to suggest familiar words, most of which continued to elude Sarkis. He seemed to make out an eerie prolongation of "offer" and "escape," as if these vocables were uttered by some enormous, droning insect.

Then, through the strange hypnotic sound, he heard the crisp laughter of a girl and the gay chattering of human voices. Plainly several people had climbed the mountain and were coming toward him along the slope, though he could not see them as yet.

The dreamy charm was broken, and he felt a shock of actual fear as well as a deep startlement when he saw that the unknown visitors were still before him. Those intruding human voices had convinced him that the happening was no dream. He felt the involuntary recoil of the earth-born mind from things that are monstrous and inexplicable.

The voices drew nearer behind the rocks, and he thought that he recognized the tones of one or more of his fellow-campers. Then, as he continued to face the apparitions, he discerned above their grotesquely floating forms the sudden flash of sourceless coppery metals that barred the air, hanging aloft like some mechanical mirage. A maze of slanted rods and curving reticulations seemed to hover and descend about the two beings. An instant later, it was gone, and the visitants had also disappeared!

Sarkis hardly saw the approach of a woman and two men, all members of the party he had wished to avoid. To a bewilderment like that of some rudely awakened sleeper, was added the eerie consternation of one who thinks that he has met the supernatural.

A week later, Sarkis had returned to his lodgings in San Francisco and had resumed the tedious commercial art which formed his one reliable source of livelihood. This uncongenial exigency had involved the ruthless smothering of higher ambitions. He had wanted to paint imaginative pictures, had dreamt of fixing in opulent color a fantasy such as Beardsley had caught in ornate line. But such pictures, it seemed, were in small request.

The happening on Spanish Mountain had stirred his imagination profoundly, though he was still doubtful of its actuality. He gave himself to endless speculation, and often he cursed the untimely interruption that had caused the visitants to vanish.

It seemed to him that the beings (if they were not mere hallucinatory images) had appeared in answer to his own vague and undirected longings for the supermundane. Like envoys from a foreign universe, they had sought him out, had favored him with their invitation. Their attempt at verbal communication argued a knowledge of terrene language; and it was plain that they could come and go at will, no doubt by means of some occult mechanism.

What did they want with him? he wondered. What would have been his fate if he had accompanied them?

His pictorial bent for the fantastic was deeply stimulated; and more than once, after his daily stint of advertising-art was done, he tried to paint the visitants from memory. This he found peculiarly difficult: the images with which he sought to deal were without analogy; and their very hues and proportions baffled his recollection. It was as if an alien spectrum, a trans-Euclidean geometry, had somehow been involved.

One eve, he stood glowering with dissatisfaction before his easel. The picture, he thought, was a silly smudge of over-painted colors which utterly failed to convey the true outlandishness of its theme.

There was no sound or other warning, nothing that could consciously attract his attention. But turning abruptly, he saw behind him the two beings he had met on Spanish Mountain. They swayed slowly in the lamplight between the cluttered table and a somewhat shabby divan, trailing their tasseled members on an old rug whose fading floral designs were splashed with fresh paint.

With the loaded brush in his fingers, Sarkis could only stand and stare, held in the same hypnotic thrall that had swept him beyond fear or wonder on the mountain. Once more he beheld the gradual, somnolent waving of the arabesque feelers; again he heard the dreamy monotonous hum that resolved itself into long-drawn vocables, inviting him to go with the visitants. Again, on the moonfish disks, were depicted scenes that would have been the despair of a futurist.

Almost without emotion or thought of any kind, Sarkis gave an audible consent. He hardly knew that he had spoken.

Slowly, as it had begun, the waving motion of the feelers ceased. The consonant humming died; the pictures faded. Then, as before, there came the coppery flash of air-suspended machinery. Broad, oblique rods and concave meshes hovered between ceiling and floor, descended about the alien entities—and about Sarkis himself. Dimly, between the glowing bars, he descried the familiar furnishings of his room.

An instant more, and the room vanished like a film of shadow wiped away in light. There was no sense of movement or of transit; but it seemed that a foreign sky had opened above, pouring down a deluge of crimson. Redness streamed upon him, it filled his eyes with a fury as of boiling blood, it dripped over him in sullen or burning cascades.

By degrees, he began to distinguish outlines and masses. The bars and meshes were still around him, his strange companions were still beside him. They were weirdly altered now, and they swam in the crimson flood like the goblin fish of some infernal sea. Involuntarily, Sarkis shrank away from them: they were terrifying, monstrous.

He saw now that he was standing on a curiously tesselated floor that curved upward on all sides like the bottom of a huge saucer. High, outward-sloping walls, windowless and roofless, towered all about. The mechanism that surrounded him was also topless, and he perceived that it was changing. Very slowly, like dying flames, the rods and meshes sank and disappeared in a circle of small sockets that were part of the floor.

A deep vermilion heaven domed the tower, pouring down the thick, heavy light. The material of which the building was composed, whether stone, metal or some unheard-of element, flowed with lusters of liquid ruby and dissolving cinnabar.

Sarkis became aware that the air he breathed, though well-supplied with oxygen, was uncomfortably thick and seemed to choke his lungs. Also, when he tried to move, he found his weight enormously increased, as if by the gravitation of a gigantic planet.

Where he was or how he had gotten there, he could not imagine. He had nursed an artistic longing for the weird, the otherworldly; but he had never dreamed of this utter and delirious alienation from known things. Moreover, he had not foreseen the shock to human nerves that would ensue an actual transition into another sphere. His sensations of physical discomfort were soon supplemented by a sort of optic torture: the light troubled him, it stimulated his senses cruelly, and yet it stifled and oppressed him at the same time.

A multitude of beings similar to his companions began to enter the topless tower, floating gradually down from the sky or swimming in through low doors. They crowded about him, and he found himself moving toward one of the exits, with their feelers and streamers tugging gently at his limbs. He felt an unreasoning terror at their touch, like a child in the grip of nightmare shadows. Their humming awoke in his brain the thought of some hostile horde of abominably droning insects.

Passing through the doorway, he entered a sea of light in which he was unable to discern clearly the features of the landscape. Almost vertically overhead, he saw the blinding blot of a vast sun. The throng of goblin people, increasing momently, bore him down a grassless, barren slope whose bottom was lost in the inundating crimson.

More and more, he felt an inexpressible malaise, a frightful mixture

of confusion, irritation and depression, to which all his senses contributed. He tried to recall the circumstances of his departure from earth,
tried to assure himself that there was some natural explanation of all that
had happened. The beings whose invitation he had accepted were, he
told himself, friendly and well-meaning, and he would suffer no harm.
But such thoughts were powerless to calm his agitated nerves, now subject to the assault of innumerable vibratory forces which the human system had never been meant to sustain.

The torture deepened. His journey down the slope, rendered doubly
slow by the dragging gravitational pull and the leisurely drifting of his
fantastic entourage, who seemed to obey another and more decelerated
tempo of time than man, was literally a descent into hell. Every impression became a source of pain and terror, and he found a lurking menace
of evil in all that surrounded him.

At the bottom of the slope, a second roofless bowl-shaped tower
loomed from the murk, on the shore of a stagnant sea. To him, at that
moment, it was like a shrine of alien diabolism, hateful and menacing;
and he wanted to scream aloud with a nameless horror when the goblin
creatures bore him toward it and urged him through its portals.

The interior of this tower, yawning to the red sky, was lined with
countless outlandish carvings from floor to top. In the center of the
floor, there stood a curious couch, made from a pile of mattress-thick
fabrics.

Eyeing the couch with nervous dubiety, Sarkis became aware that
the throng had melted away, as if its curiosity were appeased. A mere
half-dozen of the beings remained; and since all were equally monstrous,
he could not be sure if his original companions were among them.

They gathered around him with their hateful droning, pulling him
toward the couch. He resisted, but the tasseled streamers were unbeliev-
ably strong, and they tightened about him, clammily repulsive as the tentacles of octopi. The couch was innocent enough, and no doubt the
creatures were merely offering him a hospitality which, in their own way,

they had tried to accommodate to human needs. But Sarkis felt the terror of a fever patient, whose doctors and attendants seem like hellish torturers.

His last remnant of control gave way, and he shrieked and fought wildly. His own voice assumed an uncanny volume in the thick air, returning upon him deafeningly, surrounding him with ventriloquistic clamors; and he seemed to lift a Sisyphean load as he struggled.

Very gently but firmly, the creatures laid him on the couch. Fearing he knew not what, he still tried to resist them. Two of the beings proceeded to join their streamers across his recumbent body, interlacing the divided ends like fingers; and two others arranged their members in like fashion across his legs. Floating just above the floor, they held him securely to the couch, like doctors who have tied down a delirious patient.

Lying helpless, he saw the remaining two swim skyward and vanish beyond the tower's rim. After awhile he ceased his futile struggling; but his attendants still held him bound with their flat, clammy streamers.

Sarkis lived in an aching torment, whose duration was not to be measured by earthly time. The red sky appeared to descend upon him, heavier and closer; and the enigmatic details of the sculptures on the tower walls perturbed him with sly suggestions of alien foulness and fear. He saw Satanic faces that leered or frowned obscenely, and faceless gargoyle things that seemed to palpitate with malignant life in the cataracting crimson.

The sky took on an awful, ardent glowing. With intolerable slowness, the huge sun, rising to its meridian, filled with its orb the cup that was formed by the tower's rim. The intricate carvings ran with redoubled light, the stellar monsters and gargoyles dripped a venomous ruby that maddened the staring eyes of Sarkis, till he closed his lids against it, and still saw in his branded brain the corrosive, inexorably irritant color. Finally a great blackness came upon him: a sluggish and leaden Lethe, through which he sank interminably, still pursued by floating blots of acrid crimson, before losing himself.

He awoke in a sort of stupefaction, drugged and exhausted, as if his nerves had been burnt out by that cruel debauch of red. With nightmare effort, he opened his eyes to a heaven of funereal violet. The red sun had been succeeded by a purple binary of equal magnitude, whose orb was now intersecting the topless tower with a mournfully glaring crescent.

Sarkis could not collect his shattered thoughts; but a shapeless fear, an awareness of something irremediably wrong and baleful, rose in his mind. He was still held by the streamers of his four attendants; and moving his head, he saw that several others were floating patiently beside the couch. With their adroit members, more supple and capacious than hands, they bore a multitude of strange articles.

Seeing that he had awakened, they swam toward him, proffering certain smooth, elongated, fruit-like objects. One of them held to his lips a shallow bowl filled with a semi-viscid liquor, which he was plainly expected to drink.

Utterly astray and unstrung, Sarkis shrank in renewed terror from these beings. Bathed in that lugubrious violet, their outré forms were cadaverous as dead things from another star. An infinite melancholia poured from the purple sun, cascaded from the sloping walls, jetted from the monstrous carvings. The humming of his attendants, who doubtless sought to reassure him, was heavy with a dirge-like horror. Refusing the offered food and drink, he closed his eyes and lay inert beneath the dismal madness that had fallen upon him.

All that followed was as if part of this madness, and not to be separated from its teeming phantasms. Sarkis was lifted from the couch by his attendants, who formed a sort of cradle with their streamers, in which they carried him from the tower and along some endless road. At intervals he opened his eyes to ghastly-looking plants that swam and swayed in the violet air like sea-weed in an ocean-stream.

Presently he knew that his bearers were descending a steep incline, as if to some deeper circle of this dolorous inferno. Walls that might have been those of a slanted catacomb, lit with a bluish, deathly lambence, stifled him with their closeness.

He found himself at length in a great chamber, whose furnishings, to his distraught eyes, bore the aspect of frightful and multiform instruments of torture. Sarkis' alarm was increased when the flat-bodied people stretched him on a slightly hollowed slab of pale mineral whose fittings of machinery at sides and ends were reminiscent of some medieval rack.

A stony fear weighed down his faculties, arrested his breathing; and he did not resist. One of his presumable torturers was floating above him in the hell-blue light, while the others swam in a sort of ring about the slab. The floating creature laid the fringy tips of its middle streamer on his mouth and nostrils, and he felt an odd shock from the contact. An icy coldness flowed across his face, into his brow and head, into his neck, his arms, his body. It seemed that a strange, benumbing force had been exerted by the creature: the flowing coldness was followed by a loss of all sensation, and a singular detachment from the terror and malaise that had tormented him. Without alarm or speculation, he considered the beings about him, who were now removing his garments and applying to his body the sinister little disks and needle-studded plates that formed part of the slab's mechanical equipment.

It was all meaningless to him; and in some fashion that he did not even try to understand, the whole scene took on an ever-growing dimness and remoteness, as if he were floating away from it—and from himself—into another dimension.

II

His return to awareness was like a new birth. Strangeness there was, such as an infant would find in its surroundings; but fear and pain were wholly gone. He found nothing monstrous or unnatural or menacing in the world that was now revealed to his senses.

Later, when he had learned to communicate easily with the people of Mlok, they told him of the singular and radical operations which they had deemed it necessary to perform upon him: operations involving his nerves and sense-organs, so as to alleviate, by changing all his impressions and even certain subconscious functions, the torment he had suffered from the images and vibratory rays of a world in which the human senses were not prepared to function properly. At first they had not understood his sufferings, since they themselves, being far more adaptive than men, endured little discomfort in passing from one world to another. But, having diagnosed his condition, they had hastened to palliate it through the resources of a preterhuman science.

Just what had been done to him, Sarkis could never wholly grasp; and the results of the operations, admitting him to an entire new range of perceptions, were well-nigh ineffable. His otherworld hosts had wished to make him hear, see, feel and perceive in much the same manner as themselves.

Perhaps the profoundest change was in his visual images. He saw new colors of supernal softness and beauty. The red daylight, which had almost maddened him, was now a clear and nameless hue which he somehow associated with emerald green. The light of the violet binary no longer depressed him, and its ultra-spectral color was remotely allied to pale amber.

His ideas of form had undergone a corresponding alteration. The bodies and members of the alien people, which he had thought almost two dimensional, and which had terrified him with their goblin grotesquery, presented many subtle planes and curves, together with a depth that argued the addition of at least one totally new dimension. The whole effect was aesthetically pleasing, with a fundamental symmetry such as he had previously discerned in well-shaped human bodies. The vegetation, scenery and architecture no longer impressed him as abnormal or monstrous.

His sense of time had now become synchronized with the slow

tempo of the heavy planet, and the speech and movement of the people had lost that former sense of undue prolongation. The thick air, the weighty gravitation, had also ceased to discomfit him.

Moreover, he had acquired several new senses. One of these can best be described as a combination of hearing and touch: many sound images, especially those of high pitch, were perceived by his ears as a local tactility. The sensation was that of a gently varied tapping. Another sense was that of audible color: certain hues were always accompanied by an overtone of sound, often highly musical.

His intercourse with the people of Mlok was carried on through several mediums. After the operations, they could impress telepathic words and images upon his mind. Their other modes of communication, which involved for them less expenditure of energy than pure telepathy, were mastered more gradually by Sarkis. The reflex of thought-pictures, thrown on their bodies as on a screen, became intelligible to him; and the sound-vibration of their arabesque feelers, which served them in lieu of vocal cords, was now fully articulate, with its higher notes perceivable as a graduated tactile pressure.

He learned that his hosts, who called themselves the Mloki after their planet, were an old and highly developed race for whom the marvels of scientific masterdom had become secondary to the delights of pure perception and reflection. Mlok, they told him, was the third planet of a binary solar system in a galaxy so remote, astronomically speaking, that its light had never reached the earth.

The manner in which they had visited the earth and had taken Sarkis to their own world was indeed strange, and involved the use of an arcanic force, which, by projecting itself through the fifth dimension, could exist simultaneously in opposite corners of the universe. The apparatus of coppery-looking bars and meshes which had descended upon Sarkis was composed of this force. How it was controlled and manipulated, he never quite understood, apart from the fact that it was closely obedient to a certain nervous power possessed by the Mlok.

They had often visited the earth, as well as many other alien planets, through curiosity. In spite of their divergent sense-development, they had acquired a surprising knowledge of terrene conditions. Two of them, whose names were Nlaa and Nluu, had found Sarkis on Spanish Mountain, and had perceived telepathically his dissatisfaction with mundane life. Being sympathetic in their way, and also curious concerning the result of such an experiment, they had invited him to accompany them on their return to Mlok.

The real events of Sarkis' life among the Mloki were his new and wonderful sensations. The outward happenings were all very simple, for the existence of this people, apart from their excursions to remote worlds, was almost wholly contemplative.

For his food and drink, they supplied him with many fruits and vegetable juices. The Mloki themselves drew their nourishment directly from the air and light; and their topless towers were designed to collect and focus all the solar rays, the absorption of which was to them a rare, Epicurean pleasure. To a limited extent, the alteration of Sarkis' nerves had given him a similar faculty; but he still depended mainly on grosser foods.

One very remarkable feature of the sensory change in Sarkis was the vagueness which attended his impressions of his own body. He seemed to possess a dream-like immateriality, and to drift rather than walk in his movement from place to place.

He spent much of his time in converse with certain of the Mlok especially Nlaa and Nluu, who took a tutelary interest in their protégé, and never wearied of imparting to him their immensely recondite and various knowledge. He acquired undreamt-of conceptions regarding time, space, life, matter and energy, and was also instructed in novel aesthetics and in highly complicated arts which made painting appear a silly and barbarous pastime.

How long he remained in Mlok, he never knew. His instructors, a long-lived people to whom centuries were no more than years, gave little importance to the formal measurement of time. But many of the long, double days and brief, irregular nights had gone by, before a homesickness for the lost earth began to torment him. Amid all the beguilements and novelties of his existence, beneath his altered senses, a nostalgia rose in his brain, which was still, at bottom, the brain of an earth-man.

The feeling came upon him by degrees. His memories of the world he had formerly detested and from which he had longed to escape, took on a haunting charm and poignancy, and were touched with an enchantment such as belongs to early childhood. He recoiled from the sensory opulence of the world about him, and yearned for the simple scenes and faces of the human sphere.

The Mloki, well aware of the growth of this feeling, tried to distract him with new impressions and took him on a tour of their planet. In this tour, they employed a vessel which swam through the thick air like a submarine in some tellurian ocean. Nlaa and Nluu accompanied the earth-man, solicitous, and eager to point out the marvels of each latitude.

The effect however, was merely to aggravate Sarkis' nostalgia. Peering down on the domeless Karnaks and Babylons of this ultra-cosmic world, he thought of the earth-cities with a craving which, in his quondam aversion for the works of man, he would never have believed possible. Drifting among prodigious mountains, where mundane peaks would have been lost like boulders, he recalled the Sierras with a sick yearning that moved him almost to tears.

After rounding the equator of Mlok, and visiting the iceless poles, the expedition returned to its starting-point, which lay in the tropic realms. Sarkis, now desperately ill and languishing, implored Nlaa and Nluu to send him back by means of the occult force-projector to his own world. They tried to dissuade him, saying that his homesickness was merely a brain-wrought illusion that would wear off in time.

In order to relieve him permanently and speedily from his suffering, they proposed a certain treatment of his brain-cells. By the injection of a rare vegetable serum, they could alter his very memories and mental reactions. These, as well as his sense-impressions, would then approximate those of the Mloki.

Sarkis, though he shrank in a way from the proposed mental transformation, which would have removed him utterly and forever beyond humanity, might well have consented. But certain untoward happenings, wholly unforeseen, were to bring about another eventuation than this.

The planetary system to which Mlok belonged was on the very extreme of its native island universe. In the short intersolar nights, this universe could be seen as a nebulous star-cloud, filling half of the heavens; but the other half was dark and rayless as the Coal Sack familiar to terrene astronomers. It seemed that there were no living stars in the sable gulf, unless at a distance that had not yet permitted their rays to reach the observatories of Mlok.

Nevertheless, there came from this void the first invasion that had ever threatened the security of the two-sunned planet. The first warning of this invasion was a dark cloud—a thing hitherto unknown in Mlok, whose humid element was constant in the thick seas and heavy air, without evaporation or precipitation. The cloud, which had the form of a trapezium, drew down and widened rapidly above the southern zones, doming the sky with intense ebon. It broke on the lands beneath in a rain of black, liquid globules, which acted like a mordant chemical. Flesh, stone, soil, vegetation, everything that was touched by the rain, dissolved instantly, forming tarry pools and rills that soon merged in an ever-spreading sea.

The news of this catastrophe became known immediately all over the planet. The corrosive sea was watched from air-vessels, and every effort was made to curb its inroads. Dykes of atomic energy were built to enclose it; and belts of elemental fire were centered upon the pollution, to burn it away. But all such measures were in vain: the sea like a liquid cancer, ate steadily into the huge planet.

Some of the black fluid was obtained by Mloki who sacrificed their own lives in submitting it to analysis. Even as the element began its ravages upon their bodies, they announced their findings as to its nature. The globules that had fallen from space, they thought, were protoplasmic organisms of an unknown type, which had the power of liquefying all other forms of matter in what was seemingly an illimitable process of assimilation. This process had formed the eroding sea.

Another rain of globules was soon reported, this time in the northern hemisphere. A third precipitation, following swiftly, made certain the eventual doom of Mlok. The people could only flee from the dissolving littorals of the three oceans, which were widening in ravenous circles and would sooner or later unite and surround the planet. It became known, also, that the other worlds of the system, which were not peopled by intelligent beings, had been attacked by the lethal organisms.

The Mloki, a philosophic race, long given to equable meditation on cosmic change and death, were resigned to the coming annihilation. Though they could have fled to alien worlds by means of their space-projectors, they preferred to perish with their planet.

Nlaa and Nluu, however, as well as their fellows in general, now became anxious for the return of Lemuel Sarkis to his own sphere. It was not just or proper, they argued, that he should share the doom of an ultra-terrene people. They had promptly abandoned the idea of subjecting him to further medical treatment, and could only urge his immediate departure.

In a state of oddly bewildered emotions, he was taken by Nlaa and Nluu to the tower through which he had entered Mlok. From the hill on which this tower stood, he could discern the black arc of the encroaching sea of dissolution on the far horizon.

Enjoined by his preceptors, he took his place amid the circle of floor-sockets that formed the generators of the transporting mechanism. With much regret and sadness, he said farewell to Nlaa and Nluu, after vainly pressing them to accompany him.

Since, as they told him, they could determine by means of their thought-images the very spot in which he was to land, he had expressed a desire to return to Earth via his studio in San Francisco. Moreover, since travel in time was no less feasible than space-transit, his mundane reappearance would occur on the morning that had followed his departure.

Slowly, and having now a different form and hue for his altered eyes, the bars and meshes sprang from the tower floor and surrounded Sarkis. All at once, the air darkened strangely. He turned again toward Nlaa and Nluu for a parting glimpse—and found that they, as well as the tower, had vanished. The transition had already taken place!

The pseudo-metallic rods and meshes began to dissolve about him, and he looked for the familiar outlines and furnishings of his studio. A puzzlement assailed him, and then a hideously growing doubt. Surely Nlaa and Nluu had made a mistake, or else the projecting power had failed to return him to his chosen bourn. Seemingly he had been landed in a totally unknown sphere or dimension.

Around him, in a sullen light, he saw the looming of dark, chaotic masses, whose very contours were touched with nightmare menace. Surely this place was not his studio room—these crazily angled cliffs that closed him in were not walls, but the sides of some infernal pit! The dome above, with its dolorously distorted planes, pouring down a hellish glare, was not the skylighted roof that he recalled. The bulging horrors that rose before him along the bottom of the pit, with obscene forms and corrupt hues, were surely not his easel, table and chairs.

He took a single step, and was alarmed by the horrible lightness which he felt. As if by some miscalculation of distance, the step carried him against one of the looming objects, and he ran his hands over it, finding that the thing, whatever it might be, was clammily repulsive to the touch as well as repugnant to sight. Something about it, however, on close inspection, was remotely familiar. The thing was like an overswollen, geometric travesty of an armchair!

Sarkis felt a nervous perturbation, a vague and all-surrounding terror comparable to that of his first impressions in Mlok. He realized that Nlaa and Nluu had kept their word, and had returned him to his studio; but the realization merely increased his bewilderment. Because of the profound sensory changes to which he had been subjected by the Mloki, his perceptions of form, light, color and perspective were no longer those of an earth-man. Therefore the well-remembered room and its furnishings were irredeemably monstrous to him. Somehow, in his nostalgia, and the haste and flurry of his departure, he had failed to foresee the inevitability of this change of aspect in all earthly things.

A hideous vertigo swept upon him with the full understanding of his predicament. He was, virtually, in the position of a madman who knows well his own madness, but is utterly without power to control it. Whether or not his new mode of cognition was closer to ultimate reality than the former human mode, he could not know. It mattered little, in the overwhelming sense of estrangement, amid which he sought desperately to recover the least hint or vestige of the world that he remembered.

With the doubtful groping of one who seeks an exit from some formidable maze, he searched for the door, which he had left unlocked on the evening when he accepted the invitation of Nlaa and Nluu. His very sense of direction, he found, had become inverted; the relative nearness and proportion of objects baffled him; but at last, after many stumblings and collisions with the misshapen furniture, he found an insanely faceted projection amid the perverted planes of the wall. This, he somehow determined, was the door-knob.

After repeated effort he opened the door, which seemed to be of unnatural thickness, with convex distortions. Beyond, he saw a yawning cavern with lugubrious arches, which he knew to be the hall of the apartment house in which he lived.

His progress along the hall, and down the two flights of stairs to the street-level, was like a pilgrimage in some ever-deepening nightmare. The time was early morning, and he met no one. But apart from the maddening visual distortion of everything about him, he was assailed, as he went on, by a multitude of other sense-impressions that confirmed and increased his neural torture.

He heard the noises of the awakening city, set to an alien tempo of delirious speed and fury: a hurtling of cruel clangors, whose higher notes beat upon him like the pounding of hammers, the volleying of pebbles. The ceaseless impingement stunned him more and more; it seemed that the thronging strokes would batter in his very brain.

He emerged at length on what he knew to be the city street: a broad avenue that ran toward the ferry building. The early traffic had begun; and to Sarkis, the passing cars and pedestrians seemed to whirl with lightning speed, like the driven souls of the damned in some nether chasm of an insane hell. For him, the morning sunlight was a balefully tinted gloom that flowed in forky rays from a demonian Eye that brooded above the chasm.

The buildings, with pestilent hues and outlines, were full of the terror of delirium, the abomination of ill dreams. The people were ghastly creatures whose headlong movement barely permitted him to form a clear impression of their bulging eyes, their bloated faces and bodies. They terrified him, even as the people of Mlok beneath the maddening vermilion sun.

The air was thin and bodiless to him, and he suffered a peculiar discomfort from the lessened pressure and gravity, which now added to his feeling of hopeless alienation. He seemed to move like a wildered phantom through the dismal Hades to which he had been committed.

He heard the voices of the monsters who went flying past: voices that partook of the same giddy acceleration as their movements, so that the words were indistinguishable. It was like the sound of some vocal record, played too fast on a phonograph.

Sarkis groped his way along the pavement, searching for some familiar landmark in the alien-angled masses of the buildings. Sometimes he thought that he was about to discover a remembered hotel or shop-front—and then, a moment later, the broken similitude was lost in a mad bizarrerie.

He came to an open space, which he had known as a small park, with well-kept trees and shrubbery amid the greening grass. He had been fond of the place, and its memory had often haunted him in his cosmic homesickness. Now, stumbling upon it in that city of delirium, he sought vainly to retrieve the longed-for charm and loveliness.

The trees and shrubs were like towering fungi of Gehenna, loathsome, unclean, and the grass was a vermin-grey foulness from which he turned in sick revulsion.

Astray in that labyrinth of fear, and virtually out of his senses, he fled at random, and tried to cross an arterial where cars were hurtling by at the apparent speed of projectiles. Here, with no warning that his eyes or ears could perceive, something struck him down like a sudden bolt, and he slid into merciful oblivion.

He awoke an hour later in the hospital to which he had been taken. The injuries which he had sustained, from being knocked down by the slowly driven car before which he had thrust himself as if deaf and blind, were not serious, but his general condition puzzled the doctors.

When, with reviving consciousness, he began to scream horribly, and to shrink away as if in mortal terror from his attendants, they were inclined to diagnose the case as delirium tremens. His nerves were obviously in a bad way; though, curiously enough, the doctors failed to detect the presence of alcohol or any known drug to support their diagnosis.

Sarkis failed to respond to the powerful sedatives which they administered. His sufferings, which seemed to take the form of terrific hallucinations, were prolonged and progressive. One of the internes noted a queer deformation of his eyeballs; and there was much speculation regarding the singular long-drawn *slowness* of his screams and writhings. However, though baffling, his case was readily enough dismissed by the doctors when, a week later, he persisted in dying. It was merely one more of those unsolved enigmas that sometimes occur even in the best-regulated of professions.

THE LAKE OF ENCHANTED SILENCE

It lies within a land that is seen only by the sun and moon and the horizon-questing stars. The sky-wrested mountains, like sentries of Eternity, surround with their immemorial zone of azure-shadowed snows the serenity of the lake's unfathomable dream. They bar therefrom the sound of the aeons that thunder on the shores of Eternity, and the winds that ring with the rumor of iron years, and shut from view all save the azure infinity, and the fires and clouds and shadows of the sky.

The lake is fed with the snows of the mountains, and with silence which flows from the mien of space, and is filled with the blue splendor of the sky. Infinity finds itself doubled therein.

On the shores of the lake grow the blue and white amaranths of a perennial summer, and there is no life save that of butterflies and the most beautiful birds. He who penetrates this land may drink the silence of the lake, and look upon it till the image of infinity fills imperturbably the depths of a mind that has become as calm and smooth as the waters.

THE ETERNAL WORLD

Christopher Chandon went to his laboratory window for a last look at the mountain solitude about him, which, in all likelihood, he would never see again. With no faltering of his determination, and yet not wholly without regret, he stared at the rugged gully beneath, where the Gothic shade of firs and hemlocks was threaded by the brawling silver of a tiny stream. He saw the granite-sheeted slope beyond, and the two nearer peaks of the Sierras, whose slaty azure was tipped by the first autumn snow; and saw the pass between them that lay in a line with his apparent route through the space-time continuum.

Then he turned to the strange apparatus whose completion had cost him so many years of toil and experiment. On a raised platform in the center of the room, there stood a large cylinder, not without resemblance to a diving-bell. Its base and lower walls were of metal, its upper half was made wholly of indestructible glass. A hammock, inclined at an angle of forty degrees, was slung between its sides. In this hammock, Chandon meant to lash himself securely, to insure as much protection as would be feasible against the unknown velocities of his proposed flight. Gazing through the clear glass, he could watch with comfort whatever visual phenomena the journey might offer.

The cylinder had been set directly in front of an enormous disk, ten feet in diameter, with a hundred perforations in its silvery surface. Behind it were ranged a series of dynamos, designed for the development of an obscure power, which, for want of a better name, Chandon had called the negative *time-force*. This power he had isolated with infinite labors from the positive energy of time, that fourth-dimensional gravity which causes and controls the rotation of events. The negative power, amplified a thousand-fold by the dynamos, would remove to an incalculable distance in contemporary time and space anything that stood in its path. It would not permit of travel into the past or future, but would cause an instant projection *across* the temporal stream that enfolds the entire cosmos in its endless, equal flowing.

Unfortunately, Chandon had not been able to construct a mobile machine, in which he could travel as in a rocket-ship and perhaps return as to his starting-point. He must plunge boldly and forever into the unknown. But he had furnished the cylinder with an oxygen-apparatus, with electric light and heat, and a month's supply of food and water. Even if his flight should end in empty space, or in some world whose conditions would render human survival impossible, he would at least live long enough to make a thorough observation of his surroundings.

He had a theory, however, that his journey would not terminate in the midst of mere ether; that the cosmic bodies were nuclei of the time-gravity, and that the weakening of the propulsive force would permit the cylinder to be drawn to one of them.

The hazards of his venture were past foreseeing; but he preferred them to the safe, monotonous certitudes of earthly life. He had always chafed beneath a feeling of limitation, had longed only for the unexplored vastnesses. He could not brook the thought of any horizons, other than those which have never been overpassed by man.

With a strange thrilling in his heart, he turned from the alpine landscape and proceeded to lock himself in the cylinder. He had installed a timing-device, which would automatically start the dynamos at a given hour.

Lying in the hammock beneath leather straps that he had buckled about his waist, ankles and shoulders, he still had a minute or so to wait before the turning-on of the power. In those moments, for the first time, there swept upon him in an unleashed flood the full terror and peril of his experiment; and he was almost tempted to unbind himself and leave the cylinder before it was too late. He had all the sensations of one who is about to be blown from a cannon's mouth.

Suspended in a weird silence, from which all sounds had been excluded by the air-tight walls, he resigned himself to the unknown, with many conflicting surmises as to what would occur. He might or might not survive the passage through unfamiliar dimensions, at speed to which the velocity of light would be laggardly. But if he did survive, he might reach the farthest galaxies in a mere flash.

His fears and surmises were terminated by something that came with the suddenness of sleep—or death. Everything seemed to dissolve and vanish in a bright flare; and then there passed before him a swarming, broken panorama, a babel of impressions, ineffably various and multiplied. It seemed to him that he possessed a thousand eyes with which to apprehend in one instant the flowing of many aeons, the passing of countless worlds.

The cylinder seemed no longer to exist; and he did not appear to be moving. But all the systems of time were going by him, and he caught the scraps and fragments of a million scenes: objects, faces, forms, angles, and colors which he recalled later as one recalls the deliriously amplified and distorted visions of certain drugs.

He saw the giant evergreen forests of lichen, the continents of Brobdingnagian grasses, in planets remoter than the systems of Hercules. Before him there passed, like an architectural pageant, the mile-high cities that wear the sumptuous aerial motley of rose and emerald and Tyrian, wrought by the tangent beams of triple suns. He beheld unnamable things in spheres unlisted by astronomers. There crowded upon him the awful and limitless evolutionary range of transstellar life, the cyclorama of teeming morphologies.

It seemed as if the barriers of his brain had been extended to include the whole of the cosmic flux; that his thought, like the web of some mammoth and divine arachnidan, had woven itself from world to world, from galaxy to galaxy, above the dread gulfs of the infinite continuum.

Then, with the same suddenness that had marked its beginning, the vision came to an end and was replaced by something of a totally different character.

It was only afterwards that Chandon could figure out what had occurred, and divine the nature and laws of the new environment into which he had been projected. At the time (if one can use a word so inaccurate as time) he was wholly incapable of anything but a single contemplative visual impression—the strange world upon which he looked through the clear wall of the cylinder: a world that might have been the dream of some geometrician mad with infinity.

It was like some planetary glacier, fretted into shapes of ordered grotesquery, filled with a white, unglittering light, and obeying the laws of other perspectives than those of our own world. The distances on which he gazed were literally interminable; there was no horizon; and yet nothing seemed to dwindle in size or definitude, whatever its remoteness. Part of the impression received by Chandon was that this world arched back upon itself, like the interior surface of a hollow sphere; that the pale vistas returned overhead after they had vanished from his view.

Nearer to him than any other object in the scene, and preserving the same relative distance as in his laboratory, he perceived a large circular section of rough planking—that portion of the laboratory wall which had lain in the path of the negative beam. It hung motionless in air, as if suspended by a field of invisible ice.

The foreground beyond the planking was thronged by innumerable rows of objects that were suggestive both of statues and of crystalloid formations. Wan as marble or alabaster, each of them presented a mélange of simple curves and symmetric angles, which somehow seemed to include the latency of almost endless geometrical development. They were gigantic, with a rudimentary division into head, limbs and body, as if they were living things. Behind them, at indefinite distances, were other forms that might have been the blind buds or frozen blossoms of unknown vegetable growths.

Chandon had no sense of the passing of time as he peered from the cylinder. He could remember nothing, could imagine nothing. He was unaware of his body, or the hammock in which he lay, except as a half-seen image on the rim of vision.

Somehow, in that strange, frozen impression, he felt the inert dynamism of the forms about him: the silent thunder, the unlaunched lightnings, as of cataleptic gods; the atom-folded heat and flame, as of unlit suns. Inscrutably they brooded before him, as they had done from all eternity and would continue to do forever. In this world, there could be no change, no event: all things must preserve the same aspect and the same attitude.

As he realized later, his attempt to change his own position in the time-stream had led to an unforeseen result. He had projected himself *beyond time* into some further cosmos where the very ether, perhaps, was a non-conductor of the time-force, and in which, therefore, the phenomena of temporal sequence were impossible.

The sheer velocity of his flight had lodged him on the verge of this eternity, like some Arctic explorer caught in everlasting ice. There, obedient to the laws of timelessness, he seemed fated to remain. Life, as we know the term, was impossible for him; and yet—since death would involve a time-sequence—it was equally impossible for him to die. He must maintain the position in which he had landed, must hold the breath he had been breathing at the moment of his impact against the eternal. He was fixed in a catalepsy of the senses; in a bright Nirvana of contemplation.

It would seem, according to all logic, that there was no escape from his predicament. However, I must now relate the strangest thing of all; the thing that was seemingly unaccountable; that defied the proven laws of the timeless sphere.

Into the glacial field of Chandon's vision, athwart the horizonless ranks of immutable figures, there came an intruding object; a thing that drifted as if through aeons; that grew upon the scene with the slowness of some millennial coral reef in a crystal sea.

Even from its first appearance, the object was plainly alien to the scene; was obviously, like Chandon's cylinder and the wall-section, of non-eternal origin. It was black and unlustrous, with more than the blackness of infra-stellar space or of metals locked from light in the core of planets. It forced itself upon the sight with ultra-material solidity; and yet it seemed to refuse the crystal daylight, to insulate itself from the never-varying splendor.

The thing disclosed itself as a sharp and widening wedge, driven upon the adamantine ether, and forming, by the same violent act of irruption, a new visual image in Chandon's paralytic eyes. In defiance of the mental laws of his surroundings, it caused him to form an idea of duration and movement.

Seen in its entirety, the thing was a large, spindle-shaped vessel, dwarfing Chandon's cylinder like an ocean-liner beside a ship's dinghy. It floated aloof and separate—a seamless mass of unbroken ebon, swelling to an orb-like equator, and dwindling to a point at each end. The form was such as might have been calculated to pierce some obdurate medium.

The substance of which it had been wrought, and its motive power, were destined to remain unknown to Chandon. Perhaps it was driven by some tremendous concentration of the time-force with which he had played so ignorantly and ineptly.

The intruding vessel, wholly stationary, hung now above the rows of statuesque entities that were foremost in his field of vision. By infinite gradations, a huge circular door seemed to open in its bottom; and from the opening there issued a crane-like arm, of the same black material as the vessel. The arm ended in numerous pendent bars, that somehow gave the idea of finger-like suppleness.

It descended upon the head of one of the strange geometric images; and the myriad bars, bending and stretching with slow but limitless fluidity, wrapped themselves like a net of chains about the crystalloid body.

Then the figure was dragged upward as if with herculean effort, and vanished at length, together with the shortening arm, in the vessel's interior.

Again the arm emerged, to repeat the bizarre, impossible abduction, and draw another of the enigmatic things from its everlasting station. And once more the arm descended, and a third entity was taken, like the theft of still another marble god from its marble heaven.

All this was done in profound silence—the immeasurable slowness of motion being muffled by the ether, and creating nothing that Chandon's ear could apprehend as sound.

After the third disappearance with its strange prey, the arm returned, extending itself diagonally and to greater length than before, till the black fingers barred the glass of Chandon's cylinder and closed upon it with their irresistible clutch.

He was scarcely aware of any movement; but it seemed to him that the ranks of white figures, the unhorizoned and never-dwindling vistas, were sinking slowly from his ken, like a foundering world. He saw the ebon bulk of the great vessel, toward which he was drawn by the shortening arm, till it filled his entire vision. Then the cylinder was lifted into the night-black opening, where it seemed that light was powerless to follow.

Chandon could see nothing; he was aware of nothing but solid darkness, enfolding the cylinder even as it had been enfolded by the white, achromatic light of timelessness. He felt about him the sense of long, tremendous vibration; a soundless pulsing that seemed to spread in circles from some dynamic center; to pass over and beyond him through aeons, as if from some Titanic heart whose beats defied the environing eternity.

Simultaneously, he realized that his own heart was beating again, with the same protraction as this unknown pulse; that he drew breath and exhaled it in obedience to the cyclical vibration. In his benumbed brain, there grew the nascent idea of wonder; the first beginning of a natural thought-sequence. His body and mind were beginning to function once more, beneath the influence of the power that had been strong enough to intrude upon the timeless universe and pluck him from that petrifying ether.

The vibration began to swiften, spreading outward in mighty ripples. It became audible as a cyclopean pounding; and Chandon somehow conceived the idea of giant-built machinery, turning and throbbing in an underworld prison. The vessel seemed to be forging onward with resistless power through some material barrier. Doubtless it was wrenching itself free from the eternal dimension, was tearing its way back into time.

The blackness had persisted for awhile, like a positive radiation rather than the mere absence of light. Now it cleared away and was replaced by an all-revealing, ruddy illumination. At the same time, the loud, engine-like vibration died to a muted throbbing. Perhaps the darkness had been in some manner associated with the full development of the strange force that had enabled the vessel to move and function in that ultra-temporal medium. With the return into time, and the diminishment of the power, it had vanished.

The faculties of thought, feeling, cognition and movement, under their normal time-aspects, all came back to Chandon like the loosing of a dammed-up flood. He was able to co-relate all that had occurred to him, and infer in some measure the meaning of his unique experiences. With growing awe and astonishment, he studied the scene that was visible from his position in the hammock.

The cylinder, with the weird, crystalloid figures looming near at hand, was reposing in a huge room, probably the main hold of the vessel. The interior of this room was curved like a sphere; and all about and above, gigantic, unfamiliar machineries were disposed. Not far away, he saw the retracted crane or arm. It seemed that the force of gravitation inhered everywhere in the vessel's inner surface; for certain peculiar beings passed before Chandon as he watched, and ran upward on the walls till they hung inverted from the ceiling with the nonchalance of flies.

There were perhaps a dozen of these beings within sight. No one with earthly biological prepossessions could even have imagined them very readily. Each of them possessed a roughly globular body with the upper hemisphere swelling mid-way between pole and equator to form two neckless, conical heads. The lower hemisphere terminated in many limbs and appendages, some of which were used for walking and others solely for prehension.

The heads were featureless, but a glittering, web-like membrane hung between them, trembling continually. Certain of the nether appendages, waving like inquisitive tentacles, were tipped with organs that may have served for eyes, ears, nostrils and mouths.

These creatures shone with a silvery light and appeared to be almost translucent. In the center of the pointed heads, a spot of coal-bright crimson glowed and faded with pulse-like regularity; and the spherical bodies darkened and lightened as if with the rhythmic interchange of rib-like zones of shadow beneath their surfaces. Chandon felt that they were formed of some non-protoplasmic substance, perhaps a mineral that had organized itself into living cells. Their movements were very quick and dexterous, with an inhuman poise; and they seemed able to perform many different motions with perfect simultaneity.

The earth-man was stricken to renewed immobility by the strangeness of it all. With vain, fantastical surmises, he sought to fathom the mystery. Who were these creatures, and what had been their purpose in penetrating the eternal dimension? Why had they removed certain of its inhabitants, together with himself? Whither was the vessel bound? Was it returning, somewhere in time and space, to the planetary world from which it had set forth on its weird voyage?

He could be sure of nothing; but he knew that he had fallen into the hands of super-scientific beings, who were expert navigators of space-time. They had been able to build a vessel such as he had merely dreamt of building; and perhaps they had explored and charted all the unknown deeps, and had deliberately planned their incursion into the frozen world beyond.

If they had not come to rescue him, he would never have escaped from the doom of timelessness, into which he had been hurled by his own clumsy effort to cross the secular stream.

Pondering, he turned to the giant things that were his companions. He could scarcely recognize them in the red glow: their pallid planes and angles seemed to have undergone a subtle re-arrangement; and the light quivered upon them in bloody lusters, conferring an odd warmth, a suggestion of awaking life. More than ever, they gave the impression of latent power, of frozen dynamism.

Then, suddenly, he saw an unmistakable movement from one of the statue-like entities, and realized that the thing had begun to alter its shape! The cold, marble substance seemed to flow like quicksilver. The rudimentary head assumed a stern, many-featured form, such as might belong to the demi-god of some foreign world. The limbs lengthened, and new members of indeterminate use were put forth. The simple curves and angles multiplied themselves with mysterious complexity. A diamond-shaped eye, glowing with blue fire, appeared in the face and was quickly followed by other eyes. The thing seemed to be undergoing, in a few moments, the entire process of some long-suspended evolution.

Chandon saw that the other figures were displaying singular alterations, though in each case the ensuing development was wholly individual. The geometric facets began to swell like opening buds, and flowed into lines of celestial beauty and grandeur. The boreal pallor was suffused with unearthly iridescence, with opal tones that raced and trembled in ever-living patterns, in belted arabesques, in rainbow hieroglyphs.

The human watcher felt the insurgence of a measureless *élan*, of a super-stellar intellection, in these remarkable beings. A thrill of terror, electric, eerie, ran through him. The process he had just seen was too incalculable, too tremendous. Who, or what, could limit and control the unsealed activities of these Eternal Ones, aroused from their slumber? Surely he was in the presence of beings akin to gods, to the demons or genii of myth. That which he beheld was like the opening of the sea-recovered jars of Solomon.

He saw that the marvellous transformation had also been perceived by the owners of the vessel. These creatures, thronging from all parts of the spheroid interior, began to crowd around the timeless entities. Their mechanical, darting motions, the lifting and levelling of certain members that ended in eye-shaped organs, betrayed an unhuman excitement and curiosity. They seemed to be inspecting the transfigured forms with the air of learned biologists who had been prepared for such an event and were gratified by its consummation.

The Timeless Ones, it appeared, were also curious regarding their captors. Their flaming eyes returned the stare of the periscopic tentacles, and certain odd horn-shaped appendages of their lofty crowns began to quiver inquisitively, as if with the reception of unknown sense-impressions. Then, suddenly, each of the three put forth a single, jointless arm, emitting in mid-air seven long, fan-like rays of purple light in lieu of a hand.

These rays, no doubt, were capable of receiving and conveying tactile impressions. Slowly and deliberately, like groping fingers, they reached out, and each of the fans, curving fluctuantly where it encountered a rounded surface, began to play with a rhythmic flaring about the foremost of the double-headed creatures.

These beings, as if in alarm or discomfort, drew back and sought to elude the searching rays. The purple fingers lengthened, encircled them, held them helpless, ran about them in broadening, clinging zones, as if to explore their whole anatomy. From the two heads to the disk-like pads that served them for feet, the beings were swathed around with flowing rings and ribbons of light.

Others of the vessel's crew, beyond reach of the curious beams, had darted back to a more secure distance. One of them lifted certain of his members in a swift, emphatic gesture. As far as Chandon could see, the being had not touched any of the vessel's machinery. But as if in obedience to the gesture, a huge, round, mirror-like mechanism overhead began to revolve in its frame on massive pivots.

The mechanism appeared to be made of some pale, lucid substance, neither glass nor metal. Ceasing its rotation, as if the desired focus had been secured, the mighty lens emitted a beam of hueless light, which somehow reminded Chandon of the chill, frozen radiance of the eternal world. This beam, falling on the timeless entities, was plainly repressive in its effect. Immediately the finger-like rays relinquished their quarry, and faded back to the jointless arms, which were then retracted. The eyes closed like hidden jewels, the opal patterns grew cold and dull, and the strange, half-divine beings appeared to lose their complex angles, to regain their former quiescence, like devolving crystals. Yet, somehow, they were still alive, they still retained the nascent lines of their preternatural efflorescence.

In his awe and wonder before this miraculous tableau, Chandon had automatically freed himself from the leather bands, had risen from the hammock, and was standing with his face pressed against the wall of the cylinder. His change of position was noted by the vessel's crew, and their eye-tentacles were all raised and levelled upon him for a moment, following the devolution of the Timeless Ones.

Then, in response to another enigmatic gesture from one of their number, the giant lens rotated a little further, and the glacial beam began to shift and widen, till it played upon the cylinder though still including in its hueless range the dynamic figures.

The earth-man had the sensation of being caught in a motionless flood of something that was inexpressibly thick and viscid. His body seemed to congeal, his thoughts crawled with painful slowness through some obstructing medium that had permeated his very brain. It was not the complete arrest of all the life-processes that had been entailed by his impingement upon eternity. Rather, it was a deceleration of these processes; a subjection to some unthinkably retarded rhythm of time-movement and sequence.

Whole years seemed to intervene betwixt the beats of Chandon's heart. The crooking of his little finger would have required lustrums. Through tediously elongated time, his brain strove to form a single thought: the suspicion that his captors had been alarmed by his change of posture, and had apprehended some troublous demonstration of power from him, as from the Timeless Ones. Then, through further decades, he conceived another thought: that he himself was perhaps regarded as one of the god-like beings by these alien time-voyagers. They had found him in eternity, amid the measureless ranks; and how were they to know that he, like themselves, had come originally from a temporal world.

With his altered sense of duration, the earth-man could form no proper conception of the length of the voyage in time-space. To him, it was almost another eternity, punctuated at lustrum-long intervals by the humming vibration of the machinery. To his delayed visual perception, the crew of the vessel seemed to move with incredible sluggishness, by imperceptible gradations. He, with his weird companions, had been set apart by the chill beam in a prison of slow time, while the ship itself was plunging through fathomless dimensions of secular and cosmic infinitude!

At last the voyage came to an end. Chandon felt the gradual dawning of an all-pervasive light that drowned the vessel's ruddy glow in fierce whiteness. By infinite degrees, the walls became perfectly transparent, together with the machinery, and he realized that the light was coming from a world without. Immense images, multiform and intricate, began to crowd with the slowness of creation itself upon the glaring splendor. Then—doubtless to permit the removal of the guarded captives—the retarding ray was switched off, and Chandon recovered his normal powers of cognition and movement.

He beheld an awesome vision through the clear wall, whose transparence was perhaps due to the complete turning-off of the vessel's motive-power. He saw that the vessel was reposing in a diamond-shaped area, surrounded with architectural piles whose very magnitude imposed itself like an irremovable weight upon his senses.

Far up, in a fiery orange sky, he saw the looming of bulbous Atlantean pillars with platform capitals; the thronging of strange cruciform
towers; of unnatural cupolas that were like inverted pyramids. He saw
the spiral pinnacles that seemed to support an unbelievable burden of
terraces; the slanting walls, like fluted mountain-scarps, that formed the
base of imagineless cumuli. All were wrought of some shining, night-
black stone, like a marble quarried from an ultra-cosmic Erebus. They
interposed their heavy, lowering, malignant masses between Chandon
and the flames of a hidden sun that was incomparably more brilliant
than our own.

Blinded by the glare and dizzied by those lofty piles; aware also of a
queer heaviness in all his bodily sensations, doubtless due to an increased gravity, the earth-man turned his attention to the foreground.
The diamond area, he now saw, was thronged with people similar to the
crew of the time-vessel. Like giant, silvery, globular-bodied insects, they
came hurrying from all directions on the dark pavement. Arranged in a
ring about the vessel, were colossal mounted mirrors, of the same type
that had emitted the retarding ray. The gathering people stopped at some
little distance, leaving a clear space between the ray-machines and the
ship, as if for the landing of the crew and captives.

Now, as if in response to some hidden mechanism, a huge, circular
door was opened in the seamless wall. The folded crane began to
lengthen, and covered one of the timeless beings with its mesh of tentacles. Then the mysterious entity, still quiet and unresisting, was lifted
through the aperture and deposited on the pavement outside.

The arm returned, and repeated this procedure with the second figure, which, in the meanwhile, had apparently realized the cessation of
the retarding beam, and was less submissive than its fellow had been. It
offered a rather tentative resistance, and began to swell as the tentacles
enfolded it, and to put forth pseudopodic members and finger-like rays
that plucked gently at the tightening mesh. However, in a few moments,

the second being had joined its companion in the world without.

At the same time, a startling change had begun to manifest itself in the third figure. Chandon felt as if he were present at the epiphany of some aeon-veiled and secluded god, revealing himself in his true likeness from the molten chrysalis of matter. The transformation that occurred was as if some chill stalagmite should burgeon forth in a thousand-featured shape of cloud and fire. In one apocalyptic moment, the thing seemed to expand, to rush upward, to change its entire substance, to develop organs and attributes such as could belong only to a super-material stage of evolution. Aeons of star-life, of world-life, of the slow alchemy of atoms, were abridged in that instant.

Chandon could form no clear conception of what was happening. The metamorphosis was too far beyond the normal interpretative range of human senses. He saw something that towered before him, filling the vessel to its roof and pressing terribly against the curved transparent surface. Then, with inestimable violence, the entire vessel broke in a thousand flying, glittering, glass-like fragments, that shrieked with the high, thin note of tortured things as they hurtled and fell in all directions.

Before the last fragments had fallen, the time-cylinder was caught and drawn upward from the wreck as if by some mighty hand. Whether the looming giant had reached down with one of its non-human members, or whether the cylinder had been lifted by magnetic force, was never wholly clear to Chandon. All he could remember afterwards was the light, aerial soaring, in which he experienced a sudden and complete relief from the heavy gravitation of that unknown planet. He seemed to float very swiftly to an elevation hard to estimate, from the absence of familiar scale; and then the cylinder came to rest on the cloud-like shoulder of the Timeless One, and clung there as securely as if it had landed on the shore of some far-off, separate world, aloof in space.

He was beyond awe or surprise or bewilderment. As if in some cataclysmic dream, he resigned himself to the unfolding of the swift miracle. He peered out from his airy vantage, and saw above him, like the

topmost crag of a lofty cumulus, with stormy suns for eyes, the head of
the being who had shattered the alien time-vessel and had risen above
its ruins like a loosed and rebellious genie.

Far down, he beheld the black diamond area that swarmed with the
silvery people. Then, from the pavement, there rushed heavenward, like
the pillared fumes of a monstrous explosion, the mounting and waxing
forms of the other Timeless Ones. Tumultuous, awful, cyclonic, they
rose beside the first, to complete that rebel trinity. Yet, vast and tall as
they had grown, the pylons around them were taller; the terrace-bearing
pinnacles, the topsy-turvy pyramids, the cruciform towers, still frowned
upon them from the glowing, coal-bright air like the dark, colossal
guardians of a transgalactic hell.

Chandon was aware of a thousand impressions. He felt the divine
and limitless energies, waked from eternal sleep, that were flowering
with such dynamic violence in time. And he felt, warring with these,
endeavoring to subdue and constrain them, the jarring radiations and
malignly concentered powers of the new world. The very light was inimical and tyrannous in its fiery beating; the blackness of the lowering
domes and prostyles was like the crushing fall of a thousand muffled
maces, swung by sullen, cruel, silent Anakim. The lens-machines, revolving, glared upward like the eyes of boreal Cyclops, and turned their
frosted beams on the cloudy giants. At intervals, the sky lightened with
a white-hot flaring, like the reflex of a million remote furnaces; and
Chandon was aware of surly, infra-bass, reverberant, bell-toned clangors, of drum-notes loud as beaten worlds, that impinged upon him from
all quarters of the throbbing air.

The environing piles appeared to darken, as if they had gathered to
themselves a more evil and positive ebon, and were raying it forth to
stupefy the senses. But beyond this, beyond all physical perceptions,
Chandon felt the black magnetism that surged in never-ceasing waves;
that clamored before the barriers of his will, that sought to usurp his
mind, to wrest and shape his very thoughts into forms of monstrous

thralldom. Wordless, and conveyed in thronging images of terrible strangeness, he caught the biddings of inhuman bane, of transtellary hatred. The very stones of the massive buildings were joined with the brains of that exotic people in an effort to resume control of Chandon and the three Eternal Ones!

Darkly, the earth-man understood. He must not only submit to the silvery beings, he must do their will in all things. He and his companions had been brought from eternity for a purpose—to aid their captors in some stupendous war with a rival people of the same world. Even as mankind employs in warfare explosives of titanic potency, the silver creatures had desired to employ the time-loosed energies of the Eternal Ones against their otherwise equally matched foes! They had known the route through secret dimensions from time into timelessness. With wellnigh demoniac audacity, they had planned and executed the weird abduction; and they had assumed that Chandon was one of the eternal entities, with latencies of immense *élan* and god-like power.

The waves of evil monition rose ever higher. Chandon felt himself inundated, swamped. With televisic clearness, there grew in his mind a picture of the foe against whom he was being adjured to go forth. He saw the glaring perspectives of remote, unearthly lands, the mightily swarming piles of unhuman cities, lying beneath an incandescent sun that was vaster than Antares. For a moment, he felt himself hating these lands and cities with the cold, imagineless rancor of an otherworld psychology.

Then, as if he had been lifted above it by the giant upon whose shoulder he rode, Chandon knew that the black sea was no longer beating upon him. He was free from the clutching mesmerism, he could no longer conceive the alien emotions and pictures that had invaded his mind. Miraculous ease and sublime security enveloped him; he was the center of a sphere of resistant and resilient force, which nothing could subdue or penetrate.

Sitting as if on a mountain-throne, he saw that the demiurgic triad, contemptuous and defiant of the pygmies beneath, had resumed their magic growth and were shooting upward to attain and surpass the level of the topmost piles. A moment more, and he peered across the Babelian tiers of sullen stone, crowded with the silver people, and saw the outer avenues of a mammoth metropolis; and beyond these, the far-flung horizons of the unnamed planet.

He seemed to know the thoughts of the Timeless Ones as they looked forth on this world whose impious people had dreamt to enslave their illimitable essence. He knew that they saw and comprehended it all in a glance. He felt them pause in momentary curiosity; and felt the swift, relentless anger, the irrevocable decision, that followed,

Then, very tentatively and deliberately, as if they were testing their untried powers, the three beings began to destroy the city. From the head of Chandon's white, supernal bearer, there issued a circle of ruby flame, to detach itself, to spin and broaden in a great wheel as it slanted down and settled on one of the higher piles. Beneath that burning crown, the unnatural-angled domes and inverse pyramids began to quiver, and seemed to expand like a dark vapor. They lost their solid outlines, they lightened, they took on the patterns of shaken sand, they shuddered skyward in rhythmic circles of somber, deathly iris, paling and vanishing upon the intolerable glare.

From the other Timeless Ones, there emanated the visible and invisible agencies of annihilation; slowly at first, and then with cyclonic acceleration, as if their anger were mounting or they were becoming more engrossed in the awful and god-like game.

From out their celestial bodies, as from high crags, there leaped living rivers and raging cataracts of energy; there descended bolts, orbs, ellipsoid wheels of white or vari-colored fire, to fall on the doomed city like a rain of ravening meteors. The builded cumuli dissolved into molten slag, the columns and piled terraces passed in driven wraiths of steam, under the burning tempest. The city ran in swift torrents of lava; it quivered away in spirals of spectral dust; it rose in black flames, in sullen auroras.

Over its ruins, there moved the Eternal Ones, clearing for themselves an instant way. Behind them, in the black and clean-swept levels whereon they had trodden, foci of dissolution appeared, and the very soil and stone dissolved in ever-spinning, widening vortices, that ate the surface of the planet and bored down upon its core. As if they had taken into their own substance the molecules and electrons of all that they had destroyed, the Eternal Ones grew ever taller and vaster.

Chandon beheld it all from his fantastic eyrie with supernal remoteness and detachment. Enisled in a moving zone of inviolate peace, he saw the fiery rain that consumed the ultra-galactic Sodom; he saw the belts of devastation that ran and radiated, broadening ever, to the four quarters; he peered from an ever-loftier height upon vast horizons, that fled as in reeling terror before the timeless giants.

Faster and faster played the lethal orbs and beams. They spawned in mid-air, they gave birth to countless others. They were sown abroad like the dragon's teeth of fable, to follow the longitudes of the great planet to its poles. The stricken city was soon left behind, and the giants marched on monstrous seas and deserts, on broad plains and high mountain-walls, where other cities shone far down like littered pebbles.

There were tides of atomic fire that went before to wash down the prodigious Alps. There were vengeful, flying globes that turned the seas into instant vapor, that smote the deserts to molten, stormy oceans. There were arcs, circles, quadrilaterals of annihilation, growing always, that sank downwards through the basic stone.

The fire-bright noon was muffled with chaotic murk. A bloody Cyclops, a red Laocoön, battling with serpent-coils of cloud and shadow, the mighty sun seemed to stagger in mid-heaven, to rush dizzily to and fro as the world reeled beneath that intolerable trampling of macrocosmic Titans. The lands below were veiled by mephitic fumes, riven momentarily to disclose the heaving and foundering continents.

Now to that stupendous chaos the very elements of the doomed world were adding their unleashed energies. Clouds that were black Himalayas with realm-wide lightning, followed behind the destroyers. The ground crumbled to release the central fires in volcanic geysers, in skyward-flowing cataracts. The seas ebbed, revealing dismal peaks and long-submerged ruins, as they roared in their nether channels to be sucked down through earthquake-riven beds to feed the boiling cauldrons of internal disruption.

The air went mad with thunders as of Typhon breaking forth from his underworld dungeon; with roaring as of spire-tongued fires in the red pits of a crumbling inferno; with moaning and whining as of djinns trapped by the fall of mountains in some unscalable abyss; with howling as of frantic demons, loosed from primordial tombs.

Above the tumult, higher and higher, Chandon was borne, till he looked down from the calm altitude of ether; till he gazed from a sun-like vantage upon the seething and shattered orb, and saw the huge sun itself from an equal height in space. The cataclysmic moan, the mad thunder, seemed to die away. The seas of catastrophic ruin eddied like a shallow backwash about the feet of the Timeless Ones. The furious, all-devouring maelstroms were no more than some ephemeral puff of dust, stirred by the casual step of a passer-by.

Then, beneath him, there was no longer even the nebulous wrack of a world. The being upon whose shoulder he still clung, like an atom to some planetary parapet, was striding through cosmic emptiness; and spurned by its departure, the ruinous ball was flung abyssward after the receding sun around which it had revolved with all its vanished enigmas of alien life and civilization.

Dimly the earth-man saw the inconceivable vastness to which the Eternal Ones had attained. He beheld their glimmering outlines, the vague masses of their forms, with stars behind them, seen as through the luminous veil of comets. He was perched on a nebular thing, huge as the orbit of systems, and moving with more than the velocity of light, that strode through unnamed galaxies, through never-charted dimensions of space and time. He felt the immeasurable eddying of ether, he saw the labyrinthine swirling of stars, that formed and faded and were replaced by the fleeing patterns of other stellar mazes. In sublime security, in his sphere of dream-like ease and miraculous volancy, Chandon was borne on without knowing why or whither; and, like the participant of some prodigious dream, he did not even ask himself such questions as these.

After infinities of flying light, of whirling and falling emptiness; after the transit of many skies, of unnumbered systems, there came to him the sense of a sudden pause. For one moment, from the still gulf, he gazed on a tiny sun with its entourage of nine planets, and wondered vaguely if the sun were some familiar astronomic body.

Then, with ineffable lightness and velocity, it seemed to him that he was falling toward one of the nearer worlds. The blurred and broadening mass of its seas and continents surged up to meet him; he seemed to descend, meteor-like, on a region of rough mountains sharp with snowy pinnacles that rose above somber spires of pine.

There, as if he had been deposited by some all-mighty hand, the cylinder came to rest; and Chandon peered out with the eerie startlement of an awakened dreamer, to see around him the walls of his own Sierran laboratory! The Timeless Ones, omniscient, by some benignant whim, had returned him to his own station in time and space; and then had gone on, perhaps to the conquest of other universes; perhaps to find again the white, eternal world of their origin and to fold themselves anew in the pale Nirvana of immutable contemplation.

THE CHAIN OF AFORGOMON

It is indeed strange that John Milwarp and his writings should have fallen so speedily into a sort of semi-oblivion. His books, treating of Oriental life in a somewhat flowery, romantic style, were popular a few months ago. But now, in spite of their range and penetration, their pervasive verbal sorcery, they are seldom mentioned; and they seem to have vanished unaccountably from the shelves of bookstores and libraries.

Even the mystery of Milwarp's death, baffling to both law and science, has evoked but a passing interest, an excitement quickly lulled and forgotten.

I was well acquainted with Milwarp over a term of years. But my recollection of the man is becoming strangely blurred, like an image in a misted mirror. His dark, half-alien personality, his preoccupation with the occult, his immense knowledge of Eastern life and lore, are things I remember with such effort and vagueness as attends the recovery of a dream. Sometimes I almost doubt that he ever existed. It is as if the man, and all that pertains to him, were being erased from human record by some mysterious acceleration of the common process of obliteration.

In his will, he appointed me his executor. I have vainly tried to interest publishers in the novel he left among his papers: a novel surely not inferior to anything he ever wrote. They say that his vogue has passed. Now I am publishing as a magazine story the contents of the diary kept by Milwarp for a period preceding his demise.

Perhaps, for the open-minded, this diary will serve to explain the enigma of his death. It would seem that the circumstances of that death are virtually forgotten, and I repeat them here as part of my endeavor to revive and perpetuate Milwarp's memory.

Milwarp had returned to his house in San Francisco after a long sojourn in Indo-China. We who knew him gathered that he had gone into
places seldom visited by Occidentals. At the time of his demise he had
just finished correcting the typescript of a novel which dealt with the
more romantic and mysterious aspects of Burma.

On the morning of April 2nd, 1933, his housekeeper, a middle-aged
woman, was startled by a glare of brilliant light which issued from the
half-open door of Milwarp's study. It was as if the whole room were in
flames. Horrified, the woman hastened to investigate. Entering the
study, she saw her master sitting in an armchair at the table, wearing the
rich, somber robes of Chinese brocade which he affected as a dressing-
gown. He sat stiffly erect, a pen clutched unmoving in his fingers on the
open pages of a manuscript volume. About him, in a sort of nimbus,
glowed and flickered the strange light; and her only thought was that his
garments were on fire.

She ran toward him, crying out a warning. At that moment the weird
nimbus brightened intolerably, and the wan early dayshine, the electric
bulbs that still burned to attest the night's labor, were alike blotted out.
It seemed to the housekeeper that something had gone wrong with the
room itself; for the walls and table vanished, and a great, luminous gulf
opened before her; and on the verge of the gulf, in a seat that was not
his cushioned armchair but a huge and rough-hewn seat of stone, she
beheld her master stark and rigid. His heavy brocaded robes were gone,
and about him, from head to foot, were blinding coils of pure white fire,
in the form of linked chains. She could not endure the brilliance of the
chains, and cowering back, she shielded her eyes with her hands. When
she dared to look again, the weird glowing had faded, the room was as
usual; and Milwarp's motionless figure was seated at the table in the posture of writing.

Shaken and terrified as she was, the woman found courage to approach her master. A hideous smell of burnt flesh arose from beneath his
garments, which were wholly intact and without visible trace of fire. He

was dead, his fingers clenched on the pen and his features frozen in a stare of tetanic agony. His neck and wrists were completely encircled by frightful burns that had charred them deeply. The coroner, in his examination, found that these burns, preserving an outline as of heavy links, were extended in long unbroken spirals around the arms and legs and torso. The burning was apparently the cause of Milwarp's death: it was as if iron chains, heated to incandescence, had been wrapped about him.

Small credit was given to the housekeeper's story of what she had seen. No one, however, could suggest an acceptable explanation of the bizarre mystery. There was, at the time, much aimless discussion; but, as I have hinted, people soon turned to other matters. The efforts made to solve the riddle were somewhat perfunctory. Chemists tried to determine the nature of a queer drug, in the form of a grey powder with pearly granules, to whose use Milwarp had become addicted. But their tests merely revealed the presence of an alkaloid whose source and attributes were obscure to western science.

Day by day, the whole incredible business lapsed from public attention; and those who had known Milwarp began to display the forgetfulness that was no less unaccountable than his weird doom. The housekeeper, who had held steadfastly in the beginning to her story, came at length to share the common dubiety. Her account, with repetition, became vague and contradictory; detail by detail, she seemed to forget the abnormal circumstances that she had witnessed with overwhelming horror.

The manuscript volume, in which Milwarp had apparently been writing at the time of death, was given into my charge with his other papers. It proved to be a diary, its last entry breaking off abruptly. Since reading the diary, I have hastened to transcribe it in my own hand, because, for some mysterious reason, the ink of the original is already fading and has become almost illegible in places.

The reader will note certain lacunæ, due to passages written in an alphabet which neither I nor any scholar of my acquaintance can transliterate. These passages seem to form an integral part of the narrative, and they occur mainly toward the end, as if the writer had turned more and more to a language remembered from his ancient avatar. To the same mental reversion one must attribute the singular dating, in which Milwarp, still employing English script, appears to pass from our contemporary notation to that of some premundane world.

I give hereunder the entire diary, which begins with an undated footnote:

This book, unless I have been misinformed concerning the qualities of the drug *souvara,* will be the record of my former life in a lost cycle. I have had the drug in my possession for seven months, but fear has prevented me from using it. Now, by certain tokens, I perceive that the longing for knowledge will soon overcome the fear.

Ever since my earliest childhood I have been troubled by intimations, dim, unplaceable, that seemed to argue a forgotten existence. These intimations partook of the nature of feelings rather than ideas or images: they were like the wraiths of dead memories. In the background of my mind there has lurked a sentiment of formless, melancholy desire for some nameless beauty long perished out of time. And, coincidentally, I have been haunted by an equally formless dread, an apprehension as of some bygone but still imminent doom.

Such feelings have persisted, undiminished, throughout my youth and maturity, but nowhere have I found any clue to their causation. My travels in the mystic Orient, my delvings into occultism have merely convinced me that these shadowy intuitions pertain to some incarnation buried under the wreck of remotest cycles.

Many times, in my wanderings through Buddhistic lands, I had heard of the drug *souvara,* which is believed to restore, even for the uninitiate, the memory of other lives. And at last, after many vain efforts, I managed to procure a supply of the drug. The manner in which I obtained it is a tale sufficiently remarkable in itself, but of no special relevance here. So far—perhaps because of that apprehension which I have hinted—I have not dared to use the drug.

March 9th, 1933. This morning I took *souvara* for the first time, dissolving the proper amount in pure distilled water as I had been instructed to do. Afterwards I leaned back easily in my chair, breathing with a slow, regular rhythm. I had no preconceived idea of the sensations that would mark the drug's initial effect, since these were said to vary prodigiously with the temperament of the users; but I composed myself to await them with tranquility, after formulating clearly in my mind the purpose of the experiment.

For awhile there was no change in my awareness. I noticed a slight quickening of the pulse, and modulated my breathing in conformity with this. Then, by slow degrees, I experienced a sharpening of visual perception. The Chinese rugs on the floor, the backs of the serried volumes in my bookcases, the very wood of chairs, table and shelves, began to exhibit new and unimagined colors. At the same time there were curious alterations of outline, every object seeming to extend itself in a hitherto unsuspected fashion. Following this, my surroundings became semi-transparent, like moulded shapes of mist. I found that I could see through the marbled cover the illustrations in a volume of John Martin's edition of *Paradise Lost,* which lay before me on the table.

All this, I knew, was a mere extension of ordinary physical vision. It was only a prelude to those apperceptions of occult realms which I sought through *souvara.* Fixing my mind once more on the goal of the experiment, I became aware that the misty walls had vanished like a drawn arras. About me, like reflections in rippled water, dim sceneries wavered and shifted, erasing one another from instant to instant. I seemed to hear a vague but ever-present sound, more musical than the murmurs of air, water or fire, which was a property of the unknown element that environed me.

With a sense of troublous familiarity, I beheld the blurred unstable pictures which flowed past me upon this never-resting medium. Orient temples, flashing with sun-struck bronze and gold; the sharp, crowded gables and spires of medieval cities; tropic and northern forests; the costumes and physiognomies of the Levant, of Persia, of old Rome and Carthage, went by like blown, flying mirages. Each succeeding tableau belonged to a more ancient period than the one before it—and I knew that each was a scene from some former existence of my own.

Still tethered, as it were, to my present self, I reviewed these visible memories, which took on tri-dimensional depth and clarity. I saw myself as warrior and troubadour, as noble and merchant and mendicant. I trembled with dead fears, I thrilled with lost hopes and raptures, and was drawn by ties that death and Lethe had broken. Yet never did I fully identify myself with those other avatars: for I knew well that the memory I sought pertained to some incarnation of older epochs.

Still the phantasmagoria streamed on, and I turned giddy with vertigo ineffable before the vastness and diuturnity of the cycles of being. It seemed that I, the watcher, was lost in a grey land where the homeless ghosts of all dead ages went fleeing from oblivion to oblivion.

The walls of Nineveh, the columns and towers of unnamed cities, rose before me and were swept away. I saw the luxuriant plains that are now the Gobi desert. The sea-lost capitals of Atlantis were drawn to the light in unquenched glory. I gazed on lush and cloudy scenes from the first continents of Earth. Briefly I relived the beginnings of terrestrial man—and knew that the secret I would learn was ancienter even than these.

My visions faded into black voidness—and yet, in that void, through fathomless eons, it seemed that I existed still like a blind atom in the space between the worlds. About me was the darkness and repose of that night which antedated the earth's creation. Time flowed backward with the silence of dreamless sleep. . . .

The illumination, when it came, was instant and complete. I stood in the full, fervid blaze of day amid royally towering blossoms in a deep garden, beyond whose lofty, vine-clad walls I heard the confused murmuring of the great city called Kalood. Above me, at their vernal zenith, were the four small suns that illumed the planet Hestan. Jewel-colored insects fluttered about me, lighting without fear on the rich habiliments of gold and black, enwrought with astronomic symbols, in which I was attired. Beside me was a dial-shaped altar of zoned agate, carved with the same symbols, which were those of the dreadful omnipotent time-god, Aforgomon, whom I served as a priest.

I had not even the slightest memory of myself as John Milwarp, and the long pageant of my terrestrial lives was as something that had never been—or was yet to be. Sorrow and desolation choked my heart as ashes fill some urn consecrated to the dead; and all the hues and perfumes of the garden about me were redolent only of the bitterness of death. Gazing darkly upon the altar, I muttered blasphemy against Aforgomon, who, in his inexorable course, had taken away my beloved and had sent no solace for my grief. Separately I cursed the signs upon the altar: the stars, the worlds, the suns, the moons, that meted and fulfilled the processes of time. Belthoris, my betrothed, had died at the end of the previous autumn: and so, with double maledictions, I cursed the stars and planets presiding over that season.

I became aware that a shadow had fallen beside my own on the altar, and knew that the dark sage and sorcerer Atmox had obeyed my summons. Fearfully but not without hope I turned toward him, noting first of all that he bore under his arm a heavy, sinister-looking volume with covers of black steel and hasps of adamant. Only when I had made sure of this did I lift my eyes to his face, which was little less somber and forbidding than the tome he carried.

"Greeting, O Calaspa," he said harshly. "I have come against my own will and judgment. The lore that you request is in this volume; and since you saved me in former years from the inquisitorial wrath of the time-god's priests, I cannot refuse to share it with you. But understand well that even I, who have called upon names that are dreadful to utter, and have evoked forbidden presences, shall never dare to assist you in this conjuration. Gladly would I help you to hold converse with the shadow of Belthoris, or to animate her still unwithered body and draw it forth from the tomb. But that which you purpose is another matter. You alone must perform the ordained rites, must speak the necessary words: for the consequences of this thing will be direr than you deem."

"I care not for the consequences," I replied eagerly, "if it be possible to bring back the lost hours which I shared with Belthoris. Think you that I could content myself with her shadow, wandering thinly back from the Borderland? Or that I could take pleasure in the fair clay that the breath of necromancy has troubled and has made to arise and walk without mind or soul? Nay, the Belthoris I would summon is she on whom the shadow of death has never yet fallen!"

It seemed that Atmox, the master of doubtful arts, the vassal of umbrageous powers, recoiled and blenched before my vehement declaration.

"Bethink you," he said with minatory sternness, "that this thing will constitute a breach of the sacred logic of time and a blasphemy against Aforgomon, god of the minutes and the cycles. Moreover, there is little to be gained: for not in its entirety may you bring back the season of your love, but only one single hour, torn with infinite violence from its rightful period in time. . . . Refrain, I adjure you, and content yourself with a lesser sorcery."

"Give me the book," I demanded. "My service to Aforgomon is forfeit. With due reverence and devotion I have worshipped the time-god, and have done in his honor the rites ordained from eternity; and for all this the god has betrayed me."

Then, in that high-climbing, luxuriant garden beneath the four suns, Atmox opened the adamantine clasps of the steel-bound volume; and, turning to a certain page, he laid the book reluctantly in my hands. The page, like its fellows, was of some unholy parchment streaked with musty discolorations and blackening at the margin with sheer antiquity;

but upon it shone unquenchably the dread characters a primal archimage had written with an ink bright as the new-shed ichor of demons. Above this page I bent in my madness, conning it over and over till I was dazzled by the fiery runes; and, shutting my eyes, I saw them burn on a red darkness, still legible, and writhing like hellish worms.

Hollowly, like the sound of a far bell, I heard the voice of Atmox: "You have learned, O Calaspa, the unutterable name of that One whose assistance can alone restore the fled hours. And you have learned the incantation that will rouse that hidden power, and the sacrifice needed for its propitiation. Knowing these things, is your heart still strong and your purpose firm?"

The name I had read in the wizard volume was that of the chief cosmic power antagonistic to Aforgomon; the incantation and the required offering were those of a foul demonolatry. Nevertheless, I did not hesitate, but gave resolute affirmative answer to the somber query of Atmox.

Perceiving that I was inflexible, he bowed his head, trying no more to dissuade me. Then, as the flame-runed volume had bade me do, I defiled the altar of Aforgomon, blotting certain of its prime symbols with dust and spittle. While Atmox looked on in silence, I wounded my right arm to its deepest vein on the sharp-tipped gnomon of the dial; and, letting the blood drip from zone to zone, from orb to orb on the graven agate, I made unlawful sacrifice, and intoned aloud, in the name of the Lurking Chaos, Xexanoth, an abominable ritual composed by a backward repetition and jumbling of litanies sacred to the time-god.

Even as I chanted the incantation, it seemed that webs of shadow were woven foully athwart the suns; and the ground shook a little, as if colossal demons trod the world's rim, striding stupendously from abysses beyond. The garden walls and trees wavered like a wind-blown reflection in a pool; and I grew faint with the loss of that life-blood I had poured out in demonolatrous offering. Then, in my flesh and in my brain, I felt the intolerable racking of a vibration like the long-drawn shock of cities riven by earthquake, and coasts crumbling before some chaotic sea; and my flesh was torn and harrowed infinitely, and my brain shuddered with the toneless discords sweeping through me from deep to deep.

I faltered, and confusion gnawed at my inmost being. Dimly I heard the prompting of Atmox, and dimmer still was the sound of my own voice that made answer to Xexanoth, naming the impious necromancy which was to be effected only through its power. Madly I implored from Xexanoth, in despite of time and its ordered seasons, one hour of that bygone autumn which I had shared with Belthoris; and imploring this, I named no special hour: for all, in memory, had seemed of an equal joy and gladness.

As the words ceased upon my lips, I thought that darkness fluttered in the air like a great wing; and the four suns went out, and my heart was stilled as if in death. Then the light returned, falling obliquely from suns mellow with full-tided autumn; and nowhere beside me was there any shadow of Atmox; and the altar of zoned agate was bloodless and unde-filed. I, the lover of Belthoris, witting not of the doom and sorrow to come, stood happily with my beloved before the altar, and saw her young hands crown its ancient dial with the flowers we had plucked from the garden.

Dreadful beyond all fathoming are the mysteries of time. Even I, the priest and initiate, though wise in the secret doctrines of Aforgomon, know little enough of that elusive, ineluctable process whereby the pre-sent becomes the past and the future resolves itself into the present. All men have pondered the riddles of duration and transience; have won-dered, vainly, to what bourn the lost days and the sped cycles are con-signed. Some have dreamt that the past abides unchanged, becoming eternity as it slips from our mortal ken; and others have deemed that time is a stairway whose steps crumble one by one behind the climber, falling into a gulf of nothing.

Howsoever this may be, I know that she who stood beside me was the Belthoris on whom no shadow of mortality had yet descended. The hour was one newborn in a golden season; and the minutes to come were pregnant with all wonder and surprise belonging to the untried future.

Taller was my beloved than the frail, unbowed lilies of the garden. In her eyes was the sapphire of moonless evenings sown with small golden stars. Her lips were strangely curved, but only blitheness and joy had gone to their shaping.

She and I had been betrothed from our childhood, and the time of the marriage-rites was now approaching. Our intercourse was wholly free, according to the custom of that world. Often she came to walk with me in my garden and to decorate the altar of that god whose revolving moons and suns would soon bring the season of our felicity.

The moths that flew about us, winged with aerial cloth-of-gold, were no lighter than our hearts. Making blithe holiday, we fanned our frolic mood to a high flame of rapture. We were akin to the full-hued, climbing flowers, the swift-darting insects, and our spirits blended and soared with the perfumes that were drawn skyward in the warm air. Unheard by us was the loud murmuring of the mighty city of Kalood lying beyond my garden walls; for us the many-peopled planet known as Hestan no longer existed; and we dwelt alone in a universe of light, in a blossomed heaven. Exalted by love in the high harmony of those moments, we seemed to touch eternity; and even I, the priest of Aforgomon, forgot the blossom-fretting days, the system-devouring cycles.

In the sublime folly of passion, I swore then that death or discord could never mar the perfect communion of our hearts. After we had wreathed the altar, I sought the rarest, the most delectable flowers: frail-curving cups of wine-washed pearl, of moony azure and white with scrolled purple lips; and these I twined, between kisses and laughter, in the black maze of Belthoris' hair; saying that another shrine than that of time should receive its due offering.

Tenderly, with a lover's delay, I lingered over the wreathing; and, ere I had finished, there fluttered to the ground beside us a great, crimson-spotted moth whose wing had somehow been broken in its airy voyaging through the garden. And Belthoris, ever tender of heart and pitiful, turned from me and took up the moth in her hands; and some of the bright blossoms dropped from her hair unheeded. Tears welled from her deep blue eyes; and seeing that the moth was sorely hurt and would never fly again, she refused to be comforted; and no longer would she respond to my passionate wooing. I, who grieved less for the moth than she, was somewhat vexed; and between her sadness and my vexation, there grew between us some tiny, temporary rift. . . .

Then, ere love had mended the misunderstanding; then, while we stood before the dread altar of time with sundered hands, with eyes averted from each other, it seemed that a shroud of darkness descended upon the garden. I heard the crash and crumbling of shattered worlds, and a black flowing of ruinous things that went past me through the darkness. The dead leaves of winter were blown about me, and there was a falling of tears or rain. . . . Then the vernal suns came back, high-stationed in cruel splendor; and with them came the knowledge of all that had been, of Belthoris' death and my sorrow, and the madness that had led to forbidden sorcery. Vain now, like all other hours, was the resummoned hour; and doubly irredeemable was my loss. My blood dripped heavily on the dishallowed altar, my faintness grew deathly, and I saw through murky mist the face of Atmox beside me; and the face was like that of some comminatory demon. . . .

March 13th. I, John Milwarp, write this date and my name with an odd dubiety. My visionary experience under the drug *souvara* ended with that rilling of my blood on the symboled dial, that glimpse of the terror-distorted face of Atmox. All this was in another world, in a life removed from the present by births and deaths without number; and yet, it seems, not wholly have I returned from the twice-ancient past. Memories, broken but strangely vivid and living, press upon me from the existence of which my vision was a fragment; and portions of the lore of Hestan, and scraps of its history, and words from its lost language, arise unbidden in my mind.

Above all, my heart is still shadowed by the sorrow of Calaspa. His desperate necromancy, which would seem to others no more than a

dream within a dream, is stamped as with fire on the black page of recollection. I know the awfulness of the god he had blasphemed, and the
foulness of the demonolatry he had done, and the sense of guilt and
despair under which he swooned. It is *this* that I have striven all my life
to remember, this which I have been doomed to re-experience. And I
fear with a great fear the further knowledge which a second experiment
with the drug will reveal to me.

EDITOR'S NOTE. The next entry of Milwarp's diary begins with a
strange dating in English script: "The second day of the moon Occalat,
in the thousand-and-ninth year of the Red Aeon." This dating, perhaps,
is repeated in the language of Hestan: for, directly beneath it, a line of
unknown ciphers is set apart. Several lines of the subsequent text are in
the alien tongue; and then, as if by an unconscious reversion, Milwarp
continues the diary in English. There is no reference to another experiment with *souvara*. but apparently such had been made, with a continued
revival of his lost memories.

. . . What genius of the nadir gulf had tempted me to this thing and had
caused me to overlook the consequences? Verily, when I called up for
myself and Belthoris an hour of former autumn, with all that was at-
tendant upon the hour, *that bygone interim was likewise evoked and repeated for*
the whole world Hestan, and the four suns of Hestan. From the full midst of
spring, all men had stepped backward into autumn, keeping only the
memory of things prior to the hour thus resurrected, and knowing not
the events future to the hour. But, returning to the present, they recalled
with amazement the unnatural necromancy; and fear and bewilderment
were upon them; and none could interpret the meaning.

For a brief period, the dead had lived again; the fallen leaves had
returned to the bough; the heavenly bodies had stood at a long-aban-
doned station; the flower had gone back into the seed, the plant into the
root. Then, with eternal disorder set among all its cycles, time had resumed its delayed course.

No movement of any cosmic body, no year or instant of the future, would be precisely as it should have been. The error and discrepancy I had wrought would bear fruit in ways innumerable. The suns would find themselves at fault; the worlds and atoms would go always a little astray from their appointed bourns.

It was of these matters that Atmox spoke, warning me, after he had staunched my bleeding wound. For he too, in that relumined hour, had gone back and had lived again through a past happening. For him the hour was one in which he had descended into the nether vaults of his house. There, standing in a many-pentacled circle, with burning of unholy incense and uttering of accurst formulæ, he had called up a malign spirit from the bowels of Hestan and had questioned it concerning the future. But the spirit, black and voluminous as the fumes of pitch, refused to answer him directly and pressed furiously with its clawed members against the confines of the circle. It said only: "Thou hast summoned me at thy peril. Potent are the spells thou hast used, and strong is the circle to withstand me, and I am restrained by time and space from the wreaking of my anger upon thee. *But haply thou shalt summon me again, albeit in the same hour of the same autumn;* and in that summoning the laws of time shall be broken, and a rift shall be made in space; and through the rift, though with some delay and divagation, I shall yet win to thee."

Saying no more, it prowled restlessly about the circle; and its eyes burned down upon Atmox like embers in a high-lifted sooty brazier; and ever and anon its fanged mouth was flattened on the spell-defended air. And in the end he could dismiss it only after a double repetition of the form of exorcism.

As he told me this tale in the garden, Atmox trembled; and his eyes searched the narrow shadows wrought by the high suns; and he seemed to listen for the noise of some evil thing that burrowed toward him beneath the earth.

Fourth day of the moon Occalat. Stricken with terrors beyond those of Atmox, I kept apart in my mansion amid the city of Kalood. I was still

weak with the loss of the blood I had yielded to Xexanoth; my senses
were full of strange shadows; my servitors, coming and going about me,
were as phantoms, and scarcely I heeded the pale fear in their eyes or
heard the dreadful things they whispered. . . . Madness and chaos, they
told me, were abroad in Kalood; the divinity of Aforgomon was angered.
All men thought that some baleful doom impended because of that unnatural confusion which had been wrought among the hours of time.

This afternoon they brought me the story of Atmox's death. In
bated tones they told me how his neophytes had heard a roaring as of a
loosed tempest in the chamber where he sat alone with his wizard volumes and paraphernalia. Above the roaring, for a little, human screams
had sounded, together with a clashing as of hurled censers and braziers,
a crashing as of overthrown tables and tomes. Blood rilled from under
the shut door of the chamber, and, rilling, it took from instant to instant
the form of dire ciphers that spelt an unspeakable name. After the noises
had ceased the neophytes waited a long while ere they dared to open the
door. Entering at last, they saw the floor and the walls heavily bespat-
tered with blood, and rags of the sorcerer's raiment mingled everywhere
with the sheets of his torn volumes of magic, and the shreds and mang-
lings of his flesh strewn amid broken furniture, and his brains daubed in
a horrible paste on the high ceiling.

Hearing this tale, I knew that the earthly demon feared by Atmox
had found him somehow and had wreaked its wrath upon him. In ways
unguessable, it had reached him through the chasm made in ordered
time and space by one hour repeated through necromancy. And because
of that lawless chasm, the magician's power and lore had utterly failed
to defend him from the demon. . . .

Fifth day of the moon Occalat. Atmox, I am sure, had not betrayed me:
for in so doing, he must have betrayed his own implicit share in my
crime. . . . Howbeit, this evening the priests came to my house ere the
setting of the westernmost sun: silent, grim, with eyes averted as if from
a foulness innominable. Me, their fellow, they enjoined with loath gestures

to accompany them. . . . Thus they took me from my house and along the thoroughfares of Kalood toward the lowering suns. The streets were empty of all other passers, and it seemed that no man desired to meet or behold the blasphemer. . . . Down the avenue of gnomon-shaped pillars, I was led to the portals of Aforgomon's fane: those awfully gaping portals arched in the likeness of some devouring chimera's mouth. . . .

Sixth day of the moon Occalat. They had thrust me into an oubliette beneath the temple, dark, noisome and soundless except for the maddening, measured drip of water beside me. There I lay and knew not when the night passed and the morning came. Light was admitted only when my captors opened the iron door, coming to lead me before the tribunal. . . .

. . . Thus the priests condemned me, speaking with one voice in whose dreadful volume the tones of all were indistinguishably blended. Then the aged high-priest Helpenor called aloud upon Aforgomon, offering himself as a mouth-piece to the god, and asking the god to pronounce through him the doom that was adequate for such enormities as those of which I had been judged guilty by my fellows.

Instantly, it seemed, the god descended into Helpenor; and the figure of the high-priest appeared to dilate prodigiously beneath his mufflings; and the accents that issued from his mouth were like thunders of the upper heaven:

"O Calaspa, thou hast set disorder amid all future hours and aeons through this evil necromancy. Thereby, moreover, thou hast wrought thine own doom: fettered art thou forever to the hour thus unlawfully repeated, apart from its due place in time. According to hieratic rule, thou shalt meet the death of the fiery chains: but deem not that this death is more than the symbol of thy true punishment. Thou shalt pass hereafter through other lives in Hestan, and shalt climb midway in the cycles of the world subsequent to Hestan in time and space. But through all thine incarnations the chaos thou hast invoked will attend thee, widening ever like a rift. And always, in all thy lives, the rift will bar thee from reunion with the soul of Belthoris; and always, though merely by an hour, thou shalt miss the love that should otherwise have been oftentimes regained.

"At last, when the chasm has widened overmuch, thy soul shall fare no farther in the onward cycles of incarnation. At that time it shall be given thee to remember clearly thine ancient sin; and remembering, thou shalt perish out of time. Upon the body of that latter life shall be found the charred imprint of the chains, as the final token of thy bondage. But they that knew thee will soon forget, and thou shalt belong wholly to the cycles limited for thee by thy sin."

March 29th. I write this date with infinite desperation, trying to convince myself that there is a John Milwarp who exists on Earth, in the twentieth century. For two days running, I have not taken the drug *souvara*: and yet I have returned twice to that oubliette of Aforgomon's temple, in which the priest Calaspa awaits his doom. Twice I have been immersed in its stagnant darkness, hearing the slow drip of water beside me, like a clepsydra that tells the black ages of the damned.

Even as I write this at my library table, it seems that an ancient midnight plucks at the lamp. The bookcases turn to walls of oozing, nighted stone. There is no longer a table . . . nor one who writes . . . and I breathe the noisome dankness of a dungeon lying unfathomed by any sun, in a lost world.

Eighteenth day of the moon Occalat. Today, for the last time, they took me from my prison. Helpenor, together with three others, came and led me to the adytum of the god. Far beneath the outer temple we went, through spacious crypts unknown to the common worshippers. There was no word spoken, no glance exchanged between the others and me; and it seemed that they already regarded me as one cast out from time and claimed by oblivion.

We came ultimately to that sheer-falling gulf in which the spirit of Aforgomon is said to dwell. Lights, feeble and far-scattered, shone around it like stars on the rim of cosmic vastness, shedding no ray into the depths. There, in a seat of hewn stone overhanging the frightful verge, I was placed by the executioners; and a ponderous chain of black unrusted metal, stapled in the solid rock, was wound about and about me, circling my naked body and separate limbs, from head to foot.

To this doom, others had been condemned for heresy or impiety . . . though never for a sin such as mine. After the chaining of the victim, he was left alone for a stated interim, to ponder his crime—and haply to confront the dark divinity of Aforgomon. At length, from the abyss into which his position forced him to peer, a light would dawn, and a bolt of strange flame would leap upward, striking the many-coiled chain about him and heating it instantly to the whiteness of candescent iron. The source and nature of the flame were mysterious, and many ascribed it to the god himself rather than to mortal agency. . . .

Even thus they have left me, and have gone away. Long since the burden of the massy links, cutting deeper and deeper into my flesh, has become an agony. I am dizzy from gazing downward into the abyss— and yet I cannot fall. Beneath, immeasurably beneath, at recurrent intervals, I hear a hollow and solemn sound. Perhaps it is the sigh of sunken waters . . . of cavern-straying winds . . . or the respiration of One that abides in the darkness, meting with his breath the slow minutes, the hours, the days, the ages. . . . My terror has become heavier than the chain, my vertigo is born of a twofold gulf. . . .

Aeons have passed by and all the worlds have ebbed into nothingness, like wreckage borne on a chasm-falling stream, taking with them the lost face of Belthoris. I am poised above the gaping maw of the Shadow. . . . Somehow, in another world, an exile phantom has written these words . . . a phantom who must fade utterly from time and place, even as I, the doomed priest Calaspa. I cannot remember the name of the phantom.

Beneath me, in the black depths, there is an awful brightening. . . .

THE RETURN OF THE SORCERER

I had been out of work for several months; and my savings were per-
ilously near to the vanishing-point. Therefore I was naturally elated
when I received from John Carnby a favorable answer inviting me to
present my qualifications in person. Carnby had advertised for a secre-
tary, stipulating that all applicants must offer a preliminary statement of
their capacities by letter; and I had written in response to the advertisement. Carnby, no doubt, was a scholarly recluse who felt averse to contact with a long waiting-list of strangers; and he had chosen this manner
of weeding out beforehand many if not all of those who were ineligible.
He had specified his requirements fully and succinctly; and these were
of such nature as to bar even the average well-educated person. A
knowledge of Arabic was necessary, among other things; and luckily I
had acquired a certain degree of scholarship in this unusual tongue.

I found the address, of whose location I had formed only a vague
idea, at the end of a hill-top avenue in the suburbs of Oakland. It was a
large, two-story house, overshaded by ancient oaks and dark with a mantling of unchecked ivy, among hedges of unpruned privet and shrubbery
that had gone wild for many years. It was separated from its neighbors
by a vacant, weed-grown lot on one side and a tangle of vines and trees
on the other, surrounding the black ruins of a burnt mansion.

Even apart from its air of long neglect, there was something drear
and dismal about the place—something that inhered in the ivy-blurred
outlines of the house, in the furtive, shadowy windows, and the very
forms of the misshapen oaks and oddly sprawling shrubbery. Somehow,
my elation became a trifle less exuberant, as I entered the grounds and
followed an unswept path to the front door.

When I found myself in the presence of John Carnby, my jubilation was still somewhat further diminished; though I could not have given a tangible reason for the premonitory chill, the dull, somber feeling of alarm that I experienced, and the leaden sinking of my spirits. Perhaps it was the dark library in which he received me as much as the man himself—a room whose musty shadows could never have been wholly dissipated by sun or lamplight. Indeed, it must have been this; for John Carnby himself, in a manner, was very much the sort of person I had pictured him to be.

He had all the ear-marks of the lonely scholar who has devoted patient years to some line of erudite research. He was thin and bent, with a massive forehead and a mane of grizzled hair; and the pallor of the library was on his hollow, clean-shaven cheeks. But coupled with this, there was a nerve-shattered air, a fearful shrinking that was more than the normal shyness of a recluse, and an unceasing apprehensiveness that betrayed itself in every glance of his dark-ringed, feverish eyes and every movement of his bony hands. In all likelihood his health had been seriously impaired by over-application; and I could not help but wonder at the nature of the studies that made him a tremulous wreck. But there was something about him—perhaps the width of his bowed shoulders and the bold aquilinity of his facial outlines—which gave the impression of great former strength and a vigor not yet wholly exhausted.

His voice was unexpectedly deep and sonorous.

"I think you will do, Mr. Ogden," he said, after a few formal questions, most of which related to my linguistic knowledge, and in particular my mastery of Arabic. "Your labors will not be very heavy; but I want someone who can be on hand at any time required. Therefore you must live with me—I can give you a comfortable room, and I guarantee that my cooking will not poison you. I often work at night; and I hope you will not find the irregular hours too disagreeable."

No doubt I should have been overjoyed at this assurance that the secretarial position was to be mine. Instead, I was aware of a dim, un-reasoning reluctance and an obscure forewarning of evil as I thanked John Carnby and told him that I was ready to move in whenever he desired.

He appeared to be greatly pleased; and the queer apprehensiveness went out of his manner for a moment.

"Come immediately—this very afternoon, if you can," he said. "I shall be very glad to have you—and the sooner the better. I have been living entirely alone for some time; and I must confess that the solitude is beginning to pall upon me. Also, I have been retarded in my labors for lack of the proper help. My brother used to live with me and assist me; but he has gone away on a long trip."

I returned to my down-town lodgings, paid my rent with the last few dollars that remained to me, packed my belongings, and in less than an hour was back at my new employer's home. He assigned me a room on the second floor, which, though unaired and dusty, was more than luxurious in comparison with the hall bedroom that failing funds had compelled me to inhabit for some time past. Then he took me to his own study, which was on the same floor, at the further end of the hall. Here, he explained to me, most of my future work would be done.

I could hardly restrain an exclamation of surprise as I viewed the interior of this chamber. It was very much as I should have imagined the den of some old sorcerer to be. There were tables strewn with ar-chaic instruments of doubtful use, with astrological charts, with skulls and alembics and crystals, with censers such as are used in the Catholic Church, and volumes bound in worm-eaten leather with verdigris-mott-led clasps. In one corner stood the skeleton of a large ape; in another, a human skeleton; and overhead a stuffed crocodile was suspended. There were cases overpiled with books, and even a cursory glance at the titles showed me that they formed a singularly comprehensive collection of ancient and modern works on demonology and the Black Arts. There were some weird paintings and etchings on the walls, dealing with kindred themes; and the whole atmosphere of the room exhaled a medley of half-forgotten superstitions. Ordinarily I should have smiled if confronted with such things; but somehow, in this lonely, dismal house, beside the neurotic, hag-ridden Carnby, it was difficult for me to repress an actual shudder.

On one of the tables, contrasting incongruously with this mélange of medievalism and Satanism, there stood a type-writer, surrounded with piles of disorderly manuscript. At one end of the room there was a small, curtained alcove with a bed in which Carnby slept. At the end opposite the alcove, between the human and simian skeletons, I perceived a locked cupboard that was set in the wall.

Carnby had noted my surprise, and was watching me with a keen, analytic expression which I found impossible to fathom. He began to speak, in explanatory tones.

"I have made a life-study of demonism and sorcery," he declared. "It is a fascinating field, and one that is singularly neglected. I am now preparing a monograph, in which I am trying to correlate the magical practices and demon-worship of every known age and people. Your labors, at least for awhile, will consist in typing and arranging the voluminous preliminary notes which I have made, and in helping me to track down other references and correspondences. Your knowledge of Arabic will be invaluable to me, for I am none too well-grounded in this language myself, and I am depending for certain essential data on a copy of the *Necronomicon* in the original Arabic text. I have reason to think that there are certain omissions and erroneous renderings in the Latin version of Olaus Wormius."

I had heard of this rare, well-nigh fabulous volume, but had never seen it. The book was supposed to contain the ultimate secrets of evil and forbidden knowledge; and, moreover the original text, written by the mad Arab Abdul Alhazred, was said to be unprocurable. I wondered how it had come into Carnby's possession.

"I'll show you the volume after dinner," Carnby went on. "You will doubtless be able to elucidate one or two passages that have long puzzled me."

The evening meal, cooked and served by my employer himself, was a welcome change from cheap restaurant fare. Carnby seemed to have lost a good deal of his nervousness. He was very talkative, and even began to exhibit a certain scholarly gaiety after we had shared a bottle of mellow Sauterne. Still, with no manifest reason, I was troubled by intimations and forebodings which I could neither analyze not trace to their rightful source.

We returned to the study; and Carnby brought out from a locked drawer the volume of which he had spoken. It was enormously old, and was bound in ebony covers arabesqued with silver and set with darkly glowing garnets. When I opened the yellowing pages, I drew back with involuntary revulsion at the odor which arose from them—an odor that was more than suggestive of physical decay, as if the book had lain among corpses in some forgotten graveyard and had taken on the taint of dissolution.

Carnby's eyes were burning with a fevered light, as he took the old manuscript from my hands and turned to a page near the middle. He indicated a certain passage with his lean forefinger.

"Tell me what you make of this," he said, in a tense, excited whisper.

I deciphered the paragraph, slowly and with some difficulty, and wrote down a rough English version with the pad and pencil which Carnby offered me. Then, at his request, I read it aloud:

> It is verily known by few, but is nevertheless an attestable fact, that the will of a dead sorcerer hath power upon his own body and can raise it up from the tomb and perform therewith whatever action was unfulfilled in life. And such resurrections are invariably for the doing of malevolent deeds and the detriment of others. Most readily can the corpse be animated if all its members have remained intact; and yet there are cases in which the excelling will of the wizard hath reared up from death the sundered pieces of a body hewn in many fragments, and hath caused them to serve his end, either separately or in a temporary re-union. But in every instance, after the action hath been completed, the body lapseth into its former state.

Of course, all this was errant gibberish. Probably it was the strange, unhealthy look of utter absorption with which my employer listened, more than that damnable passage from the *Necronomicon,* which caused my nervousness and made me start violently when, toward the end of my reading, I heard an indescribable slithering noise in the hall outside. But when I finished the paragraph and looked up at Carnby, I was more than startled by the expression of stark, staring fear which his features had assumed—an expression as of one who is haunted by some hellish phantom. Somehow, I got the feeling that he was listening to that odd noise in the hallway rather than to my translation of Abdul Alhazred.

"The house is full of rats," he explained, as he caught my inquiring glance. "I have never been able to get rid of them, with all my efforts."

The noise, which still continued, was that which a rat might make in dragging some object slowly along the floor. It seemed to draw closer, to approach the door of Carnby's room; and then, after an intermission, it began again and receded. My employer's agitation was marked—he listened with fearful intentness and seemed to follow the progress of the sound with a terror that mounted as it drew near and decreased a little with its recession.

"I am very nervous," he said. "I have worked too hard lately, and this is the result. Even a little noise upsets me."

The sound had now died away somewhere in the house. Carnby appeared to recover himself in a measure.

"Will you please re-read your translation?" he requested. "I want to follow it very carefully, word by word."

I obeyed. He listened with the same look of unholy absorption as before; and this time we were not interrupted by any noises in the hallway. Carnby's face grew paler, as if the last remnant of blood had been drained from it, when I read the final sentences; and the fire in his hollow eyes was like phosphorescence in a deep vault.

"That is a most remarkable passage," he commented. "I was doubtful about its meaning, with my imperfect Arabic; and I have found that the passage is wholly omitted in the Latin of Olaus Wormius. Thank you for your scholarly rendering—you have certainly cleared it up for me."

His tone was dry and formal, as if he were repressing himself and holding back a world of unsurmisable thoughts and emotions. Somehow I felt that Carnby was more nervous and upset than ever, and also that my rendering from the *Necronomicon* had in some mysterious manner contributed to his perturbation. He wore a ghastly brooding expression, as if his mind were busy with some unwelcome and forbidden theme.

However, seeming to collect himself, he asked me to translate another passage. This turned out to be a singular incantatory formula for the exorcism of the dead, with a ritual that involved the use of rare Arabian spices and the proper intoning of at least a hundred names of ghouls and demons. I copied it all out for Carnby, who studied it for a long time with a rapt eagerness that was more than scholarly.

"That, too," he observed, "is not in Olaus Wormius." After perusing it again, he folded the paper carefully and put it away in the same drawer from which he had taken the *Necronomicon*.

That evening was one of the strangest I have ever spent. As we sat for hour after hour discussing renditions from that unhallowed volume, I came to know more and more definitely that my employer was mortally afraid of something, that he dreaded being alone and was keeping me with him on this account rather than for any other reason. Always he seemed to be waiting and listening with a painful, tortured expectation; and I saw that he gave only a mechanical awareness to much that was said. Among the weird appurtenances of the room, in that atmosphere of unmanifested evil, of untold horror, the rational part of my mind began to succumb slowly to a recrudescence of dark ancestral fears. A scorner of such things in my normal moments, I was now ready to believe in the most baleful creations of superstitious fancy. No doubt, by some process of mental contagion, I had caught the hidden terror from which Carnby suffered.

By no word or syllable, however, did the man admit the actual feelings that were evident in his demeanor; but he spoke repeatedly of a nervous ailment. More than once, during our discussion, he sought to imply that his interest in the supernatural and the Satanic was wholly intellectual—that he, like myself, was without personal belief in such things. Yet I knew infallibly that his implications were false—that he was driven and obsessed by a real faith in all that he pretended to view with scientific detachment, and had doubtless fallen a victim to some imaginary horror entailed by his occult researches. But my intuition afforded me no clue to the actual nature of this horror.

There was no repetition of the sounds that had been so disturbing to my employer. We must have sat till after midnight with the writings of the mad Arab open before us. At last Carnby seemed to realize the lateness of the hour.

"I fear I have kept you up too long," he said apologetically. "You must go and get some sleep. I am selfish, and I forget that such hours are not habitual to others, as they are to me."

I made the formal denial of his self-impeachment which courtesy required, said good-night, and sought my own chamber with a feeling of intense relief. It seemed to me that I would leave behind me in Carnby's room all the shadowy fear and oppression to which I had been subjected.

Only one light was burning in the long passage. It was near Carnby's door; and my own door at the further end, close to the stair-head, was in deep shadow. As I groped for the knob, I heard a noise behind me, and turned to see in the gloom a small, indistinct body that sprang from the hall-landing to the top stair, disappearing from view. I was horribly startled; for even in that vague, fleeting glimpse, the thing was much too pale for a rat and its form was not at all suggestive of an animal. I could not have sworn what it was; but the outlines had seemed unmentionably monstrous. I stood trembling violently in every limb, and heard on the stairs a singular bumping sound, like the fall of an object rolling downward from step to step. The sound was repeated at regular intervals, and finally ceased.

If the safety of the soul and body had depended upon it, I could not have turned on the stair-light; nor could I have gone to the top steps to ascertain the agency of that unnatural bumping. Anyone else, it might seem, would have done this. Instead, after a moment of virtual petrification, I entered my room, locked the door, and went to bed in a turmoil of unresolved doubt and equivocal terror. I left the light burning; and I lay awake for hours, expecting momentarily a recurrence of that abominable sound. But the house was silent as a morgue; and I heard nothing. At length, in spite of my anticipations to the contrary, I fell asleep and did not awaken till after many sodden, dreamless hours.

It was ten o'clock, as my watch informed me. I wondered whether my employer had left me undisturbed through thoughtfulness, or had not yet arisen himself. I dressed and went downstairs, to find him waiting at the breakfast table. He was paler and more tremulous than ever, as if he had slept badly.

"I hope the rats didn't annoy you too much," he remarked, after a preliminary greeting. "Something really must be done about them."

"I didn't notice them at all," I replied. Somehow, it was utterly impossible for me to mention the queer, ambiguous thing which I had seen and heard on retiring the night before. Doubtless I had been mistaken, doubtless it had been merely a rat after all, dragging something down the stairs. I tried to forget the hideously repeated noise and the momentary flash of unthinkable outlines in the gloom.

My employer eyed me with uncanny sharpness, as if he sought to penetrate my inmost mind. Breakfast was a dismal affair; and the day that followed was no less dreary. Carnby isolated himself till the middle of the afternoon; and I was left to my own devices in the well-supplied but conventional library downstairs. What Carnby was doing alone in his room I could not surmise; but I thought more than once that I heard the faint, monotonous intonations of a solemn voice. Horror-breeding hints and noisome intuitions invaded my brain. More and more the atmosphere of that house enveloped and stifled me with poisonous, miasmal mystery; and I felt everywhere the invisible brooding of malignant incubi.

It was almost a relief when my employer summoned me to his study. Entering, I noticed that the air was full of a pungent, aromatic smell and was touched by the vanishing coils of a blue vapor, as if from the burning of Oriental gums and spices in the church censers. An Ispahan rug had been moved from its position near the wall to the center of the room, but was not sufficient to cover entirely a curving violet mark that suggested the drawing of a magic circle on the floor. No doubt Carnby had been performing some sort of incantation; and I thought of the awesome formula I had translated at his request.

However, he did not offer any explanation of what he had been doing. His manner had changed remarkably, and was more controlled and confident than at any former time. In a fashion almost business-like he laid before me a pile of manuscript which he wanted me to type for him. The familiar click of the keys aided me somewhat in dismissing my apprehensions of vague evil, and I could almost smile at the recherché and terrific information comprised in my employer's notes, which dealt mainly with formulae for the acquisition of unlawful power. But still, beneath my re-assurance, there was a vague, lingering disquietude.

Evening came; and after our meal we returned again to the study. There was a tenseness in Carnby's manner now, as if he were eagerly awaiting the result of some hidden test. I went on with my work; but some of his emotion communicated itself to me, and ever and anon I caught myself in an attitude of strained listening.

At last, above the click of the keys, I heard that peculiar slithering in the hall. Carnby had heard it, too, and his confident look had utterly vanished, giving place to the most pitiable fear and agitation.

The sound drew nearer and was followed by a dull, dragging noise, and then by more sounds of an unidentifiable slithering and scuttling nature, that varied in loudness. The hall was seemingly full of them, as if a whole army of rats were hauling some carrion booty along the floor. And yet no rodent—or number of rodents—could have made such sounds, or could have moved anything so heavy as the object which came behind the rest. There was something in the character of those noises—something without name or definition—which caused a slowly creeping chill to invade my spine.

"Good Lord! What is all that racket?" I cried.

"The rats! I tell you it is only the rats!" Carnby's voice was a high, hysterical shriek.

A moment later, there came an unmistakable knocking on the door, near the sill. At the same time I heard a heavy thudding in the locked cupboard at the further end of the room. Carnby had been standing erect; but now he sank limply into a chair. His features were ashen, and his look was almost maniacal with fright.

The nightmare doubt and tension became unbearable. I ran to the door and flung it open, in spite of a frantic remonstrance from my employer. I had no idea what I should find as I stepped across the sill into the feebly litten hall.

When I looked down and saw the thing on which I had almost trodden, my feeling was one of sick amazement and actual nausea. It was a human hand which had been severed at the wrist—a bony, bluish hand like that of a week-old corpse, with garden-mould on the fingers and under the long nails. *The damnable thing had moved,* it had drawn back to avoid me, and was crawling along the passage somewhat in the manner of a crab! And following it with my gaze, I saw that there were other things beyond it, one of which I recognized as a man's foot and another as a fore-arm. I dared not look at the rest. All were moving slowly, hideously away in a charnel procession—and I cannot describe the fashion in which they moved. Their individual vitality was horrifying beyond endurance. It was more than the vitality of life—yet the air was laden with a carrion taint. I averted my eyes and stepped back into Carnby's room, closing the door behind me with a shaking hand. Carnby was at my side with the key, which he turned in the lock with palsy-stricken fingers that had become as feeble as those of an old man.

"You saw them?" he asked in a dry, quavering whisper.

"In God's name, what does it all mean?" I cried.

Carnby went back to his chair, tottering a little with weakness. His lineaments were agonized by the gnawing of some inward horror, and he shook visibly like an ague patient. I sat down in a chair beside him; and he began to stammer forth his unbelievable confession, half-incoherently, with inconsequential mouthings and many breaks and pauses:

"He is stronger than I am—even in death . . . even with his body dismembered by the surgeon's knife and saw that I used . . . I thought he could not return after that . . . after I had buried the fragments in a dozen different places . . . in the cellar . . . beneath the shrubs . . . at the foot of the ivy-vines. But the *Necronomicon* is right . . . and Helman Carnby knew it. He warned me before I killed him—he told me he could return—*even in that condition.* But I did not believe him. I hated Helman, and he hated me too. He had attained to higher power and knowledge and was more favored by the Dark Ones than I. . . . That was why I killed him—my own twin-brother, and my brother in the service of Satan and of Those who were before Satan. We had studied together for many years. We had celebrated the Black Mass together . . . we were attended by the same familiars. . . . But Helman Carnby had gone deeper into the occult . . . into the forbidden, where I could not follow him. I feared him, and I could not endure his supremacy.

"It is more than a week—it is ten days since I did the deed. But Helman—or some part of him—has returned every night. . . . God! his accursed hands crawling on the floor! . . . his feet, his arms, the segments of his legs, climbing the stairs in some unmentionable way to haunt me! . . . Christ! his awful, bloody torso lying in wait! . . . I tell you, his hands have come even by day to tap and fumble at my door . . . and I have stumbled over his arms in the dark.

"Oh, God! I shall go mad with the awfulness of it . . . But he wants me to go mad, he wants to torture me till my brain gives way. That is why he haunts me in this piecemeal fashion. He could end it all at any time, with the demoniacal power that is his. He could re-knit his sundered limbs and body and slay me as I slew him.

"How carefully I buried the portions, with what infinite forethought! And how useless it was! . . . I buried the knife and saw, too, at the further end of the garden, as far away as possible from his evil, itching hands . . . . But I did not bury the head with the other pieces—I kept it in that cupboard at the end of my room. Sometimes I have heard it moving there—as you heard it a while ago. . . . But he does not need the head—his will is elsewhere, and can work intelligently through all his members.

"Of course, I locked all the doors and windows at night when I found that he was coming back. . . . But it made no difference. And I have tried to exorcise him with the appropriate incantations—with all those that I knew. Today I tried that sovereign formula from the *Necronomicon* which you translated for me . . . I got you here to translate it. Also, I could no longer bear to be alone . . . and I thought that it might help if there were someone else in the house. . . . That formula was my last hope. I thought it would hold him—it is a most ancient and most dreadful incantation. But . . . as you have seen . . . it is useless. . . ."

His voice trailed off in a broken mumble, and he sat staring before him with sightless, intolerable eyes in which I saw the beginning flare of madness. I could say nothing—the confession he had made was so ineffably atrocious. The moral shock, and the ghastly supernatural horror, had almost stupefied me. My sensibilities were stunned; and it was not till I had begun to recover myself that I felt the irresistible surge of a flood of loathing for the man beside me.

I rose to my feet. The house had grown very silent, as if the macabre and charnel army of beleaguerment had now retired to its various graves.

Carnby had left the key in the lock; and I went to the door and turned it quickly.

"Are you leaving? Don't go," Carnby begged in a voice that was tremulous with alarm, as I stood with my hand on the door-knob.

"Yes, I am going," I said coldly. "I am resigning my position right now; and I intend to pack my belongings and leave your house with as little delay as possible."

I opened the door and went out, refusing to listen to the arguments and pleadings and protestations he had begun to babble. For the nonce, I preferred to face whatever might lurk in the gloomy passage, no matter how loathsome and terrifying, rather than endure any longer the society of John Carnby.

The hall was empty; but I shuddered with repulsion at the memory of what I had seen, as I hastened to my room. I think I should have screamed aloud at the least sound or movement in the shadows.

I began to pack my valise with a feeling of the most frantic urgency and compulsion. It seemed to me that I could not escape soon enough from that house of abominable secrets, over which there hung an atmosphere of smothering menace. I made mistakes in my hurry, I stumbled over chairs, and my brain and fingers grew numb with a paralyzing dread.

I had almost finished my task, when I heard the sound of slow, measured footsteps coming up the stairs. I knew that it was not Carnby, for he had locked himself immediately in his room when I had left, and I felt sure that nothing could have tempted him to emerge. Anyway, he could hardly have gone downstairs without my hearing him.

The footsteps came to the top landing and went past my door along the hall, with that same dead, monotonous repetition, regular as the movement of a machine. Certainly it was not the soft, nervous tread of John Carnby.

Who, then, could it be? My blood stood still in my veins; I dared not finish the speculation that arose in my mind.

The steps paused; and I knew that they had reached the door of Carnby's room. There followed an interval in which I could scarcely breathe; and then I heard an awful crashing and shattering noise, and above it the soaring scream of a man in the uttermost extremity of fear.

I was powerless to move, as if an unseen iron hand had reached forth to restrain me; and I have no idea how long I waited and listened. The scream had fallen away in a swift silence; and I heard nothing now, except a low, peculiar, recurrent sound which my brain refused to identify.

It was not my own volition, but a stronger will than mine, which drew me forth at last and impelled me down the hall to Carnby's study. I felt the presence of that will as an overpowering, superhuman thing—a demoniac force, a malign mesmerism.

The door of the study had been broken in and was hanging by one hinge. It was splintered as by the impact of more than mortal strength. A light was still burning in the room, and the unmentionable sound I had been hearing ceased as I neared the threshold. It was followed by an evil, utter stillness.

Again I paused, and could go no further. But this time it was something other than the hellish, all-pervading magnetism that petrified my limbs and arrested me before the sill. Peering into the room, in the narrow space that was framed by the doorway and lit by an unseen lamp, I saw one end of the Oriental rug, and the gruesome outlines of a monstrous, unmoving shadow that fell beyond it on the floor. Huge, elongated, misshapen, the shadow was seemingly cast by the arms and torso of a naked man who stooped forward with a surgeon's saw in his hand. Its monstrosity lay in this: though the shoulders, chest, abdomen and arms were all clearly distinguishable, the shadow was headless and appeared to terminate in an abruptly severed neck. It was impossible, considering the relative position, for the head to have been concealed from sight through any manner of foreshortening.

I waited—powerless to enter or withdraw. The blood had flowed back upon my heart in an ice-thick tide, and thought was frozen in my brain. An interval of termless horror; and then, from the hidden end of Carnby's room, from the direction of the locked cupboard, there came a fearsome and violent crash, and the sound of splintering wood and whining hinges, followed by the sinister, dismal thud of an unknown object striking the floor.

Again there was silence—a silence as of consummated Evil brooding above its unnamable triumph. The shadow had not stirred; there was a hideous contemplation in its attitude; and the saw was still held in its poising hand, as if above a completed task.

Another interval; and then, without warning, I witnessed the awful and unexplainable *disintegration* of the shadow, which seemed to break gently and easily into many different shadows ere it faded from my view. I hesitate to describe the manner, or specify the places, in which this singular disruption, this manifold cleavage, occurred. Simultaneously, I heard the muffled clatter of a metallic implement on the Persian rug, and a sound that was not that of a single body but of many bodies falling.

Once more there was silence—a silence as of some nocturnal cemetery, when grave-diggers and ghouls are done with their macabre toil, and the dead alone remain.

Drawn by that baleful mesmerism, like a somnambulist led by an unseen demon, I entered the room. I knew with a loathly prescience the sight that awaited me beyond the sill—the double heap of human segments, some of them fresh and bloody, and others already blue with beginning putrefaction and marked with earth-stains, that were mingled in abhorrent confusion on the rug. A reddened knife and saw were protruding from the pile; and a little to one side, between the rug and the open cupboard with its shattered door, there reposed a human head that was fronting the other remnants in an upright posture. It was in the same condition of incipient decay as the body to which it had belonged; but I swear that I saw the fading of a malignant exultation from its features as I entered. Even with the marks of corruption upon them, the lineaments bore a manifest likeness to those of John Carnby; and plainly they could belong only to a twin brother.

The frightful inferences that smothered my brain with their black and clammy cloud, are not to be written here. The horror which I beheld—and the greater horror which I surmised—would have put to shame the foulest enormities of nether hell in their frozen pits. There was but one mitigation and one mercy—I was compelled to gaze only for a few instants on that intolerable scene. Then, all at once, I felt that something had withdrawn from the room; the malign spell was broken, the overpowering volition that had held me captive was gone. It had released me now, even as it had released the dismembered corpse of Helman Carnby. I was free to go; and I fled from that ghastly chamber and ran headlong through an unlit house and into the outer darkness.

SOLILOQUY IN AN EBON TOWER

The poet speaks, addressing a framed picture of Baudelaire upon a bookcase:

The lamp burns stilly in the standing air,
As in some ventless cavern. Through wide windows
The midnight brings a silence from the stars,
And perfumes that the planet dreams in sleep.
The hounds have ceased to bay; and the cicadas
To ply their goblin harps. The owl that whilom
Hooted his famine to a full-chapped moon,
Has pounced upon his gopher, or has gone
To fresher woods behind a farther hill;
And Hecate has grounded all the witches
For some glade-hidden Sabbat.

                              In my room
The quick, malign, relentless clock ticks on,
Firm as a demon's undecaying pulse,
Or creak of Charon's oar-locks as he plies
Between the shadow-crowded shores. Evoked
Within the vaults of my funereal brain,
Voices awaken, sibilant and restless—
Tongues of the viper's charnel-fostered brood,
Half-grown, amid the shreds of winding-sheets
And crumbling wicker of old bones. They sing,
Those little voices, all the poisonous,

Importunate melodies you too have heard,
O Baudelaire, in midnights when the moon
Sank, followed by some cloudy hearse of dreams,
Into the skyless nadir of despond.
Black-flickering, cloven tongues! Though we distill
Quintessences of hemlock or nepenthe,
We cannot slay the small, the subtle serpents,
Whose mother is the lamia Melancholy
That feeds upon our breath and sucks our veins,
Stifling us with her velvet volumes.

                                    Now
My thoughts pursue the santal and sad myrrh
Sighed by the shrouds of all hesternal sorrows.
Busied with old regrets, they carry on
Such commerce as the burrowing necrophores
Conduct from grave to grave; or pause to mumble
Snatches of ancient amorous elegies,
Deploring still some splendid, stately love—
Gone like the pomps of void Ecbatana—
That only lives in epodes, but will rise
To ghost the goldless morrows, clothed about
With hues of suns declining and decayed,
And crowned with ruinous autumn.

                                    Other thoughts
Exhume the withered wing-shards of ideals
Brittle and light as perished moths, or bring
To sight the mummied bats of blear mischance,
By dismal eves and moons disastrous flying,
But fallen now, and dead as are the heavens
Their vans have darkened. On beloved deaths
I muse, and through my twice-wept tears re-gather

The threads that Clotho and Lachesis have spun
And Atropos has cut; and see the bleak
Sinister gleaming of the steely shears
Behind the riven arrasses of time. . . .

What weapon can we arm us with? What bulwark
Build against grief and time? What moat renewed
With waters mortal as those that shroud Gomorrah,
Will the sea-going termite never ferry
To gnaw the ebon tower, the ebon ark
Holding the Muses' covenant? Splendor-brimmed,
What grail of God or Satan will suffice
For all the breadless days, the unguerdoned labors?

Yet, for a toll so light, by Song transported,
To sail beyond Elysium and Theleme,
And see, from oblivion looming, balmier shores
Of fables infinite! To light our dreams
At rose Aldebaran or sky-huge Antares,
Then quench their heat, or temper Damascus thought
In cold aphelions and apastrons far!
To pace the sun's Typhoean ramparts vast!
To couch on Saturn's outmost ring, or roll
With Pluto through his orb of eventide
Whose Hesper is the dwindled sun! To flaunt
Before the blind an immarcescible purple
Won from the murex of Uranian seas,
And fire-plucked vermeil of Vulcan, worn against
These aguish mists and wintry shadows! Thus
We triumph; thus the laurel overtops
The upas and the yew; and we decline
No toil, no dolor of our votive doom.

*   *   *

High-housed within the Alchemic Citadel,
We are served by Azoth and by Alkahest.
Out of the gleamless mire and sand we make
Pactolian metal. Fumed from our alembics,
The world dissolves like vapors opium-wrought,
Or drips, condensed, to philtres and to venoms
That Circe nor Simaetha dreamed. We build,
Daedalus-like, a labyrinth of words
Wherein our thoughts are twi-shaped Minotaurs
The ages shall not slay. Our ironies,
Like marbled adders creeping on through time,
Shall fang the brains of poets yet to be.
Our nacred moons and corposants of beauty
Shall float on ever-mootful lands retained
By Lar and Lemur; where Chimera flies,
And still the Sphinx unanswerably rules;
Where the red phantoms we have loosed from Dis
Still haunt the thickets and the cities; where
Our phosphor lamps may serve as well as any
Along the rutted way to Charon's wharf.

Appendix

Appendix

THE ARCANA OF ARKHAM-AUBURN

R. A. Hoffman

Preface

There was a strange collaboration of writers on an article published in *The Acolyte* under the name R. A. Hoffman. One of the writers was none other than Clark Ashton Smith himself, uncredited for his efforts save for a passing reference by editor Francis T. Laney that CAS had checked and revised the manuscript. However, even this statement seemed vaguely doubtful, surrounded as it was by obviously imaginative elements.

Laney had asked me for an article describing the 1941 and subsequent visits with Smith. I sent him off some notes and also a copy of a facetious letter I had written for the amusement of Paul Freehafer and other fans upon my second encounter with the Master. When I hesitated at putting such a thing together for publication, Laney edited the material together by providing connecting narrative and returned it to me for further changes, additions, or deletions. I patched things together as best I could and mentioned this article to CAS on my next visit. He asked to see the manuscript, so that he might perhaps contribute some suggestions. He was quite taken with the idea of an article about him, which, as it was shaping up, portrayed him as sort of a ghoul. Laney and I had felt that we should get his permission for such a characterization, but on the contrary, Smith derived impish delight in participating in the fanciful creation of his own myth.

Our next meeting in Smith's cabin found us examining the entire manuscript, word by word, which we entitled "The Arcana of Arkham-Auburn." The word "arcana" Smith himself preferred, as it suggested ancient mysteries. He spiritedly began to make suggestions—a different choice of wording here, a better sentence construction there—all to the advantage of the myth we were constructing. Soon he took the manuscript in hand and proceeded to write two or three lengthy insertions.

I have recently compared the published version with the manuscript and discovered a number of misprints which we hope are corrected in this reprinting. As an added comment, note that in some manner, both the manuscript and the *Acolyte* version display no hyphen in "Klarkash-Ton," although CAS himself customarily included the hyphen in any writings to me.

(NOTE. It is difficult to preface an article of this sort, for there are many alien and inimical factors to reconcile. One must steer a precarious course between those of true faith on the one hand, and those misled atheists who profess to disbelieve in even *Great Cthulhu* and *Tsathoggua*. Moreover, a carelessly turned tho innocent phrase might bring from Him Who is not to be Named a dire and unspecifiable vengeance. Though this is strictly a factual article, the casual reader may note certain most disturbing implications, which, if followed to their logical conclusions will shatter his conception of the cosmos. If you be such a one, it is recommended that you take as fact only those portions of the narrative which you *can* believe without upsetting your equilibrium. But if you be an adept in nameless rites, you will *know* that, if anything, this account is grossly understated. To such as you, it is not necessary to state that Klarkash-Ton himself checked and revised this narrative. To such as you, this account will bring joyful tidings, for it shows conclusively that the time is coming soon when They will once more walk the earth in their rightful shapes. Iä! Shub Niggurath! Iä! Tsathoggua! Iä! Cthulhu! . . . FTL.)

I.

On December 27, 1941, four seekers of hidden knowledge made a pilgrimage to Auburn. On that murky, midwinter day Henry Hasse, Emil Petaja, Paul Freehafer, and R. A. Hoffman sought out the renowned mage, former Lord High Priest of Poseidonis, Klarkash-Ton—known to modern men as Clark Ashton Smith.

The wise-cracking with which we had left Los Angeles gradually became transformed into hushed awe as we approached Auburn. The clouds seemed to darken and descend upon us from the surrounding hills. On each side of the road was row after row of certain ambiguous bare trees apparently comprising some kind of orchard—with short, squatty bases. I say "bases." It seemed difficult to think of them as tree-trunks, for from them dark, gnarled branches rose, appearing as myriad hands clawing angrily up through the earth at the storm.

Then the road took us through a tunnel, and after traversing a mile or so of winding road, we came upon—Arkham. The signpost said "Auburn," but we knew that this was merely to preserve the sanity of casual passers-through. I have never seen a more archaic community. Weatherworn frame buildings line the narrow, torturous ways, and side alleys plunge into steep inclines. The storm-emptied streets made us think we had entered a ghost town, but a wan glimmer of light in a drugstore promised human companionship and guidance. In order that no one of us should be left alone in this strange town, Paul and Henry went boldly in to ask the way to Smith's dwelling while Emil and I cowered in the car.

They looked worried when they returned, for the sardonic, half-concealed amusement of the druggist as they told of their quest, and the mysterious way in which he had directed them, were scarcely sedative. The manner in which he had told them that by following certain directions we would be "within a hundred yards of it" seemed to intimate that the place might not always be visible to—human beings.

The druggist had advised us, if ever we reached a certain point in the journey, to inquire at a farmhouse opposite a dairy farm. Presently we saw the dairy sign, and Paul and Henry followed a muddy path up to the farmhouse door. Emil and I, staying in the car out of the rain, heard a weird animal-howl as the other two approached the house; but when we asked them later about this, they denied having heard any such sound themselves. They could get no directions at this place, for the person who came to the door said that the family had moved in only recently, and had not yet become acquainted with the territory. We wondered then just how many families in the past had moved in but had shortly . . . left.

The dairyman proved to be our benefactor. After vainly attempting to tell us the way, he took us there in his car. He angled into rough and narrow side roads, then turned and bounced off across country, where no road was visible to our human eyes. Just as we were considering ourselves lost, the car suddenly slowed and turned around. To all appearance we had reached a desolate upland of rotting tree stumps and weather-worn rocks.

"There's his place," the man said, "but I doubt if he's home. There's no smoke from his chimney." I looked in the direction he was pointing. There, a short distance down the hill, stood a weathered frame cabin with shingled sides, the only structure in sight.

The dairyman disappeared across the field as we drove on and came to a halt in front of the cabin. As we stepped out onto the soggy ground, I became aware of something moving up the hill from the right. A momentary loss of consciousness assailed us, and when we were again in control of our senses, we were confronted by a man wearing a dark coat and a beret. (Later we found that our minds had been explored telepathically and that we should have met an unimaginable end had they been found hostile.) As the man approached, we saw that he held a small section of light cardboard, on which was hand-printed the name "Clark Ashton Smith." Oddly enough, an arrow beneath the name now appeared to be pointing at the bearer, who introduced himself as Clark Ashton Smith.

He explained that he had just set out with the sign, intending to place it for our guidance where the road turned off into the field.

After we had introduced ourselves, Smith led us into his cabin. We passed through an opening in a stone wall on top of which were long-bleached skulls of some unknown animals. Entering a porch, we went through a dark room into one even darker, lighted only by the glimmering from the storm-darkened sky—the light coming from two small windows, one at each end of the long and narrow room. The meager heat from a woodstove in the center of the den barely dispelled the damp and clammy chill. The far side of the room was broken by two closed doors. Shoulder-high shelves of books lined the walls, and all other wall space was covered by fascinating originals by Smith and other weird artists. On a shelf beneath a window was a group of grotesque stone statuettes; some stood, some sat, some leaned or craned at weird angles. Many were merely heads. Smith had made them himself from native rocks, he informed us, and he named for us the various gods which were represented there in stone.

"This is Tsathoggua," he said very matter-of-factly, as he fondled a squat and ugly little image. We noted that he did not say that it was *supposed* to be Tsathoggua, merely that it *was*.

When we had examined most of the statuary, we turned to study the pictures on the walls. From somewhere, CAS suddenly produced a lighted candle in a tallow-crusted heavy brass holder, and he held this up so that we could see the pictures in clearer detail. Most of the drawings were his own, and he seemed to delight in demonstrating the types of vegetation on alien worlds and the odd life forms in hitherto-undiscovered lands.

Now, all this time there was a certain stiffness about us all, including CAS, and as we examined the statuary and the pictures there was a tension in our conversation. Smith's first words had been hushed almost to a whisper, and we automatically talked in the same low tones. Although there was no definite feeling of hostility, still there was no air of friendliness and informality, but a sense of restraint. Undoubtedly Smith sensed this too, for he suggested that he and Paul go back to Auburn (Arkham!) to get some wine, and that they bring back an interesting Barnacle-Bill-the-Sailor type friend of his. Perhaps he felt that he was being stared at too intensively, and wanted someone else there to share the center of interest.

Those low mutterings in which we had been conversing were getting on my nerves, so after the two had left for town, I spoke in my normal tone of voice. The others joined in laughter at the realization of how still it had become, and thereafter even after Smith had returned, we conversed in ordinary tones.

While the others were gone, we took advantage of our chance to snoop behind the two mysterious doors we had noticed in the far side of the room. We opened one. The room beyond was furnished very simply with a bed and one or two other articles of furniture. Piled high on the bed were great stacks of letters in a dishevelment which had apparently existed for some time. And so we began to wonder where Klarkash-Ton slept—if he slept! We commenced to search for a coffin. Only Henry saw behind the other door, and all he will say even now is that "it was like the other room." He did not look long, and I know Emil and I had no desire to explore further after Henry had turned to face us again.

The three of us gathered once more around the fire. I noticed that the chimney—about eight inches in diameter—passed through a yard-square hole in the ceiling and then went through the roof, which was lost in the darkness above. Thus we knew that there was an attic above us, but as we saw no way of ascent, we do not know what strange Things it might have harbored.

Presently Paul and CAS returned, bringing with them some burgundy and the boot-clad seaman. Sailor Frank Partridge appeared to be an uneducated man in his fifties, but Smith and the wine soon opened the seaman's mouth in almost endless intelligent conversation. Once again we assembled around the fire. The conversation soon led to Partridge's remarkable theory about Atlantis and the origin of man. It is much too lengthy to set forth here. Also, he told of an interesting dream in which he was a spectator to a barbaric sacrifice. And he related an atavistic experience in which he was told that he had while drunk conversed with someone in Gaelic, though to his knowledge he cannot speak this language.

Although the seaman was interesting, we were more interested in CAS, and so sometimes Partridge's audience dwindled to just one or two. Whenever I could evade the sailor, I was able to talk with Smith. I asked him what he thought of C. L. Moore, "A remarkable writer," he said, "with a strange gift for suggesting the atmosphere of cosmic alienage."

He showed us numerous illustrations of his various stories by several artists, including at least half-a-dozen original Finlays. He also had his own original illustrations to some of his stories which had appeared in *Weird Tales*. He expressed high admiration for both Bok and Finlay, commending the stark simplicity of the former's black and whites, and the rare combination of imaginative power and technical richness in the earlier work of the latter. He also spoke very highly of Roy Hunt.

When asked if he were interested in having his stories appear in *Unknown Worlds*, he said he was, and mentioned also that he likes the work of Fritz Leiber Jr., in that magazine. He showed us his five-hundred line poem, "The Hashish-Eater," which has been published only in *Ebony and Crystal*, and mentioned that he would like to see it, and a number of his other works, reprinted in *Weird Tales*.

Someone asked Klarkash-Ton if there were any special rules as to the pronunciation of the names of his various entities. He replied that usually the accent is on the penultimate syllable.

The sky's clearing shortly before sunset gave us opportunity to take several pictures, in which Smith dutifully posed with his different paintings and sculptures. I asked him if he liked music (we had not noticed a radio or phonograph in his house.) "Oh yes," he said, interestedly, "—Gustav Holst's 'The Planets.' And Debussy." "And Wagner?" my devotion forced me to inquire. "Oh, yes," he replied, "—very much." I was satisfied.

———

We took Smith and Partridge back to town with us when we left, letting them off at an ancient post office. As we drove out of the old village, we saw the two delvers in Atlantean lore disappear mysteriously around the corner of one of the steep and narrow sidestreets.

The sun was setting. We hastened from this archaic town, for it is said that strangers must not linger after darkness has come to the streets of Auburn.

II.

(NOTE. Of the four, Hoffman was the only one whose vibrations were enough in tune with certain vague cosmic necessities and appetites to be *allowed* to return to Arkham-Auburn. Smith would have of course welcomed the other three, but even the great Klarkash-Ton is not as yet all-powerful and his position is not such that he cares yet to match his strength against that of Him Who is not to be Named and his dread messenger of a thousand shapes, Nyarlathotep. The remainder of this article covers three or four visits to Auburn during the summer of 1943, and the marked change in style and viewpoint shows conclusively that the Hoffmaniac has been marked by the Great Old Ones, and has been subtly altered as he progresses through his discipleship. Section II was written as an actual letter to Freehafer following Hoffman's first return to Auburn. Freehafer had written Hoffman what instructions he could recall as to finding Smith's place, with the added admonishment that he might find himself "in Yuggoth or some such place." FTL)

Dear Paul (the letter commences) How can I begin? Only yesterday I set out, my heart at ease, to see him. And after the awful things I saw and the strange places I ventured into, I know that I shall never go back willingly. I say willingly, because I sometimes feel a strange compulsion as though someone or some *thing* from Outside were calling me toward the place where. . . .

Your suspicions were not far off, you know. Oh, I found the road alright, and a pathway leading off it. But we had not gone that way before; we had driven around the woods. Now I know where Averoigne *really* is. Most unsuspectingly I followed the rocky pathway, which apparently had not been used for weeks, across the sun-deadened, stiff grass. Grasshoppers and other insects crossed my path, and the sun was beating down so heavily that I took off my cap, swinging it at my side as I made my way through the tall, rustling, dry grass. I took mental note of the small woods ahead into which the path led.

The change came upon my consciousness unnoticed at first, and I was suddenly aware of it while I was enjoying the cool umbrage afforded me by the trees. There was no sound whatsoever in that glade except the noise made by my own footsteps. But I kept on, though the pathway could scarcely be seen now in the vegetation. Once I envisioned a beautiful woman standing beside a tree trunk, but as I approached, the image vanished, leaving no trace. I then attempted to follow the path once more, but discovered that in my anxiety to find where the beauteous creature had gone I had irrevocably lost the fading trail.

In despair, I called upon the gods whose names had been whispered to me by my family since my childhood—upon Tsathoggua, Cthulhu, and Ubbo-Sathla, whence all terrestrial things cometh. At mention of that amorphous creature's name, a roaring crescendo of sound crashed upon my ears from every side, and the trees shook, and the earth trembled beneath my feet. The emerald gloom of the woods was suddenly tinged with a brilliant rosy light, then pale amber, then delicate azure and a kaleidoscope which happened so rapidly that I lost all sense of time and direction and seemed lost in space. . . .

I must have screamed then. Soon came awareness that I was kneeling on the peak of a towering mountain, a black sky above and tremendous winds rushing past me. My knuckles throbbed with pain, and I discovered that I had been beating my hands upon the rocky surface where I knelt until they were wet with blood. My throat felt strained from screaming, and how long I had been there I did not know.

Then, as suddenly, I found myself again in the woods, running madly under the trees. I noticed that the hush had come the forest once more, and the natural gloom had replaced the play of auroral colors. I slackened my pace and became cognizant of my surroundings. I was once again on the path, and the wood was thinning before me. Remembrance of that awful moment on the peak came to me, and I looked at my hands, but they showed no sign of blood or bruise.

Presently I saw someone coming down the path toward me. As we drew nearer each other, I knew of a certain that this was not the same Clark Ashton Smith I had met during the yuletide of 1941. No, here was not that lean, cadaverous individual who showed us his paintings by candlelight. Here now before me was a man with a well filled out face, his thick, brown hair flowing over his brow. He greeted me with a natural, outspoken voice—not that hushed library voice he had used before.

And then I knew that this was the real Clark Ashton Smith, and I feared to think what that thing really was we talked to in his house that chill December day. Yes, we had been wise to leave before dusk.

I have decided that I had best tell you a fictional story of what transpired subsequently, for you would never believe what really happened. And for your peace of mind, and for my sanity's sake, I shall distort my relating of the events which happened after that, for there are some things which should never appear in writing. (Iä! Shub-Niggurath!) And so I shall make no reference to the strange things which occurred within the walls of Smith's cabin, but shall alter them so that you will be able to understand them in terms of this world. For you have not been to the Forest of Averoigne and seen the siren that dwells therein, and you have not seen the cold, rocky mountain peak which lies near the Leng plateau.

And this is what happened as I must tell it to you. . . .

III.

After our difficulties in locating Smith's home before, I was surprised to have no trouble discovering the little road junction where one turns to get there. Soon I took a strange path through the trees, and before I had come to the end of it, there was CAS coming toward me, carrying some trash to bury behind the rocks. He expressed no sign of surprise, and greeted me in a friendly voice. We went to his cabin. Gone was the funereal atmosphere of that December visit. Gone also the rain, gloom, and chill. Now the sun shone brightly, though the day was cool. The trees now lush green were a wholesome change from those former claw-like things reaching out of the earth while the enveloping fog rolled down from the hills. Gone now the mystery and the glamour. Here was a friend. I found myself talking to him as though I had known him for years.

When I mentioned the contrast between the two visits, CAS explained. "Maybe it was my stooge, deputy, and doppelganger Sinorn the Sylan, whom you met that day. He takes my place sometimes when I'm off visiting Nycea, Moriamis, Sephora, or some other enchantress or lamia of Averoigne."

I asked him what a Sylan was. "Sylans are a kind of elemental," he elucidated. "If you have read Cabell's *The Silver Stallion,* you may remember the Sylan, Glaum-without-bones, who usurped the physical semblance, property, etc., of Guivric the Sage, leaving the latter to wander as a homeless phantom. Sinorn is a bit tricky, like all his kind, and I may have to give him the Double Exorcism sooner or later."

As we approached the cabin, I became aware of some grey animal-shape disappearing around the side of the structure. I asked Klarkash-Ton what it was I saw—suggesting that perhaps it was one of his grimalkins.

"Oh, that must have been one of my familiars," he told me. He stated this with such finality that I did not interrogate him any further on the subject.

I took my copy of *Out of Space and Time* along with me, and CAS inscribed a brief message to me inside the cover. Preparation of the next Klarkash-Ton collection of tales will commence shortly. After the war, Arkham House also plans to publish a volume of Smith's verse. This will include all his verse ever printed in books and magazines, and also some verse as yet unpublished (CAS writes many love poems to his enchantress friends).

Upon perusing a large book on witchcraft, we noticed a sixteenth-century portrait of Nostradamus, and were both struck by the uncanny resemblance to . . . Lovecraft! We looked up two or three different photos of HPL, and without a doubt they both had exactly the same features—the nose, the eyes, the mouth, and most characteristically, the jaw. Thus we knew conclusively that Lovecraft WAS Nostradamus in his twentieth-century manifestation, since the master of prophecy could not have made his predictions of the future without having made complete use of time travel.

We discussed many things and people: stories, letters, HPL, McIlwraith, R. E. Howard, Arkham House, Acolyte, painting, statuettes. . . . I took a number of pictures. Smith pointed out to me the Nunnery of Averoigne at the foot of the hill on which we stood, and commented on the quaintness of its juxtaposition with his pagan hermitage. Afterwards we walked into town, passing the house of the Devotee of Evil, which stands half-obscured by oaks and cypresses on its hilltop.

After spending some time with CAS, he becomes an old friend and one loses all awe of his very real place in American letters. His personality is so charming, his viewpoint so youthful, that I can easily imagine him as fitting into the LASFS as one of the members. The Great Old Ones built better than they knew when they appointed Klarkash-Ton as their ambassador to Averoigne, for it is he who will usher in the millennium, he who will lead the human followers of Tsathoggua!

Acknowledgments

"The Arcana of Arkham-Auburn" by R. A. Hoffman. *Acolyte* 2, No. 2 (Spring 1944): 8–12.

"Beyond the Singing Flame." *Wonder Stories* 3, No. 6 (November 1931): 752–61. In *Out of Space and Time* (Arkham House, 1942). Text taken from *A Vintage from Atlantis* (Night Shade Books, 2007).

"The Black Lake." In *Ebony and Crystal* (The Auburn Journal, 1922). Text taken from *In the Realms of Mystery and Wonder* (Centipede Press, 2017).

"The Chain of Aforgomon." *Weird Tales* 26, No. 6 (December 1935): 695–706. In *Out of Space and Time* (Arkham House, 1942). Text taken from *The Last Hieroglyph* (Night Shade Books, 2010).

"The City of the Singing Flame." *Wonder Stories* 3, No. 2 (July 1931): 202–13. In *Out of Space and Time.* (Arkham House, 1942). Text taken from *The Door to Saturn* (Night Shade Books, 2007).

"The Devotee of Evil." *The Double Shadow and Other Fantasies* ([Auburn Journal Print], 1933). In *The Abominations of Yondo* (Arkham House, 1960). Text taken from *The End of the Story* (Night Shade Books, 2006).

"A Dream of Lethe." In *Ebony and Crystal* (The Auburn Journal, 1922). Text taken from *In the Realms of Mystery and Wonder* (Centipede Press, 2017).

"The Eternal World." *Wonder Stories* 3, No. 10 (March 1932): 1130–37. In *Genius Loci* (Arkham House, 1948). Text taken from *A Vintage from Atlantis* (Night Shade Books, 2007).

"The Face by the River." *Lost Worlds* No. 1 (2004): 3–7. Text taken from *The End of the Story* (Night Shade Books, 2006).

"The Garden and the Tomb." In *Ebony and Crystal* (The Auburn Journal, 1922). Text taken from *In the Realms of Mystery and Wonder* (Centipede Press, 2017).

"Genius Loci." *Weird Tales* 21, No. 6 (June 1933): 747–58. In *Genius Loci* (Arkham House, 1948). Text taken from *The Maze of the Enchanter* (Night Shade Books, 2009).

"A Good Embalmer." In *Strange Shadows,* ed. Steve Behrends (Greenwood Press, 1989). Text taken from *The Door to Saturn* (Night Shade Books, 2007).

"The Hunters from Beyond." *Strange Tales of Mystery and Terror* 2, No. 3 (October 1932): 292–303. In *Lost Worlds* (Arkham House, 1944). Text taken from *The Door to Saturn* (Night Shade Books, 2007).

"The Lake of Enchanted Silence." *Crypt of Cthulhu* No. 20 (Eastertide 1984): 52. Text taken from *In the Realms of Mystery and Wonder* (Centipede Press, 2017).

"A Murder in the Fourth Dimension." *Amazing Detective Tales* 1, No. 10 (October 1930): 908–37. In *Tales of Science and Sorcery* (Arkham House, 1964). Text taken from *The End of the Story* (Night Shade Books, 2006).

"The Ninth Skeleton." *Weird Tales* 12, No. 3 (September 1928): 363–66. In *Genius Loci* (Arkham House, 1948). Text taken from *The End of the Story* (Night Shade Books, 2006).

"The Old Water-Wheel." *Poetry* 61, No. 3 (December 1942): 492. In *The Dark Chateau* (Arkham House, 1951). Text taken from *The Complete Poetry and Translations* (Hippocampus Press, 2007–08).

"The Phantoms of the Fire." *Weird Tales* 16, No. 3 (September 1930): 363–66. In *Genius Loci* (Arkham House, 1948). Text taken from *The End of the Story* (Night Shade Books, 2006).

"The Resurrection of the Rattlesnake." *Weird Tales* 18, No. 3 (October 1931): 387–90. In *Other Dimensions* (Arkham House, 1970). Text taken from Text taken from *The End of the Story* (Night Shade Books, 2006).

"The Return of the Sorcerer." *Strange Tales of Mystery and Terror* 1, No. 1 (September 1931): 99–109. In *Out of Space and Time.* (Arkham House, 1942). Text taken from *The Door to Saturn* (Night Shade Books, 2007).

"The Root of Ampoi." *Arkham Sampler* 2, No. 2 (Spring 1949): 3–16. In *Tales of Science and Sorcery* (Arkham House, 1964). Text taken from *The End of the Story* (Night Shade Books, 2006).

"The Secret of the Cairn." *Wonder Stories* 4, No. 11 (April 1933): 823–29 (as "The Light from Beyond"). In *Lost Worlds* (Arkham House, 1944). Text taken from *The Maze of the Enchanter* (Night Shade Books, 2009).

"Soliloquy in an Ebon Tower." In *The Dark Chateau* (Arkham House, 1951). Text taken from *The Complete Poetry and Translations* (Hippocampus Press, 2007–08).

"A Star-Change." *Wonder Stories* 4, No. 12 (May 1933): 962–69 (as "The Visitors from Mlok"). In *Genius Loci* (Arkham House, 1948). Text taken from *The Maze of the Enchanter* (Night Shade Books, 2009).